Also by Laura Joh Rowland

Black Lotus

Laura Joh Rowland

St. Martin's Paperbacks

To my brother, Larry Joh

BLACK LOTUS

ISBN: 0-312-97958-4

Printed in the United States of America

St. Martin's Press hardcover edition / April 2001
St. Martin's Paperbacks edition / March 2002

St. Martin's Paperbacks are published by St. Martin's Press, 175 Fifth Avenue, New York, NY 10010.

10 9 8 7 6 5 4 3 2 1

Edo

Genroku Period,
Year 6, Month 8

(Tokyo, September 1693)

Prologue

The day of tragedy dawned with an iridescent sheen in the eastern sky. As the heavens gradually lightened from indigo to slate blue, stars disappeared; the moon's crescent faded. The dim outlines of forested hills framed Zōjō Temple, administrative seat of the Buddhist Pure Land sect in Shiba, south of Edo Castle. Across a vast tract of land spread the domain of ten thousand priests, nuns, and novices who occupied the more than one hundred buildings of Zōjō proper and the forty-eight smaller subsidiary temples clustered around it. Above countless tiled and thatched roofs soared the tiered spires of pagodas and the open framework structures of firewatch towers. The Zōjō

temple district was a city within a city, deserted and silent in
the waning darkness.

On the platform of a firewatch tower stood a lone figure in
the unpopulated landscape: a young priest with a shaven head,
a round, innocent face, and keen-sighted eyes. His saffron robe
billowed in the cool early autumn wind that carried the scent
of fallen leaves and night soil. His high perch afforded him a
splendid view of the narrow lanes, walled compounds, and
courtyards that comprised the district.

"Namu Amida Butsu," the priest repeated over and over
again. "Praise to the Buddha."

The chant would ensure his entry into paradise after his
death, but also served the practical purpose of keeping him alert
during a long night of guarding the religious community
against Edo's most dangerous hazard: fire. The priest's stomach
rumbled with hunger; still chanting, he stretched his cold, stiff
muscles and longed for food, a hot bath, and a warm bed.
Looking forward to the end of his vigil, he turned slowly on
the platform.

Around him revolved the panorama of morning. As the sky
brightened to luminous pearl, colors appeared in the landscape:
green foliage and multihued flower beds in gardens; scarlet
woodwork on buildings; white monuments in cemeteries; the
hazy violet mirrors of ponds. The first tentative waking trills
of birds rose to a chorus of songs. Sparrows darted over the
peaked and gabled roofs; pigeons cooed and fluttered in the
eaves; crows winged in the blue distance above the hills,
against rosy wisps of cloud. It would be a clear, warm day.
Another night had passed safely. Yet even as the thought
soothed the priest's mind, his sharp gaze sighted an aberration
in the tranquil scene.

A small, dark cloud hovered low over the western sector of
the district. While the priest watched, it thickened and spread
with disturbing speed. Now he smelled the bitter tang of smoke.
Frantically, he pulled the rope that dangled from inside the roof
of his tower. The brass alarm bell clanged, echoing across the
district.

Fire!

*   *   *

The insistent ringing of a bell jarred her from deep, black unconsciousness into dazed stupor. She lay facedown on the ground, with damp, fragrant grass pressed against her nose and cheek. Where was she? Panic shot through her, followed by the certainty that something was terribly wrong. Pushing herself up on her elbows, she groaned. Her head throbbed with pain; soreness burned on her buttocks and calves, between her thighs, around her neck. Aches permeated her muscles. The world spun in a dizzying blur. Thick, acrid air filled her lungs. Coughing, she fell back on the ground and lay still until the dizziness passed. Then she rolled over, looking around in bewilderment as her surroundings came into focus.

Tall pine trees pierced the dim blue sky above her. Smoke veiled stone lanterns and orange lilies in the garden where she lay. She smelled smoke and heard the crackle of fire. Moaning, she sat upright. Nausea assailed her; the pain in her head intensified, and she covered her ears to muffle the loud clangs of the bell. Then she saw the house, some twenty paces distant, beyond red maples circling a pond.

It was a rustic, one-story cottage built of plaster and weathered cypress, with bamboo lattice over the windows and deep eaves shading the veranda. Fire licked the foundations and crept up the walls, curling and blackening the paper windowpanes. The thatched roof ignited in an explosion of sparks and flame. Instinctively she opened her mouth to call for help. Then the first hint of returning memory stifled her voice to a whimper of dread. Through her mind flashed disjointed impressions: a harsh voice; the taste of tears; a lantern glowing in a dark room; loud thumps and crashes; a violent thrashing of naked limbs; her own running feet and fumbling hands. But how had she arrived here?

Baffled, she examined herself for clues. Her brown muslin kimono was wrinkled and her long black hair tangled; her bare feet were dirty, her fingernails torn and grimy. She struggled to piece the fragmented recollections into a comprehensible whole, but terror obliterated the images. The burning house radiated menace. A sob rose from her aching throat.

She knew what had happened, yet she did not know.

*   *   *

As the firebell pealed its urgent call, an army of priests clad
in leather capes and helmets, carrying buckets, ladders, and
axes, raced through the crooked lanes of the Zōjō temple district. A burgeoning cloud of black smoke rose from one of the
subsidiary temples enclosed in separate walled compounds. The
fire brigade stormed through the gate, whose portals bore the
circular symbol of a black lotus flower with pointed petals and
gold stamens. Inside, priests and novice monks stampeded the
lanes between the temple's many buildings, up the broad central flagstone path leading to the main hall, toward the rear of
the compound and the source of the smoke. Children from the
orphanage followed in a chattering, excited flock. Nuns in
hemp robes chased after the orphans, trying in vain to herd
them away from danger.

"Let us through!" ordered the fire brigade commander, a
muscular priest with stern features.

He led his troops through the chaos, around the main hall
and past smaller buildings, into a wooded area. Beyond a cem-
etery of stone grave markers, he saw flames through the trees.
The priests of the Black Lotus Temple had formed a line from
a cylindrical stone well, along a gravel path, and across a garden to the burning house. They passed buckets down the line
and hurled water at the fire, which had climbed the timbers and
engulfed the walls. The fire brigade quickly positioned ladders
to convey water to the blazing roof.

"Is anyone in the building?" shouted the commander.

Either no one knew or no one heard him over the fire's roar
and the din of voices. Accompanied by two men, he ran up the
steps to the veranda and opened the door. Smoke poured out.
Coughing, he and his companions fastened the face protectors
of their helmets over their noses and mouths. They groped
through the smoke, down a short corridor, through fierce heat.
The house contained two rooms, divided by burning lattice and
paper partitions. Flaming thatch dropped through the rafters.
The commander rushed through the open door of the nearest
room. Dense, suffocating smoke filled the small space. Amid
the indistinct shapes of furniture, a human figure lay on the
floor.

"Carry it out!" the commander ordered.

While his men complied, he sped to the second room. There,

the fire raged up the walls and across the tatami mats. The heat seared the commander's face; his eyes stung. From the threshold he spied two figures lying together in the corner, one much smaller than the other. Burning clothing enveloped them. Shouting for assistance, the commander waded through the fire and beat his thick leather sleeves against the bodies to extinguish the flames. His men came and helped him carry the two inert burdens out of the house, just before the roof collapsed with a great crash.

Away from the other priests still fighting the blaze, they laid the bodies on the ground beside the one previously carried out. Choking and coughing, the commander gratefully inhaled the cool, fresh air. He wiped his streaming eyes and knelt beside the victims. They lay motionless, and had probably been dead before he'd entered the house. The first was a large, naked samurai with a paunchy stomach; knotted gray hair looped over his shaved crown. There were no burns on him. But the other two . . .

The commander winced at the sight of their blistered, blackened faces. Breasts protruded through the shreds of charred cloth clinging to the larger corpse: It was a woman. The last victim was a very young child. With its hair burned away and the remains of a blanket swaddling its body, the commander couldn't discern its sex or exact age.

Priests and nuns gathered near the sad tableau. Shocked cries arose from them, then the click of rosary beads as they began chanting prayers. Someone passed the commander three white funeral shrouds. He murmured a blessing for the spirits of the deceased, then tenderly covered the bodies.

Lying huddled behind a boulder, she watched the priests continue throwing water on the house while the fire brigade hacked apart the burning shell with axes. The flames and smoke had diminished; ruined walls and timbers steamed; the odor of charred wood filled the air. Soon the fire would be out. But she felt neither relief nor any desire to call out to the firemen, who were walking around the site, examining the wreckage with worried expressions. In her confusion and terror, she felt an overwhelming urge to flee.

She raised herself on her elbows and knees. Her throbbing head spun. Nausea convulsed her stomach; she retched, but nothing came up. Moaning, she crawled. Her body felt enormously heavy and cumbersome as she dragged herself across the ground. Gasps heaved her lungs. She mustn't let anyone find her here. She had to get away. Gritting her teeth against the pain and sickness, she inched across coarse white gravel and damp lawn, toward shadowy woods and the temple's back gate.

Then she heard purposeful footsteps approaching from behind her. Strong hands lifted her up, turned her around. She found herself looking at a fireman in leather robe and helmet. His stern face was daubed with soot; his eyes were red.

"What are you doing here, little girl?" he demanded.

His accusing glare sent tremors of fear through her. Whimpering, she writhed and kicked in a feeble attempt to escape, but he held her tight. She tried to speak, but panic choked her voice; her heart pounded. Dizziness overcame her. The world grew dim and hazy. As she descended into unconsciousness, her captor's face blurred.

She wished she had a good answer to his question.

1

*I have come into this impure and evil world
To preach the ultimate truth.
Hear, and you shall be released from suffering
And attain perfect enlightenment.*

——FROM THE BLACK LOTUS SUTRA

"There was lamp oil spilled along the path to the cottage and on the ground around it." In the private audience chamber of Edo Castle, Sano Ichirō addressed Shogun Tokugawa Tsunayoshi, Japan's supreme military dictator. "The fire brigade found a ceramic jar containing a small quantity of oil hidden in some bushes nearby. And a search of the garden turned up what appeared to be a torch: a stump of pinewood with a charred rag wrapped around the end. I've examined the scene and the evidence. The fire was definitely the result of arson."

"Ahh, this is most serious." A frown crossed the shogun's mild, aristocratic features. Dressed in an embroidered bronze satin kimono and the cylindrical black cap of his rank, he stirred

uncomfortably upon the dais, where he sat with his back to a
mural of blue rivers and silver clouds, facing Sano, who knelt
on the tatami floor below. Attendants rearranged the silk cushions around the shogun, filled his silver tobacco pipe, and
poured more sake into the cup on the low table beside him,
but he waved them away and turned toward the open window,
contemplating the crimson sunset descending upon the garden.
From the distance came the neigh of horses, the footsteps of
patrolling guards, the muted bustle of servants. "I did hope that
the, ahh, suspicions of the fire brigade would prove un-
founded," the shogun continued morosely, "and that the fire
was just an accident. But alas, you have confirmed my, ahh,
worst fears."

That morning, a messenger had brought word of the fire at
the temple of the Black Lotus sect, along with a report from
the fire brigade commander, which stated that the blaze had
been set deliberately. Zōjō was the Tokugawa family temple,
where the clan worshipped and its ancestors lay entombed, and
any crime against the main temple or its subsidiaries constituted
an attack against the shogun. In addition, Tsunayoshi was a
devout Buddhist, a generous patron of religion, and took a
strong personal interest in the Zōjō community. Therefore, he'd
assigned Sano to investigate the fire. Sano had begun inquiries
at the Black Lotus Temple and had just returned.

Now the shogun said, "I suppose you have also confirmed
the, ahh, identity of the man who died in the fire?"

"I regret to say that I have," Sano said. "It was indeed
Oyama Jushin, chief police commander. When I viewed the
body, I recognized him immediately."

Prior to becoming the shogun's *sōsakan-sama*—Most Honorable Investigator of Events, Situations, and People—Sano
had served on Edo's police force as a *yoriki*, a senior police
commander. He and Oyama had been colleagues, although
Sano hadn't particularly liked Oyama. As a hereditary Tokugawa vassal whose family had served the shogun's clan for
generations, Oyama had scorned Sano, who was the son of a
rōnin, a masterless samurai. Oyama had been promoted to his
present higher rank last winter. From priests at the Black Lotus
Temple, Sano had learned that Oyama had recently joined the
sect. Now the death of an important official transformed the

arson into a politically sensitive murder case and grave offense against the *bakufu*, Japan's military dictatorship. Fate had brought Sano the responsibility of catching the killer.

"The other two victims haven't been identified yet," Sano said. "One was a woman and the other a small child, but they were badly burned, and at the moment, it seems that no one knows who they are. Membership in the sect has grown rapidly; there are presently four hundred twenty holy men and women living on the premises, with more arriving every day, plus ninety servants and thirty-two orphans. Nobody seems to be missing, but I got the impression that the sect has difficulty keeping its records up to date. And because of the crowds that frequent the temple, they can't efficiently monitor who's in the compound at any given time."

This situation sometimes occurred as a sect grew in popularity among people in search of spiritual guidance or a new diversion. The many new followers of the Black Lotus Temple could worship or even live together while remaining virtual strangers. Two particular individuals might have easily gone unnoticed by the sect leaders.

"Ahh, there are so many Buddhist orders nowadays that it is difficult to keep them all straight," the shogun said with a sigh. "What distinguishes the Black Lotus from the rest?"

Sano had familiarized himself with the sect while at the temple. He said, "Its central doctrine is the Black Lotus Sutra." A sutra was a Buddhist scripture, written in prose and verse, parables and lectures, containing the teachings of the Sākyamuni, the historical Buddha who had lived in India approximately a thousand years before. There were some eighty-four thousand sutras, each of which elucidated different aspects of his wisdom. Various orders structured their practices around various texts. "The sect members believe that the Black Lotus Sutra represents the final, definitive teaching of the Buddha, and contains the essential, perfect, ultimate law of human existence and cosmic totality. They also believe that worshippers who absorb the truth contained in the sutra will attain nirvana."

Nirvana was a state of pure peace and spiritual enlightenment, the goal of Buddhists. The state could not be articulated, only experienced.

This explanation seemed to satisfy Tsunayoshi. "Will you

keep trying to identify the dead woman and child?" he ventured timidly. A dictator with little talent for leadership and less self-confidence, he hesitated to make suggestions that he feared might sound stupid.

"I certainly will," Sano reassured his lord. Who the unknown victims had been might prove critical to the investigation. For reasons involving Tokugawa law, Sano forbore to mention that he'd sent all three bodies to Edo Morgue for examination by his friend and adviser Dr. Ito.

"This is a sorry state of affairs," lamented the shogun, fumbling with his pipe. A manservant lit it for him and placed the stem between his lips. "Ahh, I wish the Honorable Chamberlain Yanagisawa were here to offer his opinion!"

Yanagisawa, the shogun's second-in-command, had gone to Echigo Province on a tour of inspection with his lover and chief retainer, Hoshina; they wouldn't be back for two months. Although Sano couldn't share Tsunayoshi's wish, neither did he welcome the chamberlain's absence with the joy he might have once felt.

From Sano's early days at Edo Castle, Yanagisawa had viewed him as a rival for the shogun's favor, for power over the weak lord and thus the entire nation. He'd repeatedly tried to sabotage Sano's investigations, destroy his reputation, and assassinate him. But two years ago, a case involving the mysterious death of a court noble in the ancient imperial capital had fostered an unexpected comradeship between Sano and Yanagisawa. Since then, they'd coexisted in a truce. Sano didn't expect this harmony to continue forever, but he meant to enjoy it while it lasted. Today his life seemed replete with wonderful blessings and challenges: He had a family that he loved, the favor of the shogun, and an interesting new case.

"Have you any idea who committed this terrible crime?" asked the shogun.

"Not yet," Sano said. "My detectives and I have begun interviewing the residents of the Black Lotus Temple, but so far we've found neither witnesses nor suspects . . . with one possible exception. The fire brigade found a girl near the scene. Her name is Haru; she's fifteen years old and an orphan who lives in the temple orphanage. Apparently she tried to run away, then fainted."

Tsunayoshi gulped sake; his brow furrowed in thought. "So you think that this girl, ahh, saw something? Or did she set the fire?"

"Either alternative is possible," Sano said, "but I haven't been able to get any information from her."

By the time he'd arrived at the Black Lotus Temple, the nuns had put Haru to bed in the orphanage dormitory, a long, narrow room where the children slept on straw mattresses atop wooden pallets. Haru had regained consciousness, but when Sano approached her, the small, slender girl shrieked in terror and dived under the quilts. When two nuns pulled her out, she clung to them, sobbing hysterically.

"I won't hurt you," Sano said gently, kneeling beside the pallet where the nuns held Haru. "I just want to ask you some questions."

She only sobbed harder, hiding her face behind her tangled, waist-length hair. Sano ordered a soothing herb tea brought to her, but she refused to drink. After an hour of failed attempts to calm and question Haru, Sano told his chief retainer, Hirata, to try. Hirata was young, personable, and popular with girls, but he fared no better than Sano. Haru cried herself into a fit of choking, then vomited. Finally Sano and Hirata gave up.

As they left the dormitory, Sano asked the nuns, "Has Haru told anyone what she was doing outside the cottage, or what she saw there?"

"She hasn't uttered a word since she was found," answered a nun. "When the fire brigade and the priests questioned her, she behaved as you just saw. With us nuns she's calmer, but she still won't talk."

Now Sano explained the situation to Tsunayoshi, who shook his head and said, "Perhaps a demon has, ahh, stolen the poor girl's voice. Ahh, how unfortunate that your only witness cannot speak!"

But Sano had a different theory about Haru's behavior, and a possible solution to the problem. "Tomorrow I'll try another way of breaking her silence," he said.

*   *   *

After leaving the shogun, Sano walked down the hill on which Edo Castle perched, through stone passages between enclosed corridors and watchtowers manned by armed guards, past security checkpoints. Lanterns carried by patrolling troops glowed in the deepening blue twilight. The evening was almost as mild as summer, yet a golden haze veiled the waxing moon. The wind breathed the scent of charcoal smoke and dry leaves. In the official quarter, where the shogun's high-ranking retainers lived, Sano quickened his steps as he passed estates surrounded by barracks with whitewashed walls. He was eager for the company of his family, and he had a plan to propose.

He hurried through the gate of his estate, greeting the guards stationed there and in the paved courtyard inside the barracks. Beyond an inner gate, he entered the mansion, a large, half-timbered building with a brown tile roof. As he removed his shoes and swords inside the entry porch, he heard feminine voices singing and laughing, and the excited shrieks of a child. He smiled in bemusement while he walked down the corridor toward the private chambers. He still couldn't believe that the addition of one tiny person had transformed his peaceful household into a place of noisy activity. He stopped at the nursery door. His smile broadened.

Inside the warm, bright room, his wife, Reiko, sat in a circle with four other women—her old nurse O-sugi, two maids, and Midori, a family friend. They were singing a folk tune. Little Masahiro, eighteen months old, dressed in a green cotton sleeping kimono, his soft black locks disheveled and his round face rosy, toddled on plump legs from one woman to the next within the circle. His happy, childish whoops joined their song; his tiny hands clapped against theirs.

Reiko glanced up and saw Sano. Her delicate, lovely features brightened. "Look, Masahiro-*chan*. It's your father!"

Arms outstretched, chortling in excitement, Masahiro ran to Sano, who picked him up, tossed him in the air, and caught him. Masahiro laughed with glee. Sano hugged his son close, enjoying Masahiro's softness and sweet smell. Love clenched his heart; awe sobered him. He was a first-time father at the late age of thirty-four, and this boisterous little creature seemed a miracle.

"My little samurai," Sano murmured, nuzzling his son's face.

O-sugi and the maids gathered up the water basin and damp towels from Masahiro's bath and departed. Sano greeted Midori. "How are you tonight?"

"Fine, thank you." Midori bowed. Dimples flashed in her plump cheeks; her lively eyes danced. Eighteen years old, she was a daughter of a powerful daimyo—provincial lord—and held a post as a lady-in-waiting to the shogun's mother. Sano had met her during an investigation some years ago. She and Reiko had become friends, and Sano suspected that Midori and his retainer Hirata were somewhat more than friends. Because the shogun's mother had many other attendants to serve her, and great esteem for Sano, she allowed Midori to visit the estate often.

"I guess it's getting late," Midori said, rising. "I'd better go back to the palace." To Reiko she said, "Shall I come again tomorrow?"

Reiko smiled and nodded. "Good night."

After Midori left, Sano and Reiko played with Masahiro, discussing his appetite, bowels, and all the endearing things he'd done today. Then Reiko announced, "Bedtime!" This entailed much fussing and coaxing, but finally Masahiro was asleep on his little futon. Sano and Reiko settled in the parlor, where he ate a meal of miso soup, rice, grilled trout, and vegetables.

Reclining upon cushions, Reiko sipped tea. Tendrils of hair had escaped her upswept coiffure; fatigue shadowed her eyes; food stains blotched her maroon silk kimono. She was twenty-three years old, and motherhood had given her a new, mature beauty. "Masahiro is so lively, he wears me out," she said.

"You work too hard," Sano said between bites of fish. "Let the maids help with Masahiro."

"Oh, well. Masahiro keeps me busy." Reiko smiled, adding wistfully, "There's not much else for me to do."

Sano knew that Reiko, the only child of Magistrate Ueda, had enjoyed an unconventional girlhood. Her indulgent father had hired tutors to give her the education usually reserved for samurai sons bound for careers in the *bakufu*. Despite all her training, however, which extended even to the martial arts,

women couldn't hold government posts or work as anything
except servants, farm laborers, nuns, or prostitutes. Not until
she married had Reiko found a use for her talents: helping Sano
with his investigations.

She'd uncovered clues in places where male detectives
couldn't go. She'd gathered information through a network
composed of women associated with powerful samurai clans.
Often her discoveries led to the solution of a case. But since
Masahiro's arrival, Reiko had spent almost all her time at the
estate. The child had occupied her, and there'd been no work
for her in Sano's recent investigations.

"What did you do today?" Reiko asked.

The eager curiosity in her voice told Sano that she missed
the challenge of detective work. Now he realized with consternation that she'd lost some of her spirit. That he hadn't
noticed this before signified that they'd grown apart. Maybe a
short break from housewifery would refresh Reiko and bring
them closer together.

"I have a new case," Sano said. While he ate rice and pickled daikon, he told Reiko about the fire and the three deaths.
He described his unsuccessful interrogation of Haru, then said,
"From her behavior toward the fire brigade, the priests, Hirata,
and myself, I believe she's afraid of men. I ordered her moved
from the orphanage to the main convent at Zōjō Temple because I don't want potential suspects—as all the residents of
the Black Lotus Temple are—to influence my only witness. I'd
like you to go there and interview Haru."

Sano smiled at Reiko. "You're my only female detective,
and I'm hoping that you can get some information from her.
Do you want to try?"

Reiko sat up straight; her eyes sparkled, and she shed her
weariness like a cast-off garment. "I would love to."

"I must warn you that Haru may not cooperate with you,"
Sano said, though pleased by Reiko's enthusiasm.

"Oh, I'm sure I can persuade her to talk. How soon can we
go to the Black Lotus Temple?" Reiko looked ready to jump
up and leave immediately.

"I have to go to Edo Morgue tomorrow," Sano said, "then
make inquiries around town." Seeing Reiko's disappointed expression, he said, "But my detectives are going to Zōjō district

in the morning. They can escort you, if you like."

"Wonderful. I can hardly wait."

Reiko shimmered with happy energy. Sano saw in her the young bride who on their wedding day had pleaded to help solve a murder case, then forged ahead on her own after he'd refused. He felt a surge of love for her.

"All right," he said. "We can share our results in the evening."

A distant look came into Reiko's eyes, as if she'd mentally moved ahead in time to tomorrow. "This is a very important interview. I must be careful with Haru. Tell me everything about her, so I can decide how best to draw her out."

They discussed possible strategies, just as they had in the days before Masahiro. Sano realized he'd missed their partnership, and was glad he could include Reiko in the investigation.

2

When I heard the Law of the Black Lotus,
My mind filled with great joy,
And I was freed from care and distress.

—FROM THE BLACK LOTUS SUTRA

Zōjō Temple, located just off the Tōkaido—the highway that linked Edo with the imperial capital, Miyako—attracted a ceaseless flow of travelers, pilgrims, and mendicant monks. The approach to the temple comprised one of Edo's busiest marketplaces, where merchants sold refreshments, Buddhist relics, medicinal herbs, dishware, and many other goods. Today the market bustled in the warm weather. Beneath a sunny aquamarine sky that arched over hills green from the recent rainy season, samurai on horseback and strolling peasants browsed the stalls; nuns and priests begged alms. The crowd parted for a procession of mounted samurai escorting a black palanquin emblazoned with a flying-crane crest.

Inside the enclosed sedan chair, Reiko rode through Zōjō's main gate, an imposing structure with red lacquer woodwork and a double-tiered roof, whose three portals represented the three stages in the passage to nirvana. Anxiety undermined Reiko's pleasure in the trip.

The morning had begun badly. When she'd tried to leave the house, Masahiro had clung to her, crying and screaming. Reiko promised him that she would be back soon, nearly in tears herself from the pain of their first separation. She'd debated staying home and trying again tomorrow, but the interview couldn't be postponed. Finally the maids held Masahiro while Reiko ran out the door. All during the journey through Edo, she'd worried about her son.

Ahead loomed Zōjō Temple's white walls. Beyond them rose peaked rooftops, multiple pagodas, and a wooded slope. The procession crossed the bridge over the Sakuragawa Canal. Sano's detectives dismounted, then escorted the palanquin through the gate and up a steep flight of stone steps to the main temple precinct, past the sutra repository, worship halls, and the huge bronze bell in its wooden cage. Wrought-iron fences shielded Tokugawa family tombs. Crowds flowed in and out of a massive main hall with carved columns and doors and an undulating roof supported by complex bracketry. As she neared her destination, a new fear seized Reiko.

After her long hiatus from detective work, would she still be able to coax information from the orphan girl? Although she'd spent most of the night mentally rehearsing the interview, she felt unprepared, but it was too late for misgivings. The procession ascended more steps to the temple refectory, abbot's residence, and quarters for the priests, novices, and servants. The bearers set down the palanquin outside the convent, a two-story wooden building with covered balconies, sheltered by a pine grove.

Shaky with nerves, Reiko picked up the package she'd brought, a round box wrapped in floral paper. She climbed out of the palanquin. The detectives went on to the Black Lotus Temple to continue investigating the fire. At the door of the convent, a nun greeted Reiko with a silent bow. Reiko introduced herself and explained the purpose of her visit. The nun led her inside, along corridors with bare rafters and plank floors.

Open doors revealed the nuns' quarters, which featured barred windows, simple cabinets, and wooden sleeping pallets. Reiko heard low feminine voices, but saw no one.

"How is Haru today?" Reiko asked.

The nun's only reply was a vague half-smile. Reiko's nervousness increased. They mounted the stairs to another corridor. The nun slid open a door, gestured for Reiko to enter, then bowed and departed.

Hesitating at the threshold, Reiko saw a cell furnished with a futon on a wooden pallet, washbasin, cupboard, and charcoal brazier. A table held bowls of dried leaves that looked to be herbal medicine. By the open window knelt a small, thin girl dressed in an indigo cotton kimono printed with white ivy vines. Her long, glossy hair was loose, her back to the door. Rocking gently back and forth, she seemed transfixed by the view of bright sky through pine boughs, or lost in thought.

"Haru-*san*?" Reiko said quietly.

The girl gave a violent start. She turned toward Reiko a face whose wide brow, tilted eyes, and pointed chin gave her the appearance of a pretty kitten. When her delicate lips parted, Reiko imagined hearing a tiny mew of fright.

"I'm sorry I scared you," Reiko said, approaching with cautious steps. Sympathy for the girl eased Reiko's apprehension. In a soothing voice she said, "Don't be afraid. My name is Reiko, and I've come for a visit with you."

She knelt near Haru. The girl didn't speak, but her wary gaze betrayed a flicker of interest. Encouraged, Reiko said, "You met my husband yesterday. He's the shogun's *sōsakan-sama*, and he's investigating the fire at the Black Lotus Temple—"

Haru recoiled, huddling low to the floor. She cast a terrified glance toward the door, as if simultaneously seeking escape and anticipating danger.

Reiko belatedly realized that she shouldn't have mentioned Sano, whom she knew Haru feared, or introduced the subject of the fire so soon. In her anxiety and her eagerness for information, she'd forgotten common sense, a detective's most important tool. Yet Haru's reaction demonstrated that she had the wits to understand words, if not the ability to speak. Hastily

Reiko said, "The *sōsakan-sama* isn't here. I promise he won't bother you again."

Haru relaxed, but watched Reiko doubtfully.

"And we won't talk about the fire if you don't want to. We can just get acquainted. I'd like to be your friend." Reiko smiled, offering the package to Haru. "Here, I've brought you a present."

A shy smile curved Haru's lips. She seemed younger than her fifteen years, and she accepted the package with the eager curiosity of a child. Carefully she removed the cord and wrapping and opened the box, revealing small round cakes dusted with pink sugar. She gave a little gasp of happy surprise.

"They're filled with sweet chestnut paste," Reiko said.

Haru looked up at Reiko, a question in her eyes.

"Go ahead, try one."

Daintily picking up a cake, Haru took a bite and chewed. Delight lit up her face.

"You like it?" Reiko said.

Haru bobbed her head enthusiastically.

Knowing how girls liked sweets and guessing that orphans seldom received them, Reiko had reasoned that her own favorite treat would win Haru's appreciation. Now she congratulated herself on the success of her gift. She waited until Haru had eaten several more cakes, licked the sugar off her fingers, bowed in thanks, and set aside the box. Then she said, "Are the nuns treating you well?"

Ducking her head, Haru nodded.

"How are you feeling today?"

The girl remained silent, eyes downcast, biting her thumbnail. Reiko suppressed her impatience. Time passed; from downstairs came the scrape of a door sliding open or closed. Then Haru whispered, "Much better, thank you, Honorable Lady."

A thrill of glee ran through Reiko: She'd gotten Haru to talk! "I'm glad to hear that. And please call me Reiko."

"Reiko-*san*." Haru spoke louder this time, her voice clear and sweet.

Easing toward her subject of interest, Reiko said, "How long have you lived at the Black Lotus Temple?"

As though rendered mute again by the effort of producing

her previous words, Haru raised two fingers instead of answering. Reiko interpreted, "Two years?" At a nod from Haru, she said, "Are you happy there?"

"Oh, yes." Now Haru lifted her eyes, appraising Reiko. What she saw evidently reassured her, because she flashed Reiko a timid smile.

"That's good," Reiko said, charmed by Haru and pleased at the growing harmony between them. Not wanting to intimidate the girl or accentuate their class differences, she'd worn a modest dark green kimono printed with pine cones and dressed her hair in a simple knot. Now Reiko felt a renewed confidence in her judgment. "What do you like about the temple?"

"I like taking care of the children in the orphanage," Haru said softly. "Children are so sweet."

"Yes, I know," Reiko said. "I have a little boy."

"The nuns and priests are so kind," Haru said, "especially High Priest Anraku. He took me in when I was lost and alone. He gave me hope for the future." Faith shone in Haru's eyes. "He brought joy and meaning to my miserable life."

New sects attracted members by dispensing charity and spiritual guidance to impoverished or otherwise troubled citizens, Reiko knew. The novelty of new rituals, conducted by charismatic priests eager to gain a following, could bring these sects a wild popularity that faded when a different sect caught the public fancy. However, the minor Black Lotus sect, established nine years ago, had an unusually wide appeal. Many Edo Castle servants had joined, but the Black Lotus also boasted followers among merchants, *bakufu* officials, daimyo clans, and numerous samurai women of Reiko's acquaintance. Reiko, whose family belonged to the main temple of Zōjō, shared the prevailing view of upstart sects as diversions that posed little threat to society, because even if they exploited human weakness for material gain, their subjects received benefits in return, as Haru had.

"Anraku is the Bodhisattva of Infinite Power," Haru said reverently. A bodhisattva was a holy man who possessed the wisdom necessary to attain nirvana, but instead devoted himself to helping other people achieve spiritual enlightenment and release from suffering. Some religious leaders earned the title through doing good works or performing miracles; others merely proclaimed themselves bodhisattvas to attract followers. Reiko wondered which type the Black Lotus high priest was.

Now sadness veiled Haru's pretty features, and she clasped her arms around herself. "Anraku and the Black Lotus are the only family I have, now that my parents are gone," she said.

Even as Reiko experienced a pang of sympathy for the girl, her instincts quickened. "Would you like to tell me about your parents?" Reiko said gently. Perhaps one confidence would lead to others more relevant to the investigation.

Eagerness and worry mingled in Haru's expression. She gazed out the window. Below the convent, an old nun led a group of novices along a path. The novices giggled as one by one they scampered ahead of their elder while she remained serenely oblivious. Haru said, "Oh, but I couldn't impose on you."

"I want to hear," Reiko coaxed.

Haru bit her lip, then nodded and spoke in a voice soft with nostalgia: "My father owned a noodle shop in Kojimachi, near Yamasakana." This was a popular restaurant. "I was an only child. My mother and I helped my father cook and serve the food. We lived in rooms behind the shop. We worked very hard, and we never had much money, but we were happy. My future prospects were good. Someday, after I married, my husband and I would inherit the shop. But then . . ." Haru's voice broke. "I'm sorry," she whispered.

"That's all right," Reiko soothed.

Blinking away tears, Haru continued, "My parents took ill with a fever. There was no money for a doctor, or medicine. I nursed them as best I could, but they died. The day after the funeral, a moneylender seized the shop as payment for my father's debts. My home was gone. I was old enough to marry, but no one wants a bride without a dowry. I had no relatives to take care of me." Sobs wracked Haru's body. "I was so alone, so scared. I didn't know what to do or where to turn."

Overcome with pity, Reiko murmured, "Shh, it's all right," as she did when comforting Masahiro. Haru seemed a mere child, arousing Reiko's maternal instincts and her outrage against a cruel world. The girl's woeful story made her ashamed of her own good fortune. At the same time Reiko felt a glow of achievement because Haru trusted her enough to confide in her. "Don't cry. You're safe now."

"But I'm not!" The impassioned exclamation burst from Haru as she wept. "When the Black Lotus Temple took me in, I thought my problems were solved. I was going to be a nun someday and have a home forever." In Buddhist nunneries and monasteries, the faithful enjoyed freedom from worldly concerns and pursued spiritual enlightenment while supported by alms from the lay community. "Now I've been taken away from the people I love. I'm all alone again."

"Because of what happened at the temple yesterday?" Reiko said, circumspectly referring to the fire to avoid frightening Haru back into silence.

The girl nodded. "I'm so afraid that everyone thinks I set the fire and killed those people. My friends will turn against me. I'll be expelled from the Black Lotus. The police will arrest me. I'll be tied to a stake and burned to death!"

This was the penalty for arson, whether or not anyone died as a result. Even a small fire could spread, destroy the entire city, and take thousands of lives, as the Great Fire of Meireki had thirty-five years ago; therefore, the *bakufu* harshly punished arsonists. Fear for Haru overshadowed Reiko's triumph at getting her to talk about the fire. So far, Haru was the only suspect and thus an easy target for public outrage and official censure, whether she was guilty or innocent. Reiko experienced an increasing urgency to determine what had happened and perhaps prevent a terrible injustice. She didn't want to break her tenuous rapport with Haru, but she needed to establish one fact before proceeding.

"Did you set the fire?" Reiko asked.

Haru stared at her, aghast. "I would never do such an awful thing." Tears streamed from her eyes onto her trembling mouth. "I could never hurt anybody."

Sincerity echoed in the girl's voice, but Reiko cautioned herself against premature belief. "I'm sorry to upset you by asking that," she said, "but you can see why people might be suspicious, can't you? After all, you wouldn't talk when you were questioned about the fire yesterday. Why is that?"

"I could tell that those detectives didn't like me, that they thought I'd done something wrong. And the nuns and priests acted as if they didn't trust me anymore. I knew nobody would believe anything I said." The words tumbled from Haru in an agitated rush, and she began to breathe in rapid wheezes. Rising, she backed away from Reiko, leveling upon her a wounded gaze. "You say you want to be my friend, but you don't believe me either!"

"I didn't say that," Reiko protested. "I just want to understand—"

The girl fell to the floor, sobbing with hysterical abandon. "There's no one to help me. I'm going to die!"

Watching, Reiko experienced the unease of contradictory feelings. Criminals often claimed to be innocent and put on convincing acts to gain credibility, but a person wrongly suspected would also behave as Haru did.

"If you're innocent, then you have nothing to fear." Reiko moved over to kneel beside Haru, patting her back until the weeping subsided, then said, "I want to tell you a story." Although Haru lay curled on her side, her face hidden by her hair, alertness stilled her. "When I was very young, I loved legends about samurai heroes," Reiko said. "I often imagined myself as one of them, riding into battle with my armor and swords. But my favorite daydreams were about protecting peasants from marauding bandits and defeating evil villains in duels." Reiko smiled, recalling her childhood fantasies. "My father is Magistrate Ueda, and I used to listen to trials in his court. I convinced him that some of the people accused of crimes were really innocent. I saved them from jail, beatings, exile, or death. Since I married the *sōsakan-sama,* I've worked with him to avenge innocent victims. The great joy of my life is righting wrongs and helping people—especially women."

She didn't mention that she'd also helped her father extract confessions from criminals and Sano to deliver the guilty to justice. Instead Reiko said, "I'd really like to help you, Haru-*san*. But first you must tell me everything you know about the fire."

For a long moment Haru lay motionless, sniffling. Then she sat up and lifted a blotchy, tearstained face to Reiko. A gleam of hope brightened her eyes; doubt furrowed her brow. Shaking her head, she whispered, "But I don't know anything. I can't remember."

Reiko knew that criminals sometimes tried to hide their guilt behind pleas of ignorance and lost memory, but she concealed her instinctive skepticism. "How can that be? You were at scene while the house burned. At least you can tell me what you were doing there."

"But I can't." Fresh panic infused Haru's voice, and her face crumpled, as though she might burst into tears again. "The night before the fire, I went to bed in the orphanage dormitory, as usual. The next thing I knew, it was morning, and I was outside the burning cottage. I don't know how I got there."

The story sounded outlandish to Reiko, but she withheld objection for the moment. "Did you see anyone around the cottage before the fire brigade came?" she asked.

Haru frowned, pressing both palms against her temples in an apparent effort to recall. "No."

"Concentrate on the night before. Try to remember waking up, and if you saw or heard anything unusual."

A dazed look misted Haru's gaze. "Sometimes I think I remember things. A light. Noises. Struggling. Being afraid . . . But maybe I was dreaming." Then Haru's eyes focused and widened. She exclaimed, "Maybe the person who set the fire brought me to the cottage so everyone would think I did it!"

Reiko's skepticism increased: Criminals often swore they'd been framed. "Who would do that to you?"

The girl said sadly, "I don't know. I love everyone at the temple, and I thought they loved me, too."

That she didn't try to divert suspicion by incriminating someone else argued in favor of Haru's innocence, Reiko noted. "Did you know Police Commander Oyama? Or the woman and child who died in the fire?"

Lips pursed, Haru shook her head. Then she suggested, "Maybe someone from outside the temple burned down the cottage."

Criminals often blamed mysterious strangers for their deeds, too. Reiko contemplated Haru with growing distrust. She wanted to believe the girl, but many signs pointed toward her guilt.

Haru must have perceived Reiko's doubts, because her posture slumped and she bowed her head. "I knew you wouldn't believe me. But I really can't remember anything . . . except that someone hurt me that night."

"Hurt you?" Startled, Reiko said, "How do you mean?"

Haru took off her socks, stood, and lifted the skirt of her kimono. She turned, anxiously watching Reiko over her shoulder as she displayed raw scrapes on her heels and calves.

Although Reiko winced inwardly, she tried to maintain her objectivity. "That could have happened when you were trying to get away from the fire brigade."

"But there's more. See?" Facing Reiko, the girl tugged open the neckline of her kimono. Fresh, dark bruises smudged the flesh around the base of her throat. "And look!"

Quickly Haru untied her sash, shed her garments, and stood naked. More bruises, large and small, in shades of reddish purple, discolored her thighs, upper arms, and chest. "They weren't there when I went to bed. I don't know how I got them."

Reiko stared in horror. At the same time she noticed that despite her slender build and childish manner, Haru had the body of a woman. Her breasts were round and full, her armpits and pubic mound covered with coarse hair. This incongruity reminded Reiko of the danger of making assumptions based on initial appearances, but a new scenario occupied her mind.

"And my head hurts," Haru said, kneeling and parting her hair to show Reiko a red lump on the back of her scalp.

Perhaps the arsonist had abducted Haru from the orphanage, beaten her, and dragged her across the temple grounds—which would account for the scrapes and bruises—and put her in the cottage. Then Haru had somehow managed to escape the burning building, Reiko theorized. The head wound could explain her memory loss. Reiko's doubts began to crumble. Maybe Haru hadn't set the fire. Her injuries were evidence that she could have been an intended victim of it.

Haru wrapped herself in her kimono. She huddled on the floor, fretting, "I'm so afraid someone will hurt me again. I'm so afraid of dying!"

Her plight moved Reiko to tears. Unless facts later proved that Haru was guilty, Reiko must give her the benefit of the doubt. Impulsively, Reiko embraced Haru.

"You're not going to die, if I can prove that you're innocent and find the real arsonist," Reiko said.

3

Honor and uphold the correct Law,
Seek universal knowledge,
Behave with perfect clarity of conduct.

—FROM THE BLACK LOTUS SUTRA

Edo Jail loomed above a filthy canal amid the slums of Kodemmacho, in the northeast sector of the Nihonbashi merchant
district. Watchtowers topped its crumbling stone walls. Inside,
dilapidated offices and barracks surrounded the fortified dun-
geon where jailers tortured confessions out of prisoners and
criminals awaited execution. The morgue received the bodies
of citizens who perished in natural disasters or from unnatural
causes. Yet hidden within this realm of death, a small green
oasis flourished. In a fenced courtyard, a garden grew in neat
rows marked by bamboo stakes; butterflies and bees flitted.
Here Sano found his friend Dr. Ito tending his medicinal herbs.
Sano walked along the garden's border, enjoying its fresh aro-

mas. He could almost imagine himself in the countryside, rather than in a place shunned by society.

"Good morning, Ito-*san*," he said, bowing.

A tall, thin man in his seventies, Dr. Ito bowed and smiled. His short white hair gleamed in the sunlight; perspiration filmed his lined, ascetic face. "Welcome, Sano-*san*. I have been awaiting your arrival."

Dr. Ito, once a respected physician to the imperial family, had been caught practicing forbidden foreign science, which he'd learned through illicit channels from Dutch traders. Usually the Tokugawa punished scholars of Dutch learning with exile, but the *bakufu* instead condemned Dr. Ito to permanent custodianship of Edo Morgue. There he continued his scientific experiments, ignored by the authorities. He also administered medical treatment to the staff and prisoners, and his expertise had often benefited Sano's investigations.

Wiping his hands on his dark blue coat, Dr. Ito rose with the stiff movements of old age. "How is Masahiro-*chan*?"

"Many thanks for inquiring about my miserable, inferior child," Sano said, observing the polite custom of deprecating one's offspring. "His size, his voice, and his demands grow daily."

A twinkle in Dr. Ito's shrewd eyes acknowledged the paternal pride behind Sano's modesty. "I am glad to hear that. And I hope the Honorable Lady Reiko is well?"

"She is," Sano said, but the mention of Reiko unsettled his thoughts.

During the trip from Edo Castle, he'd begun to have misgivings about asking her to help with the investigation. Might her overeagerness frighten Haru and ruin their chances of getting the truth from this important witness and possible suspect? Sano valued Reiko's excellent intuition, but he needed an impartial judge to question Haru, and he belatedly understood how Reiko's personal biases might interfere with her objectivity. Sano wished he'd asked Reiko to wait until they could go to Zōjō Temple together, so he could listen in on the interview with Haru. Although Reiko had never yet failed him, he feared what might happen with this investigation.

Dr. Ito said, "Is something wrong, Sano-*san*?"

"No, nothing," Sano said, not wanting to burden his friend

with his troubles. He turned the conversation to the purpose of his visit. "Have you received the bodies from the fire at the Black Lotus Temple yet?"

Dr. Ito's expression turned serious. "Yes. And I regret to say that my examination has revealed some discoveries that may complicate your work."

He led Sano to the morgue, a low building with peeling plaster walls and an unkempt thatched roof. Inside, a single large room held stone troughs used for washing the dead, cabinets containing tools, and a podium heaped with books and papers. Dr. Ito's assistant Mura, a man in his fifties with gray hair and a square, intelligent face, was cleaning knives. He bowed to Sano and his master. Three waist-high tables each held a human figure covered with a white shroud. Dr. Ito walked to the largest body.

"Commander Oyama," he said, then beckoned his assistant.

Mura stepped forward. He was an *eta,* one of the outcast class that staffed the jail as wardens, torturers, corpse handlers, and executioners. The *eta*'s hereditary link with death-related occupations such as butchering and leather tanning rendered them spiritually contaminated and barred them from contact with other citizens. Mura, who performed all the physical work associated with Dr. Ito's studies, removed the shroud from Police Commander Oyama.

Although Sano had learned to control his aversion to the dead during past examinations, he felt a sense of pollution as he beheld the pale, naked corpse with its thick torso and limbs. Oyama's glazed eyes and gaping mouth gave him an imbecilic expression that belied the wits of a man recently responsible for enforcing the law in a city of one million people.

"Turn him over, Mura," said Dr. Ito.

The *eta* complied. Dr. Ito pointed to the back of Oyama's head. The hair had been shaved away, revealing a hollow in the scalp behind the left ear, with reddened, broken flesh in the center. "A blow cracked his skull," Dr. Ito said.

Because the examination of corpses and any other procedures that smacked of foreign science were illegal, Sano had forgone a detailed scrutiny of Oyama while at the Black Lotus Temple; he'd looked just long enough to identify the commander's face and hadn't noticed the injury. Now he said, "Could it have happened after Oyama died?"

Dr. Ito shook his head. "There was blood in his hair and on his skin before Mura washed him, and the dead don't bleed. Oyama was alive when the blow was struck by an object with sharp edges. An injury of such severity is usually fatal. He wasn't burned, and his color exhibits none of the pinkness I would expect to see if he'd died from breathing smoke. Therefore, I conclude that the blow, not the fire, killed Oyama."

"I found nothing resembling a weapon when I searched the site of his death," Sano said. "But it's clear that his murder was deliberate instead of an accidental result of arson. The fire must have been set to disguise the murder."

Blowing out his breath, Sano shook his head in consternation. He'd hoped that Oyama's death was a simple matter of being in the wrong place at the wrong time. Now Sano saw the scope of the case expand beyond the boundaries of the Black Lotus Temple. The list of potential arson suspects, previously headed by the orphan girl Haru and limited to the temple community, grew to include the associates of a man who must have made many enemies during his life.

As if reading his thoughts, Dr. Ito gave Sano a sympathetic look, then said, "I'm afraid that there wasn't just one murder before the fire was set."

Dr. Ito walked to the second table. Mura uncovered the body of the dead woman. A fetid odor of burnt, decaying flesh filled the air. Sano's stomach lurched. He swallowed hard as he viewed the corpse. With her garments removed except for charred strips of cloth adhering to her, the woman looked even worse than she had yesterday. She lay on her right side, bent at the knees and waist, arms angled. Burns ranging in color and texture from blistered, scabrous red to black cinder covered her limbs, torso, face, and hairless scalp. When Mura turned the dead woman on her other side, Sano saw unscathed areas on the newly exposed portions of skin.

"The places on her body that lay against the floor escaped the fire," Dr. Ito said, "as did this area here."

He pointed to the base of her neck. In the dead flesh was a deep, narrow, red indentation. Sano bent close and discerned a pattern: the coils of a thin rope. He straightened, meeting Dr.

Ito's somber gaze, and voiced their shared thought: "She was strangled to death, then left to burn in the fire."

Now Sano had not one but two deliberate murders, and while the second victim deserved justice every bit as much as Oyama did, her death posed extra difficulties. "How can I find out who wanted her dead and why, when I don't even know who she is?" Sano said.

"Perhaps she was an acquaintance of Commander Oyama," suggested Dr. Ito. "After all, they were in the cottage together. Perhaps his family knew her."

"Perhaps," Sano agreed, "but who could make a definite identification of her in her present state?"

Contemplating the body, Dr. Ito said, "She was of medium size and build." With a thin metal spatula he probed the woman's mouth, around which her burned lips formed a horrible grimace. "Two back teeth are missing on the right side and one on the left. The others are in good condition and sharp on the edges. The unburned skin is firm and unblemished. I estimate her age at around thirty years." Pointing at her foot, Dr. Ito added, "The sole is calloused, with dirt embedded in the creases, and the nails are rough. She was accustomed to walking barefoot outdoors, which suggests that she was from society's lower classes."

"I'm impressed that you can get so much information under these circumstances," Sano said. "Now I have a description of the victim."

"However, it is one that fits thousands of women," Dr. Ito said. "Maybe her clothes will tell us more." Using the spatula, he worked loose a strip of fabric stuck to the corpse's stomach, folding it back to reveal the color and pattern: dark blue, printed with white bamboo branches. "It's from the type of cheap cotton kimono sold all over town and worn by countless peasants."

"But the fact that this woman was wearing it indicates that she wasn't a nun, who would wear plain hemp," Sano said. "Maybe she came from outside the temple, which would explain why no one there seems to know who she could be."

Dr. Ito poked his spatula under the cloth. "There's something in here."

Sano heard the click of the tool against a hard surface. A small object fell onto the table. It was a round figure the size of a cherry, made of amber-colored jade and finely carved in the likeness of a curled, sleeping deer. A length of string protruded from a hole through the figure.

"It's an *ojime*," Sano said, recognizing the object as a bead used to connect the cords of the pouches or boxes that men hung from their sashes.

"She must have been wearing it around her waist," Dr. Ito said, "perhaps as an amulet."

"The design is unique, and it looks valuable," Sano said. "Maybe it will help me identify her."

Mura washed the *ojime* and wrapped it in a clean cloth. Sano tucked it into the leather pouch at his waist, then followed Dr. Ito to the table that held the third corpse, a pitifully small figure beneath its white shroud. "Was the child murdered before the fire, too?" he asked.

Dr. Ito nodded sadly. When Mura drew back the shroud, Sano felt the same powerful aversion to viewing the dead child as he had at the Black Lotus Temple. He hadn't been able to look yesterday, and he couldn't now. Abruptly, he turned away, but imagination conjured up a horrible picture of a burnt, wizened little body, its face a dreadful black mask with gaping mouth and empty eye sockets. Sano's heart began pounding; his stomach constricted. His breaths came hard and fast, inhaling the smell of smoke and burnt flesh. He felt faint. This was his first case involving the murder of a child, and fatherhood had shattered his professional detachment.

Then Sano felt Dr. Ito propelling him out of the morgue. The fresh air in the courtyard revived him. Now he felt ashamed of his cowardly reaction. "I'm sorry," he said. "I'm all right now."

He started to go back inside the morgue, but Dr. Ito gently restrained him. "It's not necessary for you to see the remains. I can summarize the results of my examination." After giving Sano another moment to recover, Dr. Ito said, "The child is male. There are old and new bruises on the unburned skin of his back. His neck is broken, probably as a result of strangulation. I estimate his age at two years, but he could be older—his body is severely emaciated, and perhaps stunted in growth. I believe the boy was mistreated and starved over a period of time before his murder."

Sano deplored the torture of any human, but since Masahiro's birth, he found the idea of violence toward children particularly abhorrent. Of all the murders, this one disturbed him most. "None of the temple orphans is missing," Sano said. "Did you notice anything that might help determine who the boy is or where he came from?"

Dr. Ito shook his head. "Because the child's body was found with the woman's, it would be logical to assume they were mother and son, but assumptions can be misleading." He added, "Unfortunately, there are among the poor of Edo many such ill-fed, maltreated children who might end up dead under dubious circumstances. I am afraid that you must employ other methods to identify the woman and boy."

"I've already begun." Sano had given orders to Hirata before leaving his estate. "Now I'll be on my way to Police Commander Oyama's home to interview his family and staff."

After bidding farewell to Dr. Ito, Sano left the jail. He mounted his horse and rode through teeming streets toward the city center, anticipating the work ahead with a keener determination than usual. Throughout his career, he'd dedicated himself to seeking truth and serving justice, a mission as important to his samurai honor as duty, loyalty, and courage. But fatherhood gave him an added incentive to solve this case. He must avenge the death of the unknown child.

If Haru was guilty of murder and arson, Sano would see that she paid for the crimes with her own life.

4

I will make the world pure,
Without flaw or defilement.
Its land will be made of gold,
Its roads bounded by ropes of silver,
And trees will bear jeweled blossoms and fruit.

—FROM THE BLACK LOTUS SUTRA

Reiko decided that the first step toward determining Haru's guilt or innocence was to discover what had happened to the girl on the night before the fire. How had she sustained her wounds and gotten to the cottage? Who benefited from letting Haru take the blame for the arson and murder? Surely the answers lay within the Black Lotus Temple.

After leaving the Zōjō convent, Reiko and her entourage traveled west through the surrounding district. Her palanquin made slow progress; the narrow streets between the walls of subsidiary temples were thronged with priests and pilgrims. Reiko's thoughts turned to Masahiro. What was he doing now?

Although she missed him, she had agreed to help Haru, whose life might depend on her.

At the gate of the Black Lotus Temple, Reiko alighted from the palanquin and entered the precinct, leaving her escorts behind. She had an uneasy feeling that Sano wouldn't approve of her mission, and she decided against speaking with Black Lotus officials because that might interfere with his work. Instead, she would seek out female members of the community who'd been close to Haru. Her strength as a detective lay in her rapport with women, who might be intimidated by Sano's men.

Reiko stood inside the gate, absorbing impressions. The layout of the compound resembled that of countless other temples. A wide flagstone path bisected the precinct. On either side stood worship halls, shrines, sutra repository, a fountain, bell cage, and other buildings, all constructed in traditional Buddhist style. A black and gold lotus symbol adorned gables and carved doors and the tall, double-roofed gateway to the main hall at the end of the path. Late-morning sunlight glittered upon gray tile roofs and a red pagoda. The difference between this and other temples Reiko had visited was the unusual landscaping.

Sycamores spread mottled branches over the main path; leafy arbors shadowed smaller paths. Pines, oaks, red maples, and cherry trees obscured buildings; lush grass and shrubbery grew between white gravel walks. Deep shadows cooled the air. The high walls and dense foliage shut out the traffic noises. Priests in saffron robes, nuns in gray, and novices in brown flitted silently, eyes downcast, through crowds of sedate worshippers. From somewhere within the compound rose the eerie rhythm of chanting. Strong incense that smelled like cloying orange blossoms permeated the air. The place had a strange, ethereal beauty that sent a shiver along Reiko's nerves.

"Greetings, Honorable Lady Sano."

Startled by the sound of a husky female voice, Reiko turned and faced a tall woman dressed in a pale gray kimono.

"Welcome to the Black Lotus Temple," said the woman, bowing. A long white drape covered her head. In her late thirties, she had square jaws and a full, sensuous mouth. Her narrow eyes glittered with hard intelligence. She wore no face powder, but her eyebrows were shaved and redrawn high on her forehead, and a thin film of rouge colored her lips. Age had etched faint lines around her mouth and brown spots marred her cheeks, but she must have been lovely in her youth and still possessed a haggard beauty. Four nuns flanked her, two on each side. "I'm Junketsu-in, the abbess of the convent. It's an honor to make your acquaintance."

Reiko felt a stab of surprise as she bowed in automatic courtesy and murmured politely, "The honor is mine." She'd never seen an abbess wearing makeup, and although holy women usually shaved their heads, she saw hair pulled back from the brow under the abbess's headdress. Also disconcerted by the prompt official reception accorded her unannounced visit, she asked, "How do you know who I am?"

"Oh, you're too modest." Abbess Junketsu-in smiled. Her voice had an arch, affected quality. "Everyone knows the wife of the shogun's *sōsakan-sama.*"

While Reiko realized that her work with Sano had caused some gossip around town, she was not exactly a public figure. Had someone eavesdropped on her conversation with Haru, then alerted the Black Lotus to expect her? Reiko didn't like the abbess's bold, appraising gaze, and instinct told her that Junketsu-in's appearance and behavior were signs of something wrong in the temple. Or was she being overly suspicious because it might harbor a killer?

"I suppose you're helping your husband investigate the fire," Junketsu-in said, adding weight to Reiko's suspicions. Since her participation in the case wasn't public knowledge, and women did visit temples for religious reasons, why should Junketsu-in make this assumption unless she knew about the interview with Haru? "Please let me assist you."

"I'm here to investigate Haru's possible role in the arson and murder," Reiko conceded.

Junketsu-in's smile widened. Sharp teeth, angled inward, gave her mouth the look of a trap. "I know Haru very well. We can talk in my chambers." The abbess gestured down a narrow lane.

"Actually, I was hoping to meet Haru's friends." Reiko guessed that the temple might wish to keep the investigation focused on Haru, either to protect the person responsible for the fire or to prevent scrutiny of the sect's business. She couldn't trust the word of any official who might sacrifice an orphan as an easy scapegoat. "If you'll just direct me to the orphanage, I needn't inconvenience you."

"That won't be necessary," Junketsu-in said, still smiling, although her gaze hardened. "I'll be happy to give you whatever information you need."

She and the nuns surrounded Reiko. It was obvious that they didn't want her roaming the temple on her own. Briefly, Reiko considered invoking Sano's authority and commanding Junketsu-in to let her do as she wished. Yet she felt uncomfortable about pretending to act on Sano's behalf when he didn't even know she was here. Across the precinct, she saw two of his detectives passing by, but enlisting their aid would put them in the dubious position of having to decide whether helping her constituted disobedience to their master. Also, Reiko knew that antagonizing a sect official could cause trouble for Sano.

"Very well," Reiko said, letting Junketsu-in escort her down the path. Perhaps she could still learn something of importance.

The path led under the arbors, between tree-shaded buildings past which Junketsu-in hurried Reiko as if not wanting her to get a good look at them or speak to the nuns passing by. "This is the nunnery," Junketsu-in said, ushering Reiko into a smaller version of the convent at Zōjō Temple.

They sat in a plainly furnished chamber upstairs. Sliding doors stood open to a balcony that overlooked the thatched roofs of more buildings. A maid served tea. The nuns knelt like mute sentries in the corners. Now Reiko noticed that the abbess's gray kimono was made of fine cotton with a subtle pattern of wavy, lighter gray lines instead of plain hemp like the nuns' robes; she wore spotless white socks in contrast to their bare feet.

"What are the practices of the Black Lotus sect?" Reiko asked, curious to know what rituals had attracted such a large following, and what doctrine allowed the abbess to violate the Buddhist practice of spurning worldly vanity.

"Human existence is full of suffering," Junketsu-in said in a lofty, pious tone. "This suffering is caused by selfish desire. By ridding ourselves of desire, we can gain release from suffering and reach nirvana. We can only do this by following the right path."

Reiko recognized these axioms as the Four Noble Truths, the foundation for all forms of Buddhism.

"We believe that every human has the potential to reach nirvana and achieve Buddhahood—the state of supreme enlightenment and supernatural power. Memorizing and chanting the Black Lotus Sutra and meditating on it makes us one with the truth contained therein. The act of chanting harnesses all our life's activities to the purpose of releasing the power that lies within the realm of the unconscious, where we can grasp the ultimate meaning of the sutra. Understanding occurs in a mystical fusion between worshipper and sutra, and thus we shall attain nirvana and Buddhahood."

"I'm not familiar with the Black Lotus Sutra," Reiko said. "Is it related to the famous Lotus Sutra?" That scripture was the basis for other sects. "What does it say?"

"The Black Lotus Sutra is a unique, ancient verse that was discovered by our high priest. It states that the correct path to Buddhahood consists of infinite parallel, intersecting, converging, and diverging paths that unite as one, and that High Priest Anraku, the Bodhisattva of Infinite Power, will show us each the path that we must follow." The abbess stirred restlessly. "But it is long, complex, and requires much time to recite and extensive study to comprehend. And I believe you wish to know about Haru and the fire?"

"Yes," Reiko said.

She noted the abbess's desire to turn the conversation away from the sect, which seemed an amalgam of established religion and new philosophy. The Pure Land sect, governed by Zōjō Temple, revered the Pure Land Sutra and believed that constantly invoking the name of Amida, the Buddha of Unlimited Light, helped humans achieve salvation. Zen sects, preferred by many samurai, practiced meditation with the goal of satori, a sudden perception of felt knowledge. The Black Lotus most resembled the Nichiren Shōshū sect, founded some four hundred years ago by a dynamic spiritual leader and still popular with commoners, which chanted the Lotus Sutra to achieve enlightenment. Reiko had read that scripture and knew it did not actually reveal the secret truth, which was indescribable, but that worshippers needn't understand the words to benefit from chanting them. Presumably, this was also the case with the

Black Lotus Sutra. None of the Black Lotus practices sounded extraordinary, and Reiko wondered why Junketsu-in didn't want to talk about them.

"I'm trying to reconstruct what happened to Haru, starting with the night before the fire, when she went to bed in the orphanage dormitory," Reiko said. "I want to know if anyone saw her between then and the time when the fire brigade found her."

Abbess Junketsu-in compressed her mouth in disgust. "Did Haru tell you that she can't remember anything? Well, I have to warn you against believing what she says, because although Haru can be very appealing, she's a shady character. If she said she went to bed when she was supposed to, she was lying. Her dishonesty, disobedience, and lack of respect for authority have been a constant problem.

"She's always breaking rules. She talks during sacred rituals and refuses to do chores. She steals food from the pantry. She's sloppy, rude, and trespasses in areas where the orphans aren't allowed." Disapproval saturated the abbess's voice. "When she's scolded for her misbehavior, Haru always denies any wrongdoing. She hates getting up early, so the nuns have to drag her out of bed for morning prayers. At night, she waits until everyone's asleep and sneaks out of the orphanage. That's what she did the night before the fire."

"How do you know?" Reiko was disturbed by this picture of Haru, which was at odds with her own impression of the girl, and Haru's portrayal of herself as a grateful orphan who loved her benefactors and got along well with everyone. The abbess's claim that Haru had deliberately left the dormitory contradicted Haru's version of events. Yet Reiko wondered whether Junketsu-in's eagerness to blacken Haru's reputation meant that the abbess had a personal stake in turning Reiko against Haru. "Did you see her?"

"No," Junketsu-in said. "It's not my duty to watch over the orphans." She spoke with haughty disdain. "But the temple guards have caught Haru roaming the grounds after dark. Twice they found her consorting with male novices. This has raised serious doubts as to whether Haru is suited for religious life. That's why she hasn't yet entered the convent."

The abbess laughed, a malicious trill. "I don't suppose Haru told you why she lives in the orphanage with the children even though she's a grown woman and old enough to be a nun."

Nor had Reiko noticed the oddity of this circumstance. She'd considered Haru a child, and therefore hadn't even wondered why she hadn't taken religious vows as she'd expressed wanting to do. Reiko knew that unmarried lower-class girls did engage in sex, and she remembered Haru's mature body, but the idea of Haru wantonly seducing young men shocked Reiko. Could the abbess be telling the truth about Haru? Had Reiko missed other significant facts during the interview? Maybe her detective skills had been dulled by the long hiatus from such work.

Hiding her dismay, Reiko said evenly, "I shall need other witnesses to confirm Haru's alleged misbehavior."

"There are four right here in this room." Abbess Junketsu-in gestured at the nuns seated in the corners; they unflinchingly met Reiko's gaze.

How convenient, Reiko thought. Obedient subordinates weren't exactly independent witnesses, and Junketsu-in's reluctance to let her seek others strengthened her suspicions about the abbess. "While the behavior you describe is unsuitable for a prospective nun, the information you've given me has no direct bearing on the arson," she said, noting that she had no more reason to doubt Haru than Junketsu-in.

The abbess said with an air of smug triumph, "A nun in charge of the orphans told me that she checked on them during the night before the fire, and Haru wasn't in bed." Junketsu-in smiled at Reiko's frown. "I'm not surprised that Haru has fooled you. She's quite an accomplished liar. If she says she's lost her memory of that night, it's because she was up to no good and trying to hide the truth."

Although shaken, Reiko wasn't ready to accept the idea that Haru had lied to her, or the abbess's implication that Haru had been out setting the fire. First she must reconstruct those missing hours of Haru's life. Reiko said, "She could have been taken to the cottage against her will. There's a lump on her head, and she's covered with bruises."

A sudden tension stiffened Junketsu-in's posture. She sipped from her tea bowl, as if needing time to think of a reply. Maybe she hadn't known about Haru's injuries and was surprised by the news. But she recovered quickly, saying, "Haru must have done it to herself. She did it once before, when she wanted us to think that a monk she'd seduced had attacked her."

Although it seemed improbable to Reiko that anyone would hurt herself so badly, Haru had displayed the wounds after her story of lost memory and claim of innocence hadn't convinced Reiko. Had she set the fire, then tried to make herself look like a victim? Reiko's sympathy for Haru vied with her knowledge that reliance on a suspect's story could lead her astray. She must consider Junketsu-in's accusations, but she wouldn't let them go unchallenged.

"Did anyone see Haru pouring oil on the cottage and lighting it?" Reiko asked.

Junketsu-in's slender hands, white and smooth as a highborn lady's, closed tightly around her tea bowl. A calculating expression came over her features, but she shook her head. "Not that I know of."

The answer brought Reiko a measure of vindication, although she knew that Sano's detectives were examining the crime scene, questioning the temple residents, and might eventually connect Haru with the arson. "If you expect me to believe Haru is guilty, then you must either produce some definite evidence or allow me to interview more witnesses," Reiko said to the abbess.

They regarded each other with mutual dislike. Then stealthy footsteps creaked the floor outside the room. There was a knock at the door, and Junketsu-in called in a sharp, irate tone, "Who is it?"

The door slid open. A man stood at the threshold. "My apologies, Honorable Abbess. I didn't know you had a guest."

He was tall and thin, with a large head that looked too heavy for the long stem of his neck. Sparse, graying hair receded from a bulbous forehead. He had a muddy, pitted complexion, and though he seemed in his late thirties, his stooped shoulders gave him a look of more advanced age.

Repugnance shadowed Junketsu-in's face, but she politely introduced the man to Reiko: "This is Dr. Miwa, the temple physician."

Upon hearing Reiko's name and the reason for her visit, Dr. Miwa squinted at her. "I shan't intrude," he said, sucking air through unevenly spaced teeth. "I'll come back at a more convenient time."

"Yes, please do." Junketsu-in sounded more relieved at the prospect of his departure than enthusiastic about his later return.

Reiko said quickly, "I would be honored to have you join us." She wanted to know why the Black Lotus sect employed a physician, which wasn't a custom of Buddhist temples, and she wanted another witness to interview.

"If you like," the abbess said with unconcealed bad grace.

Dr. Miwa slunk into the room and knelt near Reiko. She noticed stains and burns on his faded moss-green cotton kimono. A bitter chemical odor wafted from him.

"How did you come to be employed at the temple?" Reiko asked, puzzled by Dr. Miwa's poor grooming. In her experience, physicians were clean and neat, and she couldn't think of any herbal remedy that might produce his strange smell.

"I studied medicine with a prominent physician in Kamakura. After finishing my apprenticeship, I decided to seek my fortune in Edo. When I arrived, I had the good luck of meeting High Priest Anraku, and he offered me a post." The hiss of sucked air punctuated the doctor's sentences. He spoke with his head partially turned toward Reiko, as though unwilling to look straight at her. Perhaps he didn't want to offend her with his ugliness, but she sensed apprehension in him.

"What are your duties?" Reiko said.

"I am honored to assist High Priest Anraku with healing sick, blind, crippled, and insane people who come to him for salvation." Pride infused Dr. Miwa's voice. "I also treat the nuns, priests, novices, and orphans when they become ill."

"Then you know Haru?" Reiko said.

Junketsu-in shot Dr. Miwa a warning glance, which Reiko noted. "Why, yes," Dr. Miwa replied cautiously.

"What do you think of her?"

"Haru is a most interesting case." *Hiss, exhale.* The doctor's sidelong gaze moved over Reiko, who felt an unpleasant, creeping sensation. "She suffers from an extreme imbalance of the two aspects of nature, the six external factors, and the seven emotions."

According to the principles of classic Chinese medicine,

maintaining equilibrium among these elements was essential to good health, Reiko knew.

In a pedantic tone, Dr. Miwa explained, "Haru has too much *yin*, the active aspect. She is excessively influenced by *han* and *huo*, external and internal heat. Her dominant emotions are *nu* and *ching*." Anger and surprise, Reiko translated. "Although Haru is physically well, her spirit is unhealthy. I've been administering treatment in an effort to cure her symptoms."

"What are her symptoms?" Reiko said, realizing with dismay that Dr. Miwa's statement wasn't going to help Haru.

"Willfulness, selfishness, dishonesty, and delusions," Dr. Miwa said. "Sexual promiscuity, disregard for duty, and a lack of respect for authority."

He'd corroborated Junketsu-in's assessment of Haru, lending it the weight of his medical expertise. "Do you think Haru set the fire?" Reiko said.

Another glance passed between the abbess and the doctor, her expression commanding, his at once meek and resentful. "In my professional opinion, yes. Certainly Haru's hot nature gives her a strong affinity for fire and violence."

Despite their personal antagonism, Dr. Miwa and Abbess Junketsu-in were evidently united in their aim to incriminate Haru. Reiko saw lust smoldering in Dr. Miwa's squinty eyes as his furtive gaze licked at her. She stifled a quiver of revulsion and noticed Junketsu-in watching her with narrowed, angry eyes: While the abbess didn't like Dr. Miwa, she clearly wanted to be the focus of male attention and didn't welcome competition. Now she lifted her chin and fingered the loose skin underneath. Reiko had noticed similar behavior in older women who envied her for being young, pretty, and desirable.

"I'm interested to know why you're so eager to convince me that Haru is an arsonist and murderer," Reiko said to the doctor and the abbess.

"We don't want you to be taken in by her lies," Junketsu-in said.

"We want the investigation finished as soon as possible, and the culprit arrested, so that the Black Lotus Temple can recover from this distressing incident," Dr. Miwa said.

"Are you trying to protect someone?" Reiko asked bluntly. The abbess regarded her with open scorn, as though their undeclared rivalry had stripped away her polite façade. "If we wanted to protect anyone, we would have concealed Haru's history from you, because in spite of the trouble she's caused, Haru is one of us."

"The Black Lotus is a law-abiding sect. We do not harbor criminals," Dr. Miwa added, hissing.

"I don't see that Haru has ever hurt anyone or damaged property before," Reiko said, growing impatient with the pair's attempts to prejudice her even as she considered the possibility that they were right about Haru. Although the doctor and the abbess struck her as untrustworthy and their presence in the sect raised questions about its nature, perhaps they were acting with the good intentions they claimed. "Why would Haru burn the cottage?"

"For revenge," the abbess said. "We don't put up with disobedience, and we've punished Haru by making her go without meals and shutting her in a room by herself to pray. Discipline makes her angry. The fire was her way of getting even."

Dr. Miwa nodded in agreement. Reiko hid her distress. If Haru really was the sort of person they claimed, then revenge was a logical reason for her to commit arson. Was it also her motive for murder?

"Did Haru know the victims of the fire?" Reiko asked.

"Nobody knows who the woman and child were," Dr. Miwa said.

Reiko saw his gaze slither away from her and his hands twist together. The fingers were abnormally elongated, scarred from burns, stained with brown spots.

"They must have been beggars who were taking shelter in the cottage," Junketsu-in said, smoothing her robe and casting an envious glance at Reiko's silk garments. "We didn't know they were there, and Haru probably didn't, either. She doesn't care about other people. She wouldn't have checked to see if the cottage was empty before she lit the fire."

A movement behind Junketsu-in and Dr. Miwa caught Reiko's attention. Looking toward the balcony, she saw a young monk peering over the rail. His shaven head was narrow, with ears that stuck out like handles. He was looking straight at Reiko. When their gazes met, he glanced at the room's other occupants and put a finger to his lips. Instinctively, Reiko looked down at her tea bowl, hiding her surprise. She wondered why the monk had been eavesdropping.

"Did Haru know Police Commander Oyama?" When Reiko again glanced at the balcony, the monk had vanished.

Junketsu-in dismissed the notion with a sneer. "The orphans don't associate with important officials."

If Haru hadn't known Oyama or the other victims, then she would have had no reason to kill them, and the idea that their deaths were an accidental result of her deeds was pure conjecture. Reiko noticed the abbess's hands locked in a tight clasp, and Dr. Miwa's averted gaze. Why, after casting aspersions upon Haru, would Junketsu-in and Dr. Miwa offer lies that favored the girl? Did they really not know who the dead woman and child were? Perhaps they wished to avoid further discussion of the victims for personal reasons.

"Did you know Commander Oyama?" Reiko asked them.

"I've met him on one or two occasions," Junketsu-in said, adding, "I had no reason to wish him any harm. I spent the entire night before the fire in my quarters, and I didn't go near the cottage until after the fire brigade came. My attendants will confirm that." Her gesture encompassed the four mute, watchful nuns.

"And I was treating a sick priest, with the help of my nurses, from midnight until I heard the firebell," Dr. Miwa said. "Commander Oyama often came to the temple for private rituals with High Priest Anraku, in which I had the privilege of assisting. Our relations were entirely amicable."

They were quick to deny any possible motive for Oyama's murder, and to offer alibis, Reiko observed. Under her scrutiny, Dr. Miwa wrung his dirty hands. Abbess Junketsu-in held Reiko's gaze, but her expression was strained, defensive. Into the silence drifted the sound of muffled chanting. The atmosphere in the room was thick with the aura of hidden secrets and tensions. Reiko knew one good reason Junketsu-in and Dr. Miwa might incriminate Haru: to divert suspicion from themselves. What roles might they have played in the crime?

One thing was certain: They knew more than they were telling. Reiko acknowledged that she'd been too quick in wanting to trust Haru's veracity, and if the stories she'd just heard about the girl had come from some other source, she might believe them, but Miwa and Junketsu-in seemed unreliable witnesses. At the very least, they were prejudiced against Haru.

Reiko said, "I'd like to talk to High Priest Anraku." Haru credited the priest with saving her; he might be a better character witness for her than Junketsu-in and Dr. Miwa. "Would you please introduce me to him now?"

The abbess frowned. "High Priest Anraku is busy meditating, and he cannot be disturbed."

"I shall tell His Holiness that you wish an audience with him," Dr. Miwa said, "and let you know when would be convenient."

"Now, if you'll excuse us, we have business to discuss," Junketsu-in said.

The curt dismissal infuriated Reiko, as did the pair's refusal to let her interview their superior. But she was a mere woman, without official authority, outnumbered six to one, with no choice except to bow and rise. "Thank you for your cooperation," she said, hiding her anger.

The abbess's eyes signaled a wordless command to the nuns. Silently they accompanied Reiko out of the convent with the obvious intention of making sure she left the temple. Walking down the path, she saw Detective Marume enter a building, in the company of a priest: It looked as though the Black Lotus sect wasn't allowing Sano's men to conduct their investigation without official escorts. Reiko couldn't trust Haru, but neither should she rely upon the damning testimony of two people who so clearly disliked Haru and had their own secrets to hide. She wouldn't let the sect control the investigation or run her off the premises.

Stalling on the path, Reiko said, "Excuse me, but I must visit the place of relief."

The nuns hesitated, then nodded and led Reiko to a wooden privy shed nestled among pines at the back of the convent. Mounting the two steps to the door, she told the nuns, "You needn't wait." She closed herself inside the dim, cramped space. A hole in the floor stank of human waste. After waiting a moment, Reiko opened the door a crack and peered outside. The nuns stood nearby, watching the privy. Reiko sighed in exasperation. How could she shake off her guards without creating a spectacle that would offend the sect, upset Sano, and intimidate the people she hoped to question discreetly?

At the sound of a soft *tap-tap* behind her, Reiko spun around. In the back wall was a window screened with wooden slats, and through the gaps between these Reiko saw a narrow head with prominent ears. It was the monk from the convent balcony.

"Please, Honorable Lady, I must speak with you," he said in an urgent whisper. "I have important information."

Hope banished Reiko's initial fright. "About what?" she whispered back.

"Meet me outside the temple. Please."

Then, with a rustle of quick footsteps on dry pine needles, he was gone.

5

*They who are deeply attached to worldly love and desire
Cannot escape misery and suffering.*

—FROM THE BLACK LOTUS SUTRA

Masahiro's screams echoed through the house. Since his mother had left him several hours ago, the nursemaids had tried to pacify him with food, toys, and affection, but frequent tantrums continued. By noon, Midori, who had come to visit Reiko, learned that her friend had gone out, and stayed to help with Masahiro, could no longer bear the uproar. She and O-hana, the youngest maid, escaped into the garden. Sunlight filtered down on them through the red maples.

"Peace and quiet at last!" O-hana exclaimed. A girl of nineteen, she had a sharp, pretty face and a saucy smile. "Lucky you, being a lady-in-waiting. You don't have to put up with squalling brats. You can just sit around with Lady Keisho-in all day long. I don't understand why you want to be here, when the young master is driving us all mad."

"Oh, I like coming here," Midori said. She smoothed her pink silk kimono, disheveled from holding the baby. "Reiko and the *sōsakan-sama* are so kind to me. And I like Masahiro."

O-hana said slyly, "Is there someone else you like?"

Midori blushed to think that the maid had noticed her watching for Hirata. She'd met the *sōsakan-sama*'s chief retainer three years ago, after hearing stories about his expedition to Nagasaki, where he'd saved his master's life and captured a band of smugglers. He seemed like a samurai hero from history, and Midori had liked Hirata immediately. He was honest, kind, and, unlike other Tokugawa samurai, he didn't scorn her family background.

She was a daughter of an "outside lord"—a daimyo whose clan had been defeated at the Battle of Sekigahara, then forced to swear allegiance to the victorious Tokugawa. Although Midori was pretty and the powerful Niu clan one of the wealthiest, she found herself left out of the flirtations and marriage negotiations between palace ladies-in-waiting from important families and young *bakufu* samurai seeking advantageous matches. The men ignored her in favor of girls with better connections to the shogun, and she lacked the beauty and guile required to lure them in spite of her circumstances. She'd grown resigned to marrying some unattractive man who had been rejected elsewhere.

Yet Hirata had seemed wonderfully oblivious to the financial, political, and class concerns that shadowed every relationship. He behaved as though he liked Midori for herself, and her friendship with Reiko gave her the perfect opportunity to further her acquaintance with him. She spent all her free time at the *sōsakan-sama*'s estate so she could see Hirata whenever his work permitted. They shared a fondness for games, and often played cards together in the evenings. During their talk, laughter, and flirtation, Midori had fallen in love with Hirata. Now she hoped with all her heart to see him today.

A buzzing noise interrupted Midori's thoughts. Something whizzed past her ear.

"A wasp!" O-hana cried. The insect swooped down upon her, and she shrieked, covering her head with her arms.

Her panic was contagious. Midori screamed as the wasp veered straight at her face. She and O-hana clung to each other, running in circles, with the wasp in hot pursuit.

"Help! Help!" they cried.

The wasp caught in Midori's long hair, fluttering and buzzing furiously against her neck. "Get it off me!" she screamed. Anticipating the sharp sting, she fell to her knees.

O-hana stared in terror and backed away. Then a male voice said, "What's going on here?"

Midori looked up to see Hirata, sturdy and youthful at age twenty-three, his two swords at his waist, regarding them with curiosity. Joy leapt within Midori. "There's a wasp in my hair!" she cried.

Hirata knelt beside her. Carefully he picked out the wasp by its wings, carried it across the garden, and tossed it up into the air. The wasp flew away. Hirata returned to Midori and O-hana.

"You're safe," he said, laughing.

Midori scrambled to her feet, gazing upon him in bliss. He was so brave and wonderful. It didn't matter that his face was too wide and his mouth too large for him to be called handsome. She yearned for his love and longed to marry him, even though her family would shun a match with a former policeman, while Hirata's position merited a better bride than the daughter of an outside lord. However, one evening two years ago, something had happened to make her believe that her dreams could come true.

She and Hirata had been walking here in the garden together when a summer storm descended. They took refuge in the covered pavilion and stood side by side, listening to the thunder, watching the lightning flash through the dark clouds and curtains of rain.

"This is pleasant," Hirata said.

"Yes," Midori murmured. Look at me, she pleaded silently. Tell me you love me!

Hirata turned and smiled down at her. "I always feel happy when I'm with you, Midori-*san*. You're so easy to talk to, and you make life so bright."

Thrilled by his words, Midori couldn't speak. She looked down so that Hirata wouldn't guess what a stir he'd caused in her. Then his strong, warm hand closed around hers. The thunder boomed and rain streamed down while Midori waited in breathless anticipation.

Then Hirata spoke softly, as if to himself: "The *sōsakan-sama* and Lady Reiko are so happy together and so right for each other that it's as if theirs wasn't an arranged marriage but a love match. That's what I'd like someday. I wonder . . ."

Did he love her? Was she thinking that he'd like to marry her? Wild hope dizzied Midori. But Hirata fell silent. Perhaps he wasn't ready to declare his intentions, and she was too shy to encourage him. Soon the storm ended; Hirata went back to work. Several days later, before Midori could see Hirata again, fate sabotaged her dreams.

The shogun sent Sano to investigate a murder in the imperial capital. Sano had left Hirata in charge of the detective corps during his absence, and the responsibility had driven any thoughts of love from Hirata's mind. He labored night and day, overseeing the estate, investigating crimes. The shogun began to rely upon Hirata for companionship and counsel. Hirata still sought out Midori during moments in his busy schedule, but all he talked about was his work.

Then the shogun spent a few days at his villa in the hills, taking Hirata along as a bodyguard. Late one night, the shogun heard strange noises outside and became hysterical with fright. Hirata went to investigate and found burglars breaking into the house. After a bloody swordfight, he arrested them, winning the shogun's fervent gratitude. News of the incident spread. *Bakufu* officials who'd once ignored Hirata as Sano's mere assistant began cultivating his friendship. The Edo Castle women took new notice of him. Whenever he came to the palace, Midori saw him surrounded by fawning maids and ladies.

Now O-hana minced up to Hirata. "A million thanks for saving us from that awful wasp," she said, smiling coyly.

"It was a pleasure." Hirata beamed at the maid.

"To what do we owe the honor of your company?" O-hana said.

"I was just delivering some reports to the *sōsakan-sama*'s office," Hirata answered, "when I heard you screaming and stopped to see what was the matter."

O-hana giggled; Hirata laughed. Midori could almost see their mutual attraction sparkle in the air. Her spirits plummeted.

These days Hirata was always flirting with someone else instead of her. Even worse, he'd received marriage proposals from prominent clans who sought to wed their daughters to him. Sano acted as Hirata's go-between, and Midori overheard them planning *miai,* meetings with prospective brides. This competition for her beloved's favor horrified Midori, as did the change in Hirata.

All the attention had swelled his head, and on the rare occasions when Midori saw him, he seemed to have forgotten whatever he'd once felt for her. He would greet her casually, then dash off to work, a party, or another *miai.* Now, a year later, Hirata was still riding the wave of popularity.

"Look out, there's another wasp!" he exclaimed, pointing at the sky. When O-hana looked up, he made a buzzing sound and tickled her arm. The maid shrieked. Hirata laughed, and she pouted prettily at him.

Suddenly Midori couldn't bear for Hirata to ignore her. "O-hana!" she said sharply. "You're supposed to be taking care of Masahiro-*chan,* not playing around. Go!"

O-hana gave Midori a resentful look and flounced into the house. Hirata's grin told Midori that he knew why she'd sent the maid away, and enjoyed having two women vying for his attention. Midori felt ashamed of her jealousy and his vanity.

"Well, I must be on my way." Hirata radiated self-importance. "Lots of things to do, people to see."

Midori believed that deep inside his spirit he still cared for her. How could she restore him to his senses?

"When will you be back?" she said wistfully.

"Not until very late, I expect."

Midori resisted the urge to ask when she would see him again. How could she persuade him that she was as right for him as Reiko was for Sano, and that a marriage between them would be the love match he'd claimed to desire?

"Good-bye," Hirata said.

As he walked away, sudden inspiration struck Midori. "Wait," she called.

"What is it?" Impatience shaded Hirata's tone, but he stopped and faced her.

"This . . . this new case is important, isn't it?" Midori faltered. Her idea seemed brilliant, yet perhaps too bold.

"Very important," Hirata said. "Arson is a serious crime, especially at the shogun's family temple."

Taking a deep breath, Midori mustered her courage. "Maybe I could help you investigate."

Hirata stared in amazement. "You?" Then he threw back his head and laughed. "That's a good joke. You almost fooled me."

"It's not a joke," Midori said. A flush of embarrassment warmed her cheeks. Hirata's laughter hurt, but at least she'd gotten his attention, and all she had to offer him was her willingness to do anything for him. "I really want to help."

"How? What could you do?" Hirata's expression betrayed skepticism.

"Um . . ." Not having thought beyond her initial idea, Midori improvised, "Whatever you wish of me?"

He regarded her with an affectionate mockery that deepened her hurt. "Detective work is too difficult for a lady."

"But Reiko helps the *sōsakan-sama*," Midori said. Reiko's work with Sano appeared to be a key element in their happy marriage; it had given Midori the idea that she and Hirata might develop a similar arrangement.

"Reiko is the daughter of a magistrate," Hirata countered. "She learned about crime in the Court of Justice, while you know nothing about investigating a murder."

"I could learn by working with you." Midori had conceived her plan as a way for them to spend time together, so she could impress him with her devotion. She had no real desire to be a detective, but she resented Hirata's comparing her unfavorably to Reiko, because she felt inferior to her beautiful, clever friend. Now Midori wanted to prove herself as good as Reiko.

She said, "You could teach me what to do."

Hirata shook his head in exasperation. "Detective work is also dangerous," he said. "Reiko is an expert swordswoman; she can defend herself, but you wouldn't stand a chance in a fight." With gentle but unflattering scrutiny, Hirata appraised Midori's soft, slender body, which rarely performed physical activities more strenuous than fetching and carrying for Lady Keisho-in; her dainty hands, which had never held a weapon. "You could get hurt, or even killed. Did you think of that?"

Midori hadn't. She knew Hirata was only being practical, not deliberately cruel, but her spirits sank. He wouldn't accept her help, and she couldn't think of any other way to get closer to him. As her hopes for winning Hirata's love dwindled, Midori bowed her head, blinking away tears.

"Why, you're afraid of a tiny little wasp," Hirata teased. "How could you dare to go out in the world of evil criminals?" Then his voice turned gentle: "Oh, come on. Don't look so sad. You don't really want to play detective, do you?" Hirata touched Midori's chin. "Let me see your pretty smile."

Midori's lips trembled as she tried to comply.

"That's better," Hirata said. "Now you just put those silly thoughts out of your mind, all right?"

Reluctantly, Midori nodded.

"I'll see you soon." Hirata patted her head as if she were a child, or a dog. Then he strode away.

As Midori stared after him, a spark of anger burned through her humiliation. That he should patronize her this way! Now she decided to show Hirata that she was worthier than he thought. Wiping away her tears, she tossed her head defiantly. She would do whatever it took to prove herself as good as Reiko, and win Hirata's love.

Through the crowded streets of the Nihonbashi merchant district, Hirata rode upon his dappled white horse. Peasants scurried out of his way. Passing samurai, noting the Tokugawa crests on his silk garments, bowed respectfully. Hirata felt as though he owned the narrow alleys and open marketplaces; the wares colorfully arrayed in the shops; the noisy throngs; the cloudless blue sky. Beneath his wide-brimmed wicker hat, a satisfied smile broke through his dignified poise. Life had turned out much better than he'd ever believed possible.

Four years ago, Hirata had walked these same streets as a *doshin*—patrol officer, the lowest rank of the police force. He'd expected to spend his entire career breaking up brawls and arresting petty criminals, living in cramped barracks, marrying a woman from another *doshin* family, and raising a son who would inherit the humble station that he'd inherited from his own father. Then chance had brought him and the shogun's *sōsakan-sama* together. His loyalty and skill had earned him his current position as Sano's chief retainer.

Yet his early days at Edo Castle had been plagued by fear of making a mistake and disgracing himself while supervising a hundred other retainers who were mostly older, more experienced, and from better backgrounds than he. The pressure to perform well had kept Hirata in a perpetual state of anxiety, but hard work had brought eventual success and increased confidence. Now he was no longer the diffident, overly serious self upon whom he looked back with amusement. The shogun doted on him; everyone courted his favor; prominent clans vied for the privilege of marrying a daughter to him. As soon as he and Sano finished the investigation into the crimes at the Black Lotus Temple, they would decide which beautiful, wealthy lady would be his wife.

The thought of women provoked a memory that disturbed Hirata's complacency. What had gotten into Midori today? She'd always been a sweet, lighthearted girl, but now she was acting so strangely. Why did she suddenly want to be a detective? Hirata liked Midori; they'd had good times together, but her foolishness baffled him. While he dismounted outside the high stone walls and ironclad gates of police headquarters, Hirata shook his head. Women! Who could understand them?

Guards bowed to him; a groom took charge of his horse. A *doshin,* arriving with a trio of civilian assistants and a shackled prisoner, said, "Welcome, Hirata-*san,*" and let him enter the compound first. As he walked past barracks and stables, former colleagues bowed greetings to him. In the reception room of the main building, square pillars supported a low ceiling hung with unlit paper lanterns. Sun filtered through the open skylights and barred windows into a haze of smoke from the tobacco pipes of citizens gathered around a raised platform. Upon this, four clerks knelt at desks, receiving visitors and dispatching messengers.

"Good afternoon, Hirata-*san,*" said the middle-aged chief clerk, Uchida. His mobile, comic features stretched in a wide smile. "What can we do for you today?"

Hirata often used police headquarters as a source of information, and Uchida was the central repository for news and gossip. "I need your help in identifying the woman and child from the fire at the Black Lotus Temple," Hirata said.

"Then you wish to know whether any missing persons have been reported?" Uchida said. At Hirata's assent, the clerk's expression turned doleful. "Unfortunately, it's not easy to trace individuals in this city."

"I know," Hirata said. The townspeople belonged to groups of households, each with a headman in charge of recording births, deaths, arrivals, and departures among his group. Officials at Edo Castle monitored daimyo and *bakufu* households. The huge volume of data was stored at various temples that kept census records. Within the police department, two hundred forty *doshin* reported incidents in their patrol districts to their supervisors, fifty *yoriki* who maintained archives at their offices. Thus, the information Hirata sought existed, but wasn't easily accessible. "That's why I'm hoping you know something useful."

"Well, I have heard of a few disappearances." Uchida's face arranged itself into an exaggerated frown of concentration. "A sixteen-year-old courtesan escaped from the Yoshiwara pleasure quarter in the spring."

"She's too young to be the woman in the fire," Hirata said. Sano had sent him a message from Edo Morgue, describing the mystery victims.

"A dock worker from Radish Quay came in last month and begged us to find his senile mother, who'd wandered off."

"Too old."

"There was a woman who ran away from the Suruga Hill district a few days ago. She's thirty-four. Her husband is a grocer."

"That's a possibility." After getting the husband's and wife's names, Hirata said, "Have any little boys gone missing?"

"One in Kyōbashi." Hirata's hopes rose, but then Uchida said, "He's nine years old." The child in the cottage had been much younger, according to Dr. Ito. "And the only other missing persons I know of are all men."

"Oh, well," Hirata said, undaunted.

He had supreme confidence in himself and his luck, and a bright idea that could save him long hours of perusing dusty archives. He thanked Uchida and walked to a large office at the rear of the building, where twenty clerks sat at desks, preparing memoranda and reports. When Hirata entered the room, they all ceased working and bowed.

"I order you to draft a notice," Hirata said. He was gratified by the alacrity with which the clerks laid out fresh paper and took up their writing brushes. When he'd been a lowly *doshin*, these snobbish sons of high officials had begrudged him any attention. " 'The shogun's *sōsakan-sama* wishes to learn the identities of a woman and child found dead in a fire at the Black Lotus Temple,' " he dictated. After reciting Sano's description of the victims, he continued, " 'Persons with information must immediately report it to Edo police headquarters.' "

When the clerks finished writing, Hirata said, "Make a thousand copies of that. But first, write this memorandum and send copies to every *yoriki:* 'Each *doshin* shall post the notice on every public notice board and deliver the order to every neighborhood headman in his district.' "

Brushes flew as the clerks reproduced the notice. Hirata took a few copies to post along his way to Suruga Hill. As he walked through the reception room, Uchida beckoned to him. "If I may be so bold as to offer some advice?" The chief clerk spoke in a low voice so no one else would hear, his expression grave: "The higher one rises, the farther the distance to fall. By succumbing to pride and ambition, one may end up losing everything that really matters."

Hirata laughed. "Thank you for the warning, but you needn't worry about me."

He left police headquarters with a feeling of accomplishment. If the grocer's runaway wife was the murdered woman, perhaps he could soon solve the mystery of who had killed her and the other victims and set the fire. If not, he would begin searching the archives. In the meantime, public response to his notices would surely produce some useful information.

And if he had a chance, he would find out why Midori was behaving so strangely.

6

*I seek living beings consumed by the suffering
Of birth, old age, sickness, and sorrow.
To all who accept my truth,
I give supreme delight.*

— FROM THE BLACK LOTUS SUTRA

Police Commander Oyama's residence was located southeast of
Edo Castle in Hatchobori, near the *yoriki* compound where
Sano had lived while serving in the police force. The Hatchobori district was also known for its many carpenters. Sano rode
his horse past workshops where the carpenters sawed, pounded,
carved, and polished raw wood into doors, rafters, floorboards,
pillars, and furniture. Sawdust scintillated like motes of gold in
the warm afternoon sunlight. Behind high fences stood the
mansions of merchants grown wealthy by supplying timber to
a city where fires necessitated regular rebuilding. Up and down
the canals floated barges heaped with wood.

Sano stopped at a food stall for a quick meal of fish roasted on bamboo skewers over an open fire, rice, and tea. As he ate, he watched porters carry rice bales, barrels of salt, and dry goods along the quays to warehouses. The reek of the canals mingled with the greasy smoke from cooking. Through the crowds of commoners rode a *yoriki* clad in elaborate armor, accompanied by an entourage of attendants.

A wry smile quirked Sano's mouth as he recalled his brief tenure as a police detective. The *yoriki* were a hereditary class of Tokugawa retainers, famous for their grand style, but Sano, an outsider in the close-knit group, had been more interested in serving justice than in keeping up appearances. He'd been shunned by colleagues, criticized by superiors, and dismissed from the police force for insubordination, but his unconventionality and a twist of fate had ultimately won him a promotion to his current elevated post.

He finished eating and rode through a dense warren of townspeople's dwellings, to the samurai enclave surrounding police headquarters, which occupied a site in the southernmost corner of Edo's administrative district. Here stood the Oyama family home. Above a high wall surfaced with white plaster rose the tile roofs of a two-story mansion, retainers' and servants' quarters, storehouses and stables. Watchtowers overlooked the smaller residences of other police officials. Sano guessed that the enclave had been built with ill-gotten money: the *yoriki* were also famous for taking bribes. Outside the double gate swathed with black mourning drapery, Sano dismounted and identified himself to the guards.

"I'm investigating the death of Honorable Commander Oyama," he said, "and I must speak to the family."

The immediate family consisted of Oyama's two sons and daughter. Because the house was filled with friends and relatives who had come to comfort the bereaved, they received Sano in a covered pavilion in a garden of boulders and raked sand. There they knelt in a row opposite Sano. The elder son, Oyama Jinsai, was in his early twenties. With his slight frame and sensitive features, he bore no resemblance to his father, except for his straight brows. Fatigue shadowed his intelligent eyes; a black kimono and the sun slanting through the pavilion's lattice walls accentuated his sickly pallor. He had the dazed look of a person overwhelmed by sudden responsibility.

When a maid brought tea and a smoking tray, he lit his silver pipe with unsteady hands and inhaled deeply, as if eager for the calming effect of tobacco.

"My mother and grandparents died years ago," he explained, "so now the three of us are the only surviving members of the main Oyama family." He introduced the siblings seated on either side of him. The stocky younger brother, Junio, wore his hair in the long forelock of a samurai who hadn't quite attained manhood. The sister, Chiyoko, was a plain-faced woman in a modest brown kimono, somewhere between her brothers in years.

"Please allow me to express my condolences on the death of your honorable father," Sano said.

"Many thanks." Jinsai regarded him with anxious confusion, obviously wondering why Sano had come. Since Sano hadn't been close to Commander Oyama or worked with him in years, there was no apparent personal or professional connection to justify a visit. "Is there something we can do for you?"

"I'm sorry to disturb you at such a time, but I must ask you some questions relating to your father's death."

Jinsai looked mystified. "Excuse me if I don't understand. I've heard that you're investigating the fire at the Black Lotus Temple, but my father was killed because he happened to be in the cottage when it burned. His death was an accidental result of the arson. What questions could there be?"

"I regret to say that your father's death wasn't an accident. It was murder." Sano explained about the blow that had killed Commander Oyama.

"I see." Comprehension darkened Jinsai's features. Sano knew he'd served as his father's assistant; he would be familiar with basic police procedure. "The murder victim's family are the first suspects because they're usually the ones with the strongest grievances against him and the most to gain from his death." Jinsai inhaled on his pipe, expelled the smoke in an unhappy sigh, and shook his head. "But if you expect to find the killer here, you'll be disappointed. It's true that we had good reason to be upset with my father, but his death has brought this household many more troubles than benefits."

"Can you explain?" Sano asked.

For a long moment, no one spoke. The sound of low voices

drifted from the house; the air smelled of incense from the funeral altar. In the garden, boulders cast stark shadows across the sunlit sand. The younger brother and sister bowed their heads in misery. Jinsai's expression reflected his reluctance to air private family matters or speak ill of the dead, and the knowledge that he must protect himself and his siblings.

He said in a strained voice, "My father was a lavish spender. He squandered money on drink, parties, gambling, and women. He also gave large donations to the Black Lotus sect. The family finances were . . . in dire straits."

By tradition, samurai lived frugally, disdained money, and avoided discussing it. Sano pitied Jinsai, whose face was flushed with the shame of confessing his sire's extravagance. "I begged my father to economize, but he wouldn't. Now that he's dead, moneylenders have demanded full payment of his debts. My brother and sister and I inherited nothing except this house, which we can't afford to maintain. We'll have to move to a smaller place and dismiss most of the retainers and servants, who will find themselves out on the streets."

He added grimly, "Money is often a motive for murder, but it wasn't for anyone here. Our family fortune was large, built over many generations, and there should have been enough of it left to support the household even after the debts are settled, except my father bequeathed twenty thousand *koban* to the Black Lotus sect."

Many lay worshippers believed they could gain merit by assisting religious orders and thereby achieve blessings in life and nirvana in some future existence during the cycle of birth, death, and rebirth, Sano knew.

"For many years, my father suffered from terrible stomach pains," Jinsai explained. "Nothing relieved them. Then he went to the Black Lotus Temple, and the high priest cured him. It was a miracle. My father was so grateful that he joined the sect. Now I must honor his will and deliver his fortune to the Black Lotus."

Sano would have to find out whether the sect leaders had known about the will, since twenty thousand *koban* gave them a strong motive for Commander Oyama's murder. Maybe Haru was an innocent bystander at the crime scene. Sano wondered whether Reiko had succeeded in coaxing the girl to talk. Yet he wasn't ready to eliminate Oyama's family as suspects; financial gain wasn't the only motive for murder.

"As the oldest son, you inherit your father's post in the police department, don't you?" Sano said to Jinsai. "And his position as head of the clan."

A bitter smile twisted the young man's mouth as he smoked his pipe. "You're asking if I killed my father because I wanted his status, his government stipend, and his power." Throughout history, samurai had often advanced themselves by destroying their own relatives. "Well, I didn't kill him, but even if I had, I would have known better than to expect to become chief police commander, even though my father was training me to take over his duties when he retired.

"Yesterday evening, a *bakufu* delegation came and told me that I'm too inexperienced for such an important post. Another man will get it, and I'll be his assistant, with my same small stipend, until I prove myself worthy of a promotion." Jinsai said in a tone laden with regret, "It would have been better for me if my father had lived another ten years, so I could grow into his job. And although I am head of the family now—" Jinsai spread his hands in a gesture of despair "—there's little triumph in ruling a disgraced, impoverished clan."

He added, "In case you were thinking that my brother or sister wanted my father dead, I can assure you that his murder was even more untimely for them than me."

When he bent a commanding gaze upon his siblings, the younger brother spoke. "I was supposed to become Jinsai-*san*'s assistant when he succeeded to my father's post," he said in a meek, childish voice. "Now I get nothing unless another place can be found for me." His head bowed lower.

"You know that the *bakufu* is overloaded with retainers and the treasury is hard pressed to support them all," Jinsai said to Sano. "Since we've no money to bribe anyone into giving my brother a position, he'll be dependent on me."

The sister hid her face behind her fan and murmured, "I had received a marriage proposal from a high official . . ."

"The match would have brought wealth and prestige to the family," Jinsai said, "but this morning, the official canceled the marriage negotiations because he'd heard about our circumstances. It's unlikely that anyone else suitable will want to marry a bride without a dowry. My sister shall have to choose between being a poor spinster and entering a nunnery."

"You have my deepest sympathies," Sano said, because the children did seem to have suffered rather than gained by Oyama's death. "However, I must ask you all where you were the night before last and the morning after."

"We were home," Jinsai said; his brother and sister nodded.

Sano planned to have his detectives question the Oyama retainers and servants and search for witnesses who had seen anyone from the Oyama estate near the crime scene. But he expected that further inquiries would only clear the household of suspicion, and shift the focus of the investigation back to the Black Lotus Temple.

Jinsai said, "May I ask a question, *Sōsakan-sama*? We heard that two other bodies were found in the cottage. Who were they?"

"Nobody seems to know," Sano said. "I was hoping that someone here could identify the dead woman and child."

"There's no one missing from this estate," Jinsai said, "and if any women or children are missing from the families of my father's friends or colleagues, I haven't heard."

"Can you think of anyone who wanted to harm your father?" Sano asked.

"My father made many enemies during his life," Jinsai said. "There were criminals he arrested; gangsters who hated him for interfering with their illegal business; rivals for power in the police department; men whose wives he seduced." The young man mentioned a few names, and Sano noted them. "But if I were in charge of the murder investigation, I would concentrate on that orphan girl who was found near the fire."

"Why is that?" Sano asked, welcoming evidence to connect Haru with the arson and murders.

"If you don't mind, I'd like to discuss this with you alone." Jinsai glanced at his brother and sister.

At Sano's assent, the pair bowed, rose, and departed.

"I doubt if the criminals, gangsters, rivals, or angry husbands knew that my father was at the Black Lotus Temple that night, but the residents would have known. Especially the girls." His face rigid with disapproval, Jinsai explained, "My father used his status as a sect patron to take advantage of the female orphans and novices. Whenever he visited the temple, he would pick out a girl and have sexual relations with her. He took me to the temple once, telling me that I would enjoy the same privileges if I joined the Black Lotus. And he introduced Haru to me as one of his favorites."

"Did the sect leaders know about your father's relations with Haru or the other girls?" If they did, Sano thought, they hadn't mentioned it to him yesterday.

"Maybe; maybe not. You know how it is."

Sano nodded. Some unscrupulous sects used female members to attract followers, and the nuns were often little more than prostitutes whose earnings supported the temples. But the *bakufu* discouraged this practice by shutting down offending sects. It was possible that Oyama had carried on his activities without the knowledge of the Black Lotus leaders, swearing the girls to secrecy by threatening to hurt them if they told anyone. Or maybe they'd willingly consented to illicit sex because they wanted money or favors from him.

"I could tell that Haru hated my father," Jinsai continued. "She glared at him, spat on the ground at his feet, then ran away. He just laughed and said her temper made sex with her exciting. Maybe she killed him for violating her, then set the fire to cover up the murder."

"That's plausible," Sano said, yet he couldn't reconcile Jinsai's portrayal of Haru as a wronged woman out for revenge with the terrified girl he'd met yesterday. Besides, her hatred of Oyama didn't provide a motive for killing the other two victims. It was conceivable that she could have struck Oyama on the head and broken the child's neck, but she seemed too small and delicate to strangle a grown woman. Sano also wondered why, if Haru was guilty of the crimes, she hadn't fled the scene before the fire brigade arrived.

"Haru killed my father," Jinsai said in a voice crackling with controlled rage. "Whatever he did to her doesn't justify the misfortune she has brought upon this clan. I want her executed."

"If I can prove that she did indeed kill your father, she will be," Sano said.

As he exchanged farewell bows with Jinsai, he decided against going to the Black Lotus Temple to continue his inquiries. Instead he would go back to Edo Castle, because Reiko should be home by now. They would compare their results and determine whether Haru was an innocent bystander or the murderer and arsonist he sought.

7

Heed my warning that this world is a place of evil spirits and
poisonous creatures,
Of flames spreading all around,
And that a multitude of disasters
Will follow one another without end.

—FROM THE BLACK LOTUS SUTRA

Reiko waited with her entourage in the narrow lane outside the
Black Lotus Temple for an hour, but the monk didn't appear.
An attendant brought her a bowl of noodles and some tea from
a food stall, and she ate in her palanquin, watching the temple
gate. Priests, nuns, and pilgrims passed in and out, but there
was no sign of the young man who'd claimed to have important
information and begged her to meet him. Temple bells tolled
the hour of the sheep; the sun bathed earthen walls with the
bronze glow of midafternoon. Reiko grew restless. If the monk
didn't show up soon, she would go home to Masahiro.

Yet Reiko remembered the urgency in the monk's voice.
Surely he'd risked harsh punishment by spying on Abbess

Junketsu-in and Dr. Miwa. He might know who had set the
fire and hurt Haru. Now Reiko opened the door of the palanquin and stepped out.

"Wait here," she told her attendants.

She walked down the lane between the high walls, circling
the Black Lotus Temple. The monk hadn't specified exactly
where they should meet. Perhaps he feared being seen with
her. Reiko turned down the narrow alley at the rear of the
temple. Gnarled pines rose above the wall, casting deep, cool
shadows over the dusty path and the few pedestrians. The
sound of chanting rose in air scented with resin, incense, and
open sewers. Continuing along the wall, Reiko planned to
sneak through the temple's back gate and look for the monk.

A sudden movement rustled the pine boughs above her. As
she looked up, a human figure dropped out of the tree and
landed with a heavy thud in front of her. Reiko exclaimed in
surprise. It was the monk, sprawled on hands and knees, pine
needles showering his shaven scalp and protruding ears, his
eyes wild with panic. He scrambled to his feet and seized
Reiko's arm. Pulling her down the lane, he said in a breathless
voice, "Please come with me."

He was only a little taller than Reiko, with a wiry build. His
thin fingers dug into her flesh. "Where are you taking me?"
she demanded, shocked by his impertinence.

"Hurry," the monk pleaded. "Before they come."

"Who?"

Instead of answering, the monk shot a fearful glance over
his shoulder. He was about sixteen years old; a faint stubble
of whiskers darkened his chin and upper lip. His smooth skin
was flushed and beaded with sweat. Reiko's curiosity overcame
her resistance, and she let the monk hurry her away. He didn't
slow down until they reached a small Shinto shrine. He drew
Reiko through the torii gate and behind a tall stone lantern in
the precinct, where pines sheltered a prayer board, incense vat,
gong, and a rustic wooden shed that housed the spirit of the
deity. The monk fell to his knees before Reiko.

"Forgive me for imposing on you," he said, bobbing a hasty
bow, "but I'm desperate. I have no one else to turn to . . ."

His face contorted, and he began to cry in hoarse, barking
sobs. Reiko's need for information gave way to an impulse to

help a person so obviously in trouble. "I'm here to listen," she soothed. "Calm down."

"There's no time! They know I'm not where I'm supposed to be. They're after me. That's why it took me so long to get out of the temple."

"Who's after you?" Reiko asked, increasingly baffled. "Why are you afraid? At least tell me your name."

The monk gulped back sobs; he gritted his teeth to still his body's tremors. "My religious name is Pious Truth. Before I joined the Black Lotus, I was Mori Gogen." The two names marked him as a former samurai, as did his educated diction. "I saw you with the abbess and heard her say that your husband is the shogun's *sōsakan-sama*?" At Reiko's nod, Pious Truth blurted, "I need his help."

"We'll help you if we can," Reiko said, "but first, you must tell me what's wrong." She spoke calmly, but his anxiety infected her. "What is it that you want?"

"The Black Lotus sect is evil and cruel!" Passion raised Pious Truth's voice to a shout. "I can't bear it anymore. I want to leave!"

Excitement flared in Reiko. "Tell me what happened," she urged.

"My family are retainers to the Kuroda clan," Pious Truth said. He wiped his face on the frayed, soiled sleeve of his robe. "We've always been very religious. Last winter, my father befriended two Black Lotus priests. They came often to pray with our family, and invited us to the temple. When we went there and met High Priest Anraku, we became convinced that he alone knew the true way of the Buddha. I decided to enter the monastery, and my older sister Yasue became a nun. We hoped to achieve enlightenment, but life at the temple wasn't what we'd expected."

Bitterness hardened Pious Truth's voice. He rose, peered furtively around the lantern, then continued, "The priests forced us and the other novices to spend every moment chanting, meditating, and listening to them ring gongs and read prayers to High Priest Anraku. They gave us nothing to eat except seaweed soup. We were allowed to sleep for only two hours each night. There was so much incense smoke in the worship hall that we could hardly breathe. Our legs hurt from kneeling, and we all had stomach cramps and diarrhea from the seaweed. We weren't allowed to bathe. Whoever complained or disobeyed was beaten. The priests told us we were weak, stupid, and worthless, and unless we passed our training, we were doomed to be reborn again and again into lives of meaningless suffering."

Although Reiko knew that strict rules, limited diet, and physical discipline were customary in Buddhist orders, this sounded more like torture than religious instruction. "If things were as bad as you say, why didn't you leave?"

"We couldn't," Pious Truth said. "The priests kept a close watch to make sure no one left the temple."

"Surely your families wouldn't allow you to be mistreated," Reiko said, "and the law doesn't allow temples to hold people against their will."

Wringing his hands, Pious Truth shifted his weight from one foot to the other as if on the verge of flight. "No one knows what's going on. We novices aren't allowed to see or speak to anyone from outside the sect."

"The priests and nuns I saw at the temple looked healthy and contented and free to wander among the people."

Pious Truth gave a humorless laugh. "Those are the trusted initiates. They get better food and other privileges. They beg alms and recruit new followers. The authorities and the public are allowed to see them because they won't tell anybody what goes on at the temple. Their spirits have been conquered by the Black Lotus."

The story was growing more and more astonishing. Reiko said, "How many novices are there like you?"

"Hundreds. I don't know the exact number, because we live in separate groups, and I see the others only in passing."

"But where are they? How can the Black Lotus hide them from everyone?"

"Our quarters are in the buildings near the convent," Pious Truth said. "The walls are lined with cotton padding to muffle the sound. Outsiders aren't allowed there."

Reiko remembered the secluded buildings, Abbess Junketsu-in hurrying her past them, and the sound of muted chanting.

"The temple is bigger than anyone realizes." Pious Truth leaned toward Reiko, his eyes alight with the need to convince.

"What you saw is just the part that's visible on the surface. The Black Lotus has many places to hide things they don't want anyone to see. There are underground rooms, and tunnels leading outside. It's like a monstrous invisible growth, spreading everywhere!"

Shaking her head in amazement, Reiko said, "How could that happen without anyone noticing?"

"It is happening. I've seen it," the monk insisted. "After six months of training, we novices are forced to dig new tunnels. We work at night. The tunnels run beneath the roads, so our neighbors won't hear noises under their floors."

Pious Truth jittered with increasing agitation. "In the daytime, we work in a shop in the temple grounds, printing copies of High Priest Anraku's teachings to sell to the public. That's where I'm supposed to be now. I sneaked out, but before I got to the gate, they had patrols searching the grounds for me. By this time, they'll know I've left the temple. They'll look all over until they find me. They'll never let me go."

"But if there are hundreds of you, all desperate to be free, why don't you band together and walk out?" Reiko asked in confusion.

"It's not that easy. They have spies mixed in among us, to inform on people who are plotting to run away. We can't trust anyone. And after a while, all the drumming and gongs and chanting and smoke and hard work and going without sleep does something to your mind. You obey and endure because you haven't the wits to do otherwise. And they put something in the food—some kind of poison that confuses you even more. I found out by accident, when I got sick last month.

"I vomited constantly; I couldn't keep any food down. But my thoughts were completely clear for the first time since I came to the temple. I realized what had happened to me, and what I must do to free myself and my sister."

This extraordinary story about imprisonment and slavery wasn't what Reiko had hoped to hear from the monk, but his words echoed with the timbre of truth. Might the fire be connected to the practices he was describing?

"When I got well, I went back to work and behaved myself," Pious Truth said, "but I stopped eating the food. I threw it away when the priests weren't looking." Belatedly, Reiko noticed the gauntness of his face, the sharp bones under his robe. "But my spirit grew stronger, and I was determined to escape. Three nights ago, I waited in my bed until everyone was asleep and the priests who patrol the novice monks' dormitory were in another part of the building. Then I climbed out the window and sneaked into the convent.

"I woke up Yasue and led her across the temple grounds. I'd never been out there at night, and I'd expected the place to be dark and deserted, but there were lights in the buildings, and priests and nuns coming and going. We heard strange noises. Yasue was frightened and begged to go back to the dormitory, but I pulled her along. Just as we reached the main precinct, I heard running footsteps. I looked back and saw lots of priests carrying lanterns, spreading out over the grounds. They were looking for us."

The monk's breathing quickened; the memory of terror glazed his eyes. "We fled into the woods, but they were everywhere. Yasue was so confused from the mind poison that she ran away from me. Someone shouted, 'There she is!' I saw three priests grab her and drag her away. The other priests followed. I realized that they didn't know there were two of us. I wanted to rush over and rescue Yasue, but there were too many priests. I might have escaped, but I couldn't leave without her. So I sneaked back to the monks' dormitory, hoping we could get away another night.

"The next morning, I expected the priests to punish Yasue in front of everyone, the way they did other people who tried to run away, but Yasue wasn't there. When I asked where she was, the priests said she'd been transferred to a different group. But I know better."

Pious Truth pressed his fist to his mouth to stifle the sobs that choked him. "They killed her!"

Aghast, Reiko said, "How do you know?"

"The next morning, there was the fire in the cottage, and the fire brigade found a woman's body there," the monk babbled through a spate of tears. "Yesterday I overheard the priests telling the detectives that no one was missing from the temple. Today Dr. Miwa told you that no one knows who the woman was. Well, they're lying. My sister is missing. I've asked around, and I've looked all over for her, but she's not with any of the other groups of novices. No one has seen her."

Reiko felt a thrill of excitement, mixed with pity for the young man before her.

"What about the child who died in the fire?" she asked.

"I don't know who it was."

"Could it have been one of the temple orphans?"

If Dr. Miwa and Abbess Junketsu-in had lied about knowing the woman, they could have lied about the child, too.

"They're not all orphans," Pious Truth said. "Many of them are children of sect members—conceived and born at the temple."

Reiko was shocked. "The Black Lotus permits relations between the nuns and priests?" Buddhist orders usually required the clergy to observe vows of celibacy.

"The sect breeds children as future followers. At the orphanage, they're starved and beaten as part of their indoctrination. It's a test of physical and spiritual strength. The strongest ones will become the Black Lotus's leaders someday; the weaker will be their slaves. And the ones who don't survive . . ."

The monk's voice trailed off in a thin stream of despair. "I've heard of children vanishing from the nursery. Supposedly, they were adopted by kind families, but I don't believe it. The child in the cottage probably died during the indoctrination, and the priests used the fire to get rid of the body."

Fresh shock warred with skepticism inside Reiko. The notion of people bred like animals defied credibility, as did such cruelty to children. Yet even as Reiko wondered if Pious Truth was inventing tales to enlist her aid, his statements supported her theory that Haru was a victim rather than a criminal. Haru was covered with bruises. She'd claimed to be happy at the temple, but her recollection of torture could have vanished along with her memory of the night before the fire. Perhaps she, like Pious Truth's sister, had tried to run away and failed, then somehow escaped death in the fire meant to destroy her and other evidence of the sect's crimes.

"I'm just guessing about the child," Pious Truth said, "but I'm sure about Yasue. The Black Lotus priests killed her."

"To keep her from running away and telling outsiders how the novices are treated, or about the underground tunnels?"

Reiko wondered if Haru had also posed this threat to the sect.

"No, not just for that." Pious Truth's words emerged between deepening gasps and sobs: "I overheard the priests talking. The Black Lotus is working on a secret project. Yasue must have seen something. They had to silence her."

Slavery, imprisonment, torture—and now, diabolical plots. Reiko shook her head as her mind reeled from the torrent of allegations. "What is this project?"

"Last night, I went there. I saw. I heard. I know everything." Hysteria reduced Pious Truth to incoherence; his eyes were black pools of fear. "If they find out, they'll kill me, too!"

"I can't help you unless you tell me what—"

Weeping, Pious Truth grabbed Reiko by the shoulders. "The whole country is in terrible danger. You must warn everyone. Convince your husband to save us!"

The pain of his hands on her, the violence of his plea, alarmed Reiko. Afraid for her safety, she ordered, "Let go!"

She pulled away and backed toward the gate, but Pious Truth hurried after her. Falling to his knees, he grabbed the skirt of her kimono, clutching her legs, oblivious to her dismay at his effrontery. "Please don't leave! Help me!"

Then Reiko heard hurrying footsteps outside the shrine. A shadow darkened the precinct. Turning, Reiko saw two priests standing under the torii gate, blocking the sunlight from the street. One was old, with a long, gentle face; the younger was thickly muscled, his rough-hewn features blank. At the sight of them, Pious Truth inhaled a deep hiss of breath. He let go of Reiko and stumbled backward against the shrine building. Terror sharpened the bone structure of his gaunt face. His voice rose in a thin wail.

"Go away. Leave me alone!"

While the muscular priest advanced on him, the gentle-faced one addressed Reiko in a voice that exuded concern: "Did he hurt you, Honorable Lady?"

Daunted by the pair's sudden arrival and Pious Truth's reaction, Reiko faltered, "No. I'm fine."

"On behalf of the Black Lotus Temple, I apologize for any trouble caused you by Brother Pious Truth," the priest said with a kind smile. "He suffers from madness. He sneaked out of our hospital when his nurses weren't looking."

The heavyset priest grabbed Pious Truth, who struggled, crying, "Let me go! Help! They're going to kill me!"

Reiko didn't know what to think. Pious Truth seemed genuinely terrified, but the old priest sounded so reasonable. "He says he's in danger. He asked me to rescue him."

The priest shook his head sadly. "Delusions. Symptoms of his spiritual malady. It is he who is dangerous. We must restrain him to prevent him from hurting himself or others." As his comrade wrestled Pious Truth to the ground, the old priest removed thin cords from beneath his robe. He bound Pious Truth's wrists and ankles while his comrade held the shrieking, thrashing monk. "He has a habit of assaulting women. You're fortunate that we came along in time."

"Don't believe him!" Pious Truth shouted at Reiko. "Don't let them take me! The Black Lotus is evil. The mountains will erupt. Flames will consume the city. The waters will flow with death, and the air will breathe poison. The sky will burn and the earth explode. You must prevent the conflagration!"

The priest gagged him. He retched and moaned, straining against his bonds, but his captors lifted him and carried him out the gate.

"Wait!" Reiko ran after them. Pious Truth's words sounded like the ranting of a madman, but she distrusted the priests as associates of Abbess Junketsu-in and Dr. Miwa, potential murder suspects who had thwarted her investigation. She needed Pious Truth because his story would help her defense of Haru. "I want to see for myself that he'll be all right."

In the street, the priests bundled the novice into a black palanquin and shut the door. "We'll take Brother Pious Truth back to our hospital, where he'll get the care he needs," the old priest told Reiko. "For your own safety, do not attempt further contact with him."

The priests lifted the handles of the palanquin and trotted down the crowded street toward the Black Lotus Temple. Reiko helplessly watched them go. As she walked back to join her entourage, she wondered whether her inquiries would ultimately benefit or hurt Haru. Of all the conflicting statements she'd heard today, which should she believe?

8

The truth is elusive,
The door to wisdom difficult to enter.
——FROM THE BLACK LOTUS SUTRA

Dusk spread a canopy of vibrant rose and aquamarine sky over Edo. Lights glowed behind windows, at neighborhood gates, in temple grounds, and in boats along the river's gleaming dark ribbon. The moon, like a huge silver coin worn thin at its edge, shone above Edo Castle. In the torch-lit courtyard of Sano's estate, hooves clattered against the paving stones as mounted guards escorted Reiko's palanquin to the mansion.

When Reiko alighted, the nursemaid O-hana threw open the front door, crying, "Thank the gods you're back!"

Anxiety struck Reiko; she hurried into the mansion. "Is something wrong with Masahiro?"

"The young master has missed you so much that he's been

crying and fussing all day. He wouldn't drink milk from O-aki." This was Masahiro's wet nurse. "He refused to eat, and he wouldn't take a nap."

In the entryway, Reiko hastily kicked off her shoes, then ran down the corridor. While she'd been out, her beloved son had gone hungry and endured great misery. Now she heard him wailing in a continuous, mournful drone. She rushed into the nursery and found her own childhood nurse O-sugi jiggling Masahiro on her lap.

"There, there," O-sugi cooed. Masahiro squirmed, his face unhappy. Then O-sugi spied Reiko. "Look, Masahiro-*chan*," she said with obvious relief. "Mama is home."

The sight of Reiko abruptly silenced Masahiro. His eyes became round. Laughing with the joy of seeing him again, Reiko knelt and gathered his plump, warm body in her arms. She pressed her cheek to his soft hair.

"My baby," she whispered. "Oh, how I've missed you!"

A loud howl issued from Masahiro.

"What's wrong?" Puzzled, Reiko looked at her son and saw his face contorted with distress. She tried to comfort him, but more howls gave way to wild screams. His little hands pushed at her chest; his feet kicked her stomach.

"The young master is just tired and cross," O-sugi said. "He's been working himself up to a tantrum."

"No, he's angry at me for abandoning him!" Her son's rejection of her was too much for Reiko to bear, and tears sprang to her eyes. While Masahiro screamed and thrashed, she held him tighter. "I'm here now, it's all right," she murmured.

She and O-sugi and the maids cajoled and soothed. His face bright red, Masahiro beat his fists at them. Between his ear-splitting screams, Reiko heard the front door open, and men's voices in the entryway.

Sano was home.

Alarmed by the screams that had greeted his arrival, Sano sped down the corridor, fearful that harm had befallen Masahiro. He burst into the nursery. Discovering his son safe in

Reiko's arms, Sano experienced relief, but Masahiro continued shrieking. Sano saw tears in Reiko's eyes.

"What happened?" Sano knelt at his wife's side. "Is he hurt?"

Struggling to hold the squirming child, Reiko gave him a forced smile and pitched her voice above the screams: "No, he's just being difficult."

Now Sano noticed that Reiko wore an outdoor cloak. Concern about her replaced his fear for their son. "Did you just get home?"

"Yes."

"You were supposed to go to Zōjō Temple in the morning. Why are you so late? Has something happened to you?"

For a mere instant, Masahiro ceased his tantrum. His flushed face smeared with tears, mucus, and drool, he regarded his parents with curiosity. Then he let out a tremendous bellow, thrusting his arms toward Sano, who lifted Masahiro from Reiko's lap and cuddled the damp, feverish child.

"I persuaded Haru to talk," Reiko said. "After what I heard, I had to investigate further."

Masahiro squalled as Sano clumsily rocked him. At last Sano gave up and handed his son to the maids. He said to Reiko, "Let's talk elsewhere."

They went to the parlor, which was chilly; the charcoal braziers hadn't been lit. A draft swayed the hanging lanterns. From the nursery drifted the muted sounds of Masahiro's wails. Reiko explained that Haru didn't know the victims and couldn't remember anything about the fire or why she'd been at the cottage, then described her bruises.

"I think Haru was an intended victim of the arson. She's afraid she'll be attacked again, and executed for the crime. She's all alone in the world." In a voice laden with compassion, Reiko explained how Haru's parents had died and moneylenders had seized their noodle shop in Kojimachi. "I promised her I would try to clear her of suspicion and find the real arsonist."

Obviously, an emotional bond had formed between Haru and Reiko, blinding Reiko to the possibility that the girl was indeed guilty of the crimes. Sano thought of what he'd learned today, and a sinking sensation weighted his heart.

"My congratulations on breaking Haru's silence," he said,

easing into a discussion that he feared would cause discord. Encouraged by the glow of pride on Reiko's face, he said cautiously, "However, before we draw any conclusions about Haru, we need to examine other evidence."

"What evidence is that?"

Reiko's posture stiffened. The weight in Sano's heart grew heavier as he perceived that she was upset at the idea that he didn't share her inclination toward Haru's innocence. He regretted the necessity of telling her something she probably wouldn't want to hear.

"I met Commander Oyama's family," Sano said, then related what he'd learned. "The elder son's story about Oyama introducing him to Haru indicates that Haru did know at least one of the victims, despite what she told you."

Although Reiko neither moved nor altered expression, Sano could feel that she was shaken by his news, and appalled to think that Haru had lied to her.

"Oyama's son wants someone punished for his father's murder," Reiko said. "Maybe he fabricated that story about Haru because she's an obvious suspect."

"She's the only suspect," Sano amended. "Commander Oyama's death caused his family much harm and benefited them not at all. My detectives spent the whole day at the temple and haven't discovered evidence to place anyone besides Haru at the scene."

"Just because your men found nothing doesn't mean that other suspects and evidence don't exist," Reiko said. "The Black Lotus sect clearly benefits from Oyama's bequest and is trying very hard to control the investigation and incriminate Haru. After I talked to her, I went to the temple, and as soon as I got there, the abbess waylaid me. I wanted to question the nuns and orphans about Haru, but she wouldn't let me. And your detectives were having no better luck performing an independent investigation. They had Black Lotus priests following them like shadows."

"The priests were probably just assisting with their investigation," Sano said, alarmed that Reiko had gone ahead on her own. "I found them very cooperative yesterday."

Nevertheless, Sano wondered whether this cooperation signified an attempt to hide compromising facts behind a guise of helpfulness. Was the Black Lotus indeed trying to misdirect the investigation? The thought disturbed Sano and increased his concern about what Reiko had done.

"You shouldn't have gone to the temple," he said. "For you to poke around without my knowledge or permission could harm the investigation and my standing with the shogun."

"I'm sorry," Reiko said, contrite.

"And if there really is a killer at large, then it's dangerous for you to wander around the temple alone." Seeing Reiko's frown, Sano said, "I have the results of Dr. Ito's examination of the arson victims. All three were killed before the fire. The little boy was starved and tortured. His neck was broken."

Reiko recoiled in horror. "How terrible," she murmured. The sound of Masahiro's whimpers drifted through the house. Then her expression turned sharply alert as she absorbed the news. "Could a girl as frail as Haru have smashed the skull of a man, strangled a woman, and broken the neck of a boy—all on the same night, yet—then placed all their bodies in the cottage to be burned? Under what circumstances could an orphan girl starve and torture a child? Dr. Ito's findings strengthen the possibility that the killer is someone other than Haru."

His wife had a point, Sano realized: The scenario she described did sound implausible. "At this stage it's too early to eliminate any possibilities," he said, warning himself against prejudice. He could be wrong about Haru, despite what he'd learned today.

"Well, if we're looking for other suspects, then Dr. Miwa and Abbess Junketsu-in are good candidates. There's something very strange about them." Reiko described the sinister pair. "They both knew Commander Oyama. They were quick to offer alibis, and even quicker to cast suspicion on Haru."

Reiko told how the abbess and doctor had portrayed Haru as a troublemaker who suffered from spiritual disharmony, lied, fornicated, prowled at night, and had set the fire as revenge against the temple for disciplining her. Sano mentally tallied the information on Haru. To him, it was clear that the negative outweighed the positive.

He said carefully, "Maybe the abbess and doctor are telling the truth about Haru."

"I don't trust those two. Someone beat and bruised Haru; maybe they had something to do with it."

Reiko spoke with certainty, her back against a partition. Sano understood that his disputing her assessment of Haru had only caused her to cleave to the girl. He was troubled to see the case dividing him and his wife.

"You think she's guilty, don't you?" Reiko said.

"I won't decide until all the facts are in," Sano said, although he could tell that his hedging didn't convince Reiko. "So far, there's no evidence to say that anyone except Haru had a motive for the crimes."

"But there is." Brightening, Reiko described her meeting with a novice monk.

Sano shook his head in amazed disbelief. "That's not possible. There's no law against underground construction at temples as long as it doesn't extend outside the religious district, but a sect couldn't hide the kind of work you describe. The *bakufu* keeps tight control over the clergy. Officials from the Ministry of Temples and Shrines conduct frequent inspections of all temples. They would have discovered the imprisonment and mistreatment of the novices and children and disbanded the sect. And the *metsuke* watches for any activities that pose a danger to the country." The Tokugawa intelligence service had spies everywhere. "Those priests who took Pious Truth away said he was mad. That sounds like a good explanation for his story."

Reiko's chin lifted. "The fact that the child in the cottage was beaten and starved supports his claims. And his story provided a lead on the dead woman. Is there a better one?"

"No," Sano admitted. "Hirata checked out a report on a runaway wife from the Suruga Hill district. He just told me that he went there and found her alive and well—she'd returned to her husband. But the search has just begun. Maybe the woman is Pious Truth's sister; maybe not. We shouldn't jump to conclusions."

He placed his hands on Reiko's shoulders. "Please don't be so quick to believe some things you hear and disregard others, or to take the side of a suspect."

Sighing, Reiko nodded, but she replied, "You said yourself that it's too early to eliminate any possibility. If there's the slightest chance that Pious Truth is right about the Black Lotus sect, then we have to check into it. That's why I want to go back to the temple tomorrow, with you, to find Pious Truth and look for the things he described."

Sano groaned. Women had such a propensity for remembering everything a man said and throwing it back at him! And the discussion had circled back to the issue of how much Reiko should do on the case.

"Whatever investigation needs to be done at the temple, I'll handle it," Sano said. He hated to disappoint Reiko, but neither did he want her to endanger herself or steer the case in a dubious direction. "You've interviewed Haru. Your work is finished."

"Haru should hear Junketsu-in's, Dr. Miwa's, and Commander Oyama's son's statements about her. Her reaction might help us determine who's telling the truth. Maybe by tomorrow, she'll have recovered her memory. Maybe she can provide more information about the fire and the two unidentified victims." Reiko reminded Sano, "I'm the only person she'll talk to."

Her arguments were persuasive, Sano acknowledged. Haru, whether guilty or innocent, represented a key to solving the case. He needed Reiko's help.

"All right," Sano said. "Go visit Haru again. But I want you to promise me that you'll restrict your investigation to her and stay away from the Black Lotus Temple."

Reiko frowned, as if about to object, then said with winsome guile, "I promise—if you'll promise to personally investigate Pious Truth's claims."

Sano feared that the case was turning into a battle of wills. Although he hated to back down, compromise seemed necessary to forestall a war.

"Very well," he said. "You work with Haru. I'll look for torture victims, underground tunnels, and evil plots at the Black Lotus Temple." He added, "I think we're both in need of relaxation. How about a hot bath before dinner?"

Reiko gave him a strained smile, nodding. As they walked down the corridor together, Sano told himself that the case wouldn't ruin their family harmony. Everything would be fine.

9

Through the power of expedient means,
I shall pry living beings loose from false convictions,
And induce them to follow the Law of the Black Lotus.
—FROM THE BLACK LOTUS SUTRA

Distant temple bells heralded dawn. Dressed in white kimono and trousers, Reiko stood barefoot in the garden, her hand on the sword at her waist, her face upturned toward a pale sky filmed with drifting gray clouds. The estate lay dark and quiet around her. Moisture veiled the air; dew pearled the grass. Reiko concentrated on the energy spreading from the spiritual center within her abdomen, through her whole body. With a sudden rapid motion, she drew the sword. She lunged and slashed in combat against an imaginary opponent.

At first the sword felt cumbersome and her movements awkward from lack of practice. Soon Reiko was panting and drenched in sweat, but eventually she felt her skill returning.

She resolved to train daily, as she had before her pregnancy. The ritual calmed her mind while building her strength. Now she could think objectively about last night's talk with Sano, and she began to understand why she'd been so eager to refute evidence that raised valid concerns regarding Haru.

Proving that her judgment was sound had become a matter of honor. Though she knew she shouldn't let personal needs guide her, Reiko still trusted her own instincts and intelligence. Her suspicions about the Black Lotus fed her belief in Haru's innocence.

Reiko pivoted, ducked an imaginary strike, and lashed her blade against her doubts about her detective abilities. She and Sano would solve the case and deliver the real killer to justice, together.

When Reiko arrived at the Zōjō Temple convent, a nun told her that Haru was in the garden. Reiko left her entourage outside the front door. Carrying a package she'd brought, she walked around the building. The clouds cast a gloomy pall over gravel paths and autumn grasses. The breeze carried the scent of rain; nuns gathered laundry from balconies. Then Reiko heard Haru's voice—shrill, frightened—and a man's gruff, threatening one.

Reiko hurried around a cluster of pines and saw Haru standing near a lily pond in the secluded garden, her back pressed against a boulder. A priest loomed over the girl.

"Leave me alone!" Haru tried to squirm away, but the priest planted his hands on the stone surface on either side of her, preventing her escape.

"You've had your chance to cooperate voluntarily," he said. In his early forties, he was tall and strong; sinewy muscles corded his neck and bare arms. His domed head sloped to a low forehead, flat nose, full lips, and jutting chin. "Now I've run out of patience."

He clamped his big hand across Haru's throat and shoved. The girl's back arched; her head slammed against the boulder. She cried, "Help!"

Reiko dropped her package, rushed over, and grabbed the

priest's arm. It felt hot and hard, like iron newly tempered in a forge. "What are you doing?" She saw scars crisscrossing his bare scalp, the most prominent one a raised seam that ran from the corner of his eye over his ear, ending in an incrustation of flesh that resembled a lizard. Revulsion filled Reiko as she tried to pull the priest away from Haru. "Stop!"

The priest looked down at Reiko. Harsh lines carved the skin around his mouth. Heavy, slanting brows added menace to his frown. His arm shot out, flinging Reiko aside. Then he turned back to Haru, increasing the pressure on her throat.

Choked cries emanated from Haru; she clawed at the priest's hands. Outraged, Reiko drew the dagger strapped to her arm under her sleeve. She jabbed the priest's back with the blade, ordering, "Get away from her!"

He didn't even flinch. He didn't seem to notice Haru's fingernails tearing bloody scratches on his hand. "You set the fire," he said, bearing down on Haru. "Confess!"

Haru's face reddened; her eyes rolled in terror. Her voice emerged in a strangled whisper: "No!"

Reiko didn't want to injure the priest, but she had to save Haru. "Guards!" she called. Her five escorts came running. "Stop him!"

In an instant, the guards had the priest pinned facedown on the grass. Haru crumpled beside the boulder, coughing and clutching her throat.

"Are you all right?" Reiko asked, touching the girl's shoulder.

With a shaky, grateful smile, Haru nodded.

Reiko bent over the priest, holding the dagger against his neck. "Who are you?" she demanded.

Twisting his head sideways to look at Reiko, the priest regarded her with scorn, as though she were at his mercy, not the reverse. "Withdraw your weapon," he said. "Release me."

His manner made it obvious that he would say no more unless she complied. Reiko sheathed her dagger and nodded to her guards. They hauled the priest to his feet and stood around him lest he try to attack.

"Who are you?" Reiko repeated.

"My name is Kumashiro." He scrutinized Reiko with a hostile, unblinking gaze. His rough voice sounded like rocks shifting during an earthquake.

"From the Black Lotus Temple?"

The priest nodded curtly, although disdain twisted his mouth. "Who are you to ask?"

"I'm Lady Reiko, wife of the shogun's *sōsakan-sama*," Reiko said, observing the sudden wariness that hooded Kumashiro's eyes. "I'm investigating the fire at the temple. What is your position there?"

"I am second-in-command to High Priest Anraku, and chief security officer for the Black Lotus sect."

Reiko thought it odd that a Buddhist temple should be organized on such militaristic lines, or require a security staff. Did this have anything to do with prisoners, underground construction, and secret projects?

"You're a former samurai?" Reiko said, hazarding a guess based on Kumashiro's scars, physique, and arrogance.

"Yes."

"Whom did you serve?"

"My clan are retainers to Lord Matsudaira, daimyo of Echigo Province."

"What is your business with Haru?" Reiko gestured toward the orphan girl, who cowered against the boulder, biting her fingernails.

Kumashiro's contemptuous gaze flicked over Haru. "I was questioning her about the fire."

"The shogun has assigned my husband the job of investigating the arson," Reiko said, stifling her anger. Kumashiro was obviously the common type of man who disdained women as inferiors, but she sensed in him an abnormal hatred for her sex. "You've no right to interfere."

"The safety of the Black Lotus sect is my responsibility," Kumashiro said, "as is anyone who harms its members or property." He bared jagged teeth in an unpleasant smile. "You can save your husband a lot of trouble by going away and leaving Haru to me. I shall get her confession, and the *sōsakan-sama* shall get the criminal he seeks."

Here was another official who seemed determined to pin the crimes on Haru. "How can you be so sure that Haru has done harm?" Reiko asked the priest. "Where were you when the murders were committed and the fire set?"

A gleam of amusement in Kumashiro's eyes told Reiko that the priest recognized her intent to cast him as an alternative suspect. "Between sunset and dawn, I made my usual three tours of inspection around the temple grounds, and spent the rest of the time in my quarters. My lieutenants can confirm this—they never left me."

Another dubious alibi that would be hard to break, Reiko thought unhappily.

"Haru has admitted that she left the orphanage to meet Commander Oyama," Kumashiro continued with an air of satisfaction. "She admitted that they were lovers, and they used the cottage for their illicit liaisons."

Shock hit Reiko like a fist to the heart. Even if Kumashiro had forced Haru to incriminate herself, Oyama's son also claimed that Haru had been involved with the commander.

"Is it true?" Reiko anxiously asked Haru. "Were you having an affair with Commander Oyama, in the cottage where he died?"

The orphan girl ducked her head. Mute, with her face hidden behind lank strands of hair, she looked the picture of guilty shame. Reiko's heart sank.

"She wanted to be the wife of a powerful *bakufu* official, so she seduced Oyama," said Kumashiro. "When she found out that he had no intention of marrying her, she killed him for spite."

In Reiko's mind rose an image of Haru glaring at Oyama and spitting on the ground at his feet, as clear as if she'd witnessed the incident that Oyama's son had described to Sano. She remembered Abbess Junketsu-in saying that Haru had seduced novice priests. Had Oyama exploited Haru, or had Haru used sex to serve her ambitions—then committed murder and arson when her ploy failed?

Reiko envisioned the case as a lotus bud slowly opening to reveal first a white petal, then a black one, then more whites and blacks, with Haru at the center. Every piece of information contradicted or complemented another, painting Haru as either victim or criminal.

"You seem very certain of your theory," Reiko said to Kumashiro, "but perhaps the crimes stemmed from other illicit activities in the Black Lotus Temple."

"Such as?" The priest smirked, as though humoring her, but the tendons in his neck tightened.

"Such as the imprisonment and torture of novices. Or the breeding of children by nuns and priests. Or the construction of underground rooms, and the business that takes place there."

Reiko knew that by voicing these accusations she was putting the sect on its guard; yet she hoped to goad Kumashiro into an admission, because she couldn't count on Sano to investigate the temple. Regardless of his promise to her and his dedication to the truth, he thought Haru was guilty and the Black Lotus a legitimate sect; he might overlook evidence that said otherwise. The realization that she was losing trust in her husband dismayed Reiko.

"I wonder if the woman in the cottage was a novice who tried to escape, and the child an orphan who died from torture during religious indoctrination," Reiko said.

Kumashiro laughed, a sound like gravel scattering against steel. "Who told you those ridiculous rumors?"

"There's often truth in rumors." To protect Pious Truth, Reiko added, "The *metsuke* has spies everywhere."

The tendons in the priest's neck relaxed: Either he knew she had no proof to support her accusations, or he didn't fear the Tokugawa intelligence service. "Don't believe everything you hear," he said derisively. Then he strode toward Haru. "Get up. You're coming with me."

Whimpering, Haru scuttled backward on her hands and knees. Reiko stood between Kumashiro and the girl. "You're not taking her anywhere," Reiko told the priest.

"She belongs to the temple." Anger darkened Kumashiro's swarthy complexion. "I'll deal with her as I wish."

"She's under my protection now," Reiko said, "and I won't let you torment her."

Veins bulged in the priest's temples and rigid arms, as though swelling with fury. He spoke with quiet menace: "Those who interfere with the affairs of the Black Lotus sect always regret it."

"You dare to threaten me?" Reiko experienced a stab of fear despite her status as the wife of a high *bakufu* official and the protection of her guards. She saw in Kumashiro a truly dangerous man.

"It's not a threat," Kumashiro said in that same menacing tone, "just a friendly warning."

The hard sheen of his eyes told Reiko that he was capable of murdering three people and framing an innocent girl. A shiver rippled her nerves. She said to her guards, "Escort him off the premises."

The men seized Kumashiro and propelled him out of the garden. The wind swirled fallen leaves and tossed boughs; raindrops pelted the ground. Reiko knelt beside Haru and put her arms around the girl. "It's all right. You're safe now."

Haru whispered, "I was so scared I wet my kimono." Misery suffused her features. "It's my only one."

"Don't worry about that," Reiko said. "Let's go inside."

As they walked together toward the convent, Reiko picked up the package she'd dropped.

In Haru's room, the orphan girl removed her soiled garment and washed herself. Reiko opened the package and unfolded a fresh white under-robe, a jade green cotton kimono printed with mauve asters, and a mauve sash.

"Here," Reiko said, "put these on."

Haru gasped in amazement. "They're for me? But you're too generous. I can't accept."

"Oh, they're just old things of mine." In fact, the garments had never been worn. Although her kind gesture was sincere, Reiko hoped the gift would oblige Haru to be honest with her. She helped Haru into the clothes. "There. How pretty you look! Do you feel better now?"

The girl nodded, her eyes bright with happiness. Stroking the fabric, she said, "I've never worn anything so beautiful. A thousand thanks."

Although Reiko hated to spoil Haru's pleasure, it was time for serious business. "Haru-*san*," she said, "we must talk."

Haru knelt opposite Reiko. Apprehension furrowed her brow.

"Were you and Commander Oyama lovers?" Reiko asked, keeping her voice gentle.

Haru twisted the ends of her new sash. "No. I only said so because that was what Kumashiro wanted me to say."

Tentative relief eased the doubt that the priest had fostered in Reiko. "Then you weren't with Oyama the night before the fire? You didn't go to the cottage to meet him?"

"No, I wasn't. I didn't."

In her mind Reiko heard Kumashiro's voice: "Don't believe everything you hear"—and Sano's: "Don't be too quick to take the side of a suspect." Reiko said, "If you don't remember anything from that night, how can you be sure what you did?"

Hurt and confusion welled in Haru's eyes; her lips trembled. In a high, teary voice she said, "I didn't kill anyone. I didn't set the fire. I could never do those terrible things."

Feeling like a bully, having serious misgivings about the girl, Reiko forced herself to continue: "Why is Kumashiro so determined to make you confess?"

"He's afraid that people will think he killed Commander Oyama," Haru said. "They hated each other. I don't know why, but I often saw them arguing. And he hates me. He wants to get me in trouble so I'll have to leave the Black Lotus Temple."

If Kumashiro and Oyama had indeed been enemies, the priest had a motive for at least one of the murders. But Reiko could not ignore the inconsistency in Haru's story. "Yesterday you said that you love everyone in the temple, and they all love you. Why didn't you tell me about Kumashiro?"

Haru squirmed, twisting the sash; her gaze darted. She ventured hesitantly, "I forgot about him?"

The flimsy excuse increased Reiko's misgivings. "I've spoken with Abbess Junketsu-in and Dr. Miwa," she said, then related the pair's description of Haru as a troublemaker. "They think you're unfit to be a nun, and they blame you for the fire. Did you forget them, too?"

Reiko heard her voice rising in agitation, while Haru looked crestfallen. "Are they inventing lies to get you in trouble," Reiko pressed, "or did you do the things they said?"

Tension vibrated the atmosphere in the room. Rain pattered on the roof and dripped off the eaves. Reiko heard Haru's rapid breathing. Then the girl hung her head and mumbled, "It was so long ago . . . I thought I'd counteracted my bad karma."

Buddhists believed that a person's actions produced karma—energy that affected life in present and future existences—and that misdeeds could be exorcised by doing good. Foreboding touched Reiko's heart.

"What bad karma?" she said, wary of what she was going to hear.

"When I first came to the Black Lotus orphanage, I was a very difficult girl," Haru said in a voice laden with shame. "I had no religious faith. I only went to the temple because I had nowhere else to go. I was upset about my parents dying, and angry at my bad fortune. I hated the food and the chores. I wouldn't obey the rules. I was rude and disobedient. I was so lonely that I . . . I would meet boys at night and let them touch me."

Reiko's face felt numb, as if too many shocks had obliterated the sensation in her skin. But inside, painful emotions roiled. "You should have told me these things yesterday, when I asked about your life at the temple and who might want to hurt you," she said. "Instead, you misled me."

"But I didn't," Haru protested. She must have seen disbelief in Reiko's expression, because she hurried to explain: "I mean, I'm different now. I don't do those things anymore. High Priest Anraku showed me that I was wrong to act the way I did." Her eyes glowed with the same joyful radiance as when she'd spoken of the sect leader yesterday. "He taught me that I must rid myself of worldly desires and follow the path of the Black Lotus out of suffering to Buddhahood. So I reformed. I worked hard to make up for the trouble I'd caused and prove I could be a good nun."

A part of Reiko wanted to excuse Haru's behavior as the actions of a grieving child who'd had trouble adjusting to convent routine and wanted to forget a difficult period of her life. Still, Reiko was disappointed in Haru for withholding important information, and angry at herself for minimizing the possibility that Haru might be lying. Had the abbess and doctor neglected to mention the change in Haru, or had Haru not really reformed?

"I'm sorry," Haru quavered. Tears watered her eyes. "I should have told you."

Reiko's shaky self-confidence waned. Maybe her break from detective work had impaired her judgment, and she should quit the investigation, as little as she liked the idea. Abruptly she rose and walked to the window. The rainy landscape outside blurred before her eyes as she sorted out her thoughts. Before admitting her mistake to Sano, she must correct it, or he would have every right to forbid her to continue the investigation.

She turned to Haru, who huddled on the floor, watching her anxiously. "Tell me about Commander Oyama," Reiko said.

Haru shook her head. "I didn't—"

Reiko silenced her with a warning gaze. "If you want my help, you have to tell me the truth. Did you know Oyama?"

Drawing a deep, tremulous breath, Haru lowered her eyes and nodded. "I met him in the summer," she said. "He would talk to me when I was doing my chores. All the while, his eyes would be looking over me. He made me nervous, and I wished he would leave me alone. But he was an important patron, and I had to be polite to him. So when he asked me to come to the cottage one night, I obeyed."

Uneasiness stole through Reiko as she wondered if the incident Haru was describing had happened months ago, or right before the fire.

"When I got there," Haru continued, "he was waiting in the room. The lanterns were lit. There was a futon on the floor. He told me to sit, and he offered me some sake from a jar on the table. I said, 'No, thank you; I'm not allowed to drink.' So he drank the sake himself. Then he started undressing. I looked away and said, 'I think I should go back to the dormitory.' He said, 'Not yet.'

"Then he started touching my body. I begged him to stop, but he tore off my clothes and threw himself on top of me. I struggled, but he was too strong. Then he—he—"

Haru entwined her legs and crossed her arms over her bosom, as if trying to defend herself against the remembered attack. Reiko winced as she vicariously experienced Haru's pain and terror. She said, "Why didn't you tell me this yesterday?"

"I couldn't." Sobs heaved Haru's chest. "I was afraid you would think I killed Commander Oyama."

Reiko pondered the evidence against Haru. The girl had been

in the cottage and raped by Oyama at least once. That gave her reason to hate him. What if he'd raped her again on the night before the fire? That would explain Haru's bruises. Maybe, while struggling with the girl, Oyama had fallen and hit his head. Then Haru had panicked, set fire to the cottage, and later blocked out the memory.

Or maybe Haru had plotted revenge, lured him to the cottage, and struck him down in cold blood.

Weeping into her sleeve, Haru said, "I'm innocent, but everyone will think I'm guilty. It's no use hoping to be saved. I know what I must do." She lifted her head and spoke bravely: "I'm going to confess."

"What?" Reiko said, surprised.

"I owe a great debt to the Black Lotus sect for taking me in. If they want to blame me for killing those people and burning the cottage, then it's my duty to confess," Haru explained. Bowing, she said, "Thank you for trying to help. I'm sorry to cause you so much trouble, but I must ask a favor. Will you take me to the police? I'm afraid to go alone."

Reiko was caught between opposing impulses. On one hand, she now had much proof of Haru's dubious character, but none of anyone else's involvement in the crimes. Maybe Haru was guilty, and Reiko should let her accept the punishment she deserved. On the other hand, Reiko still thought that Kumashiro, Abbess Junketsu-in, and Dr. Miwa warranted further inquiries, as did the two unidentified victims. She wanted to know what High Priest Anraku had to say about the crimes, and whether Sano had discovered more suspects or anything to substantiate the novice monk's claims, before she made up her mind about Haru. She shouldn't condemn someone on the strength of inconclusive evidence or denouncements from enemies.

Reiko faltered. "I don't think you should confess."

"Then you believe I'm innocent?" Eager hope gleamed in Haru's streaming eyes.

"The investigation isn't finished," Reiko said, compromising between honesty and tact.

Desolation shadowed Haru's face: She wasn't deceived by Reiko's hedging. She hurried to the cabinet and removed a worn cotton blanket, a comb, a pair of chopsticks, and a wooden bowl. She spread the blanket on the floor and set the other items on top of it.

Reiko frowned, perplexed. "What are you doing?"

"I can't stay here. Kumashiro will come back. If I don't confess, he'll kill me." The words poured from Haru in a frantic rush as her fingers fumbled to tie the blanket around her meager possessions. "I must go."

"But where?" Reiko said, dazed by events happening too quickly, spinning out of her control.

"I don't know."

Likely, she would end up begging in the streets. The thought appalled Reiko, as did the idea of letting Sano's only suspect go. Perhaps Haru was manipulating her by volunteering to confess, then threatening to run away, yet she saw only one possible course of action.

"Come with me," Reiko said, taking the bundle from Haru. She put her arm around the girl's trembling shoulders, although aware that her affection for Haru had waned. "I'll take you to a safe place."

Afterward, she must continue investigating the Black Lotus sect—even if it meant breaking her promise to Sano.

10

There is only one truth.
There are not two, nor three, nor a million.
The others are not the truth.

—FROM THE BLACK LOTUS SUTRA

"Well, *Sōsakan* Sano, what progress have you made in your, ahh, investigation?" said the shogun.

He sat on the dais of Edo Castle's Grand Audience Hall, whose floor was divided into two levels. On the higher level immediately below the dais, in a row to the shogun's right, knelt the five members of the Council of Elders, Tokugawa Tsunayoshi's chief advisers and Japan's supreme governing body. Sano knelt near the end of this row. Opposite knelt the abbot of Zōjō Temple and four high priests. On the lower level sat a delegation of Edo's city elders: commoners who relayed communications between the townspeople and officialdom and supervised the neighborhood headmen. Sentries guarded the

doors. Secretaries occupied desks along the walls. The shogun's personal attendants awaited his orders, while servants
poured tea for the assembly and brought metal baskets of lit
coals for tobacco pipes.

Sano said, "I've learned that all three victims were murdered
before the fire," and described their injuries. "The woman and
boy haven't been identified yet; citywide inquiries have begun.
So far, the orphan girl remains the only suspect. There are
reports that Haru is a troublemaker who had a grudge against
Commander Oyama." Sano related the statements of Abbess
Junketsu-in, Dr. Miwa, and Oyama's son. "However, she
claims that she can't remember anything between the time she
went to bed and the time she was found at the fire. One of my
detectives is working with her to recover her memory."

The thought of Reiko stirred lingering worry inside Sano.
Their compromise last night hadn't restored their intimacy.
Reiko had spurned his amorous advances, saying she was tired,
but this morning he'd watched her practicing *kenjutsu*. Her
every movement seemed to proclaim her determination to
prove she was right about Haru. Now Sano wondered uneasily
what would happen when Reiko visited Haru today.

"We're continuing the search for witnesses and other suspects," Sano finished. "I shall have more to report soon."

His audience's reaction confirmed his fear that his results
sounded paltry. The priests and the Council of Elders regarded
Sano with veiled disapproval; the shogun took his cue from
the others and frowned. The city elders watched their superiors
in complicit silence.

"I expected better from you, *sōsakan-sama*," remarked Senior Elder Makino Narisada, whose pallid skin stretched over
the prominent bones of his face. Since the truce between Sano
and Chamberlain Yanagisawa, he'd taken over the role of
Sano's chief detractor. "You should certainly have solved the
mystery by this time; yet you've accomplished very little."

Murmurs of agreement came from the other council members. Sano's spirits began a familiar descent. Men in the *bakufu*
were always trying to gain by making someone else look bad.

"Also, your activities have thoroughly disrupted the temple
district," Makino said. "Isn't that correct, Honorable Abbot?"

"Our routines have been interrupted by detectives searching

for clues and interviewing everyone." The abbot of Zōjō Temple spoke reluctantly, in a humming voice trained by years of chanting sutras. He was a serene, statuesque priest whom Sano had met many years ago when he'd been a student at the Zōjō Temple school. Now he gave Sano an apologetic glance: While he didn't want to make trouble for Sano, he couldn't contradict a man as powerful as Makino, and he was understandably concerned about the effect of the investigation upon his domain. "But of course, the *sōsakan-sama* has our full cooperation, and we trust that the matter will be concluded quickly."

"Thank you, Honorable Abbot," Sano said, feeling pressured by this hint to speed up his progress.

A faint smile cracked lines in Makino's skull face. He addressed the shogun: "May I invite the city elders to express their concerns about the situation?"

"Permission granted," said Tokugawa Tsunayoshi. His worried gaze moved over the assembly while he tried to read the conversation's undercurrents.

The delegation on the lower level stirred. An elderly man with sparse white hair inched forward on his knees, bowed to the shogun, and said with visible nervousness, "A thousand thanks for the privilege of speaking, Your Excellency. During the past few months there have been fires in the Suruga, Nihonbashi, and Kanda districts, causing thirty-four deaths." The old man glanced at Makino. "We fear that the fires may be related to the one at the Black Lotus Temple."

Sano was alarmed by this theory that the Black Lotus fire might be the latest work of a habitual arsonist. However, he deduced that it was Makino who had planted it in the minds of the elders and brought them here to help make Sano's failure to solve the case seem more reprehensible.

"I thank the city elders for the news," Sano said evenly. "While there's no evidence that the Black Lotus fire involves anyone or any place outside the temple, I shall certainly check into the possibility."

"That sounds like a good, ahh, plan," the shogun ventured, as if afraid to contribute his opinion to an argument he didn't understand.

A flicker of annoyance in Makino's eyes acknowledged that his ploy hadn't worked the way he'd hoped. "You exhibit an astonishing indifference to the concerns of our citizens, *sōsakan-sama*. Perhaps you do not care about their safety. Is that why you're taking so long with your inquiries?"

The shogun frowned in confusion, but Sano felt his lord's approval swaying toward Makino. Sano said, "A thorough investigation requires time. Perhaps the Honorable Senior Elder would prefer that the job be done poorly?"

"An honorable man does not evade the blame for his mistakes." Although Makino's expression didn't change, anger radiated from him. "Nor does a good detective ignore what is before his eyes. The orphan girl is the obvious culprit, but she hasn't been arrested yet. She's free to set more fires and kill again."

The other council members nodded. The abbot gave Sano a sympathetic glance. Indecision puckered the shogun's brow.

"The evidence against Haru is a matter of circumstance and hearsay," Sano said, forced to defend the girl despite his suspicion of her. "There's no proof of her guilt."

"Why do you need proof when a confession would suffice? Are you saying that you're incapable of getting the truth out of a fifteen-year-old female peasant?" Makino emitted a cackle of laughter. "Perhaps you need a lesson in interrogation techniques."

Sano swallowed a sharp retort that would demonstrate bad manners and offend the shogun. "If Haru didn't commit the crimes, then torturing her would do us no good and her much undeserved harm. Executing an innocent person won't serve justice or protect the public."

"Yes, you must, ahh, protect the public." The shogun echoed Sano's words with the breathless relief of a man who has just run a long distance to catch up to his comrades.

Sano watched Makino hide his chagrin by puffing on his tobacco pipe.

"Therefore, you should have arrested Haru long ago," the shogun continued, giving Sano a reproachful look. "Your, ahh, procrastination makes the *bakufu* look weak. We cannot afford to let the citizens think they can get away with, ahh, murder. Haru should have already been punished as an, ahh, example of what happens to anyone who breaks the law. I am extremely disappointed in you, *Sōsakan* Sano."

Anxiety filled Sano as he saw Makino's veiled glee. He said carefully, "I'm sorry, Your Excellency. Please be assured that I have the *bakufu*'s interests at heart. Please allow me to point out that we could lose tremendous face if more fires and murders occurred after Haru's execution because the real culprit escaped justice."

"Ahh."

Comprehension brightened Tsunayoshi's face. Makino's ugly features darkened. Everyone else gazed at the floor.

Then the shogun said, "However, I must demand action, *Sōsakan* Sano. Either prove that the girl is guilty, or find out who is. Otherwise I shall put someone else in charge of the, ahh, investigation." The shogun looked around the room, and his gaze settled upon Makino.

The senior elder's humble bow didn't hide his satisfaction.

"If you do not produce results immediately," the shogun continued to Sano, "I shall also have to reconsider your, ahh, position at court."

Makino flashed a triumphant look at Sano, who realized with dismay that this case could destroy his career. He also understood that the surest way to save it was to prove that Haru was guilty, and do it fast.

"Dismissed," the shogun said, waving his fan at the assembly.

Back at his mansion, Sano summoned four detectives to his private office and said, "I have a new assignment for you: secret surveillance on the Black Lotus sect."

He'd picked these men because they hadn't been part of the arson investigation yet, and they weren't known at the temple. Now he turned to Kanryu and Hachiya, former police officers some years his senior. "You two will disguise yourselves as pilgrims and loiter around the temple."

"What are we looking for?" said Kanryu. His sleepy appearance concealed a talent for spying.

When Sano related the novice monk's story, the detective exchanged glances with Hachiya, a muscular man whose friendly disposition inspired trust, often to the detriment of people with something to hide. The pair bowed to Sano, observing the samurai tradition of unquestioning obedience to their master, but he sensed their skepticism.

"I know it sounds unbelievable," he said, "but if there is anything wrong at the temple that may have any bearing on the arson and murders, we need to know." To the two other detectives he said, "I want you to infiltrate the sect."

The two men, Takeo and Tadao, were brothers in their late teens, from a family of hereditary Tokugawa vassals, apprentices to Sano. They shared similar daring spirits and handsome faces. Now they listened attentively as Sano said, "You'll pose as religious youths who want to enter the Black Lotus monastery. Get accepted as novices and find out what goes on inside."

"Yes, master," Takeo and Tadao chorused, bowing.

"Kanryu-*san*, you're in charge of the surveillance," Sano said. "Report to me on everyone's progress."

"Will you be at the temple today?" Kanryu asked as the detectives prepared to leave.

After a moment's hesitation, Sano said, "Later, perhaps. I've got some business to take care of."

Kojimachi district occupied the central ridge of Edo, just west of the castle, along the road that led to Yotsuya, home of the secondary branches of the Tokugawa clan. Here, in a narrow corridor between the compounds of Tokugawa daimyo and retainers, commoners plied their trades. Merchants sold and delivered food; restaurants and teahouses served travelers; Hirakawa Tenjin Shrine hosted one of Edo's few evening markets. Behind the businesses thrived a populous residential area.

As Sano rode past a shop redolent of fermenting miso, light rain fell from the gray sky; umbrellas sprouted in the crowds around him. Trepidation weighed upon his spirit. He'd promised Reiko that he would personally investigate the Black Lotus, and sending detectives instead seemed a betrayal of her trust. And he hadn't told her that he was going to check Haru's background. Although he deemed this necessary for assessing the girl's character, he didn't want Reiko to think he lacked faith in her judgment or was persecuting Haru.

Still, he must determine to his own satisfaction whether Haru was guilty, so he could either arrest her and satisfy the shogun and the public, or develop other leads if she was innocent. Perhaps what he learned at her birthplace would put him and Reiko on the same side of the case.

The road led Sano to Kojimachi's most famous landmark: the hunters' market. Stalls sold the meat of wild boar, deer, monkey, bear, and fowl from the mountains outside Edo. Customers and vendors haggled; flies buzzed around carcasses hung on hooks or spread on pallets; the air reeked of blood and decay. Buddhist religion prohibited the eating of meat, with one exception: for medicinal purposes. Some diseases could be cured only by consuming stews or elixirs made from animals. Farther down the road stood the popular restaurant named Yamasakana—"Mountain Fish"—which served these remedies.

In a row of low, attached buildings near Yamasakana, Sano saw a noodle restaurant. This must be the establishment once owned by Haru's family. Short indigo curtains hanging from the eaves sheltered a raised wooden floor where diners could sit. At this hour—midway between the morning and noon meals—the restaurant was empty, but the sliding wooden doors stood open. As Sano dismounted and tied his horse to a pillar, he heard pans rattling in the kitchen at the rear; charcoal smoke wafted out. The moneylenders who had seized the restaurant as payment for Haru's father's debts had apparently sold it to someone else.

When Sano entered, a middle-aged proprietor wearing a blue cotton kimono and white head kerchief came to greet him. Sano introduced himself, then said, "I need information on the family who owned this restaurant before you. Did you know them?"

The proprietor's round, honest face looked perplexed. "Yes, master. They were my parents. They died eleven years ago. My wife and I have been running the business ever since." He gestured toward the kitchen, where a woman stirred steaming pots on a hearth amid chopping blocks heaped with sliced vegetables.

"I must have the wrong place," Sano said. "The people I'm

interested in died just two years ago. They had a daughter named Haru."

He was about to ask whether the proprietor knew the family, when the man went deathly pale, dropped to his knees, and uttered an anguished moan: "Haru-*chan* . . ."

The woman ran out from the kitchen. Small and slender, with graying hair piled atop her head, she scolded her husband, "We agreed never to speak of her again!" Then she took a second look at the man, and her rage faded into concern. "What's wrong?" She turned wary eyes on Sano. "Who are you?"

"He's the shogun's *sōsakan-sama*," the proprietor said in a choked voice. "He asked about her."

"Then you know Haru?" Sano said, baffled by the couple's reaction.

"No." The woman shot her husband a warning glance.

He lifted bleak eyes to Sano. "She was our daughter."

"Your daughter? But I understood that Haru was an orphan whose parents died of a fever."

Misery slumped the proprietor's shoulders. "Whoever told you that was wrong. We are alive. It is Haru who is dead."

Trying to make sense of the conversation, Sano shook his head. "Haru is at the Zōjō Temple convent." He explained about the fire and murders, and Haru's situation. The couple listened in blank silence: Apparently they hadn't heard the news. "I think there's been a misunderstanding," Sano said. "We can't be talking about the same—"

Grunting noises came from the man, and Sano realized that he was weeping, although his eyes were tearless. The woman pressed her hands against ashen cheeks. She murmured, "Oh, no."

In the kitchen a pot boiled over; moisture sizzled on hot coals, and clouds of steam rose. The woman rushed to the stove and removed the pot. The man stood, his movements shaky. "There's no misunderstanding," he said sadly. "The Haru you speak of is our daughter. She is dead to us, but we've known all along that she was out in the world somewhere."

So Haru had lied about being an orphan. Disturbed, but not really surprised, Sano wondered whether she'd told the truth about anything. "Did she run away?" Then another possibility occurred to him. "You disowned her."

"After what she did?" The woman returned, wiping her hands on a cloth. Indignation distorted her face. Now Sano saw a resemblance to Haru in her small build, wide brow, and delicate features. "We had no choice!"

"What did Haru do?" Sano asked.

"For you to understand, I must begin the story at the beginning," said the proprietor. "Two years ago, we had a regular customer—a wealthy Shinjuku rice broker named Yoichi. He came to Kojimachi every few days to shop at the hunters' market, and he often ate at our restaurant."

"Haru was growing up into a pretty young woman," the wife said. "Yoichi-san was a widower, and he took a liking to her. He asked for her hand in marriage."

"It was a good match," said the proprietor. "As a rich man's wife, she would live in a fine house and be secure. She could care for us in our old age. Her children would have everything, and inherit a fortune." Financial gain was always an important factor when arranging a daughter's marriage. "So we accepted Yoichi-san's proposal."

"But Haru didn't want to marry him because he was old and ugly. Such a disobedient, ungrateful girl!" Disgust tightened the wife's mouth. "But it was her duty to marry the man we chose for her."

"A month after the wedding, in the middle of the night, Yoichi-san's house burned down. The fire brigade found him and the servants dead in the ruins. But Haru turned up at our door the next morning. She was covered with soot. There were burns on her hands and clothes." Spreading his hands in a helpless gesture, the proprietor said, "Of course we took her in."

A chill spread through Sano. Fires were common, yet Haru had been involved in one that bore a sinister resemblance to the one at the Black Lotus Temple. Was it mere coincidence, or more reason to justify his suspicion of Haru?

"We knew right away that something was wrong," the wife said. "Haru was so happy to be home. She didn't seem sorry about the fire. When we asked how she'd managed to get out alive, she said she woke up and found her bedchamber filled with smoke. She said she ran through the flames, screaming for her husband, but he didn't answer, and she couldn't find him.

"She jumped off the rear balcony, and the next thing she knew, she was lying in the street, with people trying to revive her and the fire brigade throwing water on the house. But Haru couldn't explain why she woke up while the others didn't. We asked why she hadn't gotten hurt when she jumped off the balcony, and she said she'd tied a quilt to the rail and climbed down it. But if that was so, then why did she say she'd jumped? How did she get knocked unconscious? She looked nervous and guilty and said she must have fainted."

"Later we heard that the fire had started in Yoichi-*san*'s bedchamber," said the proprietor. "A neighbor saw a woman run out the gate before the fire brigade came. We asked Haru again and again what happened, and every time, she told a different story, and finally said she couldn't remember."

Despair filled the proprietor's eyes. He and his wife stood apart, but united in shame, their heads bowed. "We began to believe that Haru had set the fire."

"Other people thought so, too," the wife said. "Yoichi-*san*'s relatives demanded that Haru give them the business and money he'd left her, or they would go to the magistrate and accuse her of arson. She didn't want to give up her inheritance, but we convinced her that she must."

"If the magistrate decided she was guilty, she would be burned to death," Haru's father explained.

"And so would we," the mother added. In cases of serious crime, the offender's family shared his punishment.

"So you kept your suspicions to yourselves," Sano said. The couple nodded. "What happened then?"

"At first we pretended nothing had happened." As if sensing disapproval from Sano, the proprietor said, "Haru was our only child. We loved her." He swallowed hard. "But we couldn't bear to look at her and think she might be a murderess. Haru must have guessed how we felt, because she changed. She'd always been a good girl, but—"

"Well, she never liked hard work," Haru's mother qualified, "and I had to keep after her to do her chores. She was sometimes rude to customers. I did the best I could with her, but she just had a bad character."

So much for Haru's story of happy, harmonious family life, Sano thought.

"After the fire, Haru began leaving the shop without permission and staying out all day and night," the wife continued. "Many times she came home drunk. She stole from the cash box. Neighbors told us they'd seen her in teahouses with men. We scolded her and beat her, but we couldn't control her. She just cursed at us. We began wondering if she'd disobeyed Yoichi-*san* and he'd punished her and made her angry, and that was why he died. We were afraid of what she might do to us."

Commander Oyama had also made Haru angry, according to his son, Sano recalled.

"Finally we gave Haru some money and told her to leave." The proprietor gazed out at the rainy street. In the dim light, he looked pale and sick. "For months afterward, I worried about what would become of our daughter. I blamed myself for her evils and wondered what I should have done differently. I mourned her and prayed for her. My wife and I tried to forget her and go on with our lives.

"But now I can see that we were wrong to keep silent about Haru and send her out into the world." The proprietor spoke with remorse. "We should have known she would cause trouble again." He turned a haunted gaze on Sano. "She set the fire at the Black Lotus Temple, didn't she?"

"I'm afraid she may have," Sano said.

She might also have progressed to murder by means other than arson. The new evidence against his prime suspect gave Sano no joy. He deeply pitied Haru's mother and father. How terrible it must be to have a child go bad! Estrangement seemed almost worse than death, and parenthood fraught with hazards. Would Masahiro grow up to be an honorable samurai, or a wayward spirit like Haru? Sano also regretted coming to Kojimachi and hearing Haru's parents' story because he dreaded telling Reiko what he had learned about the girl.

11

If a person should spurn faith in the Black Lotus,
He will be plagued by many ailments.
He will find himself plundered, robbed, and punished
As he walks the evil path through life.

—FROM THE BLACK LOTUS SUTRA

Hirata splashed through the puddles in the courtyard of police headquarters, peering from beneath his umbrella at the crowd huddled in the dripping rain. He wondered what had brought so many people here in such bad weather. Under the eaves of the main building, he handed his umbrella to a servant; then he entered the reception room. It was packed with more people standing against pillars and seated on the floor, some puffing tobacco pipes, amid a loud babble of conversation. The warm, stuffy air was thick with smoke. Several *doshin* stood guard. Hirata elbowed his way up to the platform where the clerks sat elevated above the crowd.

"Why are all these people here?" he asked the chief clerk.

Uchida grinned. "They're responding to your notice asking for information about the dead woman and boy at the Black Lotus Temple."

"All of them?" Hirata, who had come to check on whether the notices had gotten any results, gazed around the room in astonishment.

"Every one," Uchida said, "and the folks outside, too."

The nearest bystanders spread the news that the man who'd issued the notices had arrived. The crowd surged toward Hirata, waving hands and shouting pleas.

"Quiet!" Hirata ordered. "Stand back! I'll see you one at a time."

Doshin coaxed and shoved the mob into a line that snaked around the room, while Hirata sat atop the platform. He saw the shaved crowns of samurai among the many commoners. He tried to count heads and stopped at a hundred. Surely all these people couldn't be connected with the two mystery victims.

The first person in line was a frail, stooped peasant woman. Looking anxiously up at Hirata, she said, "My grown son joined the Black Lotus sect last year. I haven't seen or heard from him since, and I'm so worried. Is he dead?"

"I'm sorry, I don't know," Hirata said. "The people in the fire were a woman and a little boy. That was explained in the notice."

"I can't read," said the woman. "I came because I heard you were looking for anyone with family members who disappeared at the temple."

"No. My inquiry doesn't include adult males." Hirata realized that his message had been distorted while spreading through the largely illiterate populace.

"Maybe my son is still alive, then." Hope brightened the woman's wrinkled face. "Please, will you help me find him?"

"I'll try." Hirata wrote down the woman's name, where she lived, and her son's name and age. Then he stood on the platform and addressed the crowd, explaining the purpose of his notice and describing the victims. "Everyone who's here about missing persons who don't fit those descriptions should come back later and make a report to the police."

Rumbles of disappointment stirred the crowd, but no one got out of line. A man with the coarse appearance of a laborer stepped up to the platform. "My daughter is missing," he said.

"How old is she?" Hirata asked.

Before the laborer could answer, a burly samurai shoved him aside and said to Hirata, "I refuse to wait any longer. I demand to speak to you now."

"Get in line," Hirata ordered. "Wait your turn."

"My three-year-old son disappeared in the spring." The samurai, whose garments bore a floral crest that marked him as a retainer of the Kane clan, stood firm. "His mother took him shopping in Nihonbashi. She lost him in the crowd. Storekeepers saw three Black Lotus priests putting a little boy into a palanquin. They stole my son."

"They stole my daughter, too," said the laborer. "She was playing outside. The priests and nuns are always in our street, inviting people to join the sect and giving the children candy. When they left that day, they took my girl with them."

"How do you know?" Hirata asked, intrigued by the accusations.

"Other children have disappeared after the Black Lotus visited. Everyone knows the Black Lotus steals them," said the laborer.

Shouts rang out along the line: "They took my child, too!" "And mine!" "And mine!"

Amazed consternation jolted Hirata. It hardly seemed possible that the sect was involved in so many disappearances. Had mass delusion infected these people?

"When I went to the temple to look for my son, the priests threw me out," said the samurai. "I went to the police, and they said they would look into the matter, but they've done nothing. I came here hoping you could help me."

Hirata took pity on the samurai, whose son's age fell in the range Dr. Ito had specified for the dead boy in the cottage. He wrote down the samurai's name and information, then turned to Uchida. "This is going to take forever. Will you help out?"

"Of course," Uchida said.

Hirata announced, "Everyone who's here about missing children and the Black Lotus sect, form a new line."

A general shift divided the crowd in two roughly equal portions. Hirata remembered the story that Sano had told him this morning, about a novice monk who'd accused the Black Lotus of imprisoning followers. Sano should be interested to hear of this new development.

Hirata and Uchida spent the next several hours on interviews. Many people wanted to talk about missing relatives who bore no resemblance to the murder victims, just to register complaints about the Black Lotus sect.

"With so many incidents, why didn't the police begin investigating long ago?" Hirata asked Uchida.

"Maybe they didn't know about the situation," Uchida said. "It's news to me, and I thought I knew everything that happened around town."

Upon questioning the citizens, Hirata learned that most had reported the disappearances to local *doshin* instead of coming to police headquarters. Perhaps the higher officials hadn't yet reviewed the reports and discerned the magnitude of the problem or a connection between the incidents. But Hirata, who knew about the rampant corruption in the police force, suspected a cover-up.

By noon, Uchida had compiled forty listings of missing young boys. Hirata amassed even more possibilities for the dead woman, but no one had recognized the jade sleeping-deer amulet found on the body. The line seemed endless; as people left the room, more streamed in from the courtyard. With a sigh, Hirata greeted the next person in line.

It was a carpenter in his thirties, who carried a box of tools. His eyes and mouth turned down at the corners in a permanently sad expression; wood shavings clung to his cropped hair. He took one look at the amulet and began to weep.

"That belongs to my wife. It was made by her grandfather, who was a jade carver." The carpenter wiped his eyes with a calloused hand. "Chie used to wear it on a string around her waist for good luck."

Hirata experienced a thrill of gratification, tempered by pity. "My sincere condolences," he said, climbing off the platform. "Please come with me."

Over the crowd's protests, he led the carpenter to a small vacant office with a barred window overlooking the stables. Hirata invited the carpenter to sit, and served him tea.

"Tell me about your wife," Hirata said gently.

The carpenter clutched his tea bowl in both hands and drank

thirstily, as if drawing sustenance from the hot liquid. Then he spoke with sorrowful nostalgia: "Chie and I have been married twelve years. We have two sons. My business has prospered. Chie had learned the art of healing from her mother, and she earned money by treating sick neighbors. We were very happy together. But four years ago, everything changed."

Grief twisted his face. Hirata poured him more tea. He gulped it, then said, "Nuns from the Black Lotus Temple came to our street. They said that their high priest could show us the path to enlightenment and invited us to the temple. I was too busy working, but Chie went. And she came home a different person. She went back to the temple again and again. At home, she spent hours chanting. She stopped keeping house. She ignored the children. She wouldn't let me touch her. I begged her to tell me why she was acting so strangely, but she wouldn't talk. I scolded her and ordered her to do her duty as a wife and mother. I forbade her to leave the house.

"One night, she ran away. She took all our money. I knew she'd gone to the Black Lotus Temple." The carpenter explained sadly, "It had happened in other families, you see. The high priest would cast a spell over people, and they'd forsake everything to join him. He would steal their souls and all their worldly property."

"And you just let your wife go? For four years you did nothing?" Hirata couldn't believe this.

"I tried my best to get Chie back!" The carpenter's eyes blazed with his eagerness to convince; his words rushed forth: "I asked the neighborhood headman and the police for help, but they said there was nothing they could do. I went to the temple and begged Chie to come home. She refused. The priests told me to stay away. But I went back the very next day, with the children. Chie wouldn't even look at them. The priests chased us out. I vowed never to give up, but then . . ."

Despair quenched the carpenter's animation. "Bad things started happening. My brother fell off the roof of a house we were building and broke his leg. Later, some thugs beat me up. Then there was a fire in a cloth shop where I was doing repairs. It burned all the goods, and I had to pay for the damage. I borrowed from a moneylender and went deeply into debt.

"Soon afterward, a Black Lotus priest came to my house.

He said my bad luck was caused by a spell that the high priest had cast upon the enemies of the sect. If I didn't stay away from the temple, worse misfortunes would befall me. I'd heard of the same thing happening to other people who tried to get relatives out of the temple. I couldn't risk my family's safety or livelihood. So . . ."

A ragged sigh issued from the carpenter. "I let Chie go. I hoped she would someday regain her senses and the sect would lose its power over her. But now my hope is gone. I'll never see my wife again in this world."

Hirata contemplated what he'd just heard. Assuming that the carpenter was telling the truth, how did this scenario relate to the murders? While the superstitious part of Hirata believed in magic spells, the policeman in him thought it more likely that human hands had caused the carpenter's troubles. The Black Lotus must have sent members to menace people who interfered with their business. They used violence and fire as weapons. Perhaps they'd strangled Chie and tried to burn her body in the cottage; but if so, then why?

He posed the question to the carpenter, who said, "I don't know. My Chie was a good, kind woman who loved helping people and would never have hurt anyone. But maybe she changed during those four years at the temple. Maybe she made enemies."

Hirata wondered whether these might include an orphan girl named Haru. Thinking of the two other victims, he said, "Did your wife know Police Commander Oyama, the man whose body was found in the fire?"

"If she did, she must have met him after she ran away, because I've never heard of him before."

"Have you any idea who the dead child was? You said that you and your wife have sons . . . ?"

"Chie left both our sons behind. So the dead child isn't ours. I don't know who it is." The carpenter bowed his head over his empty tea bowl. "I'm sorry I can't be of more help."

"You've been a tremendous help," Hirata said. The carpenter had put a name to the mystery woman, and he'd also identified her as a Black Lotus member, known to the priests and nuns who'd denied knowing her and claimed that no one was missing from the temple. Surely their lies and their dark reputation implicated them in the murders.

Hirata wrote down the carpenter's name and the location of his home. "I'll do my best to deliver your wife's killer to justice," he promised, then escorted the man out through the reception room.

The crowd hadn't diminished at all. Ascending the platform, Hirata braced himself for more tales of woe. He had an uneasy feeling that the fire and murders represented a tiny part of a larger evil. Almost certainly, the case involved much more than a troublesome orphan girl.

12

The Law of the Black Lotus
Is of a single flavor.
All beings, regardless of origin or nature,
Can gain the fruits of its truth.

—FROM THE BLACK LOTUS SUTRA

In the Hibiya administrative district, located south of Edo Castle, Reiko and Haru disembarked from the palanquin into thin, cold rain. An attendant held an umbrella over them while they hurried to the roofed gate of one of the walled estates that lined the street. Reiko exchanged friendly greetings with the sentries, but Haru eyed them fearfully and hung back.

"Don't be afraid." Reiko put a reassuring arm around the girl. "You're among friends here."

Accompanied by the attendant with the umbrella, she propelled Haru through the wet courtyard. There a crowd of police and shackled prisoners huddled under the eaves of the guardhouse. Haru shrank against Reiko. They entered the low, half-

timbered mansion. A maid greeted them in the entryway and
helped them remove their cloaks and shoes.

"Where is my father?" Reiko asked the maid.

"In his private office, Honorable Lady."

Reiko led Haru down the angled corridor, past chambers
where clerks worked at writing desks. She knocked on a door.

A deep, masculine voice called, "Enter!"

Sliding open the door, Reiko stepped inside a chamber lined
with shelves and cabinets full of books, ledgers, and scrolls,
pulling Haru after her. They knelt and bowed to the man seated
behind a desk on a low platform.

"Good afternoon, Honorable Father," Reiko said. "Please
excuse me for interrupting your work, but I've brought you a
visitor. We have urgent business to discuss with you."

Magistrate Ueda, one of two officials responsible for settling
disputes among citizens, conducting trials of criminals, overseeing the police force, and maintaining order in Edo, laid
down his writing brush. He was a stout, middle-aged samurai
with heavy-lidded eyes and a ruddy complexion, dressed in
formal black silk kimono.

"What a pleasant surprise to see you, Daughter," he said,
regarding Reiko with affection. "I'm eager to make your
friend's acquaintance."

Reiko introduced Haru. The girl kept her head bowed and
her hands clasped tightly in her lap. She whispered, "It's a
privilege to meet you, Honorable Magistrate."

When Reiko explained who Haru was, a slight frown marred
Magistrate Ueda's genial expression. Undaunted, Reiko said,
"Haru needs a safe place to stay, so I brought her here. I hope
you'll agree to take her in."

For a moment Magistrate Ueda contemplated Reiko in
thoughtful silence. Then he turned to Haru. "Certainly you
must accept my hospitality while you rest after your journey."
His voice, while gentle, lacked warmth. "May I offer you re-
freshment?"

"Thank you, Honorable Magistrate, but I've already eaten."
Haru mumbled the polite, conventional reply.

"But I insist." The magistrate summoned a maid, to whom
he said, "Take my guest into the parlor and serve her some
tea."

Haru shot a terrified glance at Reiko.

"Go on," Reiko said with an encouraging smile.

After Haru and the maid had left, Magistrate Ueda folded his hands atop a stack of papers on his desk. His grave expression heralded a scolding, and Reiko felt a stab of anxiety. He said, "Why did you bring Haru here?"

"She can't stay at Zōjō Temple any longer," Reiko said, describing Kumashiro's attack on Haru. "She's alone in the world, with nowhere to go and no friends except me. And I can't bring a guest into Edo Castle without official permission, which would take forever to get. This is the only place I could put her."

"You should have at least consulted me in advance instead of putting me on the spot," said the magistrate.

"I know, and I'm sorry," Reiko said contritely, "but there wasn't time."

"So you want me to take into my house the prime suspect in a case of arson and triple murder, hmm?" Ueda said. When Reiko nodded, disapproval drew his thick eyebrows together. "How can you ask such an outrageous favor? What can you be thinking, Daughter?"

"Haru hasn't been proven guilty and may very well be innocent," Reiko said, disconcerted by her father's reaction. Although she hadn't expected him to rejoice at the prospect of sheltering Haru, she hadn't foreseen opposition because he rarely refused her anything. "And I know she's in danger."

Magistrate Ueda shook his head. "If she did commit those crimes, then she's a danger to other people. I can't risk the safety of my household by bringing her under my roof. And what makes you think she's innocent?"

Reiko described her theory that Haru had been an intended victim of the fire and was now being framed as a scapegoat. She related her suspicions about the Black Lotus sect's practices. "I believe that the sect may be behind the murders and arson." Reiko added, "Does Haru look capable of smashing a man's head and strangling a woman and child?"

"We've both seen many criminals who look as harmless as Haru," Magistrate Ueda said, alluding to the numerous trials he'd conducted while Reiko watched through a screen in a room next to the Court of Justice. "You know better than to judge a person by appearance. And you offer proof of neither your theory about Haru's role in the crimes nor your accusations against the Black Lotus."

"At the moment, the sect seems as likely to be guilty as Haru does, and my intuition tells me I'm right," Reiko said. "I can remember times when it guided you." She'd often told him when defendants were guilty and to push for a confession, and when they were innocent and he should look elsewhere for the culprit. She'd whispered her advice through the screen, and her father had followed it with good results. "Do you doubt me now?"

Magistrate Ueda fixed a stern gaze on Reiko. "Intuition without reason can lead to serious mistakes. I taught you that. Please do not forget that it's dangerous to focus solely on the side of a story that pleases you. I presume there is evidence against Haru, because otherwise, the *sōsakan-sama* would have already exonerated her. Now, let's hear it."

Reluctantly, Reiko disclosed Haru's troubled past, her relationship with Commander Oyama, and the lies Haru had admitted telling.

"That's more than enough reason for me to eject Haru from my house immediately and send her to Edo Jail." Anger kindled in the magistrate's eyes. "Even if you've no concern for the welfare of my household, you should at least respect my position. My authority as magistrate would be much diminished if it became known that I harbored a murder suspect."

Unable to think of a good reply to his legitimate concern, Reiko felt her cause losing ground. Already at odds with Sano, she hated the thought of a rift between herself and the other most important man in her life. Yet Reiko couldn't let him turn Haru out.

"If I were in Haru's position, would you want people to decide I was guilty before the investigation was finished?" Reiko said. "Would you want me sent to jail?"

Magistrate Ueda gave her an affronted look. "That's hardly a plausible scenario, and I recognize your attempt to coax me by playing upon my paternal feelings."

However, Reiko sensed him relenting behind his severe façade. She said, "All I ask is that you treat Haru fairly. You needn't take my word for her innocence. Question her yourself.

Get to know her; decide whether you think she's guilty. Please, do it for my sake."

"Does your husband know about your plan to protect Haru?"

"No," Reiko admitted, "but he expects me to help Haru regain her memory, and it'll be easier for me to work with her if she's here, close to Edo Castle. He wouldn't want her to get hurt or killed, because then he might never learn the truth about the crimes. And I don't want the sect to misdirect him. Should he condemn the wrong person, his honor and reputation will suffer."

A long silence ensued. Reiko waited anxiously while her father placed the tips of his fingers together and frowned down at them.

At last Magistrate Ueda conceded, "I suppose I could assign a guard to watch Haru. If she behaves herself, she can stay for a few days."

Relief and joy flooded Reiko. "Thank you, Father." She jumped up and hugged him. "You won't be sorry."

He nodded, patting her hand.

"I'll go and get Haru settled in," Reiko said. "Then I need you to help with my inquiries. Will you, please?"

The magistrate's smile was rueful. "It seems that I am yours to command."

Hurrying to the parlor, Reiko found Haru sitting alone in front of a tray containing an empty tea bowl and a plate speckled with cake crumbs. The girl lifted woeful eyes to Reiko. "He doesn't want me here, does he?"

"He says you can stay." Watching Haru's face brighten, Reiko didn't mention her father's reluctance. "Come on, I'll show you where you'll sleep."

She led Haru to the mansion's private quarters and slid open the door of a spacious chamber. "This used to be my room."

The girl entered haltingly, gazing around at the walls decorated with painted murals of blossoming plum trees, the polished teak cabinets, lacquer tables and chests, and the raised study niche. "It's beautiful," she said in a hushed voice. "How can I ever repay your generosity?"

"Just try to recover from your bad experiences," Reiko said, hoping that these safe, pleasant quarters would help restore Haru's memory. She opened a cabinet, gazing at shelves that

held some old illustrated books; everything else of hers had
been discarded or moved to Sano's estate when she married.
"I'm sorry there's not much here to entertain you," she said.
"I'll get you some things later." Reiko saw Haru stifle a yawn
and said, "You're tired. You should rest."

She ordered a maid to make up a bed. Haru snuggled under
the quilts on the futon with a contented sigh, looking sweetly
innocent. Reiko felt sympathy toward the girl, but a lingering
distrust that she couldn't ignore. Troubled by her conflicting
inclinations, she returned to her father's office.

Magistrate Ueda looked up from his papers. "What else is
it you require from me, Daughter?"

"I need information about several members of the Black
Lotus sect," Reiko said.

"Hmm." The magistrate leveled a shrewd gaze at Reiko. "I
don't suppose the *sōsakan-sama* knows you're looking into
these people?"

"He needs background facts on them for his investigation
of the temple," Reiko said.

Her father's frown registered displeasure at her evasiveness.
Reiko tried to look humble. She waited.

At last he lifted his hands and let them fall in a gesture of
resignation. "You wish to know whether the sect members have
ever been in trouble?"

"Yes," Reiko said.

"Who are they?"

"High Priest Anraku, Abbess Junketsu-in, Priest Kumashiro,
and Dr. Miwa."

"Kumashiro." Disgust permeated the magistrate's pronun-
ciation of the name. "I am well acquainted with him."

"Has he broken the law?" Reiko asked, eager for compromising facts about the priest who'd tried to incriminate Haru
and extort a confession from her.

"Not exactly," Magistrate Ueda said. "When he was thirteen,
he decapitated a man just so he could test a new sword. Later,
as a youth in his twenties, he roamed around town picking
fights and killed three more men in as many years."

"But he was never punished because all his victims were
peasants?" Reiko guessed. Tokugawa law permitted samurai to
kill peasants on a whim.

Magistrate Ueda nodded in grim disapproval. "After the third fatal brawl, I reprimanded Kumashiro." This was the usual penalty for samurai whose misdeeds became too numerous for social acceptability. 'Kumashiro promised to control himself, yet his behavior only grew worse. He started attacking prostitutes at illegal brothels. He beat two of them to death and strangled a third.

"By then, I'd decided that Kumashiro had grossly violated honor and was a menace to the public. I imprisoned him and charged him with multiple murder. He would have been put to death, but his clan, who are prominent Tokugawa vassals, negotiated a deal with the shogun. In exchange for paying a large fine, Kumashiro would enter a monastery as the only punishment for the deaths he caused." He shook his head regretfully. "So he's joined the Black Lotus sect, hmm?"

"He's chief security officer and second-in-command to the high priest," Reiko said.

"I wouldn't be surprised to learn that he has continued his old ways," said the magistrate.

Nor would Reiko, after witnessing his brutality toward Haru. He seemed a much likelier murder suspect than the orphan girl. Surely now Sano would agree that Kumashiro merited investigation.

"What about the others?" Reiko asked.

"The name Miwa strikes my memory. I believe the doctor has appeared in my court." The magistrate rose, walked to a bookshelf, removed a ledger, and turned pages. "Yes, indeed. Here is the record of his trial, six years ago. Dr. Miwa was arrested for peddling rhinoceros-horn pills that were actually pebbles coated with gray paint and minced cat hair. Ordinarily this sort of fraud calls for death by decapitation, but since no one was hurt and it was Miwa's first offense, I ordered him to return his customers' money or spend a month in jail."

He scanned the record, then said, "That's interesting: my chief clerk has made a note that Dr. Miwa was destitute and went to jail until a priest named Anraku repaid the customers and freed Miwa."

So that was how Miwa and Anraku had joined forces, Reiko thought. She interpreted the doctor's criminal record as evidence of his shady character. He, too, warranted more investigation. "Have you ever met Abbess Junketsu-in?"

"I do not recall that I have." Magistrate Ueda perused an index of criminals and shook his head. "She does not appear here, at least not under her religious name." Upon entering a convent, women often took new names that ended with *-in.* "However, she may have a record under her previous one. What is she like?"

Reiko described Junketsu-in's inappropriate appearance and manner.

"Perhaps her history lies in trade with men," said the magistrate. After considerable time spent searching other ledgers for records containing mention of the Black Lotus, he said, "Ah. This is it. Eight years ago, a courtesan named Iris was brought before me. She and another courtesan were rivals for the favor of the same wealthy client. Iris physically attacked the other courtesan. I sentenced Iris to a flogging.

"And my clerk has again made a note on the record. Shortly after Iris returned to the pleasure quarter, a priest named Anraku discharged her debts and bought her freedom." Women sold into prostitution paid off their purchase price with their earnings, but since they also had to pay for their keep, they seldom gained liberty unless a wealthy patron interceded. "She joined his temple and took the name Junketsu-in."

"Then all three Black Lotus members have dark pasts," Reiko said, especially intrigued by the discovery of Junketsu-in's violence toward a woman. Could the abbess have strangled the female victim? Had she beaten and tried to murder Haru, whom she so obviously disliked?

After turning more pages, Magistrate Ueda said, "There are no records for High Priest Anraku."

"Such valuable information on three out of four suspects is more than I expected. Thank you for your help, Father." Reiko hid her disappointment. That Anraku recruited criminals into the Black Lotus spoke ill of his character; that his followers seemed determined to keep her away from him aroused Reiko's suspicions. Reiko had to learn more about him, but how?

Then inspiration struck. She knew two people who might be able to help. She would visit them today.

"Daughter." Magistrate Ueda regarded her with somber scrutiny. "I am worried about the use that you intend to make of the information I've given you. Religion may have reformed these criminals, but if that's not the case, then they could be dangerous. Give the information to your husband and let him deal with them."

"I will," Reiko said, wanting to reassure her father, yet determined to take matters into her own hands if necessary.

She bid Magistrate Ueda farewell, then looked in on Haru. The girl was fast asleep, a guard stationed outside her door. Would that she proved to be as innocent as she looked! Reiko left the mansion. As she rode in her palanquin toward Edo Castle, she wondered how Sano's investigation into the sect was going.

13

The multitudes shall abandon their lands,
They shall come on purpose to this place.
Here lotus blossoms adorn a clear pond,
Jeweled trees burn bright in the darkness of night.

——FROM THE BLACK LOTUS SUTRA

The rain had ceased by the time Sano arrived at the Black Lotus
Temple. Sunlight sparkled in puddles along the central path
where Sano walked. Worshippers strolled; children ran and
laughed. The colors of their clothing, the dripping foliage, and
the patches of blue sky among the fleeing clouds were bright
in the clean, fresh air.

A priest who'd escorted Sano during his inquiries on the
morning after the fire greeted him outside the main hall. "Greetings, *Sōsakan-sama*. I am at your service."

"Thank you, but I'd like to explore the temple on my own
today," Sano said.

The priest said, "Very well," bowed, and departed.

So much for Reiko's claim that the sect was trying to restrict the investigation, Sano thought. He walked to the novices' quarters. These were secluded, but looked ordinary and well kept. From inside came the sound of youthful voices, chanting: "I offer gratitude to the god of the world, the god of thunder, the god of the sun, the god of the moon, the god of the stars, and all other deities who protect the followers of the Black Lotus Sutra. I praise the supreme truth hidden in the Black Lotus Sutra and give thanks for the benefits I have received. I offer praise and deepest gratitude to High Priest Anraku, the Bodhisattva of Infinite Power. I pray for spiritual enlightenment, to erase the negative karma created by my past actions, and to fulfill my wishes in this life and in the future. I pray for the truth of the Black Lotus Sutra to bring nirvana to all mankind."

The chanting gave way to chatter. A priest greeted Sano at the door.

"I'd like to speak with the novice monks," Sano said.

"Certainly," the priest said. "It's time for our noon meal. Will you please join us?"

A noisy crowd of youths ranging from early teens to mid twenties, all sporting muslin robes, swarmed out of the building. They knelt on the veranda. When Sano introduced himself, they studied him curiously. He noted their rosy cheeks, bright eyes, and healthy bodies. Servants brought out the meal. Tasting his share, Sano found the fresh vegetables and noodle soup delicious.

"Are you happy here?" he asked the novices seated nearest him.

Amid chewing, bulging cheeks and cheerful smiles, they chorused, "Yes, master."

Sano noticed that the priest had vanished, leaving him alone with the novices. "Tell me how you spend your days."

An adolescent with a pointed face said, "We get up at sunrise and pray. Then we have our morning meal."

"We clean our rooms," offered a muscular youth of perhaps twenty years. "The priests teach us religion until noon, when we eat again."

"Is the food always like this?" Sano asked.

"We get rice and fish and eggs and pickles and fruit, too."

Other novices chimed in: "We get to play for an hour, then we study until dinner." "Afterward, we take baths." "At sunset, we have prayers." "Then we go to bed."

It seemed a reasonable routine, Sano thought, and similar to that of other Buddhist orders. "What if you misbehave?"

The young men grinned at a pudgy boy who was evidently a troublemaker. He said, "The priests lecture us on the error of our ways. Then we sit alone and meditate."

"They don't beat you?" Sano asked.

The question elicited puzzled looks and denials.

"What if you were unhappy and wanted to leave?"

A general stir of amusement indicated that the novices thought this an unlikely situation. "I missed my family at first," said the pudgy boy, "and I told the priests I wanted to go home. They sent me back to my parents' house, but after a few days of cleaning fish at my father's shop, I came back."

Evidently he hadn't been detained against his will or by force, and Sano didn't see anyone watching to make sure the novices didn't wander off. Sano said, "Is there a novice monk named Pious Truth here?"

Boys shook their heads.

"He was also known as Mori Gogen," Sano said, giving the name Reiko had said to be the monk's original one.

The lack of recognition on the boys' faces increased his doubts about the tale Reiko had told him. If there was no novice called Pious Truth here, who was it she'd met?

"What do you know about Haru, the girl who was found near the fire?" he asked the novices.

They exchanged sly glances. "She's generous with her favors," said the muscular youth. "Two novices were expelled for meeting her at night."

Reiko wouldn't welcome this confirmation of Abbess Junketsu-in's story about the girl, Sano knew. He finished his meal, thanked the novices for their company, then chatted with others, who gave similar answers to the same questions. Afterward, he walked to the novice nuns' quarters.

There, he found girls sitting inside a room, sewing while a nun read aloud a story about an emperor who entices his subjects to flee a city threatened by a flood, then rewards them with great wealth after they escape drowning. If this was a passage of the Black Lotus Sutra, it seemed to Sano that the scripture borrowed heavily from the famous Lotus Sutra and its Parable of the Burning House, but doctrinal imitation was no crime.

The novices burst into giggles at the sight of a man invading their domain. The nun readily granted Sano's request to interview them by himself. At his prompting, they described their daily life, which followed a routine similar to that of the boys. Apparently, they all felt free to leave if they wished, and they corroborated Haru's reputation for seducing young men. They looked healthy and contented; Sano detected no evidence of starvation or drug-induced stupor here, either.

"Is there someone named Yasue among you?" Sano asked.

Heads turned toward a chunky girl of about fifteen, seated near the window. She blushed at finding herself the center of attention.

"Don't be nervous," Sano told her. For Reiko's sake, he was sorry that he'd apparently found the novice Yasue alive and well; yet he was glad to disprove the story about her murder at the hands of the Black Lotus priests. "I just need to know if you've ever tried to run away from the temple."

"Oh, no, master." Yasue's surprised expression asked why she would do such a thing.

"Perhaps your brother suggested that you both should leave?" Sano said.

Confusion puckered the girl's forehead. She murmured, "I'm sorry, but I haven't got a brother."

Then she wasn't the sister of Pious Truth, whoever he might be. "Is there any other Yasue here?"

The novice nuns shook their heads, gazing earnestly at him.

"Is anyone ever punished for trying to run away?"

A wave of denials swept the room. Sano became more convinced than ever that Reiko had been deceived, perhaps by someone masquerading as a monk. What was going on? Sano decided he'd better pursue the matter further, partly because he mustn't ignore possible clues, but mostly because he needed facts to allay Reiko's suspicions about the sect.

Sano bid farewell to the novice nuns and walked to a low, thatch-roofed building. The priests had supposedly taken Pious

Truth to the temple hospital, and Reiko would expect Sano to look for the monk there.

Inside the hospital were thirty mattresses on wooden pallets, all occupied. Three nuns bathed the sick, served them tea, and massaged backs. Sano walked along the rows, inspecting the patients. They were male and female, all middle-aged or old.

"Are there any other patients elsewhere?" Sano asked a nun.

"No, master," she said.

"Has a young novice monk named Pious Truth been recently treated here?"

"No, master."

A physician in a dark blue coat entered, knelt beside a bed containing an elderly man, and spooned liquid from a bowl into the patient's mouth.

Sano walked over to the doctor and asked, "What ails your patient?"

"He has a fever," the doctor said, adding, "I'm giving him willow-wood juice."

This was a standard remedy. "Do you ever perform medical experiments on the sect members?" Sano asked.

"Never."

The doctor looked genuinely shocked by Sano's suggestion that he would endanger his patients' lives. The nuns came over to join them, and Sano asked the group, "Has anyone from here disappeared recently?"

"No, master," said the doctor.

The old man in bed mumbled something.

"What did you say?" Sano asked.

"Chie," said the old man. His bony cheeks were flushed, his eyes dazed. "She's one of the nurses. Used to take care of me. Haven't seen her in days."

"He's delirious," the doctor told Sano apologetically. "There has never been a nurse named Chie here."

Sano looked at the nuns, who murmured in agreement. "Has Haru ever been treated here?" Sano said.

"Yes," said the doctor. "Haru is a patient of Dr. Miwa, our chief physician. Her spiritual disharmony causes bad behavior."

Sano considered the possibility that everyone at the temple was part of a conspiracy bent on hiding secrets from him and smearing Haru's reputation, but these people seemed honest.

After leaving the hospital, he wandered through the temple precinct. He observed nuns and monks tending the gardens and washing dishes in the kitchen. They appeared as normal as the clergy at any other temple, and their activities mundane. Sano continued on to the orphanage. He thought of his interview with Haru's parents, and guilt tugged at him, because he was about to do something else he hadn't mentioned to Reiko.

Children's laughter and shouts greeted his entry into the garden surrounding the orphanage. Under the supervision of two nuns, the thirty-one orphans were running, jumping, and skipping in play. They ranged in age from a toddler, who reminded Sano of Masahiro, to two girls of ten or eleven years tossing a leather ball with some younger boys. One of the boys missed a catch, and the ball flew toward Sano. He caught it. The group turned to him, wary at the sight of a stranger.

"Watch," Sano said.

He kicked the ball high in the air. The children squealed in delight, and a boy caught the ball. He clumsily imitated Sano's kick, booting the ball into some bushes.

"Here, I'll show you," Sano said. With his coaching, the children mastered the trick and began a lively contest to see who could kick the ball highest. Someone sent the ball soaring over the orphanage roof. The boys ran to retrieve it, and Sano turned to the two girls.

"Is Haru a friend of yours?" he asked.

The girls moved close together, suddenly shy. The taller, who was delicate and pretty, blurted, "We don't like Haru. Nobody does."

"Why not?" Sano asked.

"She's mean." the other girl said, her round face puckering in dislike. "If we don't do what she says, she hits us. Um, the littler ones are afraid of her because she picks on them."

Sano listened in consternation. Their story contradicted the one Haru had given Reiko, who he knew would be upset to learn that the orphans Haru had professed to love considered her a bully. Sano also knew that these bad character references could help him convict Haru. If she was cruel to children, she might have killed the little boy found in the fire. More mixed feelings plagued Sano. He was eager to solve the case, yet disturbed to think of himself and Reiko compiling evidence for and against Haru like warlords stocking arsenals for a battle. Although he didn't relish the idea of losing, he wondered if Reiko was right about the Black Lotus in one respect.

It appeared that Haru had offended many people here. Maybe they were seeking revenge, as she'd claimed, by implicating her in murder and arson.

The boys had returned with the ball. One of them said, "It's no use telling the nuns or priests how Haru treats us. They won't stop her."

"Why not?" Sano said.

"Haru is High Priest Anraku's favorite. She can do whatever she wants."

Sano saw that he must speak with Anraku. The high priest had been secluded in prayer rituals during his previous visits to the temple, and he'd willingly postponed an interview because he'd considered Anraku neither a witness nor a suspect, but now it was imperative that he question the high priest about Haru.

"I'm trying to find out who set the fire," Sano said to the children. "Do you know anything that might help me?"

The boys shook their heads. Glances passed between the two girls. "Haru did it," said the pretty one.

Children often made up stories and repeated things they'd heard, Sano knew; as a father, he felt a certain responsibility toward these children who had no parents. He sent the boys off to play ball, then asked the girls, "What are your names?"

"Yukiko," said the pretty one.

"Hanako," said the round-faced one.

"Yukiko-*chan* and Hanako-*chan,* it's wrong to accuse someone unless you have facts to prove your accusation," Sano said. "Do you think Haru set the fire just because other people say so?"

Again the girls looked at each other. Hanako said, "Um, the night before the fire, we went to bed in the dormitory, but instead of going to sleep, we watched Haru."

"She sneaks out at night all the time," said Yukiko. "We wanted to follow her and see where she went."

"We thought that if we could catch her doing something really bad, we could, um, report her," Hanako said. "High Priest Anraku would find out that she's no good and expel her."

Sano was startled by the vindictive cunning of these innocent-looking girls, and his expression must have revealed disapproval, because Yukiko said hastily, "Oh, we wouldn't really have reported Haru. We were just going to tell her that we would unless she stopped hurting us."

Their childish blackmail scheme disconcerted Sano even more. How early they'd learned the ways of the world! "What happened?" he asked.

"When the temple bell rang at midnight, Haru got out of bed and left the dormitory," Yukiko said. "We went after her."

"She tiptoed through the precinct," Hanako said. "She kept looking around like she was, um, afraid to be seen."

"We followed her down the path," Yukiko said, "then Hanako got scared."

Hanako said defensively, "I knew that if Haru saw us, she would be angry. She would, um, be even meaner to us. So I made Yukiko go back to the dormitory with me."

"Then you didn't see what Haru did?" Sano said.

"No," Yukiko said, "but we followed her as far as the garden outside that cottage that burned down."

"She acted sneaky, like she was doing something wrong," Hanako said. "She must have set the fire."

Maybe Haru had gone to the cottage to meet Commander Oyama, Sano thought. If so, what had happened between them? How did the murdered woman and boy fit into this scenario?

"Did you see anyone else near the cottage?" Sano asked.

"No, master," said Yukiko.

"Did you hear any unusual noises?"

The girls shook their heads. If they were telling the truth—and Sano saw no indications otherwise—then this was confirmation of Abbess Junketsu-in's claim that Haru had sneaked out of the dormitory that night.

"What did you do then?" Sano said.

"We, um, went back to bed."

Still, the girls couldn't account for the later missing hours in Haru's life. Sano thanked them, then toured the temple, inspecting the buildings and grounds. He found no doorways to underground passages. On a path he met a pilgrim carrying a pack on his back and a walking staff in his hand. The face under his wicker hat belonged to Detective Kanryū. He bowed to Sano, showing no sign of recognition, shook his head slightly, then walked on. Sano interpreted this signal to mean that his surveillance team hadn't yet discovered anything amiss in the temple.

At the abbot's residence, an attendant told Sano that High Priest Anraku was engaged in meditation. Sano was annoyed at being put off, but he didn't want to disrupt the temple routine and offend the shogun's religious sensibilities, so he scheduled an appointment with Anraku for tomorrow afternoon. Then he walked to the hall that served as headquarters for his investigation. There, three of his detectives were questioning Black Lotus members.

"Any luck?" Sano asked them between interviews.

"We've questioned about half the sect," said a detective. "So far, there's nothing to indicate that any of Commander Oyama's family or known enemies were here at the time of the fire. And there doesn't appear to be anyone with cause or opportunity to have committed the crimes."

Except Haru, Sano thought grimly. He joined his detectives in interviewing nuns and priests, aware that until he found evidence against someone else, Haru remained his only suspect, and he would somehow have to detach Reiko from her.

14

*He who denounces those who embrace the Law of the Black
  Lotus
Will not be believed,
For he speaks not the real truth.*

—FROM THE BLACK LOTUS SUTRA

The shogun's mother, his two hundred concubines, and their attendants lived in a secluded area of the palace known as the Large Interior. Reiko entered by its private gate. Walking through a garden green and fresh from the rain, she came upon a group of young women dressed in bright kimonos, gathering asters and reeds in the late-afternoon sunshine. Among the women Reiko spied Midori, who smiled and hurried to greet her.

"Hello, Reiko-*san*," Midori said. "What brings you here?"

"I need to see His Excellency's mother," Reiko said.

"Then I must warn you that Lady Keisho-in is in one of her moods. We've had a terrible time keeping her entertained. Now she's sent us out to pick flowers for her to arrange." Midori sighed at the plight of herself and the other ladies-in-waiting. "Maybe a visit from you will improve her temper."

Reiko and Midori walked toward the building, a wing of the palace with a gabled tile roof over plaster and timber walls. Midori said hesitantly, "Have you seen Hirata-*san* today?"

"Yes, as I was leaving the house this morning," Reiko said.

"Did he . . ." Midori looked down at the flower basket in her hands. "Did he say anything about me?"

"We didn't speak at all," Reiko said, sparing her friend the knowledge that Hirata never mentioned Midori anymore. Reiko had noticed Hirata's lack of attention to her friend, and Midori's growing despondency. She knew Midori was in love with Hirata, but although she and Sano had cherished hopes of a match between them, social considerations and Hirata's indifference made the possibility of their marriage remote.

"I don't know what to do!" Midori cried. Tears spilled down her cheeks. "How can I make him like me again?"

Reiko privately thought Hirata had turned into a conceited boor who wasn't worth such anguish, but she wanted to help her friend. "Maybe you should show special interest in his life."

"I've already tried that." Midori sniffled. "I offered to help him solve a case, but he just laughed."

"Well, maybe that's not such a good idea," Reiko said, quailing at the thought of delicate, innocent Midori involved in dangerous detective work.

"You mean you don't think I'm capable either?" Midori said, pouting.

"It's not that," Reiko said hastily. "But most men don't admire cleverness in a woman or want her meddling in their business, and I doubt if Hirata-*san* does, either. Maybe you should just look as pretty as possible and be cold and aloof toward him. That should spark his interest in you."

Comprehension shone in Midori's eyes. "Of course! He'll want me because he thinks I don't want him. Oh, thank you," she exclaimed, hugging Reiko. "I can't wait to see Hirata-*san* and show him how little he means to me!"

Inside the Large Interior, rooms were crammed with pretty young women playing cards, combing their hair, and chattering among themselves. Their shrill voices deafened Reiko as she walked through the narrow, winding corridors with Midori. A cypress door, resplendent with carved dragons, marked the entrance to Lady Keisho-in's private chambers. Two sentries—among the few men allowed in the Large Interior—stood outside. From inside came gay samisen music. Keisho-in's crusty old voice yelled, "I'm sick of that song. Play something else," then subsided into phlegmy coughing.

Another tune began. The sentries admitted Midori and Reiko to a room filled with tobacco smoke. Through its haze Reiko saw the samisen player seated amid other ladies-in-waiting. Around them lay cards, tea bowls, and plates of food. Lady Keisho-in lolled upon cushions. She was a small, squat woman clad in a cobalt silk kimono; a silver tobacco pipe protruded from her mouth. Puffing, she squinted at the doorway.

"Midori-*san*? Don't just stand there, come over here." Ill temper coarsened her voice. "Who is that with you?"

Reiko and Midori knelt before the shogun's mother and bowed. "I present the Honorable Lady Reiko," Midori said.

"Splendid!" With a grunt, Lady Keisho-in pushed herself upright. Her dyed black hair, thick white face powder, and crimson rouge gave her a guise of youth, but her sixty-seven years showed in her sagging bosom and double chin. She smiled, revealing gaps between her cosmetically blackened teeth; her rheumy eyes sparkled.

"Life is so melancholy these days, and it cheers me to see you," she said to Reiko. She signaled the attendants, who poured tea for Reiko. "Have some refreshments."

"Thank you," Reiko said, glad of Lady Keisho-in's welcome. She'd visited Keisho-in before, but never without invitation, and she'd feared offending the mother of her husband's lord.

"My, it's been ages since we last met." Keisho-in shifted to a more comfortable position for a good chat. The samisen music continued; Midori and the other attendants sat in polite silence. "What have you been doing?"

"Taking care of my son," Reiko said. "He's eighteen months old now, and he keeps me quite busy."

"I recall my own dear boy at that age," Keisho-in said with fond nostalgia. "He loved his mama so much that he couldn't bear to be separated from her. He was so obedient and docile."

He hasn't changed much, Reiko thought. The shogun depended on his mother for advice on how to rule Japan, and Lady Keisho-in was one of his most influential companions. Her word could elevate or destroy the careers of *bakufu* officials. Fortunately, Sano had earned her goodwill, and it was this goodwill that Reiko hoped to benefit from today.

"How is your health?" Keisho-in asked. "Do your breasts give plenty of milk? Hmm, your figure looks fine." With a lewd cackle, she added, "I bet you and your husband have resumed marital relations."

Blushing in embarrassment, Reiko nodded. The woman had such a vulgar habit of discussing intimate subjects!

"Move closer so I can get a better look at you," Keisho-in said. Reiko obeyed. Keisho-in scrutinized her, then declared, "Motherhood becomes you." Heightened interest lit her gaze. "In fact, it has increased your beauty."

"Many thanks for the undeserved praise," Reiko said politely. "I know I look terrible."

"Oh, you're too modest." Lady Keisho-in dimpled. "Now tell me, what news is there of the *sōsakan-sama*?"

"He's investigating the fire and murders at the Black Lotus Temple," Reiko said, leading the conversation to the topic of importance to her.

"Men," scoffed Keisho-in. She inhaled on her pipe, exhaled smoke, and coughed, shaking her head. "Always so absorbed in business. Do you know that Priest Ryuko has gone off somewhere and left me by myself all day?"

Ryuko was Keisho-in's spiritual adviser and lover. Evidently, his abandonment had caused her bad mood. Now she fluttered a silk fan in front of her face. Above it, her eyes twinkled at Reiko. "I bet your man has left you to your own devices, too."

"Actually, he's asked me to help with the case," Reiko said.

She explained about Haru, and her belief that the Black Lotus sect was involved in the crimes. Lady Keisho-in listened eagerly, uttering exclamations: "Shocking!" "Remarkable!" Her attention encouraged Reiko to hope that Keisho-in would grant the favor she wanted.

"I need to speak with High Priest Anraku, the leader of the sect," Reiko said, "but his subordinates wouldn't let me."

"Disgusting!" Keisho-in grimaced. "Those people take too much authority upon themselves."

"Perhaps if I had assistance from a person of influence . . . ?" Reiko hinted.

"I suppose that might help," Keisho-in agreed cheerfully.

"Someone to whom the high priest owes a duty could convince him to grant me an audience," Reiko said.

Smiling, Keisho-in nodded, but it was obvious that she had no idea what Reiko meant. Mirth shimmered behind the stoic faces of the ladies-in-waiting. Reiko gave up on subtlety. "The high priest would see me if you ordered him to," she said.

"Of course he would." Comprehension brightened Keisho-in's face. "He has to do what I say. All of his kind must."

Lady Keisho-in was an avid Buddhist who had taken a religious name; she'd also directed the shogun to build temples and give generous endowments to religious orders. The clergy didn't dare disobey her, lest they lose Tokugawa patronage.

"Just leave that priest to me," Keisho-in said, "and you shall have whatever you want." She fixed an insinuating, covetous gaze on Reiko.

Keisho-in was flirting with her! The belated realization flabbergasted Reiko. Everyone knew that the shogun's mother liked women as well as men, but Reiko had never imagined herself as an object of Keisho-in's romantic interest. The dowager had always treated her with maternal kindness, yet now it seemed that Keisho-in had taken a fancy to her.

"A thousand thanks," Reiko stammered in dismay. Keisho-in often had affairs with her attendants, the wives of *bakufu* officials, and even her son's concubines. No lover could give her as much affection as she needed, and she punished them harshly for their failure. Everyone had heard tales of maids and concubines thrown out on the streets; ladies-in-waiting dismissed and doomed to spinsterhood because Keisho-in forbade anyone to marry them; officials demoted because their wives had displeased her. Reiko wasn't physically attracted to women, and she found the shogun's mother repugnant. She was horrified to discover that she'd put herself and Sano in peril.

The only solution was to get away as quickly and gracefully as possible. Reiko said, "Your help will surely benefit the investigation, and I truly appreciate it, but I must—"

"We shall go to the Black Lotus Temple tomorrow," Keisho-in announced. "I'll order the sect to let you see the high priest, and we'll both visit him."

"What?" Reiko hoped she'd misheard the shogun's mother.

"A little trip is just the diversion I need," Keisho-in said. Giggling, she leaned closer to Reiko as she whispered, "Traveling together will give us time to get better acquainted."

Reiko stared at her, dumbstruck. She didn't want to spend any more time with Lady Keisho-in. Nor did she want Keisho-in around to meddle in the investigation.

"But you don't have to go to the temple," Reiko said, fighting anxiety. "It's such a long way, and a message from you to High Priest Anraku would do just as well as a personal visit. Please don't trouble yourself."

"A favor for you is no trouble." Some of the happiness faded from Lady Keisho-in's face. "Don't you want my company?"

"Of course I do," Reiko said quickly, because she dared not offend Keisho-in. "I'm just so overwhelmed by your generosity."

"Then it's all settled. We'll leave at the hour of the dragon." Her good humor restored, Keisho-in extended her hands to the ladies-in-waiting. "Help me up so I can choose my costume for the occasion." As the women pulled her to her feet, Keisho-in simpered at Reiko. "I want to look nice."

Riding in her palanquin through the streets of Edo Castle's official district, Reiko gazed absently out the window at the walled estates and mounted samurai. She tried to think how to avoid taking Lady Keisho-in along to the Black Lotus Temple, and failed. Unless she honored Keisho-in's wishes, she wouldn't get an interview with High Priest Anraku. She dreaded tomorrow and wondered how to discourage Keisho-in's attentions. What would she tell Sano? Maybe she shouldn't have approached the shogun's mother.

Then Reiko shook her head. It was too late for regrets and self-recrimination. She would just have to think of a way to handle Lady Keisho-in. Meanwhile she had another favor to ask of someone else.

Outside an estate near Sano's and similar in design, but grander, the captain of her military escort announced her arrival to the sentry stationed at the gate: "The wife of the *sōsakan-sama* wishes to visit the wife of the Honorable Minister of Temples and Shrines." Soon Reiko was seated in a cozy chamber with her friend Hiroko, daughter of Magistrate Ueda's chief retainer and now wife of the official in charge of monitoring the clergy.

"It's good to see you again," Hiroko said, pouring tea. She was two years Reiko's senior and had rounded features that reflected her tranquil disposition. Maids brought her two little boys, aged one and three years, for Reiko to admire. Hiroko inquired about Masahiro, then said with a gentle, knowing smile, "Somehow I doubt that you've come here for the mere pleasure of passing the time with me."

A fond, sisterly understanding had existed between them since their childhood, when Reiko had taken the lead in games while Hiroko tried to curb Reiko's willfulness and often shared the consequences of it.

"I need information about the Black Lotus sect," Reiko said. "I was hoping that the honorable minister might have some knowledge that would help solve the mystery of the fire and murders at the temple. May I speak to him?"

A frown marred Hiroko's smooth forehead. "You know I would give you anything you wanted of me, Reiko-*san,* but . . ." She paused, seeking words to refuse a favor to the daughter of her father's master. "My husband is very busy, and women shouldn't meddle in men's affairs."

"I understand," Reiko said, "and I don't like asking you to do something that might cause trouble in your marriage, but a life may depend on what I can learn about the Black Lotus." Reiko described Haru's plight and her own suspicions about the sect. "Unless I can find out who committed the crimes, a person who may be innocent will be executed."

Hiroko glanced at her children playing in the next room, her gaze clouded with indecision.

"Will you at least ask your husband if he'll spare me a moment?" Reiko asked, though she hated to pressure her friend.

Fortunately for Reiko, obedience was ingrained in Hiroko. A sigh issued from her, and she conceded, "I'll ask him."

She left the room, but soon returned. "He agreed to see you," she said, her relief clear in her voice. "Come with me."

Reiko accompanied her friend to the mansion's private office and knelt before the man seated behind a desk in the raised study niche. Twenty years older than his wife, he had a lean, rigid figure clad in a gray kimono. The swarthy skin of his face stretched taut over high cheekbones. His eyes, deeply set beneath his shaved crown and heavy brows, had a hard intelligence.

"Honorable Husband, I present Lady Reiko, daughter of Magistrate Ueda and wife of the shogun's *sōsakan-sama*." Hiroko bowed. She said to Reiko, "Please allow me to introduce the Honorable Minister of Temples and Shrines," then rose and left the room.

Reiko stifled an urge to call her back. Minister Fugatami's formidable appearance alarmed her. He must think her a presumptuous little fool.

"I am honored to make your acquaintance," she said, bowing. Nervousness quavered her words; her heart pounded.

Minister Fugatami also bowed, regarding her with stern disapproval. Reiko guessed that he'd agreed to see her only because her father was a respected colleague and her husband a member of the shogun's inner circle. "I understand that you have an interest in the Black Lotus sect," he said. His voice was quiet, cold. "Please explain why."

When Reiko began faltering through a recitation about Haru, he raised a hand, stopping her. "My wife has already told me about this girl," he said. "That does not concern me. What I wish to know is why you think the Black Lotus is capable of murder." With a touch of scorn, he added, "The law requires evidence to support such a presumption, but I wouldn't expect a woman to understand that. Are you slandering the sect just to remove the blame from your little friend?"

That he should judge her so prematurely and underestimate her knowledge of the law! Indignation gave Reiko courage. She said politely but firmly, "No, Honorable Minister, I am not." Surprise raised his thick brows: She was probably the first woman who'd ever stood up to him. "I have reason to believe that the Black Lotus is evil."

As she described her encounter with the novice monk, and

his tales of imprisonment, torture, and murder, Minister Fugatami leaned forward, listening intently, until she finished her account with Pious Truth's claim that the sect was engaged in a dangerous secret project.

"You heard this from a source inside the sect," he said. A strange elation inflected his voice. Now he regarded her with a warmth akin to affection. "Please forgive my initial doubt, and allow me to thank you for coming to me."

His sudden transformation aroused in Reiko a distrust that must have shown on her face, because Minister Fugatami said, "I owe you an explanation. My own interest in the Black Lotus dates back to a time six years ago, when the sect began its rapid expansion." He seemed to have forgotten her inferior status; in his enthusiasm for his subject, he spoke as if addressing an equal. "Like yourself, I believe the Black Lotus is involved in bad business."

He turned to the shelves behind him and lifted down four thick ledgers. "These are the records of my research on the sect, but alas, my information comes from sources outside the temple. Your story about the novice monk is the first I've heard of any member speaking out against the Black Lotus. It is a welcome sign that the wall of silence surrounding the sect is beginning to crumble, and I shall finally obtain the evidence I need to shut down the temple."

Reiko felt a thrill of excitement that this powerful official shared her suspicion about the Black Lotus. Perhaps Sano would finally take the allegations against the sect seriously. "May I ask what you know about High Priest Anraku?" she said.

The room was growing dim as the day faded into evening. Fugatami lit lanterns, then opened a ledger.

"This is my dossier on Anraku, whose original name was Yoshi, born thirty-seven years ago to the unmarried daughter of a laborer in Bizen Province," he said. "At age fourteen he became a novice at the local monastery, where he got a rudimentary education and exercised such strong control over the other novices that they considered him their spiritual leader and refused to obey the priests. Anraku beat any novices who resisted his authority. He was expelled after a year, without taking religious vows.

"Next he set himself up as an itinerant priest, wandering through the countryside, begging alms and cheating peasants at card games. Then came a period of eight years during which Anraku seems to have disappeared. He eventually resurfaced in Edo and began selling charms that would supposedly bring prosperity, but actually did nothing.

"Anraku roamed through town for the next several years, attracting many followers. He established the Black Lotus sect in a makeshift temple in a Nihonbashi storefront. His followers distributed his writings, begged alms, and sold his dirty bath-water, advertised as 'Miracle Juice' that could cure diseases. Anraku also charged money for transferring his divine energy to his followers via secret rituals."

"Didn't the authorities care?" Reiko said, recalling Dr. Miwa's arrest for fraud.

Shaking his head in regret, the minister said, "Anraku was good at controlling people and influencing them to believe they'd benefited from his rituals and remedies. Since no one complained about him, there was no reason to censure Anraku. Eventually he raised a fortune. He also forged connections with Zōjō priests. In exchange for a share of his wealth, they adopted the Black Lotus sect as a subsidiary and allowed Anraku to build his temple in their district. But I believe he's still pursuing his criminal ways, on a larger scale."

"Why is that?" Reiko asked eagerly.

Minister Fugatami laid his hand on another ledger. "These are complaints about the Black Lotus, filed with my office, from citizens and neighborhood headmen. According to them, the sect kidnaps children, extorts donations, and imprisons followers. Its neighborhood shrines are allegedly fronts for gambling dens and brothels. I am convinced that so many independent accounts tell the truth."

Here was confirmation of Pious Truth's tale, yet disbelief undercut Reiko's gladness. "How can this have been going on for years?" she said. "Why has no one stopped it?"

"Because these reports are all hearsay." With a gesture of repudiation, Fugatami shoved the ledgers aside. "I have not been able to obtain solid evidence to justify censuring the sect. I've interviewed the nuns and priests, who claim that all is well. I've inspected the temple and found nothing objectionable. I'm sure Anraku has spies who warn him that I'm coming, so that he can hide anything he doesn't want me to see."

Perhaps the cover-up also hid evidence pertaining to the fire and murders, Reiko speculated, and explained why Sano hadn't found any suspects except Haru. "Can't you ban the sect anyway?" she said, because she'd thought that the minister of temples had authority to act on his own judgment.

"Unfortunately, Anraku has loyal followers among my superiors," said Fugatami. "They've persuaded the shogun to require material proof of my suspicions and testimony from sect members—exactly the things I've failed to get—before he'll approve a ban on the Black Lotus."

Reiko hadn't realized that the Black Lotus had such strong influence within the *bakufu.* "Can Anraku's spurious cures and teachings really have won the favor of so many high officials?" she said, disturbed by the thought of their power opposing her effort to clear Haru and expose the sect's misdeeds.

"Oh, yes." Irony twisted Fugatami's mouth. "Some of my colleagues are as credulous as peasants. Besides, I suspect they've accepted monetary gifts from Anraku."

Corruption was rampant, and criminals often bribed officials to sanction their illegal activities, Reiko knew. "What's to be done?" she asked.

"It is my duty to protect the public from physical and spiritual harm by evil religious frauds." The cold fire of dedication burned in Minister Fugatami's eyes. "With your help, maybe I can at last shut down the Black Lotus Temple, dissolve the sect, and punish the leaders. I must definitely see your novice monk."

"My husband promised to find Pious Truth." Reiko wondered whether Sano had succeeded.

"Good. Still, an inside witness represents only half the proof I need." Fugatami stroked his chin thoughtfully, then said, "Many new complaints have come from Shinagawa." This was a village near Edo. "I plan to investigate them tomorrow. I shall ask the *sōsakan-sama* to accompany me so I can gain his support for my cause." He took up a writing brush. "Will you convey my letter of invitation to him?"

"Gladly." Reiko hoped Minister Fugatami could convince Sano that the Black Lotus was worth investigating, yet she doubted that her husband would agree to spend hours on a trip. "But he may not have time to go."

"He can send one of his retainers," Fugatami said, writing characters on paper.

A sudden inspiration quickened Reiko's heartbeat. She and Lady Keisho-in were going to see High Priest Anraku tomorrow morning, but she had nothing to do afterward, and Shinagawa wasn't far from the Zōjō district. "I could go as my husband's representative," she suggested.

"You?" Surprise lifted Minister Fugatami's voice; he stopped writing and stared at Reiko with the same disapproval as when they'd first met. "That would be most inappropriate."

"We wouldn't have to travel together," Reiko said, understanding that a woman couldn't join an official procession. "Nor would I interfere with your business." That would be an even worse breach of social custom. "I propose simply to watch and report back to my husband."

The minister hesitated, studying her in the flickering lantern light. Reiko could see him estimating how much influence she had over Sano and weighing his desire for his mission's success against the impropriety of honoring her request. At last he nodded.

"Very well," he said reluctantly. He wrote the letter and handed it to Reiko. "If the *sōsakan-sama* cannot go to Shinagawa, and you happen to be there, I won't prevent you from observing my investigation."

15

Though wisdom be hard to fathom,
Be firm in power of will and concentration,
Have neither doubt nor regret,
And you shall perceive the truth.

——FROM THE BLACK LOTUS SUTRA

"So the murdered woman was a peasant folk-healer named Chie," Sano said to Hirata as they walked through the outer courtyard of Sano's estate. "That was a good idea to post notices around town. I commend your excellent work."

"Oh, it was just luck," Hirata said modestly.

In the deepening twilight, lanterns burned outside the barracks; detectives led horses to the stables. Sano said, "A patient at the temple hospital says a nurse named Chie disappeared. Her name and vocation match those of the wife of the carpenter you interviewed."

"Therefore, the murdered woman was connected with the

Black Lotus," Hirata said, "which contradicts the sect leaders' claim that nobody is missing from the temple."

"Apparently." Consternation filled Sano. Had the many priests and nuns he'd interviewed today, who'd all said they knew nothing about the crimes or the mystery victims, lied to him? Was the peaceful harmony he'd observed at the temple an illusion that hid the activities that a young man purporting to be a novice monk had described to Reiko? The identification of the woman lent support to Reiko's theory of a Black Lotus conspiracy designed to sabotage the investigation; yet Sano still couldn't agree with Reiko that Haru was an innocent victim, after what he'd learned about the girl today.

He and Hirata entered the mansion and found Reiko in the corridor, removing her cloak and talking to Midori and a maid. When Reiko saw Sano, she started nervously. "Oh. Hello," she said.

"Hello," Sano said, concerned because she'd obviously stayed out late again and wondering why.

The maid took Reiko's cloak, bowed, and left. There was an uncomfortable silence as Hirata smiled at Midori, she looked away from him, and tension gathered between Sano and Reiko.

"It seems that we have things to discuss," Sano said at last. "Let's go to my office."

There he sat at his desk on the raised platform. Hirata knelt opposite him to his right, Reiko to his left. Midori, who'd apparently thought his invitation included her, sat beside Reiko. Sano said to his wife, "What have you learned today?"

"This morning I went to see Haru." Although she feared how Sano would react to what she was going to say, Reiko managed to match his controlled manner. She described how she'd found Priest Kumashiro trying to force Haru into confessing. She explained that Haru had admitted misbehaving at the Black Lotus Temple but had reformed, and been forced into sex with Commander Oyama. "Kumashiro says he has an alibi, but he and Oyama were enemies. He seems more likely a killer than Haru. He actually threatened me. I believe Haru is in danger from him, so I took her to stay at my father's house."

"You did *what*?" Alarm shattered Sano's calm façade.

"Haru was so afraid of Kumashiro that she wanted to run away," Reiko said. "You wouldn't have wanted me to let her go, would you? I had to put her someplace she would feel safe. My father agreed to take her in. What's wrong with that?"

Hirata frowned; Midori looked baffled. Sano drew and slowly released a deep breath, as though willing self-control. "Today I met Haru's parents," he said.

Startled, Reiko said, "What are you talking about?"

"Haru's parents," Sano repeated, adding with a touch of reproach, "are alive and well in Kojimachi. Haru isn't an orphan at all."

"Oh. I see." Badly shaken, Reiko said, "You've proved that Haru is a liar, but the fact that a person lied about one thing doesn't mean she couldn't be telling the truth about others."

"There's more." Sano told how Haru had been a disobedient daughter, married off against her will to an old merchant. "He and his servants died in a fire. Haru's parents, the neighbors, and the man's relatives believe Haru set the fire to kill her husband and free herself from the marriage. She took refuge in the Black Lotus Temple because her family disowned her. Whether or not Haru is responsible for the deaths at the temple, I fear you've installed a murderess in your father's house."

Every sentence drove deeper into Reiko the undeniable knowledge that Haru was as deceitful as her enemies claimed— and possibly as evil. Nonetheless, Reiko glimpsed room for doubt in Sano's story. "Did anyone actually see Haru setting the fire?" she said.

"No," Sano admitted.

"Those people could be mistaken about Haru. Maybe everyone's suspicion forced her to leave home and pretend to be an orphan. This new evidence against Haru is just as questionable as the evidence in the Black Lotus fire."

The expression on Sano's face revealed that he'd already thought of this and didn't appreciate her reminder of the weakness in his argument.

Relief lessened Reiko's fear that she'd misjudged Haru and endangered her father. "Haru could very well be innocent."

Sano nodded reluctantly, but said, "Haru's past isn't the only reason I believe she may be guilty." He described Haru's abuse of the orphans, and the two girls who'd seen her sneaking out to the cottage on the night before the fire. "It's clear that she got there under her own power. I've almost finished questioning everyone else at the temple, and she's still the only person who had cause and opportunity for arson."

While Reiko tried to hide her dismay at this new revelation, Sano spoke before she could frame a reply. "You can argue that those girls were jealous of Haru and wanted to get her in trouble, just like everyone else in the Black Lotus. Besides, they were near the cottage, too. They could have burned it. Why trust them instead of Haru? Because they weren't found near the cottage during the fire." Exasperation underlay Sano's reasonable tone. "I checked into them, and they've no history of bad behavior, or of relations with Commander Oyama. Nor are they perpetual liars with a fire in their past. You must stop trying to dismiss evidence against Haru."

"I wish *you* would stop disregarding evidence against the Black Lotus," Reiko said. The strife between herself and Sano frightened her, yet she saw no way to dispel it without backing down. She felt ready to abandon Haru, who'd betrayed her trust and was probably guilty of something, if not everything, but her surrender would mean letting the sect escape justice. "Did you investigate Pious Truth's story?"

"I did. I saw no signs of starvation, torture, murder, imprisonment, or underground secret projects. I've assigned men to spy on the temple, but I doubt they'll find anything either. And I was unable to locate any novice monk named Pious Truth. Apparently, he doesn't exist."

"But I saw him," Reiko said, confused. "I spoke with him. He was real. Where is he?"

Raising his eyebrows, Sano turned his hands palms up. "I did find a novice nun called Yasue. She was not only alive but apparently happy at the temple. And she has no brother."

"That could have been a different person with the same name as Pious Truth's sister," Reiko said.

Hirata cleared his throat. "*Sumimasen*—excuse me," he said. "Today at police headquarters, I interviewed many citizens who say that the Black Lotus kidnaps children, enchants followers, and attacks families that try to get them back. Even if this person who called himself Pious Truth isn't a novice at the temple, he may be right about the sect."

"There!" Reiko exclaimed. "Witnesses to confirm my suspicions."

"Haru's guilt or innocence is a separate issue from whatever the sect has allegedly done," Sano said to Hirata. "Hearsay about the Black Lotus doesn't necessarily weaken the case against Haru."

"Yes, *Sōsakan-sama*." Hirata's strained expression indicated that he wasn't convinced, but his samurai loyalty required him to agree with Sano. "I just thought I should mention what I discovered."

"Who cares about you?" Midori blurted. Everyone turned toward her, surprised, as she addressed Hirata with disdain: "You're not as smart or important as you think you are."

Hirata's jaw dropped. Reiko noted with dour amusement that Midori had begun her new scheme to regain Hirata's interest. She could have chosen a better time, but at least she'd gotten his attention.

Sano ignored this little drama. "Until we have more clues besides tales from superstitious peasants and mysterious vanishing monks that the Black Lotus is involved in illegal activities, we cannot charge them with any crimes."

"But we do have more clues," Reiko said.

She described Dr. Miwa's and Abbess Junketsu-in's criminal records. As she summarized her talk with Minister Fugatami, incredulity dawned on Sano's face.

"You barged in on the Minister of Temples and Shrines?" she said.

"I was granted an audience. He wants you to go to Shinagawa with him tomorrow to investigate the latest complaints against the Black Lotus." Reiko took the letter out from beneath her sash and handed it to Sano.

He read it, and his expression darkened. Then he crumpled the paper. Rising, he paced the room, regarding Reiko as if she'd lost her wits. "Imposing on Minister Fugatami was a dangerous breach of propriety. Survival in *bakufu* politics depends on good relationships with colleagues. High officials are quick to take offense. How could you place my career and our livelihood at risk?"

Reiko stood and followed Sano; Hirata and Midori sat watching them. "Please accept my apologies," Reiko said, now aware of how seriously she could have compromised Sano. "But Minister Fugatami was glad to see me. I wish you would go to Shinagawa and decide for yourself whether the complaints are valid. Surely his opinion counts for something."

"Minister Fugatami has a reputation for being overzealous," Sano said in an icy tone. "Many in the *bakufu* frown upon him as a fanatic because he has criticized, hounded, and tried to abolish sects that later turned out to be perfectly harmless and legitimate. Chances are, he's persecuting the Black Lotus for no good reason as well."

Reiko had been so awed by Minister Fugatami that she hadn't questioned his judgment. Was he wrong to believe the peasants' stories? Was she wrong to have believed him?

"By approaching Minister Fugatami you obligated me to him." Sano stopped pacing. "I can't go to Shinagawa because that would further obligate me to support his crusade whether or not I should. But if I don't go, I'll make an enemy. You've put me in a bad position."

Favors were the currency of the *bakufu*, and Reiko knew that Sano must pay his debts or lose the goodwill of colleagues. Guilt spurred her to reassure him. "Minister Fugatami asked nothing except a chance to convince you that he deserves your support. He understood that you might not be able to go. He said I could go in your place."

Shaking his head, Sano said, "Absolutely not. That would violate propriety, and you've done enough harm already."

Yet Reiko couldn't waste the lead she'd discovered. "If I don't go to Shinagawa, how will we get the truth about the Black Lotus?"

Hirata suggested hesitantly, "I could go."

"No," Sano said, his manner decisive. "Sending any representative is the same as going myself, with the same consequences. Besides, there's no need for anyone to go. We'll soon have a report from the surveillance team at the temple."

"By that time it may be too late," Reiko said. In spite of Sano's failure to locate Pious Truth, she still believed he was a novice at the temple, and in danger. "How many people must suffer before you intervene?"

"If anyone has suffered, I'll need evidence before I can take official action," Sano said, "and the detectives are more likely to provide it than are complaints from the public. I shall wait for their report."

His tone defied argument, but Reiko said, "I'll look around the temple after I see High Priest Anraku tomorrow."

"We agreed that you would restrict yourself to getting information from Haru," Sano reminded her. "You've already broken your promise." Then suspicion narrowed his eyes. "Just how did you intend to get an audience with Anraku?"

He wasn't going to like the answer, Reiko thought unhappily. "Lady Keisho-in agreed to accompany me to the temple and order Anraku to see me," she said.

"You asked the shogun's mother for this favor?" Now Sano's face took on the dazed look of a man beholding the wreckage after an earthquake. "How could you have the nerve, especially when you know that her favors don't come without a price?"

Reiko knew all too well, but she said, "I think the investigation is worth it."

Sano stared at her, uncomprehending. "Why is that girl so important that you're choosing her over your safety and my career?"

"I'm not!" Reiko cried, but his question struck close to the truth. Though she loved her husband with all her heart, her choices had in a way placed Haru before him. Somehow, events had swept her beyond reason. Perhaps they'd affected Sano, too.

"You're at least as prejudiced regarding Haru as I am. May I ask why it is so important for you to condemn her without a thorough inquiry?" Reiko went on. "Are the shogun and the Council of Elders pressuring you to convict her?"

She read in his eyes that he was indeed under pressure, and had a disturbing thought that Sano was no longer the principled, idealistic man she loved. She said, "Can you be forsaking truth and justice for the sake of politics?"

Fury leapt in Sano's gaze, and Reiko realized to her dismay that he'd perceived her rashly spoken questions as an attack on his honor. As she and Sano stood paralyzed, gazes locked, the air around them compressed into a dense, stormy space; Midori and Hirata watched them in helpless consternation.

"I'm sorry," Reiko stammered, aware that she'd had much else to apologize for recently, but nothing as bad as this. "I didn't mean . . ."

With slow, deliberate movements that betrayed his battle for control over his temper, Sano walked back to his desk and sat. His face hardened into a stony, emotionless mask. "I forbid you to go to the Black Lotus Temple or to Shinagawa," he said in a quiet tone that vibrated with suppressed rage. "Now please leave me."

Numb with shock, Reiko staggered blindly from the room.

Midori followed her. Hirata came hurrying down the corridor after them. "Midori-*san*," he said, "wait. I want to talk to you."

"Well, I don't want to talk to you." Midori tossed her head.

Trembling and sick inside, Reiko walked into her private chamber and knelt on the floor. Would that she could relive the past moments differently!

Midori burst into the room. Radiant with joy, she exclaimed, "I did what you suggested, and it's working!" She knelt near Reiko and giggled. "For the first time in ages, Hirata-*san* really noticed me." Then she took a closer look at Reiko, and her jubilation subsided. "What's wrong?"

Silent weeping twisted Reiko's mouth. How she envied Midori, who'd obviously understood little of what had happened in Sano's office. How wonderful to be so young, frivolous, and absorbed in romance!

Midori said soothingly, "The *sōsakan-sama* was very angry, but don't worry—he'll forgive you."

Reiko wanted to believe Midori, but she couldn't.

"What are you going to do?" Midori asked.

To restore peace with Sano, Reiko knew she should end her inquiries; yet circumstances had locked her into defending Haru, for right or wrong, in spite of everything she'd learned about her.

"Tomorrow I'm going with Lady Keisho-in to see High Priest Anraku," she said. "Afterward, I'll travel to Shinagawa."

Resolve calmed Reiko; she wiped her tears on her sleeve.

"But won't that make the *sōsakan-sama* even angrier at you?" Midori said, her face a picture of concern.

"I'm afraid so," Reiko said unhappily.

Carrying on her investigation against his will might permanently estrange her from Sano. The knowledge chilled Reiko. But this case now involved more than just discovering who'd committed the crimes at the Black Lotus Temple. Sano had imperiled his honor by allowing political concerns to influence him. Reiko had a duty to protect it by convincing him to pursue real justice instead of seizing the quickest solution to the case, and to save his career by preventing him from making a mistake that would disgrace the whole family.

And she was determined to find out the truth about Haru once and for all.

"Then you're going to disobey anyway?" Midori said.

"I can't stand by and see my husband ruined and Haru incriminated while a killer goes free," Reiko said. The investigation had produced two alternative culprits—Haru or the Black Lotus—and Reiko felt justified in her choice, which her intuition still favored. "I must do what's right."

"Then let me help you." Eagerness lit up Midori's eyes. "We can go out together tomorrow, and you can teach me to be a detective. We'll show the men what we can do!"

Humor leavened Reiko's unhappiness. She smiled at Midori, who apparently saw the situation as a contest of men versus women, with Hirata's love the prize.

"Many thanks for your generous offer, but I don't want to get you in trouble, so I'd better go by myself," Reiko said. Then, seeing Midori's disappointed expression, she fibbed, "I'll try to find something else for you to do."

"Oh, good!" Midori beamed.

Sano sat in his office, his elbows propped on the desk, shaken and horrified. How could Reiko speak such insults? How could he feel such rage toward her? An evil spirit had invaded their home, breeding discord and malice.

Its name was Haru.

With the impassioned regret of hindsight, Sano wished he'd never involved Reiko with Haru. He knew better than to think that Reiko would give up trying to exonerate the girl. Yet even as Sano wondered how he could separate Reiko from a murder suspect, a needle of self-doubt pierced his conscience. In his perpetual insecurity about his position, was he indeed succumbing to political pressure to arrest Haru because she represented the quickest way to solve the case? Sano cradled his head in his hands. He'd thought himself a man of honor and objective judgment, but now he questioned his own character.

Was Reiko right about him, and Haru, and the Black Lotus?

"*Sōsakan-sama,* there's something I must say," Hirata said.

Jolted out of his troubled reverie, Sano looked up at his chief retainer, who sat opposite him: He'd not noticed Hirata enter. "Go ahead," he said.

"Those citizens I interviewed were so sure that the Black Lotus is evil, I started to believe it," Hirata said haltingly. "If you'd met them, I think you would, too. I didn't want to say this earlier, but . . ." Hirata's face reflected deep conflict within him. "Their testimony is serious indication that the sect is involved in bad business. I'm sorry to disagree with you."

"That's all right." Sano endured the sting that Hirata's words caused him. The duties of a chief retainer included voicing unpleasant, necessary truths to his master.

"Ignoring the signs could ruin the investigation," Hirata added.

"I know." Sano could admit to Hirata what he couldn't to Reiko. "We'll have to check out those stories about the sect." He thought for a moment, then said, "I'll decline Minister Fugatami's invitation. I don't think a trip to Shinagawa is necessary yet, because we can tap another source of facts about the Black Lotus."

"Who is that?" Hirata asked.

"The prime suspect herself," Sano said. "It's time for another visit with Haru."

16

They who defy the Law of the Black Lotus
Will have the whip laid upon them,
Their bodies will be beaten and cuffed,
They will suffer grief and pain,
To the point of death.

—FROM THE BLACK LOTUS SUTRA

Night enfolded the Zojo temple district. Diffuse moonlight frosted the roofs and treetops, but darkness saturated the deserted alleys. Sleep had silenced ten thousand voices, slowed heartbeats, stilled movement. The autumn wind's hushed breath absorbed the exhalations of slumber.

Priest Kumashiro stood in an underground room beneath the Black Lotus Temple. In a corner huddled the monk Pious Truth. Ropes bound his wrists and ankles; swollen bruises discolored his face and naked body. Two priests, holding wooden clubs, stood over him. Pious Truth was panting, slick with sweat, his terrified gaze focused on Kumashiro.

"Has he confessed?" Kumashiro asked the priests.

They shook their heads. Pious Truth cried, "I didn't tell her anything, I swear!"

But Kumashiro believed Pious Truth had indeed revealed Black Lotus secrets to Lady Reiko. She must have told the *sōsakan-sama,* whom Kumashiro had seen prowling the temple grounds today. Entrances to the subterranean complex were well hidden, but Kumashiro had to learn the full extent of the breach in security.

He crouched before the monk and said in a quiet, menacing voice, "What did you say to her?"

Pious Truth cowered, but spoke defiantly: "Nothing."

Kumashiro struck the monk across the mouth. He yelped in pain. "I'm loyal to the Black Lotus," he protested, drooling blood. "I would never tell an outsider anything!"

Rising, Kumashiro contemplated the monk who'd already withstood two days of torture. It was time for stronger coercion. "Bring him to the medical chamber," Kumashiro ordered the priests.

They dragged Pious Truth out of the cell, following Kumashiro down a tunnel just high and wide enough for men to walk upright and two abreast. The walls and ceilings were reinforced with planks; between these, tree roots veined the soil. Hanging lamps lit the way, casting weird shadows.

"What are you going to do to me?" Pious Truth said anxiously.

No one answered. The pulse of the hand-operated bellows that pumped in air from concealed vents was a continuous, rhythmic clatter. Rancid odors tainted the air. Pious Truth mewled. Kumashiro led the group into one of a series of connected rooms in a branch tunnel. At the center of the room stood a table. A vast hearth, with a huge basin set on a charcoal brazier below a stone chimney, occupied a corner. Muted voices, clatters, and the burble of liquid issued from an adjoining room, out of which sidled Dr. Miwa. When he saw Kumashiro, wariness tensed his pocked face, but his squinty eyes brightened at the sight of Pious Truth.

"Is this a patient for me?" he said.

"He's a runaway." Kumashiro beheld the doctor with undisguised revulsion. "I want you to make him cooperate."

Bowing, Dr. Miwa displayed his uneven teeth in an ingratiating smile. "Certainly."

The priests heaved Pious Truth onto the table. He struggled, yelling, "Let me go! Help!"

No one aboveground would hear him, Kumashiro knew. The priests tied the monk down, then left. Dr. Miwa fetched a cup of liquid and held it to Pious Truth's mouth.

"No!" Pious Truth shrieked. "I don't want it!"

Kumashiro forced Pious Truth's jaws apart. Dr. Miwa poured. Although the monk gurgled and spat, most of the liquid went down.

"I've given him an extract of *fan xie yie* leaves, *ba dou* seeds, and morning glory," Dr. Miwa said. "It will purge excessive spiritual heat and evil influences from him."

"Spare me the medical gibberish," Kumashiro said, annoyed by Miwa's pretense that what they were doing constituted a genuine cure. "He's not a patient. Nor are you a healer."

Anger flushed the doctor's muddy complexion, but he remained silent, too much a coward to contradict a superior.

"You were a failure as a physician, and if you think High Priest Anraku respects your credentials, think again." Kumashiro found pleasure in wounding Miwa's vanity. "He only tolerates you because you're useful to him."

The same applied to everyone in the sect, including Kumashiro. They were all here to serve Anraku's purposes, but Kumashiro didn't mind because if not for Anraku, he would be dead, destroyed by the life he'd led.

A son of a high retainer of the Matsudaira branch of the Tokugawa clan, Kumashiro had grown up on the Matsudaira estate in Echigo Province. As a boy he'd excelled at the martial arts, but his teachers had criticized his spiritual disharmony, which blocked his progress along the Way of the Warrior. Kumashiro himself perceived something wrong inside him—an emptiness; a sense that real life lay beyond a locked magic door. This angered and frustrated him. He grew more and more aggressive during practice sword matches. Other boys on the estate avoided him because he picked fights and beat them; his own mother was terrified of his temper. Violence eased the gnawing emptiness in Kumashiro, but didn't open the door. However, Lord Matsudaira was impressed with his fighting skill and, when Kumashiro was thirteen, took him to Edo as a guard at the clan's city estate.

In Edo, Kumashiro received a new pair of swords. The law permitted samurai to test blades on peasants without being punished, so Kumashiro wandered the crowded streets of Nihonbashi, seeking a suitable target, until a beggar accidentally bumped him.

"Humble apologies, master," the beggar said, bowing.

Kumashiro drew his new long sword and slashed the beggar's arm. The man cried out in pained surprise, and Kumashiro stared at his victim's wound, transfixed by a rush of sensation. Drawing blood had opened the magic door a crack. Noises seemed louder, colors more vivid, the sun's heat newly intense. The smell of humanity quivered Kumashiro's nostrils. It was as if he'd finally gotten a taste of real life.

The frightened beggar turned to run, but Kumashiro lunged, cutting bloody gashes in the man's legs and back. Every cut opened the door a little wider. Heady new vitality filled Kumashiro as onlookers scrambled for cover. The beggar fell on hands and knees.

"Please, master," he cried, "have mercy!"

Kumashiro raised his sword high over the neck of his victim, then brought it slashing down. The blade severed the beggar's head. Warm, red blood sprayed Kumashiro. His veins, his muscles, his very bones tingled with intoxicating energy. He felt the dead man's spirit fill his empty space, and a thunderous rapture as his internal forces balanced in harmony. Killing had brought him to life, to the Way of the Warrior.

And that moment had brought him here, to this underground room, where a young monk lay tied to a table. Kumashiro watched as Pious Truth moaned, convulsing against the ropes.

"Ah, the medicine is taking effect," Dr. Miwa said.

Sweat and urine poured from Pious Truth and puddled on the table. Retching, he vomited. The stench of diarrhea arose.

"Soon the purge shall be complete," said Dr. Miwa.

Excitement crept into his voice; he was trembling as if with sexual arousal. His breath hissed faster.

"It's a fine doctor who enjoys the suffering of his patient," Kumashiro said. Yet although Miwa's perversion disgusted

him, Kumashiro knew very well the exhilarating combination
of violence and sex.

The ecstasy of his first kill had faded quickly; as the magic
door closed, Kumashiro vowed to repeat the experience. He
and a gang of fellow Tokugawa retainers roved Edo, brawling
with peasants and rival samurai. In his twenties, with three
more kills behind him, Kumashiro got a reprimand from the
magistrate. Still, his need persisted.

One night his gang visited an illegal brothel. Kumashiro disliked females—such weak, inferior creatures—but he had nothing better to do, so he went along. A prostitute took him to her
room. As she stroked him, Kumashiro found her repulsive.

"What is this?" she said, squeezing his limp organ. "A dead
snake?" Meanness edged her playful remark: She'd noticed his
feelings toward her. "Perhaps your sword is blunt, too."

At this insult, Kumashiro struck the whore's face a tremendous blow. She screamed. The door in Kumashiro swung ajar;
arousal and heightened sensation thrilled him. He beat the girl,
and she fought him, but he mounted and entered her. His hands
throttled her neck as he thrust. At the instant of climax, he
choked the life out of her, crying out in rapture as he absorbed
her spirit.

With the memory clear in his mind, Kumashiro turned his
attention to Pious Truth. "Are you ready to admit you betrayed
the Black Lotus, or do you want to suffer more?"

The monk was deathly pale, groaning in pain, too weak to
struggle, but he gasped out, "I told Lady Reiko nothing."

"The evil force is much stronger in him than in his sister,"
Dr. Miwa said. Mild torture had persuaded Yasue to confess
that Pious Truth had engineered their escape attempt. "We must
employ more drastic treatment."

Dr. Miwa summoned his assistants, two young nuns. They
untied Pious Truth and placed him in the basin of water on the
hearth. While the nuns lit the brazier, Miwa's hungry gaze lingered on them. Kumashiro wished he could throw all the females out of the temple. Experience had taught him that they
were a source of misfortune.

Over the next five years after killing the whore, he'd killed
three more prostitutes, and the magistrate charged him with
multiple murder. While in jail awaiting trial, Kumashiro came

to believe that the deaths of females had disturbed the *bakufu* more than had the other deaths he'd caused. If not for females, he wouldn't be facing a death sentence. Later, circumstances in the Black Lotus Temple had affirmed his belief in the evil of women and fornication.

He despised Abbess Junketsu-in, who bedded priests in the sect's upper echelon, sparking angry rivalries that caused him difficulty in maintaining order. Junketsu-in's other disgraceful practices also appalled Kumashiro; he couldn't cover them up forever. Sex created problems with the patrons, too. Kumashiro thought of Commander Oyama, and hatred seethed in him.

The only good thing Oyama had ever done was to destroy police reports on complaints about the Black Lotus and order his minions not to bother the sect. But this good had been negated by his habits, which caused disturbances within the temple, and public gossip. Recently, Kumashiro had waylaid Oyama outside the cottage where he'd conducted his illicit affairs. He'd ordered Oyama to leave the female sect members alone, but Oyama had refused. While they argued, exchanging threats, then blows, the girl Haru had come out of the cottage and seen them. Kumashiro was sure she'd told the police about the argument. They must already know his history, and he worried that they would think he'd murdered Oyama . . . and Chie.

What the nurse had experienced inside the temple, what she'd learned about the sect's business, had rendered her a grave danger to the Black Lotus. Kumashiro was glad that Chie and Oyama were gone, but threats remained. Haru knew too much, as did Pious Truth.

The monk sat in the basin, his head protruding from the water, which fogged the air as it gradually warmed. Anguish and terror filled his hollow eyes. Through bruised, swollen lips he mumbled, "Please, help, please, let me go, please . . ."

"The heat will purify his spirit," Dr. Miwa said with barely contained excitement.

Kumashiro addressed the monk: "If you don't cooperate, you'll boil to death." His own senses quickened as the magic door inched open. "This is your last chance to tell me what you said to Lady Reiko."

Thickening steam wafted up the chimney. Pious Truth jerked, howling while the water heated; his complexion turned scarlet. He heaved up from the basin, sank below the water's surface, and emerged, gasping.

"All right, I confess!" he blubbered. "I told her about the underground tunnels, and how the novices are treated, and that my sister was murdered in the temple."

This was serious indeed. Kumashiro feared that Lady Reiko would continue prying into temple affairs and convince her husband to act against the sect. Kumashiro must do something about the problem of Lady Reiko.

"Now that I've told you everything, please, have mercy!" Pious Truth begged.

"The cure has worked," Dr. Miwa said with satisfaction. "We can take him out."

"I promise I'll never talk to an outsider again!" Pious Truth sobbed in relief.

"No, don't," Kumashiro said to Dr. Miwa. "He's proven himself untrustworthy. Stoke the fire."

As Miwa's assistants complied, Pious Truth writhed, shrieking, "No, no, no!"

Kumashiro stood firm. He must shield the Black Lotus's interests, which had become his own on his first day at the temple.

When his clan had negotiated with the *bakufu* to spare his life by committing him to enter a monastery, Kumashiro had initially been furious and bitter. A peaceful religious existence seemed to him worse than torture, yet he didn't want to die, so he went to the Black Lotus monastery, having picked it at random. As soon as he arrived, High Priest Anraku summoned him to a private audience.

Anraku sat on a dais in a windowless chamber decorated with gold Buddha statues and carved lotus flowers, dimly lit by candles and so full of incense smoke that Kumashiro could barely see him. In a sonorous voice he said, "Honorable Samurai, do you know why you are here?"

"It was either this or execution." Kumashiro knelt, annoyed by the mystical trappings and suffocating smoke.

Resonant laughter rose from Anraku's shadowy figure. "That is not the real reason. My will brought you to the Black Lotus Temple so that you could become my disciple."

The incense clouded Kumashiro's thoughts, and Anraku's

hypnotic voice eroded skepticism. "Why choose me?" Kumashiro said, interested in spite of himself.

"There is a vacancy in you that you can fill only by the act of killing," Anraku said. "The act infuses your world with sensation otherwise denied you. Your need for that sensation is so strong you would risk death to satisfy it."

"How did you know?" Kumashiro was shocked. "I've never told anyone."

"I saw into your spirit from afar," Anraku intoned. "The Black Lotus Sutra describes the one true path to enlightenment as a convergence of many paths, each designated for a particular individual. Killing is your path. Each life you absorb brings you closer to nirvana."

Revelation awed Kumashiro. What a miracle that his obsession was actually a blessing! Maybe his coming here was meant to be.

"Become my disciple, and I shall help you achieve your destiny," Anraku said.

Bowing low, Kumashiro said, "Yes, Honorable High Priest."

Anraku had initiated Kumashiro into the priesthood and placed him in charge of policing the temple. Kumashiro eliminated any sect member who showed indication of disloyalty. Soon he became the high priest's second-in-command. He gloried in his freedom to kill, but the need never waned. His best hope was to continue along his path until Anraku's schemes transformed him and the whole world.

Now the monk's howls subsided. Losing consciousness, Pious Truth sank in the basin.

"He is almost gone," Dr. Miwa said.

Moving close to the basin, Kumashiro unsheathed the dagger that hung at his waist. The magic door was opening. Everything glowed with new color, as if lit by the sun. Kumashiro tipped the monk's head back. The pulse of fans beat louder in his ears. Swiftly he drew his blade across the monk's throat. Crimson blood gushed into the water. As Pious Truth's spirit energy filled him, Kumashiro savored the rapture, not caring that Dr. Miwa watched him. They were bound in a conspiracy of silence, forced to tolerate each other's proclivities, for the good of all.

Eventually, Kumashiro cleaned and sheathed his blade. "Let's get rid of him," he said.

Dr. Miwa and the nuns lifted the corpse from the basin and wrapped it in a white shroud. Kumashiro and Miwa carried it through the tunnels to the crematorium. Here the nuns stoked a stone furnace and worked the bellows until the fire roared hot like a dragon's breath. Kumashiro and Miwa dumped the corpse inside. As the assistants chanted, "Praise the glory of the Black Lotus," and the smell of burning flesh seared his lungs, Kumashiro felt regret that the joy of killing was so transient, and relief that he'd eliminated another threat.

To protect his way of life, he must protect the Black Lotus.

17

Behold the Bodhisattva of Infinite Power!
His body is shapely,
A thousand moons cannot rival the perfection of his face,
His eye is as brilliant as a million suns.

— FROM THE BLACK LOTUS SUTRA

Early morning traffic streamed down the boulevard that led south from Edo Castle through the daimyo district. Between the fortified estates, pedestrians and mounted samurai made way for troops escorting a huge palanquin that bore the Tokugawa crest. Inside the palanquin rode Reiko and Lady Keisho-in, seated opposite each other, bound for the Black Lotus Temple. The weather was cool and misty, and the women shared a quilt spread over their laps and legs.

"You look as if you're thinking about something unpleasant," Lady Keisho-in said. Her plump body and heavy jowls bounced with the palanquin's movement. "What's wrong?"

Reiko had been brooding about her argument with Sano yesterday and the sleepless night she'd spent alone while he stayed in his office. She suspected that Sano hated quarreling as much as she, but both of them were too proud to compromise. Recalling how he'd left the house today without even saying good-bye to her, Reiko felt the stinging pressure of more tears.

"Everything is fine," she said with false brightness. Aware of her responsibility to entertain the shogun's mother, she pointed out the window. "Look! Such pretty furniture in that shop!"

"Beautiful!" exclaimed Lady Keisho-in.

Reiko kept up the conversation while they rode through town, but as they traveled the woodland highway approaching the Zōjō district, worry grew within her. Eventually Sano would find out that she'd disobeyed his orders. The fear of losing his love plagued Reiko. She chatted with Keisho-in, all the while thinking that unless she could find new evidence in favor of Haru or against someone else, Haru would be convicted and the Black Lotus would go free. Besides, Reiko had already embarked on the forbidden trip; going the rest of the way could do little more harm.

Beneath the quilt, Keisho-in's leg bumped Reiko's. "I'm sorry," Reiko said, politely taking the blame.

She shifted position to give Keisho-in more room, but soon they bumped again. Keisho-in giggled. Reiko flinched as Keisho-in's toe tickled her thigh.

"I know a good way to pass the time," Keisho-in said coyly.

There was no mistaking her intention. Reiko drew her knees up to her chest in appalled, defensive haste. The old woman wanted her, just as she'd feared. What should she do?

Lady Keisho-in moved closer. Her age-spotted hand stroked Reiko's cheek. "Ah, you're so lovely," she said, sighing.

Turning away from Keisho-in's sour breath, Reiko stifled a cry of protest. "I can't do this." The words slipped out of her even though she knew the danger of spurning the shogun's mother.

"Why not?" Keisho-in asked. "There's plenty of time before we reach the temple." Then she drew back, and her gaze sharpened as she studied Reiko. "What you mean is you don't desire me. You think I'm old and ugly." Hurt and anger welled in her rheumy eyes. "I can see it on your face. You led me on so

I would help you, and now you reject me." She shouted out the window to their escorts: "Stop so I can throw out this sly little whore. Then take me home."

The procession halted. "Wait. Please," Reiko entreated. Being stranded on the road was a minor inconvenience compared to the dire consequences facing her unless she placated Keisho-in.

"I shall tell my son that you hurt my feelings. He'll punish your husband for your cruelty." With a dramatic gesture, Lady Keisho-in flung open the palanquin's door. "Now get out!"

Reiko envisioned Sano stripped of his position, livelihood, and honor—or executed. Dread filled her. "Forgive me, Honorable Lady, I didn't mean to reject you," she said.

Keisho-in still looked peeved, but she shut the door.

"It's just that I've never been with a woman before," Reiko said truthfully, thinking fast. "I'm too shy to do it here, where people might see or hear us. I would be too inhibited to please you now."

"I suppose you're right." Her humor restored, Keisho-in ordered their escorts to continue on to the temple. As the palanquin began moving, she settled back on her cushions. "We shall wait until later."

Reiko silently thanked the gods for the reprieve and hoped that later never came.

Outside, the traffic noises increased as the procession reached the Zōjō district; shouts drifted from the marketplace. Soon the bearers set down the palanquin, opened the door to a view of the Black Lotus Temple gate, and helped the shogun's mother out. Reiko followed. She and Keisho-in and their guards entered the temple precinct, where a group of priests came to meet them.

"Welcome, Your Highness," said a priest at the center of the group. It was Kumashiro. He frowned at Reiko, and the lizard-shaped scar on his head purpled with an influx of blood.

"We want to see High Priest Anraku," said Lady Keisho-in.

Reiko saw a flicker of displeasure in Kumashiro's gaze, then the knowledge that he couldn't refuse the shogun's mother. He said, "Of course, Your Highness. Please come with me."

At least her risky episode had gotten her this far, Reiko thought, resolving to make the interview worthwhile.

Kumashiro led her and Keisho-in to a garden of dense, twisted pines behind the abbot's residence. Reiko saw a thatched roof through the boughs. As they walked along a shaded path toward it, a suave male voice spoke: "A million thanks for gracing us with your presence, Most Honorable Mother of His Excellency the Shogun. Greetings, Lady Reiko."

Keisho-in said in surprise, "How does he know who it is without seeing us?"

"But I did see you." Amusement inflected the voice. "My knowledge comes from inner vision, not mere eyesight."

Probably the high priest employed spies to give him advance notice of visitors, Reiko speculated.

The cool, damp air in the forest was scented with pine resin. A pavilion composed of a raised tatami platform and a roof supported on wooden posts appeared. In the center, a man with a shaved head sat cross-legged, hands upturned on his thighs. Clad in a white robe, he seemed to glow in the misty daylight.

"Please join me," Anraku said, nodding at two cushions that lay be-fore him.

Keisho-in scrambled up the steps of the pavilion, left her sandals on the bare wooden floor at the edge of the tatami, and knelt upon a cushion. Following, Reiko saw Kumashiro slip away through the trees. While Anraku performed the customary social ritual of offering refreshments, Reiko studied him.

He was in his early thirties, broad-shouldered and muscular, yet slender. With his tawny golden skin, square jaw, high cheekbones, and finely sculpted nose and mouth, Anraku was a man of striking beauty. His left eye, darkly luminous, gazed upon Reiko with faint mirth, as though he perceived and enjoyed her surprise. The other eye was covered by a black cloth patch.

His good looks hadn't escaped the notice of Keisho-in. She patted her hair, simpering. Nuns appeared, bearing trays of tea and cakes, which they silently served. Keisho-in exclaimed to Anraku, "But you didn't even call them!"

"My followers have an extra sense that makes speech unnecessary because they anticipate my orders," Anraku said.

He addressed Keisho-in but looked at Reiko. She supposed that Kumashiro had sent the nuns, and she was eager to prove that the Black Lotus was evil, but she couldn't help feeling Anraku's potent, seductive charm.

"Yesterday I had a vision that showed us here as we are now." Anraku's lips curved in a faint smile at Reiko. "So you wish to speak to me about Haru and the fire?"

The abbess must have told him she'd asked for an audience, Reiko supposed. "Yes, I do."

Lady Keisho-in frowned at Reiko, clearly wanting the priest's attention for herself. "Tell me," she said to Anraku, "why do you wear that eye patch?"

His sidelong glance at Reiko suggested that they had secrets to share after he humored the shogun's mother. He said, "My right eye is blind."

"Oh, what a pity," Keisho-in said.

"Not at all," Anraku said. "My partial blindness enables me to see things invisible to other people. It is a window on the future, a passage to the many worlds within the cosmos."

Keisho-in looked impressed. "How did it happen?"

The luminosity of Anraku's good eye darkened, as if he'd diverted light inward. "Many years ago, I was banished for wrongs that weak, jealous men falsely accused me of committing. I wandered the country alone, and wherever I went, I was reviled and persecuted. Hence, I fled the world."

Reiko remembered Minister Fugatami describing how Anraku had been expelled from a monastery because he'd usurped the priests' authority, then become an itinerant monk who'd lived by cheating peasants. Certainly he'd deserved punishment, but Reiko remained silent, curious to hear how he accounted for the missing years of his life.

"I climbed Mount Hiei," Anraku said, referring to the sacred peak near the imperial capital. "I meant to seek guidance at Enryaku Temple."

In ancient times Enryaku had been a sanctuary for criminals because police weren't allowed there, Reiko knew; fugitives might still find it a good place to hide.

"Then a heavy mist descended upon the mountain. The world around me turned white and hazy. As I toiled upward, the path under my feet disappeared. I was cold, wet, exhausted, and knew not which way to go." Anraku's hushed words evoked the frightening experience of walking blind through the mist. Lady Keisho-in's eyes were round with fascination. Even Reiko felt the power of his storytelling.

"Suddenly I emerged into clear air in a woodland dell on the mountaintop. There were clouds filling the sky above me, and clouds hiding the land below. I looked around and saw a tiny cottage. An old man dressed in rags came out of the cottage and said, 'I will shelter you for the night if you work for your keep.'

"So I chopped wood, built a fire in the cottage, then cooked fish I caught in a stream. Night came, and I lay on the floor to sleep. At sunrise, I awoke to see the old man standing near me. Suddenly he was no longer old but ageless, and serenely beautiful. A brilliant light radiated from him. He was an incarnation of the Buddha."

"Astonishing," murmured Lady Keisho-in.

A story told by many religious frauds, thought Reiko; but Anraku seemed to believe his own tale.

"Then the Buddha became an old man again," Anraku said. "I begged him to make me his disciple, and he agreed. Every day for eight years, I labored at housework, but he taught me nothing. Finally I grew frustrated. I said to the old man, 'I've served you well, and now I demand a reward.' But he just laughed as if he'd played a joke on me. Then there was a loud boom of thunder. White light streamed down through a crack in the sky and transformed the old man into the Buddha. He lifted his hand and said, 'Here is the knowledge you desire.'"

Anraku's hand rose. "Out of the Buddha's palm shot a bolt of lightning. It struck my eye. I fell, shouting in agony. As the pain burned deep into me, the Buddha said, 'I designate you the Bodhisattva of Infinite Power. You will spread my teachings across the land and bring to mankind the blessing that I am giving you.' Then he recited a text, and his voice etched the words into my memory. It was the Black Lotus Sutra. The secret path to enlightenment blazed before me like a river of stars.

"When the pain stopped, the Buddha was gone. The cottage and clouds had disappeared. I could see across the land below the mountain, but only with my left eye. The right eye was burned shut. It gazed upon infinite dimensions throughout space and time. I saw things happening in distant places before I was born, and events far in the future." Emotion trembled in An-raku's voice. "I had a vision of the temple I would build here. I rose and walked down the mountain toward my destiny."

Though Reiko believed that the Buddha had many incar-nations and some humans had supernatural powers, no one knew what had happened to Anraku during those eight years; he could invent any explanation he liked. He could also invent visions.

"What is the secret of the Black Lotus Sutra?" Lady Keisho-in asked eagerly.

Anraku gave her an apologetic smile. "Alas, it cannot be explained, only experienced by devotees of the sect."

"Well, then, I'll join," Keisho-in said with characteristic im-pulsiveness.

Dismay chilled Reiko. "Perhaps it would be best to give the matter some serious thought first," she said.

"Thought is but an illusion that obscures destiny," Anraku said, and his smile gently rebuked her. "If it is Her Highness's fate to become one of us, then she shall." To Keisho-in he said, "Let me examine your life for the truth."

Keisho-in leaned forward. Anraku gazed upon her intently, and Reiko had an eerie sense of his concentration radiating through the black eye patch like an invisible weapon toward Keisho-in. Reiko tasted dread. If Anraku harmed Keisho-in, it would be her fault.

"You are a woman of humble origin whose beauty capti-vated a great lord," Anraku said. "Your son rules with the aid of your wise counsel. You are devout and charitable, respected and loved. Inside you is a rare, extraordinary potential."

"Ah!" Lady Keisho-in gasped. "That's me exactly!"

He'd said nothing that he couldn't have learned from public knowledge of her, and it wasn't hard to guess that Keisho-in considered herself special, Reiko observed.

Now Anraku turned the eerie, tactile gaze of his blind eye on Reiko. He said gravely, "There is a painful division in you. One side cleaves to a man; the other, to a girl of no kin to you. You are torn between love and honor. To choose one side is to sacrifice the other. You live in terror of choosing wrongly. You fear you've already compromised yourself beyond repa-ration."

Reiko stared in wordless shock. His subordinates would have told him that she was trying to help Haru, but how did he guess how she felt? The cool, rustling pine forest seemed suddenly astir with malignant forces and the pavilion a cage imprisoning Reiko. Did Anraku really have supernatural vision, or spies watching her? Both possibilities were alarming.

"Your spirit is in serious peril unless you reconcile your dualities," Anraku said. "The Black Lotus Sutra shows the way to spiritual unity. Honorable Lady Reiko, both you and Her Highness must join me."

"Oh, yes, let's!" Keisho-in said.

"I didn't come here to discuss myself," Reiko said, hiding her fright behind brusqueness. That Anraku could judge people so well made him dangerous, no matter how he did it. "I want to talk about the fire and murders. What do you know of them?"

Anraku's tranquil demeanor didn't alter. "I know that things were not as they seem," he said.

"What does your vision show you?"

Obviously recognizing her question as bait, Anraku smiled.

"Where were you the night of the fire?" Reiko said.

"At a shrine festival in Osaka." That city was many days' journey from Edo. Before Reiko could ask if anyone could confirm his presence there, Anraku added, "I was also in China."

Puzzled, Reiko said, "But the law forbids anyone to leave Japan, and even if you could, it's impossible to be in two places at once."

Anraku's expression disdained her logic. "I am bound by neither man's laws nor nature's. With the powers given me by the Buddha, my spirit can travel to many places simultaneously."

"Marvelous!" Lady Keisho-in said. "You must teach me how to do that."

"Where was your body while your spirit traveled?" Reiko said.

"It lay in my chamber, guarded by my disciples."

At least this was an alibi Reiko could check, but she grew more uncertain about Anraku and fearful of him. Whether or not his magic powers were genuine, he had real influence over people. According to Hirata and Minister Fugatami, citizens had accused him of extortion, fraud, kidnapping, and violence. Was Anraku a sincere mystic who was unaware of what his followers did, or a madman responsible for the sect's crimes?

"What was your relationship with Commander Oyama?" Reiko asked.

"He was a generous patron and valued disciple."

"With your powers, you must have known that he bequeathed twenty thousand *koban* to your sect." Reiko hoped to trap Anraku into admitting that he'd had reason to kill Oyama.

"Mere mortals can never know what I know," Anraku said.

Interpreting his complacent smile to mean that there was no physical proof one way or the other, Reiko said, "Then tell me what you know about the nurse Chie."

"She had a talent for healing and a wish to do good," Anraku said.

Reiko guessed that Anraku knew the murdered woman had been identified and that denials were pointless. He also knew better than to give any reason for wishing Chie or Oyama dead.

"Have you any idea who the dead child was?" Reiko said.

"None," Anraku said.

A shadow of emotion veiled his face, then receded before Reiko could interpret it, but she knew he'd lied. Still, even if he was a murderer, Anraku was a man of influence.

"I wish to prove whether or not Haru committed the crimes," she said. "What can you tell me of her character?"

Throughout the interview Anraku had sat unnaturally still, but now he flexed his lithe body, as though easing cramped muscles. "Whatever trouble Haru may have caused in the past, my guidance had cured her of bad behavior."

This wasn't exactly a testimonial to Haru's innocence, but maybe his opinion would convince Sano, Reiko hoped.

Lady Keisho-in stirred restlessly. "Enough of this unpleasant talk about murder," she said. "When can I begin my indoctrination into the Black Lotus?"

"Immediately, if you like." An acquisitive gleam brightened Anraku's single eye.

Though Reiko wanted to question him regarding Pious Truth and his accusations against the sect, she had to get the shogun's mother away from the temple. She said, "Honorable Lady, shouldn't you consult Priest Ryuko first?"

At the mention of her spiritual advisor and lover, Keisho-in hesitated, then said, "I suppose so."

"Then let's go back to Edo Castle." Reiko hoped the priest would recognize Anraku as competition for his mistress's favor and dissuade Keisho-in.

"In the meantime, I'll send a donation as a pledge of my good faith," Keisho-in promised Anraku.

"My sincere thanks." Anraku bowed. "I look forward to your return." As they made their farewells, he shot Reiko a smug glance, as if to say, *Oppose me if you will, but I shall win in the end.*

During the walk through the precinct, Keisho-in gushed, "Isn't Anraku wonderful? Like a living god. And he wants me!"

Was he a god, or a charlatan who coveted a share of the Tokugawa power and fortune? "I think he's dangerous," Reiko said.

"Oh, don't be silly," Keisho-in scoffed.

They reached their palanquin, and Reiko said, "Will you excuse me if I don't go home with you? I have an errand."

"Very well," Keisho-in said indifferently.

At least Anraku had distracted her from sex between women, yet Reiko dreaded Sano discovering that she'd involved Keisho-in with the Black Lotus almost as much as she dreaded him finding out about her own close call. And as she ordered her guards to hire a palanquin to take her to Shinagawa, she feared how he would react when he learned she'd disobeyed his order to stay out of Minister Fugatami's investigation.

18

What is real or not real?
Do not try to see or understand.
All phenomena exist and do not exist;
Only the enlightened can distinguish truth from falsehood.

—FROM THE BLACK LOTUS SUTRA

"Honorable Father-in-law, we've come to see Haru," said Sano. He and Hirata sat in Magistrate Ueda's private office. The magistrate sat behind his desk, while a maid served tea. Sano said, "How is Haru doing?"

"She's behaved herself so far," Magistrate Ueda said. He added contritely, "Forgive me if I've upset you by taking her in. I would not normally house a murder suspect, but this time I allowed myself to be persuaded against my better judgment."

"I know. It's not your fault. My wife can be very persuasive."

The thought of Reiko fueled the anger in Sano. Still wounded by her insults and furious at her contrary behavior, he nonetheless ached with lonely need for her. He didn't want them to be adversaries. If neither of them would surrender, what then?

"I hope this case hasn't caused you trouble at home," Magistrate Ueda said with concern.

"Nothing serious," Sano lied. Social custom discouraged talk of personal problems, and he was uncomfortable discussing his even with Magistrate Ueda, a close friend. "It's just that my wife has become convinced that Haru is innocent."

"And you?" The magistrate's sharp gaze indicated that he'd noticed how Sano avoided using Reiko's name and guessed how bad things were between his daughter and son-in-law.

"There's much evidence against Haru," Sano hedged, and explained what he'd discovered. He didn't want to admit that he thought Haru guilty of something, because he was afraid his decision was premature, born of his anger at Reiko and his need to prove he was right and she wrong.

Magistrate Ueda contemplated Sano with a grave expression, then said, "I will mediate between you and Reiko if you wish."

"You needn't trouble yourself, but thank you for your kind offer." Sano was grateful, although shamed by the idea that he couldn't handle his own marriage and his father-in-law must intercede to preserve the union of the two clans. "I'm sure my wife will see reason when the facts are known. Now Hirata and I would like to ask Haru for some of those facts."

Magistrate Ueda rose. "I'll take you to her."

He led the way to the private quarters of the mansion. A guard loitered outside a room Sano recognized as Reiko's girlhood chamber. Magistrate Ueda spoke through the open door: "Haru-*san*, you have visitors."

Looking into the chamber, Sano saw Haru seated at a dressing table. She wore her hair in an elaborate knot studded with floral ornaments, and a jade green kimono printed with mauve asters. White makeup covered her face, and she'd painted her lips scarlet. She looked years older and startlingly pretty. Clothes, toiletries, and boxes of sweets lay on the floor around her. The scene enraged Sano. Four people, including her husband, had died in violence, and here Haru sat, primping amid things that Reiko must have given her.

Now Haru saw Sano and Hirata. She gasped.

"The *sōsakan-sama* wants a word with you," Magistrate Ueda said, his tone kind although Sano could tell that his father-in-law shared his disapproval of Haru.

After the magistrate left, Sano crouched near Haru. "You seem to have recovered from your ordeal," he said to her.

She must have sensed his animosity, because she folded her arms and hunched her shoulders. Her fear transformed her into a child again. The sudden change angered Sano because she was an adult, using childishness as a defense.

"Perhaps you've recovered your memory, too," Sano said. "Tell me about the night of the fire."

"I—I already told Reiko-*san* that I don't remember," Haru mumbled, looking around as if in search of Reiko.

Their friendship had gone too far, Sano thought as his anger flared toward both women. "My wife's not here to pamper you. You'll answer to me. What happened?"

"I don't know." Trembling, Haru recoiled from him.

"Well, maybe you have a clearer recollection of years ago. Let's talk about your parents."

Haru's face took on a leery expression. "My parents are dead."

"Spare me the sad tale," Sano said disdainfully. "I met your parents yesterday. Did you forget that they disowned you? Or did you think no one would ever find out?"

"No!" Haru cast a longing glance at the door, but Hirata blocked it. "I mean—"

"Why did you say you were an orphan?" Sano said.

Her tongue flicked over her lips. "I wanted the people at the temple to feel sorry for me and take me in."

The manipulative little liar, Sano thought in disgust. He said, "Do you feel sorry that your husband died when you burned down his house?"

Now panic leapt in Haru's eyes. "I didn't!" The high, unnatural pitch of her voice contradicted her vehemence. "It was an accident!"

Rising, Sano stood over Haru. "You set the fire in your husband's bedchamber. You were the only survivor, and glad of it. What did the old man do to you that made you murder him?"

She began wheezing and flung up her arms as though expecting him to strike her.

"What about Commander Oyama and the woman and little boy?" Sano shouted, welcoming her terror. She couldn't get away with obstructing him any longer. To keep his position, his honor, and his family's livelihood, he must break Haru. "Did you kill them? Did you set the fire at the temple?"

"No!" Now sobs punctuated the wheezes. Haru wept and choked; tears smeared her makeup. Bending, she cradled her head in her arms. "Please, leave me alone!"

"*Sōsakan-sama.*" A warning note tinged Hirata's voice.

Sano turned and saw his chief retainer regarding him with consternation. Now he noticed that his heart was thudding, his breath rapid, every muscle tense. In the heat of anger, he'd nearly crossed the line between persuasion and violence.

Hirata said, "Let me talk to her."

Alarmed by his loss of control, Sano nodded and stepped aside. If he couldn't handle his temper and keep personal problems from interfering with his work, he might never solve the case. He fought down panic.

Hirata knelt beside Haru. "Don't cry; nobody's going to hurt you," he soothed, patting her back. "It's all right."

Soon her weeping subsided. She turned a timid, drenched face to Hirata. Taking a cloth from under his sash, he dried her tears and smiled. "There, that's better."

Weakly, she smiled back, glancing at Sano, brave now that she thought she had an ally in Hirata.

"I believe you're innocent," Hirata said gently. "Help me find out who's guilty, and I'll help you."

Haru studied his earnest, open face, and hope brightened her eyes. "Can you?"

"Yes, indeed. I'll make sure your name is cleared and you can go back to your friends at the Black Lotus Temple." Hirata's trustworthy manner had elicited confessions from many criminals. "What do you say? Will you help me?"

Nodding, Haru said, "I'll try."

However, when Hirata questioned her, Haru produced the same tale she'd told Reiko: She remembered nothing after going to bed the night before the fire. Sano battled anger and sudden unease. Haru's eagerness to help could be a pose that she'd adopted because hysteria hadn't saved her from interrogation, but she sounded so sincere. Might she be speaking the truth?

"Haru-*san,* I'm afraid that what you've told me won't help either of us," Hirata said with kind concern. "Are you sure you know nothing more about the deaths of Commander Oyama, Nurse Chie, or the boy?"

"Nurse Chie was the woman in the cottage?" At Hirata's nod, Haru started to speak, then pressed her lips together.

"What is it?" Hirata prompted.

Uncertainty puckered the girl's forehead. "I wouldn't want to get anyone in trouble."

"Don't worry. Just tell the truth," Hirata said.

"Well . . ."

Hirata waited expectantly, and Sano with suspicion. At last Haru said, "It happened in the sixth month of this year. Dr. Miwa was giving me a medical treatment. I was asleep in bed in the temple hospital, when voices woke me. I looked up and saw Dr. Miwa and Nurse Chie across the room. Chie took care of the patients, and I liked her because she was pretty and cheerful, but that day she was crying. She said, 'We can't do this. It's wrong.' Dr. Miwa said, 'No, it's glorious, right, and destined to be. We must go through with it.'

"He was all excited, but Chie said, 'I don't want to. Please don't make me!' " Clasping her hands, Haru pantomimed begging. "They didn't know I was listening. Dr. Miwa got angry and shouted at Chie, 'You'll obey or die.' He grabbed her and pulled her to him. She screamed, 'No, I can't! I won't!' Then she broke free and ran out of the room."

Haru looked hopefully at Hirata. "Will that help?"

The story might indeed help Haru because it cast aspersions on the doctor, Sano observed. If Chie had spurned sexual advances from Miwa, that might give him a reason to kill her. But Haru's recital seemed too pat. Sano wondered if the incident had really occurred.

"Did anyone besides you see what happened?" Hirata asked.

Haru shook her head. "I was the only person around."

Just as Sano had expected, there were no impartial witnesses to confirm the story. If Dr. Miwa denied arguing with Chie, it would be his word against Haru's. Although a physician had more credibility than did a peasant girl, even false accusations could harm someone with Miwa's criminal record.

"Thank you, Haru-*san*," said Hirata.

"Please don't hurt Dr. Miwa," Haru said, looking worried. "He helped me, and I'd hate to get him in trouble."

Sano eyed her with contempt. She'd already told Reiko about a violent argument between the priest Kumashiro and Commander Oyama. Now the little hypocrite had struck back at Dr. Miwa for maligning her character.

"Especially since he's not the only one who was mad at Chie," Haru added.

"Who else was?" Hirata asked.

"Abbess Junketsu-in," said Haru.

In case heaping suspicion upon Dr. Miwa wasn't enough to get her off the hook, she would incriminate Junketsu-in, Sano thought. And the abbess was another of Haru's detractors.

"She didn't want Chie in the Black Lotus," Haru said. "She was always picking on Chie and trying to get her thrown out. Once I asked Chie why Junketsu-in was so mean to her. Chie said Junketsu-in was jealous." With an air of stunned revelation, Haru exclaimed, "Oh! Maybe Junketsu-in killed Chie to get rid of her."

"Or maybe you invented the whole story," Sano interjected, unable to remain quiet while Haru evaded the question of her own guilt. As she stared at him in fright, Sano advanced on her. "You've said plenty about other people. Now let's discuss what your friends at the orphanage say about you. Hanako and Yukiko told me they followed you to the cottage on the night before the fire. They say you went under your own power, completely conscious of what you were doing."

Haru scooted nearer Hirata for protection. Her breathing quickened again. "They're wrong," she whispered.

"Yukiko and Hanako lied?"

She gave an anxious, hasty nod.

"Dr. Miwa and Abbess Junketsu-in lied when they said you're a troublemaker?"

Again Haru nodded, with less conviction.

"The neighbors who say you burned your husband's house also lied?"

Haru sat frozen, speechless.

"So everyone is lying except you." A sarcastic laugh burst from Sano. "Well, I don't believe that, and I've had enough of your stories. Now let's go over that night again. This time I want the truth."

She turned a pleading gaze on Hirata, who said regretfully, "I can't help you unless you cooperate."

An abrupt change came over the girl. Her posture took on a sinuous fluidity, and her eyes a seductive gleam. She lowered her kimono to reveal bare shoulders. Licking her lips, she said to Hirata in a husky murmur, "But I'm innocent. How can you doubt me?" She leaned close to him; her cheek touched his.

"Hey, what are you doing?" Startled, Hirata leapt to his feet.

Haru rose, sashayed toward Sano, and pressed herself against him. "The truth is that I find you most appealing. Let me show you how well I can cooperate. Perhaps then you'll be satisfied that I've done nothing wrong."

Her nerve appalled Sano. He shoved Haru away. "You can't seduce us into thinking you're innocent."

Haru looked puzzled, as if her ploy had worked in the past and she didn't understand why it had failed this time. Her face crumpled, and she let out a sob.

"Crying won't help you either," Sano said contemptuously.

Now the girl's expression turned furious. A howl erupted from her, and she launched herself at Sano. The impact of her body knocked him off balance, and he staggered. Her fingernails clawed at him; lines of pain seared his cheek.

"Stop it!" Sano shouted, fending off her flailing hands.

Hirata seized Haru. She turned on him and raked her nails down his face. "Ow!" he cried, and he let her go, clutching his left eye.

"You demon!" Sano grabbed Haru.

She was stronger than she looked, and she fought like a wild beast. "You're all out to get me!" she shrieked. "Everyone blames me for everything. I hate you all. I want to kill you!"

Satisfaction filled Sano even as the girl's fists, elbows, and knees battered him. Though he hadn't gotten answers from Haru, at least he'd forced her to reveal her true self. Hirata, his eye bleeding, grabbed her legs, and she kicked his stomach. Magistrate Ueda and a trio of guards burst into the room.

"What's going on here?" the magistrate said. Seeing Sano

and Hirata struggling with Haru, he said, "Guards. Subdue her."

With their help, Sano and Hirata overpowered Haru. Finally she stood captive, writhing in the guards' grip.

"The old man deserved it!" she shrilled, her face distorted by fury. "I didn't want to marry him, but they made me. He treated me like a slave. He beat me. He deserved to die!"

Magistrate Ueda frowned; Hirata gaped. A thrill of horror and anticipation rippled through Sano. "Are you saying you killed your husband?" he asked Haru.

Eyes crazed and hair tangled, Haru looked like a madwoman. "That policeman forced me to have sex with him in the cottage. I'm glad he's dead!" She spewed incoherent curses.

Sano said, "I interpret that as a confession of murdering her husband and Commander Oyama."

The worry of the past days fled him in a rush of relief. With the question of Haru's guilt settled, the investigation wouldn't come between him and Reiko any longer. Reiko would have to admit she'd made a mistake about Haru and abandon her dubious quest to prove that the Black Lotus was involved in crimes. Sano looked forward to regaining peace in his life.

"*Sumimasen*—excuse me, but we can't be sure that what she said is really a confession, because she didn't actually say she set the fires or hurt anyone," Hirata said.

"Attacking us is proof that she's capable of harm," Sano said, touching the bloody scratches on his face.

"Even if she did make a confession," said Magistrate Ueda, "it doesn't account for the other two murders."

Sano said to Haru, "Did you kill Nurse Chie and the boy?"

Wild sobs wracked Haru; struggling to free herself, she seemed oblivious to his words.

"Well, we've got her for her husband's murder and Oyama's," said Sano, driven by his need to solve the case and serve justice. "That's enough for now. I'm sure we can get a full confession from her later."

Magistrate Ueda spoke in a quiet, grave voice for Sano's ears alone: "She's in no shape to make a valid confession, and there's still a chance that she's innocent. For your own sake, don't let emotion impair your judgment."

These words brought Sano to the dismaying realization that his antagonism toward Haru and wish to have her gone from

his life had undermined his objectivity. He, who prided himself
on serving honor through seeking the truth, had almost compromised his principles. Although tempted to blame Reiko, he
knew the real fault was his own.

"Thank you for your advice, Honorable Father-in-law,"
Sano said, chastened.

New apprehension filled him as he wondered if this case
would destroy everything he valued. He was no longer certain
whether convicting Haru would solve his problems with Reiko.
Though he still believed in Haru's guilt, he dreaded telling his
wife about the arrest. After he took Haru to jail, he must go to
the Black Lotus Temple to speak with High Priest Anraku and
check Haru's stories with Dr. Miwa and Abbess Junketsu-in.
His prejudice against the girl required extrameticulous investigation of all angles of the case before he could discredit
Reiko's evidence in favor of Haru.

"I shall charge Haru with the murders of her husband and
Commander Oyama and order a trial to determine whether
she's guilty of those crimes, the other murders, and the arson,"
Sano decided. "The trial will be delayed until the investigation
is complete. Haru is under arrest. She'll await trial in jail."

"No!" she screamed, fighting harder. "No, no, no!" She continued screaming as the guards dragged her out of the room.

19

I will send forth believers,
Monks and nuns,
Men and women of pure faith,
To propagate my Law.
—FROM THE BLACK LOTUS SUTRA

Shinagawa was a village south of Edo, and the second of fifty-three post stations along the Tōkaidō highway. The palanquin ride from the Zōjō district brought Reiko there by afternoon. Between Edo Bay and the wooded rise of Palace Hill, the highway ran past teahouses filled with citizens greeting travelers or seeing them off on journeys. More travelers browsed shops, gathered at the stables, and lined up for inspection at the station office. Hawkers called customers to inns. Now Reiko peered through the palanquin's window at passing samurai from nearby daimyo residences, and the many monks who came to Shinagawa for illicit amusements. Looking down a side street, she saw banners stamped with the Tokugawa crest protruding from a large crowd gathered between rows of connected houses with thatched roofs.

"Stop over there," she called to her bearers.

They obeyed. Reiko alighted from the palanquin. The mist had cleared, but the sky was overcast and the air cool; a damp wind wafted charcoal smoke and the smell of horse manure from the highway. Reiko and her guards walked toward the banners. The crowd included laborers, housewives carrying babies, and curious children. Men's serious voices emanated from the center.

When the guards cleared her way through the crowd, Reiko saw Minister Fugatami, his samurai entourage, and a group of aged male commoners dressed in dark robes, standing around a well, a square wooden structure fitted with a pulley and bucket. Fugatami acknowledged Reiko's arrival with a slight nod. His sharp features were grim as he returned his attention to his companions.

"This is one of three wells that we believe were poisoned by the Black Lotus during the past year," said one of the commoners, a dignified, white-haired man. Reiko supposed that he and his comrades were village elders and he was their senior giving Minister Fugatami a report on incidents involving the sect. He lowered the bucket into the well and drew it up, full "The water has a peculiar odor."

Fugatami sniffed the water and grimaced. "Indeed." He dipped a hand into the bucket, examined the liquid that ran off his fingers, then said to his attendants, "Note that the water also has an oily texture and faint greenish hue."

"People have complained of the odd taste," said the elder "Fifty-three have become ill with diarrhea after drinking. Fortunately, none have died, and we've sealed the bad wells, but we're worried about possible future incidents."

Angry rumbles of agreement arose from the spectators; a baby cried. The elders silenced the crowd with stern looks.

"Why do you think the Black Lotus is responsible?" asked Fugatami as his attendants wrote down the data.

"There was never any problem with wells until Black Lotus priests and nuns began frequenting Shinagawa in large numbers. Neighborhood watchmen have seen them loitering at night near the wells that were later found to be bad."

Alarm and elation stirred in Reiko. Mass poisoning was a serious new addition to the list of accusations against the Black Lotus. However, it might induce Sano to investigate the sect.

"There have also been four reported instances of a pungent smoke drifting through the streets," said the senior elder. "Breathing the smoke causes chest pain, coughing, and shortness of breath. The last instance was three months ago, and a shopkeeper saw two Black Lotus nuns running away just as the smoke began."

"Was the source of the smoke identified?" Minister Fugatami asked.

"Yes. Please come this way."

With the senior elder leading, Minister Fugatami, his entourage, and the crowd headed down the street to a tiny Shinto shrine. Reiko and her guards squeezed through the torii gate. Inside stood a primitive altar that held candles, incense sticks, offerings of food, and a gong to summon the deity.

"A pile of burning rags was found there," the senior elder said, pointing to a spot beside the fence. "They reeked of the odor. The watchman who found them was almost overcome by the fumes."

Even as she regretted the townspeople's suffering, Reiko welcomed more evidence of the sect's evil nature.

"There were no deaths?" Fugatami said.

"No," said the senior elder, "but we fear that death will occur if these incidents continue. Four families were stricken with stomach pains and vomiting earlier this month, after visits from Black Lotus priests. It seems that the priests are spreading disease."

Or poisoning the food and drink of people who allow sect members into their homes, Reiko thought.

"The most serious incident was an explosion," said the senior elder.

The crowd accompanied him across a bridge over the Meguro River to a neighborhood in a poor section of town. There, amid teahouses and shops, Reiko saw a pile of charred beams, planks, roof tiles, and burnt debris where a building had once stood. A bitter, sulfurous odor lingered around the site.

"The Black Lotus sect owned that building," the senior elder said. "They held prayer sessions and recruited followers there.

Six nights ago, the building exploded with a huge boom, then caught fire. Luckily, there was no one inside or nearby, and the fire brigade put out the fire before it could spread."

"Did you examine the ruins?" Minister Fugatami asked.

"Yes. We found empty jars and some iron chests that had been blown apart, but we don't know what caused the explosion."

The sect must have used the building as a storage site for poison and headquarters for their activities in Shinagawa, but Reiko didn't understand why they'd destroyed their own property.

"Someone could have been killed or badly injured," said the senior elder. "Also, the number of kidnappings connected with the Black Lotus has increased—there have been nine this past month. Things are getting worse, but when we went to the temple to talk about the incidents, the sect denied any involvement. Honorable Minister, we beg you to help us protect our people."

The other elders echoed his plea. Minister Fugatami said, "You've done well by bringing the matter to my attention. I promise to do everything in my power to determine what is going on and put a stop to any wrongdoing by the Black Lotus. Now I must return to Edo."

As the crowd dispersed, the elders expressed their appreciation to Fugatami. The minister looked toward Reiko and nodded to her. She and her guards walked back to her palanquin. She sat inside and waited. Soon Fugatami appeared at the window.

He greeted her formally, then said, "I regret that the *sōsakan-sama* was unable to be here."

"My husband regrets that his business kept him away," Reiko fibbed politely, "but I thank you for permitting me to observe your investigation for him."

"What I've seen and heard today, added to your monk's story about the Black Lotus, should be enough to persuade my superiors to outlaw the sect," Minister Fugatami said with satisfaction. "Even those who are followers cannot justify protecting an organization associated with so many crimes."

Reiko hated to disappoint him, but she had to bring him up to date on developments since they'd spoken yesterday. "M\

husband has inspected the Black Lotus Temple. He wasn't able to locate the novice monk—according to the sect, Pious Truth doesn't exist. Nor could my husband find any sign of prisoners, torture, or underground chambers."

"Indeed." Fugatami's expression turned grave. "I suppose that the Black Lotus has permanently silenced the monk."

"You think they killed him for talking to me?" Suddenly the air seemed to turn colder; an eerie lull of quiet interrupted the shouts and laughter from inns and teahouses on the main road.

"I do," Fugatami said grimly. "And without an inside witness, my case against the sect weakens. However, there's still hope if I can enlist your husband as an ally. I will be presenting a complete report on the Black Lotus to the Council of Elders tomorrow afternoon. Will you convey to the *sōsakan-sama* my invitation to join us? I should be grateful if you could persuade him to support me tomorrow when I ask the Council of Elders to close down the sect and dismantle the temple."

"I'll do my best," Reiko promised, without much faith in her ability to persuade Sano to do anything just now. Still, if Pious Truth was alive and in danger, she must try to rescue him; if the sect had killed him, she must avenge his death. She hoped that dismantling the temple might uncover evidence that would help Haru, for she hated to think she was defending a murderer, even in a crusade against other murderers. And Reiko could not rid herself of a stubborn, visceral inclination to believe in Haru's innocence.

"These incidents and their increasing frequency attest that the evil within the Black Lotus is growing stronger and the sect is progressing toward trouble of major proportions," Minister Fugatami said. "I do not know what it might be, but I fear that Shinagawa is only the beginning."

20

I bring fulfillment to the world,
Like a rain that spreads its moisture everywhere,
To those superior and inferior,
Of proper or improper demeanor,
Of keen and dull wit,
I rain upon all equally.

—FROM THE BLACK LOTUS SUTRA

Abbess Junketsu-in stood at the open second-story window of the abbot's residence, gazing over the Black Lotus Temple. Beneath a lusterless gray twilight sky, the precinct lay deeply shadowed by its trees and arbors. As temple bells tolled for evening rites, a cool wind wavered the flames in stone lanterns along the paths. The day's pilgrims had already gone; the nuns and priests had vanished indoors. Biting her lip, Junketsu-in watched *Sōsakan* Sano and his detectives walking toward the main gate. Her nerves were still on edge from the questions he'd asked her earlier about her relationship with Nurse Chie.

"Do not be afraid of the *sōsakan-sama*," High Priest Anraku said from behind her.

Startled, Junketsu-in closed the window and turned. Anraku moved so quickly and noiselessly that she never heard and seldom saw him coming; he just appeared, as if by magic. And he could always read her mind. Now he reclined upon a raised bed draped in a canopy of red and gold tapestry and heaped with embroidered cushions. His brocade stole and saffron robe gleamed in the light from brass lamps. One wall of his room was covered by a mural in which the Buddha lay in a jeweled, flaming coffin. An altar held a huge bronze phallus and smoking incense; curtained archways led to adjoining rooms. Anraku had designed his private chambers to imitate a palace he'd seen while his spirit traveled through India. At the sight of him, desire pierced Junketsu-in. She lowered the drape that covered her hair and drew herself up to show off her elegant figure.

" 'Fear is a destroyer of the spirit,' " Anraku quoted from the Black Lotus Sutra. " 'Insignificant men derive power from people's fear of them. Resist fear, and the power is yours.' "

"But Haru has said bad things about me." Fresh anxiety filled Junketsu-in as she remembered what Sano said the girl had told him about the abbess's mistreatment of Chie.

"The *sōsakan-sama* doesn't believe her," Anraku said with a dismissive wave of his hand. "Nor did he believe her when she said that Priest Kumashiro argued with Commander Oyama, or that Dr. Miwa tried to force himself upon a woman who was also murdered."

Junketsu-in had heard that Sano had also interrogated Kumashiro and Miwa today. Perhaps they'd told Anraku; perhaps he'd divined the facts upon which he based his opinions. She almost wished Sano would believe Haru's tales about them. The doctor was a repulsive lecher, and Kumashiro treated her like filth; they envied her position close to Anraku, and she despised them both. Still, any threat to them also threatened her, and the entire sect.

"The fact that Sano is checking Haru's stories disturbs me," Junketsu-in said. Anraku frowned—he forbade his followers to challenge his wisdom—but Junketsu-in rushed on, compelled to warn him. "Sano has been here all afternoon, talking to people and poking around. If he continues this way, eventually he'll find something to support Haru's accusations." Anraku didn't like anyone to question him, but Junketsu-in ventured timidly, "What did you and Sano talk about during your meeting this afternoon?"

With a swift grace, Anraku rose and placed his hands on her shoulders. "I decide what you need to know, and I shall tell you if and when I choose." He spoke in the quiet, menacing voice reserved for followers who displeased him. "What are the Three Great Laws of the Black Lotus that I have taught you?"

"You are the Bodhisattva of Infinite Power," Junketsu-in stammered, fearful of his anger. "You alone know each person's individual path through life. They who obey the Bodhisattva of Infinite Power will achieve Buddhahood."

"Then accept my authority, or suffer punishment."

"I'm sorry. I didn't mean to offend you," she apologized hastily, knowing too well that her position as his chief female official was tenuous. "I'm just worried that Sano will blame you for the fire and murders." Whether he'd burned the cottage or killed with his own hands, wasn't Anraku ultimately responsible for everything that happened here?

"Do you dare imply that Sano is any match for me?" Anraku's expression turned ominous, and Junketsu-in cringed. "If your faith in me is so weak, I can find another woman who deserves the attentions I've bestowed upon you."

"No! Forgive me!" Junketsu-in pleaded.

The pressure of his hands enflamed her desire and awakened memories of other hands that had touched her during the years when her name hadn't been Junketsu-in but Iris. The first man had been her father, who'd owned a tofu shop in Ginza. At night Iris, her parents, and her two younger sisters had all slept together in the single room of their living quarters. When Iris was eight years old, her father crept under her quilt and began fondling her.

"Don't make any noise," he whispered.

While the rest of the family slept, he mounted and entered her. His hand over her mouth stifled her cries of agony. After he was done, he said, "If you tell anyone, I'll kill you. Be good, and I'll make you happy."

The next morning Iris was so sore she could hardly move, but she heeded her father's words and acted as if nothing had happened. Later, he bought her a beautiful doll. For the next few years Iris tolerated her father's nocturnal attentions, and he rewarded her with toys, pretty kimonos, and sweets. He petted and praised her while ignoring the other girls. She was allowed to play instead of helping her meek, subservient mother with the housework. Iris enjoyed the power that the secret gave her, until her father stopped visiting her bed and her sister Lily became his new favorite.

Suddenly Iris was the family drudge. She hated her father for abandoning her and missed her privileged position. But she was now thirteen years old and pretty. While cleaning the tofu shop, she noticed men on the street eyeing her. One, a handsome young carpenter, stopped to talk.

Iris said, "If I let you have me, what will you give me?"

He gave her copper coins and took her in the alley behind the shop. New sensations stirred in Iris, who began to realize that sex could bring physical pleasure as well as material gain. Soon she had many lovers who paid her in money and gifts. When she was sixteen her father fell ill; right before he died, he married her off to his apprentice. Iris and her husband took over the shop. He was a weak man in thrall to her; she continued her affairs and used her earnings to build herself a luxurious home.

Unbeknown to her, she'd begun a journey that had brought her to the Black Lotus Temple, to this room where she now fell to her knees before Anraku.

"My faith in you is absolute," she said, caressing his legs through the saffron robe. How she burned for him! How easily he could cast her off. "Your power and wisdom are supreme."

To her relief, Anraku's scowl dissolved into a benevolent smile. He grasped her hands, raising her. "Let us waste no more attention on trivial men like the *sōsakan-sama* when our destiny looms on the horizon."

"The time is near, then?" Excitement filled Junketsu-in.

"Very soon my prophecies will come true," Anraku replied in a hushed, dramatic tone. In the flickering light, he gleamed; his hands were smooth and hard and warm on Junketsu-in's. "Every follower of the Black Lotus shall achieve enlightenment in a celebration such as mankind has never known. You shall be at my side when I rule a new world."

Junketsu-in thrilled at the thought, but a niggling doubt disturbed her. "Everything will happen no matter what?" she asked, though afraid to offend Anraku by revealing her fears that the fire and murders might thwart him.

"Destiny waits for nothing." Dreams swirled in Anraku's eye. "No one can stop me."

Still, Junketsu-in's doubt persisted. Could Anraku not understand that Sano's investigation and Lady Reiko's meddling might ruin his plans? On rare occasions such as this, when Junketsu-in's innate common sense resurfaced, she even had misgivings about Anraku's supernatural powers. Granted, he exercised formidable control over his followers; however, his strength derived as much from their labor and the political clout of his patrons. Faith had inspired his visions, but human might and method would make them fact. Was he a fool not to know this? Or was Junketsu-in a fool who didn't understand the cosmic forces driving his schemes?

As usual, her attempt at objectivity failed. She only knew she loved Anraku, and that she owed him her life.

One spring evening twelve years ago, police officers had burst into Iris's house while she was entertaining a lover. They shackled her and dragged her out to the street. The police commander said to her, "You're under arrest for prostitution outside the licensed quarter."

It was Commander Oyama, although Iris didn't learn his name until later. His strong build and arrogant good looks attracted her. With an inviting smile, she said, "If you let me go, I'll show you how grateful I am."

He considered her offer. "Unshackle her," he ordered his men, then followed Iris into her house. But after they'd finished, he went to the door and called to the waiting police: "Take her to jail."

"Wait," cried Iris. "You promised to let me go."

Oyama laughed. "Promises to a whore mean nothing."

The magistrate sentenced Iris to work as a prostitute in the Yoshiwara pleasure quarter for ten years. She reveled in the sex, but hated the cramped quarters and the mean brothel owner who kept the money she made. She despised Oyama for using her, and plotted revenge against him, but first she had to escape the Yoshiwara.

After three years she attracted a rich merchant who promised to pay off the brothel for her keep and bribe the *bakufu* to commute her sentence, but soon another courtesan stole his affection. Iris was furious. At a party in the brothel, she attacked her rival, clawing the woman's face to shreds. The magistrate sentenced her to a flogging. Her hatred for Oyama grew, as did her need for revenge. Shortly afterward, she was sitting in the window of the brothel, on display for the passing crowds, when a priest approached her.

"Greetings, Iris," he said. "I've come for you."

She gave him a disdainful sneer, because priests were poor and therefore no use to her. But this one was very handsome, with one eye covered by a patch. "Tell the proprietor you want me," Iris said, intrigued in spite of herself.

The next thing she knew, she and the priest were riding through the Yoshiwara gate in a palanquin. The priest was Anraku, and he'd bought her freedom.

"But why?" Iris said. "Where are you taking me?"

"I am your destiny. We are going to my temple, where you will join the nunnery."

A celibate life of prayer didn't appeal to Iris, but desire for Anraku had already kindled in her, and she thought she could manipulate him into letting her go and giving her money to live on. But when they reached the temple, Anraku left her in the convent. There she joined other novices in a regimen of prayer, harsh discipline, little sleep, and no contact with anyone outside. The training confused her mind. She didn't see Anraku again until ten days later, in a private audience.

"How does your training progress?" he asked.

By this time Iris was desperate for Anraku. "Please," she murmured, reaching for him.

Anraku only smiled his enigmatic smile. "No. The time is not yet right."

Iris endured a year as a novice. She lived for brief visits from Anraku. At last he initiated her, gave her a new religious name, Junketsu-in, and revealed the secret passage of the Black Lotus Sutra that was meant for her.

"The union of male and female fosters spiritual energy," he said. "Woman is the fire, man the smoke. Her door is the flame, his member the fuel. Pleasure is the spark, and climax a sacred offering. Intercourse is a path to enlightenment. That is the path you must follow. I shall be your guide."

That night he began teaching her the thousand erotic rituals described in the Black Lotus Sutra. Never had Junketsu-in known such fulfillment. Anraku became her beloved god; his words were fact and law to her. Anraku made her abbess of the convent, where she lived in luxury, waited upon by the nuns she ruled, and performing duties ordered by the high priest. Junketsu-in thought she would live happily until the day when Anraku's prophecies were realized, but soon things began to go wrong, with results that imperiled her today.

Now Junketsu-in said to Anraku, "If the *sōsakan-sama* accuses me of the crimes, will you protect me?"

"You are protected by your faith in me," Anraku said.

Yet she needed more than that. If Sano discovered the things she'd done, he might decide she was the only person with reason to have committed all three murders and framed Haru. The girl and the victims, who had come into the Black Lotus one after the other, like a parade of demons, had turned Junketsu-in's life into hell.

The first demon was Chie.

Junketsu-in had known from the start that Anraku had many lovers; still, she'd believed that no one else could satisfy him the way she did—until Chie arrived. The humble, earthy peasant woman had exuded a powerful sexuality that had captivated Anraku. Junketsu-in argued against admitting Chie as a novice, but Anraku overrode her.

Jealousy plagued her as she spied on him wooing Chie the way he'd done her. She vented her anger on Chie, beating the meek novice, denying her food, calling her names, and spreading lies about her; she'd begged Anraku to expel Chie, in vain. Junketsu-in suffered the torment of secretly watching the pair engage in ritual intercourse. Anraku began ignoring Junketsu-in, while Chie became his new mate and chief nurse in the temple hospital. Junketsu-in had affairs with other priests, hoping to make Anraku jealous, but he proved indifferent. Then she learned that Chie was pregnant.

Anraku had sired children by other women, but Junketsu-in hadn't cared because he paid little attention to his offspring; nor had she cared that she was barren. But watching Chie grow large with the fruit of his seed was more than Junketsu-in could tolerate. She poisoned Chie's food, trying to induce a miscarriage. When that failed, Junketsu-in threw Chie on the ground and kicked her stomach. Hastened labor resulted in the birth of a son, Radiant Spirit. Though Anraku took no notice of the event, Junketsu-in ordered the nuns at the nursery to underfeed and neglect the child. While she was waiting for him to die and plotting how to regain her place with Anraku, into her life came the second demon.

Seven years had passed since Commander Oyama had arrested Junketsu-in, and they met again at the ceremony where the sect's high officials welcomed him as a patron. After the ceremony, Oyama sought out Junketsu-in for a private word.

"So you're a holy woman now," he said with the derisive laugh she recalled too well. "Life has treated you kindly."

"No thanks to you," Junketsu-in said as her hatred resurfaced.

Oyama leered at her. "I shall enjoy renewing our acquaintance."

"Not if I can help it."

But Anraku ordered her to instruct Oyama in ritual sex. She objected to servicing her old enemy, but Anraku said, "It is my will, and you must obey or leave the Black Lotus." Despite his cruelty, Junketsu-in still loved and desired him. She submitted to degrading encounters in the cottage with Oyama, who mocked her past even as he took his pleasure from her. Meanwhile, Radiant Spirit survived; Chie remained Anraku's favorite. And along came the last demon.

Angry, rebellious, and lustful, Haru disrupted the orphanage, where she couldn't get along with the other children, and the monastery, where she got along too well with the monks. Junketsu-in fought to discipline her, but Anraku fancied Haru; he adopted her as a sort of daughter and lover. Suddenly Junketsu-in had another enemy to blight her existence. Still, she persevered and schemed, and she gradually reaped success.

The murders of Chie and Radiant Spirit had removed them forever. Commander Oyama had gotten what he deserved. Haru had been arrested for the crimes, as Junketsu-in had hoped. Anraku had resumed his sexual alliance with Junketsu-in the day after the murders. She was again his mate, but she would not feel safe as long as Haru was still alive.

Anraku grazed Junketsu-in's cheek with his finger. The heat

of his touch stirred her as she recognized the onset of the sexual rite.

"Haru was arrested today," she said, cautiously broaching a topic that she knew Anraku considered none of her concern.

"I am aware of that." Anraku's finger dragged down her lips, parting them.

Junketsu-in caught her breath. As his finger moved down her chin and throat, she said, "Haru knows much about the temple's business. Perhaps too much."

"What is happening to Haru is part of the master scheme," Anraku said, untying her sash. "She will play her role perfectly."

Did he intend to do nothing about Haru? Panic tinged Junketsu-in's thoughts. Then her gray kimono and white underrobe fell away, and she stood naked before Anraku. Arching her neck, she savored the rush of arousal. Anraku shed his garments, revealing sculpted musculature. Smiling beatifically, he glowed with inner energy and immense sexual power.

"Haru has been talking to the *sōsakan-sama* and his wife," Junketsu-in said. Surely his desire for her would induce Anraku to listen to her. "She's already spoken against me because she wants me executed instead of her. To save herself, she may say enough to destroy the Black Lotus. Please stop her before it's too late."

"She will say what she is meant to say and do what she is meant to do," Anraku said. "She is crucial to the destiny of the Black Lotus. My vision has seen the path she must walk."

Now he began the ritual of Divine Marking. His sharp fingernails gouged Junketsu-in's neck, breasts, stomach, and buttocks with deep red crescents, lines, and swirls, like a mantra written in flesh. Junketsu-in exclaimed in pain and pleasure. Sensation drowned worry; she gave herself up to Anraku. She bit the tender skin of his armpits, around his navel, and behind his knees. Her teeth left dents where blood welled like tiny red beads.

"You are the fire. I am smoke," Anraku murmured as they sank onto the bed.

Lying on her back, Junketsu-in raised her legs high, spread them wide. Anraku lowered himself between them and entered her. She swooned at the pleasure. Their bodies moved with flexible ease, her legs first clasping his shoulders then flung outward, his thrusts slow then fast, arms entwining and hands stroking in the most potent ritual of all: Igniting the Flower. Junketsu-in climbed on top, rotating her body around his organ inside her. Then she was crouching and he behind her, penetrating deeply. Now they were upright, she with her knees around his waist, he standing and supporting her. Still thrusting, Anraku began to spin.

The room swirled around Junketsu-in. Glinting jewels of light from the canopy and mural circled in the hazy incense smoke. Anraku spun faster. Junketsu-in laughed in giddy exhilaration. As her passion mounted, she saw in her mind a giant black lotus, the petals on fire. The image of the burning flower shone in Anraku's eye. His face was fierce with desire. Then the climax took them. As Anraku pumped his seed into Junketsu-in and her body pulsed around him, they seemed to leave the earth and whirl through the stars. She screamed her joy. His moan echoed like thunder across mountains. The flaming lotus exploded in her head, and Junketsu-in tasted the ecstasy to come when destiny arrived and the Black Lotus sect achieved enlightenment.

Then Anraku—and she—would have power over the whole world.

21

If one should harbor doubt and fail to believe,
He will fall at once into the path of evil.

—FROM THE BLACK LOTUS SUTRA

"Haru-*san*?" Reiko called, walking down the corridor through the private quarters of Magistrate Ueda's mansion.

Night had fallen by the time she'd traveled from Shinagawa to Edo, and lanterns shone behind paper walls, but the chamber she'd given Haru was dark. Reiko, come to tell Haru what she'd learned today, slid open the door. She found clothes and sundries on the floor, but no Haru.

"She's gone," said Magistrate Ueda.

Reiko turned to see him standing near her. "Gone?" she asked, first puzzled, then alarmed. "Where?"

Shaking his head, Magistrate Ueda regarded Reiko with

somber pity. "Let's sit in the parlor. We can have tea while I explain, hmm?"

"I don't need any tea." His stalling increased Reiko's alarm. "I just want to know what happened to Haru."

"She is in Edo Jail," Magistrate Ueda said reluctantly. "This morning your husband arrested her for the crimes at the Black Lotus Temple."

"What?" Reiko stared in horrified disbelief.

"Sano-*san* interrogated Haru," he said, then described how Haru had railed against her husband and Commander Oyama, admitting she'd wanted them dead because they'd hurt her.

"That's not proof of her guilt," Reiko cried, though she knew how bad it made Haru look even if it wasn't exactly a confession.

"There was sufficient other reason to arrest Haru," Magistrate Ueda said. "She flew into a rage and attacked your husband and Hirata-*san*. Your husband received minor scratches on his cheek, but Haru managed to claw Hirata-*san*'s eye."

The girl who seemed so pathetic and harmless to Reiko presented such a different face to other people, and had now behaved in such a way as to reinforce Sano's antagonism toward her.

"Attacking my husband and Hirata-*san* was wrong of Haru, but it isn't proof that she's killed anyone," Reiko said.

Magistrate Ueda frowned. "If you were not so partial to Haru and hostile toward the Black Lotus you would see that her behavior indicates guilt rather than innocence, hmm?"

Reiko did see, but the injustice of persecution based on prejudice and inconclusive findings alarmed her. "My husband's haste will be our undoing. Why did you just let him arrest Haru?"

"I concurred with his decision. As I told you before, I believe there's a strong chance that Haru is guilty. What happened here today confirmed my opinion that she's dangerous and belongs in jail."

"I can't believe you took my husband's side against me."

Now the magistrate's expression turned sad. "I would do almost anything for you, Daughter, but I cannot shield a crim-

inal. You must leave Haru to the law. Go home and make peace
with your husband."

Upset and frantic, Reiko ran from the house. Her father had
turned against her, but she couldn't give up and let killers go
free.

When Sano rode though the gate of his estate with Hirata,
they found Detectives Kanryū, Hachiya, Takeo, and Tadao
standing in the torch-lit courtyard. Kanryū and Hachiya still
sported the tattered kimonos in which they'd disguised themselves as pilgrims. Sano dismounted, and all four prostrated
themselves at his feet.

"Please pardon us, Sōsakan-sama," they chorused.

"What's going on?" Sano said. "You're supposed to be at
the temple."

Just then, the gate opened, and bearers entered the courtyard,
carrying a palanquin. Consternation jolted Sano. Where had
Reiko gone, and what had she been doing out so late?

"The Black Lotus discovered that we were spies," Kanryū
said. "There was no use trying to conduct a secret surveillance
any longer, so we came home."

The bearers set down the palanquin, and Reiko climbed out.
Her stricken eyes told Sano that she knew about Haru. She
walked into the mansion, her back straight and head high.

"Rise," Sano ordered his men, who obeyed. Already his
heart had begun pounding in anticipation of a scene with Reiko.
"Tell me what happened."

"I had sneaked into the area of the temple where the clergy
live," Kanryū said, "when a priest suddenly appeared. He said,
'I must ask you to leave,' and escorted me out the gate."

"The same thing happened to me when I was looking for
secret tunnels under the buildings," Hachiya said.

"We told the priests we wanted to join the sect," Tadao said.
"They put us in a room with twelve other men who also wanted
to join. They asked us about ourselves, fed us a meal, then left
us so we could meditate on whether we belonged with the
Black Lotus. After a while, the priests came back and took

Takeo and me outside. They told us we weren't suited for the clergy, so we must leave."

"I could see in their eyes that they knew who we really were," Takeo said.

"It's no coincidence that they threw us all out," Kanryū said. "They'd identified us all. They knew why we were there."

Suspicion troubled Sano. "Who else besides Hirata-*san* and myself knew you were doing surveillance at the temple?"

"Just the detective corps," Hachiya said.

After dismissing the men, Sano said to Hirata, "There must be a spy among us who's reporting to the Black Lotus." That a trusted retainer would betray him disturbed Sano greatly. So did the knowledge that the Black Lotus thought it necessary to spy on him—and eject his spies from the temple. Could there be truth to the accusations against the Black Lotus? But if the sect was evil, wouldn't it have killed his spies? Then again, perhaps it feared retribution.

"We'll have to find out who the spy is and get rid of him," Hirata said, dabbing a cloth against his eye. It was red, swollen, and runny from Haru's clawing. He said unhappily, "I thought I knew those men, and I've never had cause to question their loyalty to you. If the Black Lotus can corrupt a samurai's honor, it must be strong—and dangerous."

"We'll continue looking into the sect until we discover the truth," Sano said as they walked toward the mansion. "But at least we've got the person who's responsible for the deaths we were assigned to investigate."

Inside, they found Reiko in the parlor with Midori. The pretty maid O-hana was pouring tea for them. When Sano and Hirata entered the room, the women bowed. Midori and O-hana murmured polite greetings, but Reiko neither spoke nor looked at Sano. She sat rigid, her lips compressed. Sano braced himself for a confrontation.

Midori gazed up at Hirata with a joy that turned to surprise. She exclaimed, "What happened to your eye?"

"I got injured working on the investigation," Hirata said proudly.

"Let me see." Jumping up, Midori leaned close to examine the wound. "Does it hurt much?"

"Oh, it's not too bad."

A peculiar expression crossed Midori's face, and she flounced away from Hirata. "Well, don't let it drip on anything," she said, her anxious concern turned to coldness.

Sano and Hirata both stared at her, bewildered. A muscle twitched in Reiko's cheek. O-hana hurried over to Hirata.

"But of course it hurts," she cooed. "Come to the kitchen, and I'll make an herb poultice for you."

As the pair left the room, Hirata glanced over his shoulder at Midori. She hesitated, then hurried after him. Sano knelt opposite Reiko.

"What's the matter with Midori?" Sano asked.

Reiko gazed fixedly at the tea bowl in her hands. She shrugged. Hostility radiated from her.

"Where's Masahiro?"

"In bed asleep."

Her quiet voice was tight, and Sano saw on the surface of her tea the reflected lantern light quivering with the tension of her grip. Silence descended upon them, ominous as a coming storm; the faraway voices of the maids tinkled like wind chimes in a gale.

"How could you arrest her?" Reiko said, still not looking at Sano.

"How could you go to the temple and then to Shinagawa after I told you not to?" Sano said, offended by her discourteous manner and implied criticism of his actions. "You did go, didn't you? That's why you were out so late."

Reiko ignored his questions, but Sano knew he was right. "You didn't even tell me," she said bitterly. "Had I not stopped at my father's house, I wouldn't have known about Haru."

Sano forced down the anger that roiled in him. Although he thought Reiko should accept defeat with grace, he must be generous if he wanted to restore peace. "I'm sorry for not telling you, but I didn't know what was going to happen when I questioned Haru, and afterward, there wasn't time."

"You knew you were going. You could have at least told me that much."

With an effort, Sano ignored the rebuke, and his guilty notion that maybe he'd been unfair to his wife. "Do you know that Haru attacked Hirata and me?"

Reiko nodded, unrelenting.

"It was important to put Haru in jail where she couldn't hurt anyone else," Sano said. "If you'd been there, you would have agreed."

"If I'd been there, it wouldn't have happened!" Now Reiko lifted her furious gaze to Sano and set down her tea bowl.

"You mean you would have prevented her from confessing," Sano said as exasperation overcame his good intentions. "You would have foiled my attempts to get the truth from her. That's why I didn't tell you I was going to interview Haru."

"I beg to disagree," Reiko said with icy politeness. "I would have prevented you from bullying Haru into saying what you wanted her to say. That's what you did, isn't it? And that's the real reason you didn't want me there."

Maybe he had been rough with the girl, Sano thought, but not excessively. "She said plenty on her own. She did her best to direct my suspicion toward Dr. Miwa and Abbess Junketsu-in." Sano described Haru's stories about the doctor threatening Chie and the abbess trying to get rid of the woman.

"I think Haru was telling the truth about them," Reiko said, convinced by her personal knowledge of the pair.

"Haru voluntarily incriminated herself," Sano said. "It was my duty to arrest her."

"Pardon me, but that was no confession." Reiko rose. "You choose to believe so, but . . ." She drew a deep breath in an attempt to calm down, then said in a forced conciliatory tone, "Please don't persecute Haru just because you're angry at me."

"I'm not!" Sano shouted. He stood too, incensed at her suggestion that he would let a marital feud provoke him to accuse someone unfairly. "I'm trying to serve justice, and you're obstructing it!"

"You're rushing to judgment, and I'm trying to save you from a terrible mistake!"

Hirata came into the room, holding a thick, damp cloth pouch over his injured eye. A tearful Midori followed. They watched Sano and Reiko in dismay.

"You will stop trying to sabotage my case by meddling with witnesses as you did at the temple today," Sano said.

"I'm not sabotaging you," Reiko said. "I want justice, too, and I've found information that contradicts what Haru's enemies have said about her. High Priest Anraku says her character is good."

"That's not what he told me," Sano said, recalling his interview with Anraku that afternoon. "When I told him I'd arrested Haru, he said it was for the best and offered whatever help he could provide in concluding the investigation."

Reiko's expression went from shock to disbelief, then grim understanding. She said, "Anraku must have turned against Haru after I talked to him. The Black Lotus is protecting itself by sacrificing Haru. The sect must have committed the crimes, under Anraku's orders."

Her manipulation of logic annoyed Sano. "Either Anraku is a good character witness or he's an evil slanderer. You can't have it both ways. And he didn't seem dangerous. A bit odd, but no more so than many priests."

"You would think differently if you'd seen him with Lady Keisho-in," Reiko said.

"You shouldn't have seen him with Lady Keisho-in. I told you to stay away from her. While I'm trying to protect our family's safety and livelihood, you deliberately endanger us!"

Reiko averted her gaze for an instant. In a swift change of subject, she said, "After leaving the temple, I went to Shinagawa." She described poisoned wells, noxious fumes, a mysterious epidemic, more reported kidnappings, then an explosion and fire in a building owned by the Black Lotus. "Minister Fugatami believes the sect is working up to even more serious trouble. He's going to speak to the Council of Elders tomorrow, and he invited you to attend the meeting."

"That's out of the question," Sano said, appalled that Reiko had again attempted to involve him in Minister Fugatami's crusade. "For me to publicly ally myself with a man of such shaky reputation in the *bakufu* would damage my standing in the shogun's court and strip me of power to accomplish anything at all."

"I beg you to go." Reiko extended her hands to Sano in a gesture of desperate entreaty. "We must stop the Black Lotus's attacks and make sure we find the real killer!"

"I already have found her," Sano retorted. Reiko started to protest, but Sano cut her off: "Whatever facts Minister Fugatami has, he can present them at Haru's trial. We'll have no further discussion."

A patter of footsteps penetrated the lethal atmosphere. Everyone turned as Masahiro trotted through the parlor door. Clad in a blue nightshirt, his hair tousled from sleep, he carried a small wooden container.

"Mama. Papa," he said. Beaming at them, he rattled the contents of the container. "Play!"

"Not now," Sano said.

A nursemaid hurried into the room, murmuring apologies. Reiko said, "Go back to bed, Masahiro-*chan,* that's a good boy."

The maid reached for him, but he scampered away, shrieking, "No! Me stay!"

He stuck his plump little hand inside the container and hurled into the air a fistful of the black and white pebbles used in the game of go. As Reiko and the maid chased Masahiro, begging him to stop, he gleefully pelted them with pebbles. Hirata stepped over to Sano.

"*Sumimasen*—excuse me, but I think you should meet with Minister Fugatami," Hirata said in a low voice that the others wouldn't hear. "If there's the slightest chance that the Black Lotus set the fire and murdered those people, you can't afford to disregard the minister's information until the trial. By then, it will be too late for Haru, if she's innocent. We must examine all the evidence beforehand."

Hirata was right, Sano acknowledged with a reluctant nod. In the Tokugawa legal system, most trials ended in a guilty verdict; persons tried were virtually condemned in advance. Even a wise, fair man like Magistrate Ueda wasn't immune to making errant judgments based on his ingrained faith in tradition. As strongly as he believed her to be the culprit, Sano wanted to ensure a just trial for Haru.

"All right, Masahiro-*chan,* that's enough," Reiko said, lifting her son and hugging him before she handed him to the maid. "Back to bed. Good night."

Watching, Sano saw another reason to meet with Minister Fugatami. He and Reiko and Masahiro were a family, and Sano must hold them together, even if it meant making a concession. After the maid had taken Masahiro away, Sano said to

Reiko, "I'll go to the council meeting tomorrow."

"You will?" Surprise lifted Reiko's voice as she turned to him. She looked as though she wanted to ask why, but feared that questions might change his mind. Then her face lit up with the lovely, radiant smile Sano had missed. "Thank you," she said, bowing with dignified grace.

Sano nodded, hiding mixed feelings. Hope for their marriage cheered him, though he feared they would never agree about Haru.

"Hirata-*san* and I have work to do," Sano told Reiko. He edged toward the door, eager to leave before another argument could start. Besides, he and Hirata did have to talk about how to identify the spy in their midst. "I'll see you later."

"What was that about?" Midori said.

"All is not lost. When my husband talks to Minister Fugatami, I'm sure he'll come around to my point of view." Reiko laughed in exhilaration. The world seemed suddenly bright. "There's still hope of proving the Black Lotus guilty of the crimes."

Midori sighed. "I wish I had some hope. I don't think I'll ever mean to Hirata-*san* what he means to me. You should have seen him flirting with O-hana just now." Her voice trembled, and her eyes teared.

Reiko put a consoling arm around Midori. "What about your plan to pretend you don't care for him? Give it time to work. Don't follow him around like you just did."

"It's no use," Midori said glumly. "I can't help myself. Besides, I'm not fooling Hirata-*san*. When I went into the kitchen, he laughed and said, 'Why do you try so hard to be aloof? I know you like me.' How I wish there were some way to win his love!"

As Midori brooded, Reiko turned her thoughts back to the investigation. "Today Minister Fugatami found many more examples of the Black Lotus hurting people outside the temple," she said, "but there's no one to say what goes on inside the temple because the priests and nuns won't talk. Pious Truth is gone. My husband couldn't find anything when he was there,

and his detectives were caught spying. I'm afraid that unless
he gets definite proof of the sect's wrongdoing, he'll disregard
the accusations against it and continue persecuting Haru. I wish
there were some way to see inside the temple!"

"I could go there and try."

"What?" Reiko stared at Midori, who gazed back at her with
eyes now bright with hope. "You?"

"Why not? It would solve your problem, and mine." Excited, Midori continued, "I'll hang around the temple and watch
the nuns and priests. If I can see bad things happening, the
sōsakan-sama will have to do what you want."

"I'm sorry, but I can't involve you," Reiko said firmly. "The
Black Lotus is too dangerous. I believe they kidnap people,
poison, torture, and kill them." Reiko described what she'd
heard in Shinagawa and from Pious Truth. "If they catch you
spying, there's no telling what they might do."

"Oh, I'd be careful. I wouldn't let them catch me." Daring
and confidence replaced Midori's desolation.

"My husband would never allow it," Reiko said, not wanting
to mention that she didn't think Midori could handle the task.

"He wouldn't have to know until I was done," Midori said.

"Hirata-*san* will get angry at you for doing something his
master wouldn't approve of," Reiko said.

"Looking pretty and acting aloof has gotten me nowhere
with Hirata-*san,* and I don't know what else to do." Midori
flung out her arms in a reckless gesture. "What have I got to
lose?"

"Your life," Reiko said.

Hurt dimmed Midori's expression. "You think I wouldn't
be a good spy, don't you?" Her voice quaked; tears welled in
her eyes. "You think I'm stupid."

"No, of course not," Reiko hastened to assure her.

"Then let me spy on the Black Lotus!"

Reiko was caught in a serious dilemma. Refusal would injure Midori's feelings and ruin their friendship; acquiescence
could put Midori in grave peril. Still, Reiko couldn't help noting the advantage of employing Midori as a spy. She looked
so harmless and ordinary; the Black Lotus would never look
twice at her, let alone guess that she was spying. . . .

Common sense and concern for Midori prevailed over

Reiko's need to know what was happening inside the temple. "Midori-*san*, you must promise me never to go near the temple or anyone associated with the Black Lotus," Reiko said sternly.

When Midori continued pleading, Reiko talked about the sinister people in the sect and all the evil things she believed they had done. At last Midori bowed her head and nodded, stifling sobs. Reiko tasted the bitter knowledge that although she'd made the right choice, the investigation had created bad feelings between herself and yet another person close to her.

22

If there be persons who are clean and spotless as a pure gem,
Diligent, compassionate, and reverent,
Then preach the truth to them.

—FROM THE BLACK LOTUS SUTRA

A brilliant, clear autumn sky arched over the Zōjō district. The morning sun gilded leaves turning yellow and red in the treetops. The warm weather had brought droves of pilgrims who mingled with nuns and priests in the marketplace. At the gate of the Black Lotus Temple, Midori climbed out of the palanquin that had carried her from Edo Castle. Nervous but excited, she hurried into the precinct, clutching the bulky parcel she'd brought. She paused, beholding the sights.

There were certainly more trees and plants than in other temples, but the nuns, priests, and pilgrims strolling the grounds looked normal to Midori, as did the buildings. Children's laughter enlivened the quiet. Probably Reiko had exaggerated the danger to frighten her away from the temple, Midori thought. She felt a pang of disappointment because she'd hoped for a little adventure, and a resurgence of the pain caused her by Hirata and Reiko last night. To them she would always be a handy friend but never worthy of Hirata's love or Reiko's respect . . . unless something changed. And Midori intended that it would. She was going to spy on the Black Lotus whether Hirata and Reiko approved or not. Now she marched over to a pair of nuns who stood outside the main hall.

"Good morning," Midori said, bowing. "I've come to join the nunnery."

Since yesterday she'd struggled with her conscience and decided she must break her promise to Reiko. Although her friend had lectured her on why she shouldn't go to the temple, Midori had discerned how much Reiko wished to have a spy in the sect, and she'd thought of the best way to observe without arousing suspicion. She would show Hirata and Reiko what she could do!

The nuns bowed; one of them said, "You must first be examined by our leaders. Please come with us."

Midori felt a flicker of trepidation as she followed the nuns to the back of the main hall. She had no idea how temples decided whether to admit a prospective nun.

The nuns opened a door in a wing attached to the hall. "Please wait in there," the older nun said.

Midori slipped off her shoes and entered. The door closed. She found herself in a room furnished with a wall niche containing a *butsudan*—a wooden cabinet that held a written passage of Buddhist scripture—before which knelt a plain young woman, chanting prayers in a rapid monotone. She ignored Midori. By the window stood another woman. A few years older than Midori, she was pretty in a coarse way, with pert features, tanned skin, and a watchful expression.

"She wants to show how pious she is," she said, pointing at the praying woman. "Too bad there's no one to see but us."

Midori smiled timidly.

"I'm Toshiko," the other woman said, crossing the room to stand near Midori. "What's your name?"

Midori had thought up an alias: "Umeko."

"So you're joining the nunnery too?" Toshiko's informal

manner and cheap indigo robe marked her as a peasant.

"If they'll have me," Midori said.

Toshiko looked her over, curious. "Why do you want to be a nun?"

The bold queries unsettled Midori, but she was accustomed to speak when spoken to, so she gave the story she'd prepared: "My family wanted me to marry a man I don't like, so I ran away."

"Oh." This common scenario seemed to satisfy Toshiko. "Well, I'm here because my father is poor and I'm the youngest of five daughters. No one will marry me because I have no dowry. It was either this or be a prostitute."

"I'm sorry," Midori said, truly moved by the woman's plight and admiring her matter-of-fact acceptance of it.

The door opened, and a nun entered. She beckoned to the praying woman, who silently rose. They left the room together.

"Think you'll be happy here?" Toshiko said.

"I hope so."

"I hear they're very strict," Toshiko said.

Midori recalled the rumors of starvation, torture, and murder that Reiko had mentioned last night. Earlier, they'd only added thrills to her adventure, but she felt the first stirrings of terror.

As a precaution she'd written a note to Reiko, explaining her plan to join the sect, and left it on Reiko's desk. But what if Reiko didn't find the note? No one would know where Midori was; there would be no one to rescue her if she got in trouble.

"Don't look so scared." Laughing, Toshiko linked arms with Midori. "Stick with me. I'll see you through."

Her friendliness comforted Midori, but soon the nun came for Toshiko, and Midori sat alone, waiting. The fear grew until she felt cold and shaky. She clutched her parcel, glad of something to hold. Wondering what comprised the official examination, she battled the impulse to flee. She thought of how upset Reiko would be if she knew Midori was here. Midori then thought of Hirata.

She stayed.

After what seemed ages, the nun took Midori to a building near the back of the precinct. This was a low wooden structure nearly hidden by trees, with shutters closed over the windows.

Alone, Midori entered a long room where a huge round ceiling lantern burned overhead. Five priests and five nuns were kneeling along opposite walls, and three figures sat upon a dais across the end of the room.

"Kneel beneath the lantern," ordered the big man at the dais's center.

Fluttery with nervousness, Midori obeyed, holding the parcel tight in her lap. She hadn't expected so many people. Although the light focused upon her obscured her vision, she saw that the speaker was a priest with cruel features and a scar above his ear. Reiko had described the sect officials to Midori, and she recognized him as the priest Kumashiro. The ugly man at his right must be Dr. Miwa, and the nun at his left, Abbess Junketsu-in. They looked more frightening than they'd sounded in the safety of Reiko's parlor. The other priests and nuns were nondescript strangers. Stern and foreboding, they all regarded Midori. From elsewhere in the building came the sound of muffled chanting.

"Tell us your name and why you wish to join us," Kumashiro said.

In a thin, quavery voice, Midori related her false story, adding, "I want to devote my life to religion."

"What's that you've brought?" Junketsu-in said. With her elegant robe and head drape and her classic features, she was pretty but somehow sinister.

"It's a kimono." Midori faltered. "A gift for the temple, to pay for my keep."

A nun conveyed the parcel to the dais. Junketsu-in unwrapped the pale green silk garment printed with gleaming bronze phoenixes. "Very nice," she said, laying it by her side.

Midori regretted the sacrifice of her favorite, most expensive kimono for a good cause.

"Serve us tea," Kumashiro said.

A teapot and cups sat on a tray near the dais. Midori resented these commoners for treating the daughter of a daimyo like a servant, but years as a lady-in-waiting had taught her to obey orders. She poured the tea with unsteady hands. When she presented a cup to Priest Kumashiro, the liquid sloshed on his robe.

"Stupid, clumsy girl!" he shouted.

"I'm sorry!" Terrified, Midori fell to her knees and scooted backward. "Please forgive me!"

Embarrassing herself in front of so many people mortified her. Surely they would throw her out.

"Never mind. Go back to your place," Kumashiro said. "We'll ask you questions, and you must answer honestly."

More nervous than ever, Midori knelt under the lantern. During childhood lessons, she'd never been much good at recitation. What if she didn't know the right answers?

"Suppose you were walking alone in Edo and you lost your way," Kumashiro said. "What would you do?"

Such a situation was unfamiliar to Midori, who never walked alone in the city because that was not done by young women of her class. She had never gotten lost or bothered to think what she should do if that calamity befell her. Panic gripped Midori. Quick, quick, what to say?

"I—I guess I would ask someone to help me," she ventured.

As soon as she spoke, it occurred to her that she should have said she would retrace her steps or use landmarks to help her find her way. Inwardly, Midori cursed her stupidity. The watching faces showed no reaction to her answer, but surely they thought she lacked common sense and depended on others to think for her. She clenched her fists, praying to do better on the next question.

"How would you divide three gold coins between yourself and another person?" Kumashiro said.

A resurgence of panic rattled Midori's wits, but she knew she couldn't divide three items evenly between two people. She also knew that courtesy required self-sacrifice.

"I would give two coins to the other person and keep one for myself," she said.

Then she realized that she could exchange the gold coins for coppers and divide those. She would never get into the nunnery this way!

"If a person who was older, wiser, and stronger than you and superior to you in rank gave you an order, what would you do?" Kumashiro asked.

Relief flooded Midori. This was an easy question for a girl conditioned to respect authority. "I would obey."

"What if you were ordered to do something you didn't want to do?"

"It would be my duty to obey anyway," Midori replied promptly.

"What if it meant doing something you thought was wrong?"

Frowning, Midori hesitated while she tried to figure out what answer he wanted. Anxiety knotted her stomach. "I'd obey because I would think that my superior knew what was right or wrong better than I."

"Even if what you were ordered to do was against the law?"

Midori was perspiring, although her hands and feet felt like lumps of ice. She didn't think she should say she would break the law; nor did she want the sect to believe she would rebel against authority.

"Answer," commanded Abbess Junketsu-in.

"I would obey," Midori said, hoping she'd chosen the lesser of two evils.

"Would you obey even if it meant hurting someone?" Kumashiro said.

Hurting them how? Midori wondered in frantic confusion, but she was afraid to ask. Maybe saying no now would make her earlier replies seem untruthful. "Yes," she said uncertainly.

She longed for some indication of how well she'd done so far, but none came. Junketsu-in took up the questioning. "Are you close to your parents?"

Filial piety required that Midori profess loving devotion to the parents she'd supposedly left, and regret for refusing to marry the man they'd chosen for her. She thought that was the correct response. But her real mother had died long ago; her father, Lord Niu, spent most of his time on his provincial estate, and Midori rarely saw him. If she lied, her interrogators might guess.

"No," she said, reluctantly opting for the truth.

The expressions of the assembly remained neutral. "If your parents should need your assistance, would you feel obliged to return home?" Abbess Junketsu-in said.

Lord Niu suffered from madness, and Midori couldn't imagine anything she could do for him. She said, "No," ashamed to appear such an undutiful daughter.

"Have you any brothers or sisters you would miss if you entered the nunnery?" Junketsu-in said.

Midori thought sadly of the older sister murdered, the brother slain after committing treason, and other sisters married and living far away. She couldn't miss them any more than she already did. "No," she said.

"What about friends?"

"No," Midori said. Hopefully, she wouldn't be away from Hirata and Reiko long enough to miss them.

"Suppose that you were all alone, with no place to live and no way to earn your rice," Junketsu-in said. "Then suppose that someone rescued you, sheltered and fed you. How would you feel toward them?"

"I would feel most grateful," Midori said honestly. When her stepmother had banished her from Edo, other members of the family had lacked the power or inclination to help Midori, but *Sōsakan* Sano had brought her back and gotten her a position in Lady Keisho-in's retinue. She would be forever thankful to him, and to Reiko for befriending her.

"How would you repay the favor?"

"I would do whatever I could for them when they needed me." After all, helping Reiko was one reason Midori had come here.

"Would you love them?" Junketsu-in said.

"Yes," Midori said. Sano and Reiko were like family, and she did love them.

"If you'd come to love someone, would you give your life for them?"

"Yes," Midori said with conviction. Honor required such loyal self-sacrifice. And Midori had often dreamed of dying heroically for Hirata.

The impassive façades of the people around her didn't alter, but she sensed moods shifting and the faint draft of breaths simultaneously expelled, as if they'd reached some decision. Hope and dread leapt in Midori. Had she passed or failed the test?

Oh, she knew she'd failed! They were going to say they didn't want her. Now she couldn't even hang around the temple and watch what happened, because the Black Lotus would wonder why she'd stayed. Midori was dying to go home, but she couldn't bear to have Reiko learn that she'd broken a promise and hadn't even learned anything about the sect. She couldn't face Hirata without hope of winning his heart.

"Come with me," said Abbess Junketsu-in. "You shall begin training as a novice in the convent immediately."

Midori gaped in stunned delight. She was in! She bowed to Kumashiro, Junketsu-in, and Dr. Miwa, exclaiming, "Thank you, thank you!"

As Junketsu-in led her away, Midori eagerly anticipated spying on the sect and impressing Reiko and Hirata. She hoped her new friend Toshiko had also been accepted as a novice.

23

He who denounces the Black Lotus
Will be buried beneath stones,
And spend an eternity in hell.

—FROM THE BLACK LOTUS SUTRA

Seated in his office, Sano planned out Haru's trial. He had begun drafting the speech he would make to explain the evidence against the girl, and meant to work until it was time for him to meet with Minister Fugatami and the Council of Elders, when Hirata entered.

"There's a disturbance in Nihonbashi," Hirata said. "A mob of citizens is at war with the Black Lotus sect."

Alarmed, Sano rode to Nihonbashi immediately with Hirata and a squadron of detectives. Crashing noises and angry shouts rang out over the rooftops. Peasants fled the area, while mounted troops galloped toward the site of the unrest. Smoke billowed into the blue sky. Arriving in a neighborhood of car-

pentry workshops, Sano watched from astride his horse as male
commoners wielded clubs, iron poles, and shafts of lumber
against saffron-robed priests. The priests defended themselves
with staffs or bare hands. Shrieking housewives beat brooms
on the backs of nuns.

"Down with the Black Lotus!" shouted the commoners.

An answering refrain arose from the priests, nuns, and an
army of peasant followers who fought back: "Praise the glory
of the Black Lotus! Stop the persecution of innocents!"

Cries of, "Thugs! Criminals! Murderers!" came from both
sides.

The narrow streets were a dense maelstrom of darting,
swinging figures. Children and old folk stood on balconies,
hurling rocks on priests. *Doshin* waded through the mob, sep-
arating combatants and herding them away. Flames and smoke
poured from a storefront. The fire brigade threw buckets of
water on the blaze.

"Merciful gods," Hirata said. "This will destroy the city if
it doesn't stop soon."

Near Sano, a mounted, armor-clad police commander yelled
orders to his men. Sano recognized him as a former colleague.
"*Yoriki* Fukida," he called. "How did this happen?"

The commander turned, shouting, "When the nuns and
priests came begging in the neighborhood this morning, some
carpenters attacked them. The fight turned into a mass brawl.
The crowd set fire to the Black Lotus's building."

"Where are the carpenters now?"

"Over there." The commander pointed down the street.

Sano led his party in the direction indicated. Outside the
gate at the intersection, a *doshin* and assistants stood guard over
four dirty, bruised men who lay on the ground, their wrists and
ankles shackled. Sano and Hirata dismounted. As Hirata looked
the prisoners over, his gaze settled on one with down-turned
eyes and mouth.

"Jiro-*san*," he said in surprised recognition. "You started the
brawl?" The man groaned. Hirata said to Sano, "He's the husband of the murdered woman Chie."

Walking up to the carpenter, Sano smelled a strong odor of
alcohol: Jiro was drunk. "Why did you attack the nuns and
priests?" Sano said.

"Took my wife," Jiro mumbled. "Killed her."

"What about the rest of you?" Hirata asked the other prisoners.

"The Black Lotus took my wife, too!"

"They kidnapped my son!"

"And my daughter!"

More interrogation revealed that hostility toward the sect had been growing worse in the area, and Jiro's attack had ignited a volatile situation.

"I understand your problems, but you shouldn't have taken the law into your own hands," Sano said.

"Jiro-*san,* your wife's death will be avenged," Hirata said, "as soon as we determine who's responsible."

Sano believed he already had. If he'd arrested Haru sooner, she might have already been punished, and perhaps the riot wouldn't have occurred. He accepted a measure of culpability for the violence. However, new doubt shook Sano's certainty that Haru was guilty. That so many people hated the Black Lotus suggested that the sect could indeed be responsible for the murders and arson, as well as kidnappings and torture. For the first time, Sano wondered if Reiko might possibly be right. Hearing Minister Fugatami's report on the Black Lotus might prove crucial to his investigation and not just a favor to Reiko. However, the meeting was several hours away, and he must address the problem caused by his failure to solve the case quickly enough.

"Let's go help break up the riot," he told Hirata and the detectives.

By the time the riot was quelled and Sano reached Edo Castle, the Council of Elders had already convened. He entered the chamber where the five officials sat on the dais and their secretaries knelt at desks by the window.

"My apologies for arriving late," Sano said. Kneeling on the floor before the dais, he bowed.

"This is a private session. You were not scheduled to attend." Senior Elder Makino frowned in disapproval from his place at the center of the dais. "Why are you here?"

"The Honorable Minister of Temples and Shrines invited me," Sano said. Minister Fugatami must have neglected to tell the elders, so they thought Sano was intruding on their meeting. He deplored the gross impropriety he'd inadvertently committed. Where was the minister, anyway? Sano felt extreme annoyance at Fugatami, and at Reiko for getting him into this situation.

"So you are now a comrade of the honorable minister?" Disdain wrinkled Makino's emaciated face. The other elders looked concerned.

"He's a potential witness in my investigation," Sano clarified. Just as he'd feared, his presence signaled that he'd allied himself with a man of shaky reputation, a disadvantage that Makino meant to use against him. "I've come to hear his report on the Black Lotus."

"Are you joining his crusade against the sect?" asked Elder Ohgami Kaoru, usually a supporter of Sano. His manner was cool, as though he wished everyone to forget about their alliance.

"Not at all," Sano said, grimly aware that his name was now linked with Minister Fugatami's, and relationships within the *bakufu* weren't so easily dissolved as Ohgami hoped. "I only want to collect facts from him that may be relevant to my case."

"Well, I fear that you shall be disappointed," Makino said. "We granted Minister Fugatami this meeting he requested, and he has failed to appear."

Dismay struck Sano. Standing up the Council of Elders was a serious breach of courtesy and protocol. "Has the honorable minister sent an explanation?" Sano said.

"He has not," said Makino, and his colleagues fixed disapproving stares on Sano.

"This is an inconvenience to us all," Sano said, vexed at Fugatami for leaving him to take the brunt of the council's ire. The next time Sano asked cooperation from the elders, they would remember this.

"Since you're here, you might as well report on the progress of your investigation," said Makino.

The last thing Sano wanted was to offer up his work for judgment while the elders were in a bad temper, yet he had no choice but to obey. He described his findings, then said, "Yesterday I arrested the girl Haru."

"And it took you how long to make this arrest which you should have made immediately? Four days?" Scorn twisted Makino's voice. "The girl is obviously guilty, yet you've dawdled so much that I think you are more interested in favoring criminals than in upholding the law."

That Makino thought he favored Haru, whom he disliked and believed to be guilty! "In the case of a serious crime, it's important to do a thorough investigation before accusing anyone," Sano said, bristling at the insult to his honor. "And thorough investigations take time."

"You've taken enough time for civil unrest to arise," said Makino. Obviously, he knew about the riot, and blamed Sano for it. "When is the girl's trial?"

"It will be scheduled as soon as I've cleared up a few last details," Sano said.

The elders' faces reflected severe disapproval: The *bakufu* preferred arrests to be quickly followed by punishment. "I presume that those details include Minister Fugatami's findings on the Black Lotus sect," Makino said, disgusted. "Well, that explains the new alliance between you and the honorable minister. He is using you to further his own purposes, while you use him as an excuse to delay justice."

"Justice shouldn't be dispensed without certainty of a suspect's guilt," Sano said, avoiding further discussion about Minister Fugatami. The man's findings had better be genuine and worthwhile to justify the trouble he'd caused Sano. He only hoped Reiko would appreciate his effort to placate her at the expense of his standing with the Council of Elders.

"Minister Fugatami has repeatedly failed to provide any proof of crimes committed by the Black Lotus," Makino said. "His fanatical campaign against the sect has angered its followers within the *bakufu* and offended many other officials. There's a definite possibility that a new minister of temples will soon be appointed."

Makino's meaningful look at Sano clearly implied that when Fugatami went down, Sano would too.

"Now I believe that we've waited long enough for Minister Fugatami," said Makino. "This session is adjourned. *Sōsakan-*

sama, you are dismissed." As Sano bowed in farewell, Makino added, "We do not appreciate people who abuse their authority or waste our time."

"Throw the ball to me, Masahiro-*chan*," Reiko called.

The little boy toddled across the garden, holding the stuffed cloth ball over his head. Laughing, he flung it at Reiko. The ball rose in a brief arc, plopped onto the ground, and rolled a short distance.

"Very good!" Reiko picked up the ball. "Catch!"

She tossed gently. He snatched at and almost caught the ball, then scrambled after it. Reiko smiled. The sun warmed her face, brightened the grass and red maples and pond. She'd missed playing with Masahiro, and in the few days she'd spent away from him, his strength and coordination seemed to have improved. He was growing up so fast! Yet even while Reiko enjoyed being with her son, she worried about Haru in Edo Jail and waited alertly for Sano to return from his meeting with Minister Fugatami and the Council of Elders.

Masahiro ran to the house, calling, "Papa!"

Looking around, Reiko saw Sano standing on the veranda. Anticipation leapt in her. "Oh, good, you're back." She hurried to him, but his grim expression halted her at the foot of the steps. "What's wrong?"

"The husband of the murdered woman attacked some Black Lotus priests and nuns and started a riot. And Minister Fugatami didn't show up at the meeting." Sano lifted Masahiro in his arms, but the smile he gave his son faded as he said to Reiko, "The elders are angry. Makino seized the chance to criticize my handling of the case. Minister Fugatami stands to lose his post, and if Makino exerts his considerable influence with the shogun, I may lose mine, too."

"Oh, no," Reiko said, appalled. "I'm very sorry I got you in trouble."

Sano nodded, acknowledging her fault but unappeased by the apology. "Minister Fugatami has had his chance to talk to me, and demonstrated that he has nothing to say. This will be the last time you meddle in *bakufu* politics."

Alarm constricted Reiko's heart as she realized that Sano had good reason to disregard the minister's information. "I don't believe Minister Fugatami would deliberately miss the meeting," she said. "It was so important to him to report his findings about the Black Lotus to you and the Council of Elders. Something must have prevented him from attending."

"Almost nothing short of death would excuse him," Sano said.

His words filled Reiko with sudden, overwhelming fear. She ran into the house, calling for the maids to summon her palanquin. Sano followed, carrying Masahiro.

"Where are you going?" Sano asked.

"To Minister Fugatami's house." In her chamber, Reiko threw on a cloak. "I have to know what went wrong."

Sano set down Masahiro, who ran off down the corridor. "Whatever did, I've already made it clear that I want nothing to do with the man, and your visiting him again will only further the connection."

"I won't see him. I'll ask his wife what happened."

"Just leave the matter alone." Sano blocked the door.

In desperation, Reiko said, "The Black Lotus retaliates against people who make trouble for them. Do you remember how the nurse Chie's husband was attacked after he tried to get her back from the temple? I'm afraid it's Minister Fugatami's turn now."

Sano's expression sharpened. "I'll go with you."

Whether her conviction had struck a chord of response in him, or he merely realized he couldn't stop her and wanted to control her behavior at the Fugatami house, all that mattered to Reiko was getting there.

"The Honorable Minister isn't receiving guests today," said the sentry stationed in the guardhouse at the Fugatami estate.

"Is he home?" Sano stood with Hirata and two detectives at the guardhouse window, while Reiko waited in her palanquin nearby. Now that he'd had time to think, Sano was sorry he'd let Reiko's panic influence him. Probably nothing had happened to Minister Fugatami, except that he'd reconsidered his crusade against the Black Lotus. Still angry at Fugatami, Sano hoped to ascertain his condition without personal contact.

"Yes, but he gave strict orders that he's not to be disturbed," said the sentry.

"Is all well with the Honorable Minister?" Hirata asked.

"He was fine yesterday evening, when I last saw him."

Reiko whispered to Sano, "We have to see for ourselves!"

Her insistence annoyed Sano; reluctantly, he addressed the sentry: "I'm here on official business for the shogun, and I order you to let us see Minister Fugatami."

"Very well."

The sentry summoned a guard who ushered Sano's party into the courtyard, where Reiko climbed out of the palanquin. Samurai retainers loitered outside the barracks, but when the party entered the mansion, it seemed strangely quiet.

"Where is everyone?" Sano asked the guard as they all walked down the dim corridor.

"The Honorable Minister's top retainers went off somewhere." The guard peered uneasily into vacant offices and reception rooms. "His servants should be here. I don't know why they're not."

Sano heard a murmur of distress from Reiko, walking behind him with the detectives. Beside him, Hirata frowned. A bad feeling tingled Sano's nerves. "You've seen your master today?"

"No," said the guard.

"Are you sure the family is here?"

"No one has seen them leave."

They turned a corner into the private quarters of the mansion. On a sliding paper wall ahead to the left, maroon streaks like spattered paint appeared. Sano looked down and saw dark footprints in the hall. Alarm seized him. He hurried to the open door. The fetid, metallic odor of blood assailed him. He saw a man lying on the futon, and a woman sprawled on the floor, limbs askew. Their throats had been cut, and blood had drenched their faces, hair, robes, the bedclothes, tatami, and walls. Horrified, Sano turned abruptly.

"Reiko-*san*! Don't look!" he ordered.

Too late. She was right behind Sano; she'd already seen the room. Her open mouth drew a deep, wheezing gasp, and she swayed. Sano dragged her away from the door. He held her, pressing her face against his chest. Hirata, the detectives, and the Fugatami guard looked inside the chamber; exclamations rose from them.

"Master!" the guard cried.

Sano experienced nausea and revulsion at the spectacle of violent death, but his detective instincts focused his mind on the work he must do. Still holding Reiko, he turned for a more thorough look into the chamber. Now he noticed that a quilt covered Minister Fugatami up to his shoulders. The woman had cuts on her arms and hands, as if from defending herself against a blade.

Reiko struggled in Sano's arms, crying, "Hiroko-*san*! Hiroko-*san*!"

"She's dead." Sano held Reiko tighter. "There's nothing you can do for her." He said to his men, "Secure the estate. Nobody leaves." He must find out who had done this terrible thing, and why.

"The Black Lotus killed them!" Pulling out of Sano's grasp, Reiko pointed into the room. "Look!"

On the wall above the futon, drawn in the spattered blood, was a crude representation of the Black Lotus symbol. Reiko stumbled down the corridor.

"The children," she moaned. "Merciful gods, where are the children?"

24

There will be many people who will speak ill of us,
They will address the rulers and high ministers,
Seeking to defile and banish us,
But we shall endure.

—FROM THE BLACK LOTUS SUTRA

"Minister Fugatami's two small sons are missing. We searched the estate and the entire official quarter, but found no sign of them," Sano told the shogun.

They were walking along a path through the shogun's private garden. After Sano had finished examining the crime scene and questioning the Fugatami household, he had taken Reiko home, then come to the palace for an emergency audience with the shogun. He'd already reported the murders; now, he needed the shogun to approve the course of action he deemed necessary.

"That is most, ahh, unfortunate." The shogun wore white martial arts practice clothes for his afternoon exercise routine.

As he puffed, marched, and swung his arms, attendants trailed him, carrying towels and a water jug.

"I've determined what happened," Sano said. "Last night, Minister Fugatami's three top retainers ordered the staff out of the house and dismissed the servants. Later, they sneaked into the mansion, which was deserted except for the family. They cut Minister Fugatami's throat while he lay asleep. His wife tried to run away, but the retainers killed her. All Minister Fugatami's papers are gone, and there was a large amount of ash in the kitchen stove, which suggests that the retainers burned the papers there, before they took the children and left."

"What a deplorable breach of loyalty," lamented the shogun. "And how, ahh, shocking that murder should be committed right here in Edo Castle! Are you sure the minister's retainers are to blame?"

"They arranged for the family to be alone. According to the patrol guards, those retainers were the only people to enter the house, and now they're missing."

The shogun frowned in puzzlement as he did a series of jumps. "How did they get the, ahh, children out of the castle?"

"The Fugatami gate sentry says they left the estate around midnight, carrying a large chest," Sano said. "The children must have been inside it. The retainers are trusted officials, and the castle guards let them through the checkpoints without inspecting the chest."

"Security must be improved," said the shogun, bending to touch his toes. "See to it at once."

"Yes, Your Excellency," Sano said, "but the major problem is the Black Lotus." The murder of the Fugatami had convinced him that Reiko's suspicions about the sect were justified and he must act before anyone else could be hurt. "I believe the retainers painted a Black Lotus symbol on the walls because they're members of the sect. I believe they assassinated Minister Fugatami to stop his crusade against them, then destroyed his papers so there would be no incriminating evidence left. I also believe they and the children are now hidden in the temple, where the sect is preparing to create much worse trouble."

Straightening, Tokugawa Tsunayoshi looked closely at Sano, then gave a nervous laugh. "Surely you are not serious?"

"I am," Sano said, though aware that the scenario would

have once sounded preposterous to himself. "That's why I must ask you to order all activities at the Black Lotus Temple to cease and the residents arrested while I conduct a thorough investigation of all the sect's followers and properties."

Worry creased the shogun's forehead. "Ahh . . ." He signaled to an attendant, who gave him a drink of water. "I cannot believe that a Buddhist order would do such terrible things," he fretted. "Indeed, my honorable mother has developed a great, ahh, enthusiasm for High Priest Anraku. She plans to become his disciple, and I know she would not associate herself with a sect that is as bad as you claim."

If only Reiko had not taken Lady Keisho-in to the temple. The shogun trusted his mother's judgment; he rarely opposed her, and anyone who did risked offending him.

"Anraku is a skillful trickster who can take in even the wisest persons," Sano said, recalling how he himself had been fooled by the priest. He should have listened to Reiko, who'd perceived Anraku's true nature. "The Honorable Lady Keisho-in is in grave danger."

"Surely my mother would know if she were." Annoyance soured the shogun's expression. "Do you dare challenge her wisdom?"

"Not at all," Sano said calmly, while panic shot through him. "I just want to protect her and other good, innocent citizens from harm by the sect."

"She is, ahh, not the only member of my regime who follows the way of the Black Lotus," the shogun retorted, sweaty and flustered with ire now. A nervous attendant blotted his face with a towel. "There are many who accept High Priest Anraku as their, ahh, spiritual guide. They have expressed to me their disapproval of Minister Fugatami. They would not appreciate your continuing his persecution of the sect."

Sano was alarmed to learn that the Black Lotus had supporters in high positions close to the shogun. "May I ask who these people are?"

Tokugawa Tsunayoshi's face took on a queasy look, as if he'd said too much for his own good and wanted someone to rescue him. When no one did, he huffed, "You may not ask."

Yet Sano deduced that the high-ranking Black Lotus supporters had to be members of the Tokugawa branch clans, which controlled large landholdings and wielded much political influence. Some of these Tokugawa daimyo were strong personalities who intimidated the shogun, although he would never admit it. The Black Lotus's power had spread too wide and high, and Sano guessed how this had happened.

Chamberlain Yanagisawa normally discovered and neutralized such threats to his own power with great efficiency, but he was away on his provincial inspection tour. Perhaps his affair with *Yoriki* Hoshina had distracted him from politics, and he'd forgotten to watch his back. The old Yanagisawa would never have allowed a religious order to develop so much influence, yet even now, he wouldn't ignore the Black Lotus situation. If he knew about it, he would disband the sect. With a sharp sense of irony, Sano wished his former enemy were here.

Then a disturbing thought occurred to Sano. Maybe there were secrets that even Yanagisawa with all his spies didn't know, and forces stronger than the powerful chamberlain. Sano realized for the first time how much the stability of the nation depended on Yanagisawa, and fear chilled him. If Yanagisawa couldn't control the Black Lotus, who could?

"I will not treat the Black Lotus as you advise," said the shogun. "That would be a blasphemy against Buddhism. The temple shall be allowed to continue its business."

Determined to counteract the influence of the sect's supporters, Sano said, "We must capture the men who murdered Minister Fugatami and his wife. The temple is the obvious place to begin looking for the killers and the missing children. Therefore, I need permission to search it and interrogate everyone there as potential accomplices."

"Well, ahh . . ." As the shogun hesitated, his face took on a look of labored concentration. "Probably Minister Fugatami's retainers killed him for, ahh, personal reasons, and afterward, they, ahh, painted Black Lotus symbols on the walls because they knew he was an enemy of the sect and wanted to cast suspicion upon it."

Sano thought it more likely that the symbols had been left at the murder scene because High Priest Anraku wanted to take credit for the crime and thereby warn his enemies what would happen to anyone who crossed him. And if the sect members' faith in their own power had convinced them that they were above the law, they wouldn't fear the consequences of implicating themselves in a crime.

"Perhaps they fled to the countryside, planning to ransom the children later," the shogun continued. "You had better, ahh, mount a nationwide manhunt rather than focus on the temple."

His rejoinder had an artificial tone as well as an uncharacteristic craftiness, and Sano had seen that same look on the faces of Kabuki actors trying to remember their lines. Sano realized that the shogun had already been informed about the murders, by someone who'd coached him on what to think and say. The efficiency with which the Black Lotus had moved to protect itself daunted Sano.

"There have been poisonings, kidnappings, attacks, and an explosion connected with the Black Lotus," Sano said. He described what Reiko and Hirata had learned. "Sentiment against the Black Lotus is widespread. The public attacked some priests and nuns this morning. To prevent further violence, the sect's activities should be halted and the members confined at least until I can find out what they're planning."

The shogun waved his hand in a dismissive gesture. "Enemies of the Black Lotus are spreading false rumors that have, ahh, incited violence." Again he spoke in that artificial tone. Then he gave an irritated sigh and signaled to an attendant, who handed him a sword. "Your persistence in denouncing the Black Lotus grows tiresome. You are spoiling my exercise."

Aware that he trod a hazardous path between the shogun's esteem and disfavor, Sano said, "My apologies, Your Excellency. I only wish to serve you. And unless I'm granted control over the Black Lotus, I may not be able to solve the mystery of the fire and murders at the temple as you've ordered me to do." Sano saw his path edging the brink of peril. Even a hint that he might fail in his work could turn Tokugawa Tsunayoshi against him, yet he had to demonstrate that what seemed like insubordination was really his commitment to duty. "I believe that a thorough investigation of the Black Lotus will reveal facts that we ignore at the risk of endangering society."

Holding the sword out before him, the shogun squatted; his knees creaked. "I, ahh, had the impression that you'd already identified the culprit. Haven't you arrested that girl?"

News had reached him fast; again Sano perceived the hand

of the Black Lotus at work. The shogun usually forgot things told him, and the fact that he'd retained this information attested to the sect's ability to plant notions in his weak mind.

"Yes, I have," Sano admitted.

"Then your work is done," the shogun said. He performed awkward lunges with his sword. "Arrange the girl's, ahh, trial as soon as possible. Stay away from the temple and its residents."

Without access to the temple, Sano would never learn the truth about the sect. With the Black Lotus protected from official scrutiny, he feared more murders, worsening unrest. Desperate, Sano sought a way to change the shogun's mind.

"Some of the sect members are needed to testify at the trial," he said. "Abbess Junketsu-in, Dr. Miwa, and Priest Kumashiro are important character witnesses, and two orphan girls have placed Haru at the crime scene. The law allows Haru the right to face her accusers."

"Then I revoke her right." Stabbing the air, Tsunayoshi tripped. "You may present the, ahh, testimony yourself. I shall order Magistrate Ueda to convict Haru and condemn her to death. Her execution will silence the, ahh, rumors against the Black Lotus and calm the public."

"But it won't stop whatever schemes the Black Lotus has set in motion." Throwing aside caution, Sano dropped to his knees before the shogun. If only he'd heeded Reiko's concerns earlier, he might have persuaded Tsunayoshi to act before the sect got to him. "Please, I beg you to reconsider and shut down the Black Lotus before it's too late!"

"The only schemes are in your, ahh, imagination," the shogun said peevishly. "I will hear no more of your slander. Stay away from the Black Lotus, or you shall be sorry."

He slashed a sudden, horizontal cut at Sano. The blade whistled so close over Sano's head that he felt the air current across his scalp. The attendants gasped, and Sano froze. He knew the shogun had meant to miss him, but Tsunayoshi was such an inept swordsman that he might have injured or killed Sano by accident. The tacit threat terrified Sano.

"Go now," ordered the shogun. "Vex me no more."

25

If you should be thrown into a pit of fire,
The Bodhisattva of Infinite Power will change the fire to water.
If you are pursued by evil men,
The Bodhisattva will defend you.

—FROM THE BLACK LOTUS SUTRA

Three novice monks knelt in a row in Dr. Miwa's secret underground chamber. "Praise the glory of the Black Lotus," they chanted in rapid, breathless unison. Their young faces wore beatific expressions; their glazed eyes reflected images of High Priest Anraku, who stood before them.

"Your service shall be rewarded with the enlightenment you crave," Anraku said. With a radiant smile, he laid his hand upon the head of each monk in turn. They gasped in delight and chanted faster.

Across the room, Dr. Miwa watched from beside the workbench that held the lamps, stove, dishware, utensils, and jars of herbs and potions for his experiments. He could almost feel the

spiritually charged touch of Anraku's hand and craved its blessing for himself. Somehow, Anraku always looked more real to
Dr. Miwa than did anyone else. His luminosity eclipsed Kumashiro and Junketsu-in, who hovered like dim shadows on
either side of him. Now, as Anraku turned toward him, Dr.
Miwa trembled with the dread and gladness that his master's
attention always inspired.

"So you have finally developed the right formula?" Anraku
asked.

"Yes, I believe that one of these potions will achieve the
effects you desire." Dr. Miwa pointed to three ceramic bottles
on the workbench. Sweat broke out on him, and his breath
whistled through his teeth. He saw revulsion on Kumashiro's
and Junketsu-in's faces, and he despised his uncontrollable nervous tics. His hands fumbled, assembling three cups. "I shall
test the potions now."

"The formula must work," Anraku said, his voice hard with
determination. "My vision has shown me that three signs will
herald the day of our destiny. Two of the signs have already
come to pass. The first was the sacrifice of burnt human offerings—the fire and deaths at the cottage. The second sign was
the onset of persecution against the Black Lotus faith today.
The third sign will be the siege of the temple." Anraku extended his arms, welcoming the event. His single eye shone.
"Our time draws near."

The novices chanted louder. Junketsu-in gazed at Anraku
with reverent bliss. Kumashiro stood silent and stern, his hand
on his sword. Dr. Miwa tried to open his senses to the divine
truths that Anraku perceived. He heard pulsing bellows, the
ringing axes from tunnels under excavation; he smelled rancid
steam from adjoining rooms of his chamber. But supernatural
awareness evaded him. He must rely on Anraku for knowledge.

"We must be ready for battle." Anraku leveled a fierce stare
upon Dr. Miwa. "Your success is crucial to our fate."

Dr. Miwa quaked under the pressure to perform well. Most
Black Lotus members believed that Anraku foretold the future,
and that what he prophesied would happen as a natural result
of cosmic forces in action. But his highest officials knew he
didn't trust in the cosmos to do what it should. He depended
on the efforts of mortals to ensure the desired outcome of en-

lightenment, power, and glory for himself and the sect.

"I promise I won't fail you," Dr. Miwa mumbled.

With shaking hands he poured a few drops of dark, murky liquid from the first bottle into a cup. He filled the cup with water, stirred the mixture, then carried it to the novice monks. Still chanting, they lifted eager faces to him. Dr. Miwa held the cup to the mouth of a novice, a skinny boy of fourteen whose wide eyes burned with faith. The boy gulped the draft.

"Praise the glory of the Black Lotus," he said, grimacing at the bitter taste. He and his comrades had been trained to do whatever Anraku expected, at whatever cost to themselves.

Anraku, Junketsu-in, Kumashiro, and Miwa waited silently for the potion to take effect. Dr. Miwa clenched his fists so hard that his nails dug into his palms. In his mind echoed a desperate prayer: *Please let it work this time!* He could not survive another failure in a life notable for failure.

The circumstances of his origin had set the stage for later difficulties. He'd been born the youngest and weakest of four sons, to a grocer in the city of Kamakura. The family business wasn't rich enough to support all the offspring, so Miwa had been apprenticed at age ten to a local physician who treated patients around the city, ran a small pharmacy, and already had other apprentices. Miwa, a sad, homesick outcast from his family, soon found himself an outcast in his new situation.

His two fellow apprentices were older boys, and not pleased to share the training, meager food, and humble shelter that the physician provided. Saburō and Yoshi immediately ganged up against Miwa. They mocked his homeliness and beat him. They gave him the worst tasks, like cooking the foul-smelling bear bile. Miwa, too weak to fight back, concentrated on learning the diagnosis and treatment of diseases, the medicinal herbs and potions. He showed off his knowledge during the lessons, hoping to impress his master and put his tormenters in a bad light. However, his efforts backfired.

The physician was a childless widower who aspired to wealth and prestige but achieved neither. He favored Saburō and Yoshi as if they were his sons, and rebuked Miwa constantly.

"Stop acting as if you're better than everyone else," he said. "It's disgusting, and you look a mess. Clean yourself up."

Miwa tried, but he had a remarkable affinity for grime. It stained his clothes, blackened his fingernails, and erupted in pimples on his face. Resentment toward his master and the apprentices festered in him. He swore that one day he would be a great doctor, yet his problems worsened. Medical study required treating the sick under a physician's supervision, but patients disliked him, and his master curtailed Miwa's practical training for fear of losing business. Miwa finished his apprenticeship at age twenty, with much theoretical knowledge and a chest of medicines, but little experience. When he set up his practice, only the poorest, sickest people hired him, for a pittance; he sought wealthy patrons, but found none. Lacking money and personal charm, he couldn't attract a wife or even a mistress; his sexual life consisted of encounters with prostitutes who serviced him in exchange for medical treatment. His belief in his brilliance sustained him through lean years. Eventually, he decided to move to Edo, in the hope that his career would flourish in a bigger city.

Along the way, his baggage and medicine chest were stolen. He arrived in Edo a pauper and wandered the streets seeking work with pharmacists and doctors. No one wanted him. He spent his nights sleeping under bridges and his days begging alms, growing dirtier and uglier as months passed. Then one morning he stopped at a pharmacy and overheard a conversation between a customer and the proprietor. The customer wanted rhinoceros-horn pills—a powerful, expensive aphrodisiac—but the proprietor said he had none because supplies from India were low. Desperation inspired Miwa.

"I can provide some," he said.

After he and the pharmacist struck a deal, Miwa went off and gathered pebbles, then caught a stray cat and pulled out some of its fur. He mixed the fur with mud, molded it around the pebbles, and coated them with gray paint he stole from an artisan's workshop. The pharmacist paid him a large sum for the fake rhinoceros-horn pills. Soon Miwa had a thriving business selling the aphrodisiac, and enough money to rent lodgings. He planned to quit as soon as he could finance his medical practice.

However, his customers began complaining that the pills didn't work. When the police came to his lodgings to arrest

him, they found shaved cats in cages, a supply of paint and
pebbles, and Miwa assembling more pills. The magistrate convicted Miwa of fraud and ordered him to refund his customers'
money, but he'd already spent it on medical equipment, so he
was sentenced to three months in jail.

Now, as Dr. Miwa stood in his underground chamber, the
specter of past misfortunes hovered near. If he failed this time,
he would suffer worse punishment than jail. He anxiously
watched the novice who'd drunk the potion. The novice kept
chanting, his voice still strong and his eyes bright; he showed
no physical change.

"Enough time has passed. Your formula is no good," Priest
Kumashiro said, sneering at Dr. Miwa.

"How disappointing," Abbess Junketsu-in murmured with a
quick, nasty smile.

"What seems to be the problem?" Cold fury lurked beneath
Anraku's quiet voice.

"The formula works at full strength," Dr. Miwa said defensively. His hatred of Kumashiro and Junketsu-in almost overwhelmed his fear of Anraku. They were like the two
apprentices, always needling him, always savoring his defeats.
Junketsu-in was mistress to Anraku, and Kumashiro held the
coveted post of second-in-command; thus, they both outranked
Dr. Miwa, whose medical skill was his only advantage over
them. "The low concentration is the problem. But I'm sure the
next formula will work."

An impatient gesture from Anraku signaled for him to proceed. Dr. Miwa hastily poured liquid from the second bottle,
added water, and fed the potion to another novice. He must
please Anraku. He must repay the debt he owed the high priest.

After serving two months in jail, Miwa had begun dreading
his release. His fraud had ruined his reputation; he couldn't
practice medicine in Edo. How would he earn a living? He
mourned the waste of his brilliant talent. Then one day, while
he was emptying slop buckets, a guard came to him and said,
"Someone has bought your freedom. You can go."

It was Anraku who'd repaid Miwa's customers, Anraku who
met him outside the prison gate.

"Why did you do this?" Dr. Miwa said, distrusting the
priest's good looks, and motives.

Anraku smiled. "You are a physician of great genius. I value your talents as the world cannot."

The words were a healing elixir to Miwa's wounded pride. Grateful, yet still suspicious, he said, "How do you know about me?"

"I see all. I know all." Anraku spoke with convincing simplicity; his one-eyed gaze pierced Miwa's spirit.

"What do you want from me in return?" Miwa said, beginning to fall under the priest's spell.

"My temple requires a physician. I have chosen you."

Anraku had taken Dr. Miwa to the Black Lotus Temple, newly constructed at that time, nine years ago. He gave Dr. Miwa a hospital, nurses, and authority over the medical treatment of the temple's growing population. The post brought Dr. Miwa the respect and recognition long denied him. He worshipped Anraku as his god. However, medical training had taught him the skill of scientific observation, and soon he understood the inner workings of the kingdom his god had created.

He believed in Anraku's supernatural vision, but he learned that the high priest had many spies conveying knowledge to him. These spies were followers and paid informers throughout Japan. They had reported on Miwa and identified him as potentially useful to the sect. Miwa discovered that he wasn't the only person recruited this way. Anraku scouted society's criminals and had found Kumashiro, Junketsu-in, and many of his senior priests among them. Dr. Miwa also learned how Anraku bound these wayward individuals to him.

They, like Miwa, were in desperate straits. Anraku determined what each person desired, then provided it in exchange for loyal obedience. These recruits became dependent upon him. He was all things to all people—guide, father, lover, tyrant, son, judge, savior. Because the Black Lotus Sutra said there was an infinite number of paths to enlightenment, elite disciples such as Dr. Miwa could pursue destiny however they liked. Not until they'd severed all ties with normal society and morality did they discover the dark side of their paradise: Anraku's intolerance toward anyone who didn't perform the duties he expected of his disciples.

Within two years of his arrival at the temple, Dr. Miwa was

dividing his time between the hospital and the subterranean laboratory. Aboveground, he treated the sick; below, he worked on experiments for the Black Lotus's day of destiny and tortured disobedient sect members. He found that causing pain aroused him sexually. He could never return to normal life because the temple was the only place where he could have everything he needed. But now the specter of the monk Pious Truth shadowed his memory. Dr. Miwa knew he was not exempt from similar treatment, should he displease Anraku. He watched the novices, all of them healthy and robust, and he couldn't bear to wait and see if the second formula worked.

"I shall test the last formula now," he said.

Under the daunting scrutiny of his colleagues, Dr. Miwa mixed the potion and took it to the third novice. He was fifteen years old, plump with baby fat. He drained the cup, exclaiming, "Praise the glory of the Black Lotus!"

Suddenly his face flushed crimson. His eyes became wide and blank; he swayed. His words blurred into an incoherent babble.

"The formula is working," Dr. Miwa said, filled with relief and jubilation.

The novice began shaking violently. While his comrades chanted, he retched, vomiting bile. Its sour stench tainted the air. He collapsed in a fit of convulsions.

"I see the Buddha. I see the truth," he murmured. Awe veiled his gaze. He gave a final shudder, then lay still. Dr. Miwa crouched, examined the novice, and looked up at Anraku. "He's dead."

Anraku beamed, illuminating the room as if the sun had penetrated the earth. "Good work," he said. Kumashiro nodded in grudging approval; jealousy narrowed Junketsu-in's eyes. "We shall be well prepared to meet our destiny."

Anraku glided soundlessly from the laboratory. At Dr. Miwa's orders, the surviving novices carried the corpse away to the crematorium. Their chanting faded down the tunnel. Kumashiro and Junketsu-in lingered.

"Congratulations," Kumashiro said to Dr. Miwa in a sardonic voice. "It seems you're good for something besides gratifying yourself with other people's pain."

How like Kumashiro to spoil his triumph, Miwa thought

bitterly as the priest left the room. Kumashiro was like Commander Oyama. The commander had been another arrogant, forceful man who enjoyed tormenting the weak. He'd come to the temple seeking a spiritual remedy for stomach pains, and Dr. Miwa had cured him, but Oyama gave the credit to Anraku while mocking Miwa and treating him as a mere lackey. Miwa rejoiced that Oyama had been punished for his cruel ingratitude. If only Kumashiro would die, too.

Abbess Junketsu-in said snidely, "Lucky for you that the formula worked. Anraku-*san* told me yesterday that after what happened in Shinagawa, he would give you one more chance, and if you failed again . . ."

Arching her painted brows, she let the unspoken threat hang in the air. Dr. Miwa gazed at her in helpless fury. She always flaunted her intimacy with Anraku and aggravated Miwa's insecurities. He despised her even more than he did Kumashiro because he wanted her so badly.

"Shinagawa was just an experiment," Dr. Miwa huffed. "Trial and error are necessary to scientific progress." He busied himself arranging jars of chemicals on his workbench. "You will please leave. I have things to do."

"Indeed. Your other formulas aren't working out very well, are they? Especially the one that exploded accidentally and destroyed Anraku's temple in Shinagawa." Junketsu-in laughed, then sidled near Dr. Miwa. "Why do you pretend you don't like me when we both know better?"

He smelled her musky perfume, felt the warmth of her body. Hot, unwelcome desire suffused him. Memories of other times like this roiled in his mind. Working day after day with Nurse Chie, he'd longed for her even as he saw revulsion in her eyes. She, like Junketsu-in, had aroused him without any intention of satisfying his longings. Now Junketsu-in raised her hand to his face and brushed her sleeve against his cheek.

"Be nice to me, and maybe I'll put in a good word for you with Anraku-*san*," she said, tittering.

She wouldn't touch her bare skin to him, not even to tease! The insult enraged Miwa. Chie hadn't wanted physical contact with him, either; she'd repelled his advances. She'd also threatened him and the whole sect. She, like Oyama, had deserved to die. Dr. Miwa's anger exploded.

"Leave me alone!" he shouted, lashing out his arm and knocking Junketsu-in aside. His breath hissed furiously as he picked up a jar from the workbench. "Go away, or I'll throw this acid in your face. You'll be uglier than I, and Anraku won't want you anymore. If you don't stop tormenting me, I'll tell the *sōsakan-sama* that you hated Chie and killed her."

The fear in Junketsu-in's eyes gratified him. She fled the laboratory, and Dr. Miwa clutched the edge of his workbench, breathing hard, trying to calm his temper. To succeed in his task and keep the position and respect he'd worked so hard to gain, he must control himself. He could not, and would not, fail again.

26

He of the true, clear gaze,
The gaze of great and perfect understanding,
Is a sun of wisdom dispelling all darkness.
He shall quell the wind of misfortune,
And everywhere bring pure light.

—FROM THE BLACK LOTUS SUTRA

Reiko sat in the round, sunken tub in the bathchamber, submerged up to her neck. She'd opened the window and lit lamps around the room; the hot water steamed in the cool breeze and reflected wavering flames. Sick horror still knotted her stomach, though hours had passed since she'd seen the corpses of the Fugatami; her mind continuously revisited the bloody scene. When Sano entered the chamber, she looked up at him with eyes swollen and sore from weeping.

"I keep thinking about Hiroko and Minister Fugatami," she said in a ragged voice. "This is the third bath I've taken since I left that house, but I still don't feel clean."

"I understand," Sano said gently. "The aura of death always lingers."

He stripped off his clothes. Crouching on the slatted wooden floor, he poured a bucket of water over himself, then washed his body with a bag of rice-bran soap. His vigorous scrubbing bespoke his own desire for purification.

"This afternoon I went to tell Hiroko's father what happened." Sorrow welled inside Reiko as she remembered how the dignified old man had tried to hide his grief over Hiroko's death and his anxiety about his missing grandsons. She wondered guiltily whether her contact with Minister Fugatami had somehow triggered the murders.

"Thank you for sparing me the task," Sano said, his expression bleak and strained as he washed his hair.

"What happened with the shogun?" Reiko asked.

"He refused to shut down the sect. He ordered me to stay away from the temple."

"Oh, no. What are you going to do?"

"What can I do but obey orders?" Sano said unhappily. He rinsed himself, then climbed into the tub. The water shifted and rose around Reiko as he sat opposite her. "I'll look for evidence outside the temple that will convince the shogun to change his mind. And I've sent a message to Chamberlain Yanagisawa, explaining the situation and asking him to come back to Edo. I think he'll consider the Black Lotus problem serious enough to deserve his attention."

Reiko was both glad and alarmed that Sano had taken the major step of summoning Yanagisawa, but feared that the chamberlain might not return in time to prevent a disaster. "At least some good has come of Minister Fugatami's death," she said. "You finally believe he was right about the Black Lotus." That she and Sano were at last on the same side comforted Reiko. "And Haru can be released from jail," Reiko added, now more certain than ever that the sect was guilty, which argued in favor of the girl's innocence. "She can't go back to the temple, so we'll have to find a place for her to live."

Then Reiko noticed a disturbed look on Sano's face. "What's wrong?" she said.

"Haru isn't going anywhere." Sano's tone was cautious yet decisive. "She's staying right where she is."

"But you can't keep her locked up when the case against her has weakened so much." Reiko couldn't believe she'd heard him right.

Sano shook his head. He inhaled deeply as if mustering the energy for an argument he'd hoped to avoid. "What happened today doesn't clear Haru."

"You agree that the sect killed Minister Fugatami and attacked people in Shinagawa. Isn't it logical that they also killed Commander Oyama, Chie, and the child?"

"Logical," Sano said, "but not certain. That the Black Lotus is evil doesn't necessarily mean Haru is good. Whatever the sect has done, my case against Haru remains the same."

"Then you're still sure she's guilty?" Incredulity jolted Reiko. "You still intend that she should be tried for the crimes?"

"I do," Sano said.

His expression was regretful, but Reiko heard the finality in his voice. The steaming water around them seemed to grow cold as she realized that she and Sano weren't on the same side after all. He was still in danger of condemning the wrong person, ruining his honor, and letting killers escape justice.

"Minister Fugatami probably died because he knew too much about the Black Lotus and was a danger to the sect," Reiko said. "I think the same conditions apply to Haru, Commander Oyama, and Nurse Chie. They must have seen and heard things inside the temple. High Priest Anraku decided he couldn't trust them to keep his secrets. He had Oyama and Chie murdered, then framed Haru so she would die too."

"I understand how much you want to believe that," Sano said, "but there's no proof."

Reiko perceived obstinacy beneath his gentle tone. She drew up her knees, avoiding contact with him. "Have you asked Haru what she knows of the sect's business?" When Sano shook his head, Reiko said, "Neither have I, because I didn't have the chance. Maybe if we go to the jail and ask her now, she'll give us information that will clear her and persuade the shogun to let you investigate the Black Lotus."

A current rippled the water as Sano folded his arms. "I'll not give Haru another opportunity to invent tales about other people or pretend she doesn't know what she did the night before the fire. I don't trust her to tell the truth about the Black Lotus, so I won't bother asking."

"That's unfair," Reiko said, angry now. "Haru deserves a chance to save herself, especially since the Fugatami murder is evidence in her favor."

Temper flared in Sano's eyes. "She's had plenty of chances to tell a better story about what happened to her. She'll get another chance at her trial. And I've been more than fair to her—and to you—at my own expense. I put off arresting Haru so I could check out all the possible leads. My hesitancy gave Senior Elder Makino the means to destroy my reputation. I've also delayed Haru's trial so I could hear Minister Fugatami's report on the Black Lotus, as you wished. The shogun has ordered me to convene the trial, and I intend to do so before he can punish me for disobedience. Haru is guilty, and I shall welcome her conviction."

Discord seemed to saturate the water like foul poison. Suddenly Reiko could no longer bear to stay near Sano. Rising, she climbed out of the tub in a cascade of dripping water.

"Reiko-*san,* wait," Sano said.

She heard anguish in his voice but ignored his plea. There was nothing more to say that would alter his opinion or hers. Reiko snatched a cloth from a shelf and swathed her wet body. She hurried out of the room and down the hall to her chamber. Shivering with cold and agitation, she dried herself and donned a dressing gown. Then she knelt by the charcoal brazier and tried to think how to find the Fugatami children and thwart the Black Lotus's schemes before the trial, when the machinery of the law would claim Haru. Now that neither she nor Sano could go back to the Black Lotus Temple, they had no way to see into the sect.

The thought stimulated Reiko's memory of Midori proposing to spy on the temple. Reiko suddenly realized that she hadn't seen or heard from her friend all day. Disturbed to think Midori was so offended that she was avoiding contact, Reiko decided she must seek out Midori first thing tomorrow and try to repair their friendship.

*   *   *

At the Black Lotus Temple, nuns herded a hundred novices through the precinct. The young women, dressed in white robes, their long hair loose, marched in pairs past dark, silent buildings. Their eager faces shone in the fitful light from lanterns carried by the nuns. No one spoke. The only noises were their rapid breaths, the scuff of sandals on the gravel path, and the whine of cicadas in the shrubbery. In the middle of the line, Midori walked beside Toshiko. Excitement permeated the group like an invisible force. Midori trembled with anticipation, sure that tonight she would learn something of major importance about the Black Lotus.

After she'd been accepted into the temple, she had expected the nuns to assign her the menial chores that novices usually performed at temples. She'd thought she could look around and talk with sect members; however, that hadn't happened. Instead, Midori had spent the day closed up in the nunnery with the other novices. An elderly priest had taught them verses from the Black Lotus Sutra. All speech except chanting the verses had been forbidden. Nuns armed with wooden paddles rapped the heads of anyone who talked during meals. Still, whispers buzzed among the novices. Toshiko had sat beside Midori and passed on gossip: "Enemies are slaughtering our kind." "All the nuns and priests and Black Lotus followers have been ordered to come to the temple. No one is allowed to leave." "The temple is closed to outsiders." "It will happen soon!"

"What are they talking about?" Midori whispered to Toshiko.

A paddle rapped their heads, silencing them. Through the window bars Midori saw nuns and priests hurrying by, carrying bundles. A sense of secret purpose pervaded the atmosphere. Midori longed to explore and find out what was going on, but the nuns watched her constantly; they even accompanied the novices to the privy. Then, at the evening meal, Abbess Junketsu-in had addressed the novices.

"High Priest Anraku has declared that our day of destiny is near, and we must prepare ourselves," she said. "All novices shall be initiated at a ceremony tonight."

Now, as the novices marched through the precinct, the main hall loomed ahead. The nuns led the novices up the stairs, and sudden fear came over Midori because no one had explained what would happen at the initiation ceremony. She hung back, but Toshiko pulled her along with the other girls. Priests opened the doors. Smoky golden light spilled outward, welcoming the novices inside.

There, flames leapt in brass lanterns that hung from the high, beamed ceiling. Young priests stood like an army of black-robed, shaven-headed soldiers along walls covered with ornate lacquer friezes. Mirrors above these reflected and expanded the large room. A gleaming, polished cypress floor fronted the altar, a high platform that spanned the en-tire back wall and held golden Buddha statues, thousands of glowing candles, and incense burners that filled the air with sweet, pungent smoke. Beyond these, a gigantic mural depicted a black lotus. Midori gasped in awe.

The nuns arranged the novices in ten rows facing the altar. Midori and Toshiko stood together in the second row.

"Praise the glory of the Black Lotus," chanted the priests.

Suddenly, smoke erupted from the altar's center, billowing in a thick column to the ceiling. Surprised exclamations burst from Midori and the other novices. Up through the smoke rose a human figure. It was a tall man who wore a black patch over his left eye, and a sparkling, multicolored brocade robe.

"Bow down before Honorable High Priest Anraku," ordered the nuns.

As she and her comrades dropped to their knees, pressed their foreheads to the floor, and extended their arms, Midori tried to still her body's panicky trembling and be brave. She wished Hirata and Reiko were here with her.

The high priest spoke: "Welcome, my followers." His quiet voice had a resonance that penetrated clearly through the chanting. "Raise your heads so I can look upon you."

Midori cautiously sat upright. Anraku stepped forward to the red bars of the low railing that bordered the altar. The mirrors multiplied his image all around the room. His beauty dazzled Midori. His gaze scanned the novices, and when it briefly held Midori's, she felt an instant, exhilarating connection to him.

"I congratulate you on the advent of your membership in the Black Lotus," Anraku said. "You have come here from many different circumstances of life, from places near and far, but you all have one marvelous thing in common."

He paused, and Midori shared the breathless suspense that immobilized the audience.

"You are unique among mortals," Anraku continued, spreading his arms in an all-encompassing embrace. The smoky air vibrated with the chanting and the force of his personality. "You have extraordinary perception and strong, pure spirit. You are capable of miracles. You are destined for greatness."

Pride swelled the chests of the hundred novices and brought smiles to their faces. Anraku's words stirred Midori despite her role as an outsider and spy. The drifting incense smoke suffused her lungs; she felt giddy. Perhaps she really was special, and Anraku was the first to recognize the fact.

"You have all paid a price for being special." As Anraku leaned toward the audience, he seemed to grow in stature; his voice reverberated. "The world is cruel to those who are different. You have suffered slights, mockery, and rejection. You have been ostracized, banished, and punished unjustly. Your lives have been filled with pain."

Sobs punctuated the chanting. Midori saw grief contorting the faces of the young women. Their misery infected her. She recalled Hirata's hurtful teasing and his neglect of her, Reiko's condescension, the Edo Castle ladies-in-waiting who snubbed her, the family she rarely saw. Tears spilled from her eyes.

"Those who have hurt you have done so because they envy you," Anraku said. "They wish to destroy the superiority that you possess and they can never achieve."

Revelation stunned Midori. Such a perfectly logical explanation for her troubles! All around her she saw comprehension dawning on tearful faces.

"But your suffering has a purpose. The divine forces have sent misfortunes to test your spirits. By surviving, you have passed the test. Now fate has chosen you to join an elite order of people like yourselves. You have come to your true home. Here you shall find the fulfillment you deserve."

Anraku smiled, radiating a benevolence that healed past hurts. Now the novices wept for joy, and Midori with them. Perhaps fate really had brought her here, and this was indeed the one place where people would appreciate her.

"Look around you at your new clan," Anraku said with a

sweeping gesture of his hand. "Know that you belong here, together, among others of your kind."

Warm, affectionate glances passed among the novices. Midori felt the bliss of a comradeship she'd never known before. She chanted, "Praise the glory of the Black Lotus!"

"You share an important purpose," Anraku said. "You all seek spiritual awareness, divine knowledge, and the ultimate expression of the powers within. With me as your guide, you shall attain all those blessings. You are ready to begin the first step of your journey."

Eager stirrings rippled the audience. Anraku said, "The Black Lotus Sutra describes the path to enlightenment as a tapestry woven from an infinite number of threads. Approach me one by one so that I may look into your spirit and discern which thread bears your name."

Two nuns walked to the first row of novices. They led a young woman up to the altar. Midori experienced sudden alarm. She'd gotten so carried away by the ritual that she'd forgotten why she was here. Anraku leaned down, grasped the novice's face between his hands, and stared intently into her eyes. The chanting accelerated. Midori saw Anraku's lips move as he spoke to the novice and knew she couldn't go up there. When her turn came, Anraku might guess she was a spy!

Anraku released the novice, who stumbled back to her place, weeping. Nuns led other novices to the altar. After the high priest spoke to them, some moaned, cried, or acquired wondering, dazed expressions; some fainted. What was he saying to them? Midori wondered. Soon the nuns came for her. Filled with dread, she rose, swaying dizzily as if she were drunk. The nuns supported her as she wove to the altar. Mirrored lights and smoke spun around Midori; the chanting echoed through her. Heart racing, she stood before Anraku.

He seemed tall as a mountain, his robe bright as fire against the huge black lotus flower. Then he leaned down, and his hard, warm hands clasped Midori's cheeks. Midori dared not look straight at him, lest he realize her deception, yet his gaze captured hers. His single eye was a beacon that illuminated every corner of her soul. Perceiving unfathomable dimensions behind the black patch, Midori whimpered in terror.

Then Anraku smiled, and the sense of deep connection with

him soothed Midori. He said in a soft, hypnotic voice, "Love is the force that compels you. Unrequited love saddens your heart. For love you would walk through fire, travel to the end of the earth, wait for an eternity. Love brought you to me."

How could he know? Midori thought wildly. Had he found out who she was? She longed to run away, but his firm grasp paralyzed her.

"Love is your path to enlightenment," Anraku said. "It is a path through much darkness and trouble, but I shall guide you safely to your destiny. Follow me, and you shall win your heart's desire."

Wisdom illuminated his face. His power flowed from his hands into Midori like a charge of energy. As she stared at him, his image transformed. Suddenly it was Hirata holding her, smiling down at her. Joy exhilarated Midori. The high priest really could grant her anything she wanted, even Hirata! Then the vision dissolved, and Anraku released her.

Midori experienced a sensation of falling away from him at great speed as lights swirled around her. Abruptly, she found herself kneeling in the row of novice nuns. Breathless from shock, she tried to figure out what had happened, but rational thought eluded her. She knew the high priest was drawing her into his realm of enchantment and she must resist, yet she desperately wanted what he offered.

Novices continued going to and from the altar. Moans, sobs, and emotion agitated the group. Midori wondered what he'd promised everyone else. That he could know them all and give them everything made no sense; yet it made perfect sense. Midori felt her will weakening, her spirit cleaving to Anraku.

When the ritual ended, Anraku surveyed the novices with proud satisfaction. They raised rapt faces to him, and Midori knew they felt toward him the same fear, trust, and attraction as she did. Anraku said, "Now you each know the path that is yours to follow. Before you embark on your journey, you must take the vows that are required from all members of the Black Lotus sect." He lifted his hands. "Rise, my children."

Midori clambered to her feet. Still dizzy, she wobbled. The unsteady bodies of Toshiko and other young women bumped her.

"Repeat after me," Anraku said: "I pledge to embrace the

Black Lotus faith and shun all other faiths forever."

As an untrained newcomer Midori had no idea what comprised her new faith, but that seemed less important than saying whatever was necessary to earn the reward Anraku had promised. Her voice joined the loud, heartfelt chorus of repetitions.

"I pledge to forsake my family, friends, and the entire outside world," Anraku said.

Even as visions of her sisters, Hirata, Reiko, Sano, and Masahiro flitted through Midori's mind, she recited the oath.

Distorted perception magnified Anraku to colossal stature; his mirrored, glittering reflections filled the room with his presence. He intoned, "I pledge to dedicate my life to the service of the Black Lotus."

The novices echoed him with increasing fervor. Midori felt her whole self blending into the group.

"I pledge to obey High Priest Anraku from now until forever," Anraku said.

Shouting the vow, Midori could no longer distinguish her voice from the voices of her comrades. Her heart beat in rhythm with theirs; they breathed together like a single being.

"I pledge my loyalty to the Black Lotus sect," Anraku said.

Hysteria transformed the people around Midori into a hot, dense mass of swaying bodies and reaching hands. "I pledge my loyalty to the Black Lotus sect!"

With stern gravity, Anraku said, "This is your last, most important pledge: If I should break my vows, may death strike me down and doom me to an eternity in hell."

Thunderous response shook the room. Excited beyond rationality, Midori couldn't bear for the ritual to stop. Body and spirit demanded something more, though she didn't know what.

"Now we shall affirm your vows with the sacred initiation rite of the Black Lotus," Anraku said.

Chanting priests formed ranks behind the rows of novices. Two nuns climbed steps to the altar. Anraku spread his arms, and they removed his brocade robe. He stood proudly nude and magnificent. Midori stared because she'd never seen a naked man before. The sight of Anraku's manhood shamed and fascinated her.

"I welcome you as a follower of the true faith." Anraku extended his open hands. Towering amid the candles and smoke, he looked like an idol come to life. "Share my power. Receive my blessing."

The two nuns knelt on either side of Anraku. The priest behind Midori closed a hand over her shoulder. Twisting away, she looked around at him. He was a few years older than she, with a sly face. He grasped her shoulders and turned her to face the altar. Midori saw other priests holding the other novices. She recoiled from her priest, whimpering—this seemed wrong. Around her, novice nuns, wrapped in the arms of their priests, sighed with pleasure. The sensual atmosphere enfolded Midori. The priest's cheek grazed hers. When she again turned to look at him, she saw that he was Hirata.

Midori exclaimed in bewilderment and joy. Hirata embraced her the way she'd imagined in her secret fantasies; his eyes smoldered with desire. Midori's whole body tingled at his touch. Moaning, she leaned back against Hirata. Such a miracle to have him at last! Midori didn't care how he'd gotten here, or who saw them.

Novices and priests arched, writhed, intertwined limbs, and thrust against one another. Groans and cries rose above the chanting that emanated from nowhere and everywhere. The nuns on the altar stroked Anraku's organ; it swelled and lifted.

"Come close," Anraku said, his voice hoarse with excitement. "Release the spiritual energy that dwells within me."

Couples moved toward him. Hirata whispered to Midori, "I love you. You are mine. I am yours."

The words filled Midori with bliss. When he led her to the altar, she didn't resist. She would do anything for him, anything for Anraku, who'd given Hirata to her. The couples crowded around the altar, chanting, "Praise the glory of the Black Lotus!"

Anraku stood, chest heaving, glistening with sweat, as the nuns each clasped a hand around his organ and pumped him. Suddenly he tensed, threw back his head, flung out his arms, and bellowed, "Let my power flow from me to you!"

His seed spurted. Hirata held Midori tighter. She cried out in heartfelt bliss, all her romantic dreams fulfilled. Uproar from the crowd echoed them.

The nuns on the altar clothed Anraku in his brocade robe.

He held his fists out to the crowd. "Come and receive my spiritual force!" he shouted.

He opened his fists. Blood trickled from the palms. The crowd surged forward. Novices eagerly licked at Anraku's hands; blood smeared their faces, stained their robes. Midori's dizziness increased, but Hirata held her upright. Will and caution deserted her as Anraku pressed his palm to her mouth.

She swallowed thick, salty blood. Anraku, the nuns, and the priests chanted the Black Lotus Sutra, but Midori couldn't comprehend the words. Lights, smoke, and voices blurred into a single overpowering sensation. Drowsiness descended upon Midori; her vision dimmed. She was remotely aware of Hirata lifting her in his arms, carrying her away. She realized that something bad had happened, but she'd lost the power to appreciate the difference between right and wrong. Something had gone very amiss with her plans . . . what those plans were, she couldn't recall. As Midori sank into dark unconsciousness, fleeting thoughts surfaced in her mind: She must stay at the Black Lotus Temple. She wished she could remember why.

27

If you are imprisoned,
Hands and feet bound by chains,
The Bodhisattva of Infinite Power will release you.
——FROM THE BLACK LOTUS SUTRA

A full moon pocked and scored with shadows broke through veils of cloud above Edo Jail, which dominated the dark, empty streets in northeast Nihonbashi. Lights burned in watchtowers along the jail's high stone walls, and within passages patrolled by guards. A bonfire of refuse smoked in a courtyard. Wails issued from the dilapidated prison buildings.

In a cell in the prison, Haru lay on a pile of straw. Moonlight filtered through the tiny barred window onto her frightened face. Shivering in the cold, she hugged herself and pulled her bare feet under her skimpy muslin robe. The stench of human waste nauseated her. Up and down the corridors outside her locked door, other female prisoners moaned, coughed, and snored. A woman wailed, "Help! Let me out!" The pleas echoed Haru's own desperation. She clung to hope that had waned as the hours passed.

After her arrest, she'd struggled and screamed so wildly that the soldiers had bound and gagged her. They'd transported her along the streets on an oxcart, through jeering crowds. When she arrived at the prison, the jailers had untied her and thrown her into this cell. Haru had beat her fists on the door, rampaged around the cell, shrieked, wept, and tried to climb the wall to the window until exhaustion overcame her. She'd fallen asleep, then awakened after dark to lucid misery. Now, weak from hunger and thirst, her body aching, she thought of the events that had brought her here.

She'd worked so hard to convince Reiko that she was good and innocent. Reiko was like a kind, loving older sister, and Haru was grateful to Reiko for trying to help. If only the *sōsakan-sama* hadn't found her parents! And if only Abbess Junketsu-in, Dr. Miwa, Priest Kumashiro, and the orphans hadn't said bad things about her. They and the *sōsakan-sama* hated her and wanted her to die. Now Haru pinned her hopes of rescue on High Priest Anraku.

When she'd first come to the Black Lotus Temple, Anraku had selected her to be his personal attendant. She'd served his meals, run errands for him, and become his lover. Her position as one of his favorites gave her privileged status. She didn't have to do chores, spend long hours studying and praying, or obey rules. Anraku had given her what she most wanted and life had until then denied her: to be treated as special. Her parents had considered her just another pair of hands to help out in the noodle shop. Her husband had treated her like a slave. Only Anraku understood that she deserved better.

"Your path through life is the one that interweaves and unites all other paths," he'd told her. "You are the lightning that begins the storm, the spark that shall ignite the conflagration, the weight that shall tip the balance between good and bad. The ultimate destiny of the Black Lotus depends upon you."

He'd never explained what he meant, but Haru was content to serve him and enjoy her privileges. Anraku was beautiful, wise, and strong, and she loved him. His power had shielded her from other people's disapproval and the consequences of her behavior. Haru had believed in her importance to him and relied on his protection, but now it seemed that Anraku had forsaken her.

After the fire at the cottage, Haru had expected Anraku to make everything all right for her. But instead, Anraku had let the police interrogate her and take her away from him. At Zōjō Temple and Magistrate Ueda's house, Haru had waited in vain for him to bring her home. Had Kumashiro, Junketsu-in, and Miwa turned him against her?

Terror and misery roiled inside Haru. She tried to tell herself that Anraku wouldn't listen to accusations from her enemies. With his divine powers, wouldn't he know that what had happened at the cottage had been a necessary event along the path of her life? Yet perhaps he'd had a new vision that altered his feelings toward her. A sob choked Haru. She could think of no other reason to explain why she was now alone and in grave peril.

The woman down the corridor stopped wailing. The prison slumbered; in the distance, dogs howled. Haru closed her eyes. As sleep overtook her, she drifted to another place and time. She was struggling with Commander Oyama in the cottage. He pushed her down on the floor, laughing at her screams, his fleshy face red with lust as he pawed her . . .

Suddenly the scene changed to the bedchamber of the house where Haru had lived during her marriage. Oyama turned into her husband: withered, toothless, irate. Haru wanted to push him off her, but his servants held her down. Grunting, he thrust himself between her legs . . .

She ran through darkness. Fire exploded behind her, and she heard pursuing footsteps. Now she was standing on a pile of lit coals, tied to a stake. Flames burned her robe; angry spectators cheered. In the rising fire she saw an image of priests tearing a little boy from the arms of Nurse Chie, who screamed, "No, no!" The flames leapt higher, searing her skin, igniting her hair . . .

With a gasp, Haru bolted awake and upright, her heart pounding. Even as she realized that she'd been dreaming, quick, stealthy footsteps came down the corridor. She heard a metallic scraping sound as the iron bar that secured the door to

her cell withdrew. Instinctive alarm launched Haru to her feet.
She scuttled into the cell's back corner and stood still, arms
pressed to her sides, trying to make herself invisible.

The door cracked open, and they slipped into the cell—three
men wearing cloths tied over their hair and the lower portions
of their faces. The last one in shut the door quietly. Haru saw
their eyes glint in the moonlight and fix on her. She could scent
aggression in their sweaty, pungent odor, hear malevolent purpose in their harsh breathing. Squealing in fear, she shrank into
the corner. The tallest man swiftly crossed the room toward
her. He seized the front of her robe, jerked her close to him,
and clamped a hand over her mouth.

"Don't fight, and don't make a sound," he whispered
hoarsely, "or I'll kill you. Understand?"

He held her trapped between his body and the walls. His
hard fingers squeezed her jaw shut and mashed her lips against
her teeth. As terror constricted her chest, Haru nodded.

"I've come to tell you what you're going to do," the man
said, his mouth moving behind the cloth. "So listen well."

Haru didn't recognize his eyes or his voice. The other men
standing on either side of him seemed vaguely familiar, but
with their features hidden Haru couldn't be certain.

"When you go to your trial, you will confess to murdering
those people and burning the cottage," said her captor.

An involuntary mewl of protest issued from Haru's throat.
The man shoved her, banging her head against the wall. The
blow stunned Haru; her ears rang.

"You think you can save yourself by saying you didn't do
it," he said as if reading her thoughts, "but if you don't confess,
and the magistrate spares your life, you'll come to wish you
had been executed after all."

Who was he, and why did he want her to die? The questions
flitted unanswered through Haru's confusion and fright.

"We're going to give you a taste of what you can expect
unless you do as I say," the man hissed.

He yanked her out of the corner, spun her around, and flung
her away from him. His companions caught her. She cried out
and clawed at them, but one man locked muscular arms around
her while the other gagged her with a cloth. Haru retched. Her
heart thudded in panic. The two men held her by the wrists;

stretched between them, she twisted and struggled.

The man who'd spoken struck her cheek. Haru's head snapped back. Pain shot through her face. He hit her nose and ears; more pain rocked her. Warm, salty blood streamed out of her nostrils, clogged her throat. Certain that they would hurt her even more if she made noise, Haru fought the urge to scream. She wept while the man attacked her with a short leather whip that lashed lines of agony across her breasts and stomach, her back and buttocks and legs. The only sounds in the cell were the crack of the whip, her tormenters' harsh breathing, and her own muffled sobs.

Then the two men let go of her. Haru collapsed, her whole body quivering in agony. Now the men were rolling her on her back, tearing open her robe, spreading her legs. The tall man straddled her, and reality merged with the horrors of her nightmare.

"No!" she pleaded through the gag.

She flailed, but the other men grabbed her wrists and ankles. They held her still while their comrade shoved his organ into her. Haru gave a shrill cry of pain. He smacked her head.

"Quiet!" he growled, plunging and heaving.

He was Commander Oyama; he was her husband. His foul stench sickened Haru as the brutal mating continued. Gritting her teeth, she thought how much she hated them all.

"Confess, or expect much worse than this," he rasped in her ear.

But she could never tell all that she'd done and seen, because she would lose what mattered as much as her life.

"If you escape execution, I'll come after you," the man said. "Wherever you go, whatever you do, I'll find you. I'll punish you until you plead for the mercy of death. Then I'll kill you."

He grunted, and Haru felt his hardness break inside her. As he withdrew and rose from her, she moaned in relief, but then one of the other men mounted her. Again came the savage thrusting, the pain. And again, when the third man took his turn. Haru's crotch was sore and slick with blood. The frantic tossing of her head loosened the gag.

"Stop! Leave me alone!" she screamed.

She heard stirrings in the other cells as prisoners awakened. The man on top of her froze.

"Help! Help!" Coherency deserted her, and she shrieked in hysterical bursts.

Down the corridor came hurrying footsteps. Male voices conversed somewhere nearby. The man leapt off Haru, cursing. As her assailants rushed to the door, the tall one paused.

"Remember what I told you," he said.

Haru kept shrieking; she couldn't stop. Three guards burst into the cell, carrying lanterns that lit the room. Through a daze of pain and tears, Haru saw their shocked faces as they stared down at her exposed body.

Her assailants were gone.

28

Those who are not fully versed in all matters
Cannot identify the truth from among ten million falsehoods.

—FROM THE BLACK LOTUS SUTRA

The next morning, before Reiko could to go to the palace women's quarters to look for Midori, she passed Sano's office and heard Hirata's voice say, "There's news from Edo Jail. Haru was attacked last night."

Alarm halted Reiko. She quickly backtracked and entered the office. Inside, Sano was seated at his desk, and Hirata kneeling opposite him. The pair saw her, and their faces took on uneasy expressions.

"Please excuse us. We're discussing business," Sano said.

He and Reiko had spent another night in separate rooms, and Reiko guessed from his drawn features that he hadn't slept any better than she. His tone clearly said that he didn't want her there, but she ignored the hint.

"What's happened to Haru?" she said.

"Haru isn't your concern anymore," Sano said with controlled patience. "Please go."

Reiko didn't budge. After a tense moment, Sano reluctantly nodded to Hirata.

"The prison guards found Haru screaming in her cell," Hirata said. "She'd been beaten."

"Who did it?" Reiko said, horrified.

"There was no sign of her attacker," Hirata said, "and Haru seems unable to speak."

Sano rose. "We'd better look into this."

"I'm going with you," Reiko said. She would talk to Midori later. Right now she had to offer Haru whatever help she could.

"A wife can't tag along on official business," Sano said, visibly irritated. "And Edo Jail is no place for you."

"No harm will come to me as long as you're there to protect me," Reiko pointed out. "It sounds as though Haru is in the same condition she was in after the fire. If she won't talk to the jailers, she probably won't talk to you, either. She needs someone who will at least listen to her side of the story."

Sano hesitated, and Reiko saw him weighing his desire to keep her apart from Haru against his need for facts. At last he nodded in resignation. "All right."

An hour later, they arrived at Edo Jail. Sano, Hirata, and three detectives rode their horses across the rickety wooden bridge that spanned the canal fronting the prison. Guards followed on foot, escorting Reiko's palanquin. Outside the iron-banded gate, the riders dismounted, and Sano went to the guardhouse to speak to the sentries. Reiko stepped out of the palanquin, looking curiously up at cracked, mossy stone walls and dilapidated roof gables that rose above the slums of Kodemmacho district. This notorious place of death and defilement didn't look as bad as she'd imagined.

The sentries opened the gate. Sano and his men walked into the compound. Following with her guards, Reiko entered a courtyard. There loitered rough-looking prison guards, armed with daggers and clubs. They bowed to Sano and stared rudely at Reiko. Wishing she weren't so conspicuous, she stuck close behind her husband until he and Hirata entered a dingy wooden building. As Reiko waited, she heard lewd mutters from the prison guards. She became aware that the place stank of sewage. Piteous cries drifted from the tiny barred windows of a huge fortress with dingy plaster walls. Reiko shuddered. At last Sano and Hirata returned, accompanied by an older samurai, presumably the warden. He frowned at Reiko in surprise.

"My wife has come to administer charity to the prisoner," Sano explained curtly.

The warden's face assumed a blank expression that hid whatever he thought about the unconventional behavior of the shogun's *sōsakan-sama*. He said, "Please come with me."

As the whole party moved toward the fortress, Reiko listened to the conversation between Sano and the warden, who walked with Hirata several paces ahead of her.

"Have you found out who hurt Haru, or why?" Sano said.

"Not yet," the warden said.

"What is Haru's condition?"

"She's very shaken and still won't talk."

They reached the prison fortress, and sentries opened the heavy door. A cacophony of screams and moans burst upon Reiko. As she followed Sano and the other men down a labyrinthine corridor, the stink of feces, urine, vomit, and rotting garbage engulfed her; flies swarmed. She held her sleeve over her nose. In the meager sunlight that shone through high windows, she saw dirty water leaking from under the closed doors of the cells that lined the corridor. Within these Reiko heard women muttering, pacing, thumping the walls. She lifted the hem of her kimono out of the filth and trudged on.

The warden opened the door of a cell, then stood aside to let Sano and Hirata enter. Reiko slipped in after them. She saw Haru lying on a pile of straw on the floor, facing away from the door. There were raw welts on her bare legs and bloodstains on her gray robe. Her body shook in continuous tremors. Appalled, Reiko forgot her own discomfort.

"Haru-*san*!" she exclaimed, moved by pity.

The girl turned her head. Reddish-purple bruises ringed both eyes. Her nose and lips were swollen and caked with blood. At the sight of Sano and Hirata, she recoiled in terror. Then she saw Reiko. A weak, plaintive cry issued from her. Heedless of the dirty floor, Reiko knelt and gathered Haru in her arms. Haru sobbed and clung to her, while Reiko angrily eyed the warden, who'd let this happen.

"I want a basin of hot water and cloths so I can clean her," Reiko said to him.

The warden looked surprised that she'd spoken, then affronted. He turned to Sano.

"You found her like this?" Sano asked him.

"Yes."

"And you've not treated her injuries?" Disapproval cooled Sano's voice.

"It's not our practice to pamper criminals," the warden said defensively.

"Get the bath supplies," Sano ordered, "and fetch Dr. Ito."

The warden left to obey. Reiko's anger extended to Sano. He didn't really care about Haru; he just wanted to keep her alive for her trial. Having arrested her, he was partly responsible for her suffering. Reiko averted her eyes from him and soothed Haru until the girl quieted.

"What happened, Haru-san?" Reiko said gently.

Haru pressed her damp, feverish face against Reiko's shoulder. She mumbled, "There were three men. They hurt me."

She began weeping again. Reiko patted her back. "It's all right, you're safe now." She would have liked to give Haru more time to tell the story at her own pace, but Sano and Hirata were waiting for information, and Reiko feared they would intercede if she delayed too long. "Who were the men?"

"I don't know. They wore masks." Huge sobs convulsed Haru. "I tried to fight back, but they—they—"

Her hand moved down over her pubis. Now Reiko noticed how much blood there was on the lower portion of Haru's robe, and understood what else the gang had done. She whispered, "Oh, no." Glancing up, she saw her own comprehension and pity reflected on Sano's face, but his reaction didn't ease her ire toward him.

"We need to question all the jail personnel," Sano said to Hirata. "Assemble them outside."

Hirata departed. Two prison guards brought in clean rags and a basin of steaming water. An elderly man with a stern face and white hair accompanied them. He wore the dark blue coat of a physician and carried a wooden chest.

"Good morning, Sano-*san*," he said.

"Thank you for coming, Ito-*san*," said Sano. "Please allow me to introduce my wife."

Reiko and Dr. Ito exchanged bows, regarding each other with mutual interest. "It's an honor to meet you," Reiko said.

"The honor is mine," Ito replied sincerely. He saw Haru, and concern deepened the creases in his forehead. "This is my patient? Perhaps you would be kind enough to assist while I treat her?"

Haru shrank away from him, whimpered, and clung to Reiko.

"Don't be afraid," Reiko said. "We're going to make you feel better."

She leveled a cool gaze at Sano, hinting that Haru needed privacy and he should remove himself. He gave her a warning look, bade farewell to Dr. Ito, then left the room, closing the door firmly behind him.

In the prison's main courtyard, Sano found Hirata with the hundred men who staffed Edo Jail. The few samurai officials stood together. Forty guards had lined up in rows nearby. These were petty criminals—thieves, gangsters, brawlers, confidence men—sentenced to work in the jail. They sported cropped haircuts, cotton kimonos and leggings, and various clubs, daggers, and spears. Apart from the rest knelt the eta. Everyone bowed to Sano.

"Who was on duty in the women's wing last night?" Sano asked them.

Three men stepped forward from the ranks of the guards.

"You found Haru after she was attacked?" Sano said.

"Yes, master," chorused the guards.

"Do you know who attacked her?"

They shook their heads, but Sano saw their feet shift uneasily. He didn't think they had beaten Haru, but he guessed whom

they would want to protect. He walked along the rows of
guards, scrutinizing them, until one caught his attention. This
guard was in his twenties, with slitty eyes under a low brow.
While the other men wore old, faded, patched kimonos, the
indigo fabric of his garment was dark and new.

"Where were you last night?" Sano asked him.

"Asleep in the barracks." The guard stood with his hands
clasped behind him.

Sano grabbed the guard's hands, yanked them around, and
inspected them. Raw, red scratches marked the wrists. "How
did you get these?"

"I was playing with a cat," the guard muttered, pulling out
of Sano's grasp.

"A cat named Haru?"

On a hunch, Sano lifted the guard's kimono. He saw a dingy
loincloth covered with brownish bloodstains: The man had
changed his outer clothes after assaulting Haru, but not his
underwear. Disgust filled Sano. His belief that Haru was a killer
limited his sympathy for her, but he abhorred people who
preyed on the helpless.

"Who were your accomplices?" he demanded.

Down the row, another guard started running toward the
gate. Hirata and two other detectives chased and caught him.
They forced him to the ground. Sano walked over to the captive, who lay facedown while the detectives held him.

"He's one of the attackers," Hirata said, pointing to the
scratches on the guard's arms.

The warden joined them. "These two men are known for
sporting with female prisoners," he said.

Then the attack on Haru was an ordinary incident of violence at Edo Jail and unrelated to the murder case, Sano
thought. Still, he needed to be certain. He addressed the guard:
"Why did you torture Haru?"

"We just wanted a little fun," the man whined.

"Who was the third accomplice?"

"We didn't do anything that doesn't happen here all the
time," the man said.

"Never mind the excuses," Sano said. "Answer me."

"There wasn't anyone else. Just the two of us."

* * *

While her guards stood watch outside the cell, Reiko had helped Dr. Ito undress Haru and bathe her. Dr. Ito had applied healing salve to her wounds, bandaged them, and fed her a potion containing herbs to strengthen her system and opium to relieve pain. He'd promised to check on Haru later, then left. Now Haru lay on fresh straw, wearing a clean robe, covered by a blanket. Reiko sat beside her.

"Have you any idea why those men attacked you?" Reiko asked.

Haru's bruised face relaxed as the sedative began to take effect. She said in a soft, drowsy voice, "He wanted me to confess to killing those people and setting the fire. He said that if I didn't, he would hurt me even worse, then kill me."

An ominous chill passed through Reiko. Apparently, Haru was talking about the gang's leader, who'd had a purpose more sinister than blood sport. "Why did he want you to confess?"

"I don't know." Haru yawned. "He didn't say."

"Who was he?"

". . . I don't know."

However, Reiko could think of a good explanation. The Black Lotus must have decided that forcing Haru to confess would stop the investigation into the sect. The thugs must be followers of High Priest Anraku, sent by him to threaten Haru. This scenario strengthened Reiko's belief that Haru knew too much about the sect's clandestine business, and Anraku wanted her to take her secrets to the grave. Reiko became determined to remove Haru from Edo Jail. Therefore, she must convince Sano that Haru needed special protection and had knowledge that would further his investigation.

"Haru-*san*, you must tell me what you saw and heard while you were living at the Black Lotus Temple," Reiko said.

The girl stirred. She murmured, "What kinds of things?"

"Secret underground rooms and tunnels," Reiko said. "Novices being starved, imprisoned, tortured, or killed."

Haru tossed her head from side to side. Sleepy anxiety puckered her face.

Reiko thought she knew the reason for the girl's agitation.

"High Priest Anraku took you in and you feel indebted to him, but if you want to save yourself, you must tell the truth."

"Anraku . . ." Haru's voice trailed off on a sad, lonely note. "Why has he forsaken me?"

"What is the sect planning?" Reiko asked urgently. "Did Anraku order the attacks in Shinagawa? Is he going to do something worse?"

"No," Haru protested weakly. "He's good. He's wonderful. I love him. I thought he loved me."

She closed her eyes as if the conversation had exhausted her, and Reiko saw the veil of sleep descending upon her. Reiko believed that Haru knew more than a misguided sense of loyalty allowed her to tell. Might Anraku have enchanted Haru as he had other followers? Could Haru have been involved in his schemes? The cold touch of suspicion disturbed Reiko, yet as she looked down at Haru's small, battered figure, her instincts insisted that Haru could still be basically good, despite the mistakes she'd made. Besides, it seemed improbable that the sect would have entrusted important facts to her. Still, Reiko wondered how strong was Anraku's hold on Haru, and what Haru might have done for the high priest.

"Haru-*san*," she said, "if you tell me what the Black Lotus is up to, I may be able to get you out of jail."

The girl lay asleep, her breathing slow and even. Her eyelids fluttered, and a moan issued from her parted lips. She said, "I didn't know he was there."

"Who?" Reiko said, startled.

"Radiant Spirit," Haru murmured. Her eyes remained closed; she was apparently talking in her sleep. "Chie's little boy."

"Chie had a child named Radiant Spirit?" Reiko wondered if this was fact, or a fabrication of Haru's dreams.

Under the blanket, Haru twitched. "I didn't want to him to get hurt," she cried. "He wasn't supposed to be there. It was an accident!"

"Where?" Premonition solidified into a cold, sinking weight inside Reiko.

"In the cottage," Haru said.

Then she sighed, and her restless movements ceased. She slept peacefully while Reiko beheld her in horror. It sounded as though Haru meant she'd set the cottage on fire and accidentally burned the child because she hadn't known he was inside. Had she started the fire to destroy the bodies of Commander Oyama and Chie—the people she really had intended to hurt, and had indeed killed?

The terrible possibility held Reiko in a stunned thrall. Over the pounding of her heart, she heard women shouting down the corridor, and a guard ordering them to be quiet. All her doubts about Haru rose up in her. The lies, the fire that had killed her husband, her repeated attempts to incriminate other people, her bond with High Priest Anraku—these all validated Reiko's sudden notion that Haru had admitted while asleep a guilt her conscious mind refused to recall.

But Reiko didn't want to believe that she'd mistakenly interfered with Sano's attempts to serve justice. Perhaps she'd misinterpreted what Haru had said. The blows Haru had received to her head and the medicine Dr. Ito had given her might have confused her. One thing was certain. Much as Reiko hated to breach the code of honesty in her marriage with Sano, she couldn't tell him about Haru's unconscious ramblings, for that would escalate his campaign against Haru, and the Black Lotus would never be exposed.

29

*If there be those who trouble and disrupt the proponents of the
true Law,*
Their blood will spill like rivers.

—FROM THE BLACK LOTUS SUTRA

Midori awakened to groggy consciousness. A heavy fog of
sleep weighed upon her. Through it she heard distant chanting.
Her head ached; her mouth was dry and her stomach queasy.
Rolling onto her side, she opened her eyes.

She was lying on a futon on a wooden pallet, in a large
room illuminated by shafts of sunlight from barred windows.
Around her, other women lay asleep on beds arranged in rows.
Midori frowned in confusion. Who were they? Where was she?
Then she realized that she must be in the Black Lotus convent,
and the women were her fellow novices. The fog in her mind
lifted, and she recalled the initiation ceremony with lucidity and
horror.

She'd enjoyed that man touching her, thinking he was Hirata! She couldn't believe she'd behaved so disgracefully! There must have been poison in the incense that had driven her mad. Anraku's blood must have contained a sleeping potion, because she couldn't recall anything that had happened after drinking it.

Now Midori noticed that the sleeping women were dressed in gray robes instead of the white ones they'd worn last night. Some of them were bald: Their heads had been shaved. Midori's heart lurched as she recalled that now they were all nuns. Her hand flew to her own head. She felt long, silky hair and sighed in relief, though she wondered why she'd been spared. Examining herself, she saw that she, too, wore gray. Someone had changed her clothes while she slept. Misery and shame swelled inside Midori. She'd thought herself such a clever spy, yet she'd succumbed to the Black Lotus.

A nun walked up the aisle, banging a gong. "Get up!" she ordered. "It's time to begin your new life!"

Amid murmurs and yawns, the new nuns stirred. Midori sat up, wincing as vertigo engulfed her. Servant girls passed out steaming bowls of tea and rice gruel.

"No talking," the nun announced.

Midori received her portion and realized she was hungry, but feared that the food contained poison. If she wanted to keep her wits, she must not consume anything the sect gave her.

"If you're not going to eat yours, can I have it?" someone whispered.

Looking up, Midori saw Toshiko kneeling on the bed beside hers. Toshiko looked sleepy; she still had her hair, too. Midori noticed that all the prettier girls did. Concerned for her friend's safety, Midori whispered urgently, "No, you can't! It might be bad!"

"Bad?" Toshiko frowned. "What do you mean?"

The nun patrolled the aisles. Midori didn't want to find out what the punishment was for breaking rules. She realized that she couldn't leave Toshiko at the mercy of the Black Lotus. When she left the temple, she must take her friend with her. "I'll explain as soon as I can." Then curiosity overrode caution. "What did Anraku promise you?"

Toshiko never got a chance to answer, because the nun

herded everyone outside to use the privies and fetch water from the well to wash themselves. Then she took them to the main hall. The precinct was full of nuns and priests bringing in rice bales, loads of charcoal and wood, urns of oil, barrels of pickled vegetables and dried fish. Midori wondered why they needed so many provisions. She saw no pilgrims around, and felt a stab of fear.

The Black Lotus had indeed expelled everyone except its members. She must be the only outsider here. The weather was clear and bright, but Midori sensed an undercurrent in the atmosphere, as if from an invisible storm brewing. She longed to run away before anything worse happened to her, but she couldn't go home with nothing to tell except the details of the initiation ceremony, and she'd rather die than have anyone know that. If she returned empty-handed, everything she'd gone through would be for naught. Besides, she'd come to believe that the Black Lotus really was evil, and she wanted to help defeat it. She must be brave and stay long enough to gather the information she'd promised Reiko.

Inside the main hall, her group joined a crowd of monks and nuns who were kneeling on the floor. An elderly priest led them in chanting. Midori secured a place next to Toshiko and chanted the monotonous prayer. The hall looked different today. Curtains covered the mirrors, and only a few candles burned on the altar, yet the emotional intensity she'd felt last night still charged the air. Senior nuns and priests guarded the doors or patrolled narrow aisles between the ranks of kneeling figures. Head bowed, Midori nudged Toshiko.

"The Black Lotus is dangerous," she whispered. "It kills people. Something bad is going to happen."

"How do you know?" Toshiko whispered back.

The thought of revealing her true identity and purpose scared Midori, but she didn't think Toshiko would believe her unless she did. "I'm Niu Midori, a spy for the wife of the shogun's sōsakan-sama. She told me," Midori said. "I'm here to find out what's happening. As soon as I do, I'm leaving. You have to come with me because if you stay, you could get hurt."

They kept chanting as Toshiko flashed Midori a frightened glance. Then Toshiko whispered, "All right. What are we going to do?"

"I'll sneak away later and look around," Midori answered. "Then I'll come back for you."

At intervals during the prayers, groups of nuns and priests filed out of the hall and others filed in, worshipping in shifts. Eventually, the nun led Midori's group to a building that housed a workshop for printing prayers. Inside, nuns cut sheets of paper and mixed pots of acrid black ink. Others worked at long tables, spreading ink on wooden blocks incised with characters and pressing the blocks against paper. Midori and Toshiko were assigned to cut the printed prayers into strips that bore the message, "Hail the new era of the Black Lotus." Two priests roved the room, overseeing the work. Midori waited until the priests were busy at the other end of the room, then edged toward the door.

"Where are you going?" demanded a loud, female voice.

Startled, Midori looked around and saw a nun glaring at her from the printing table. The priests moved toward her. "To the privy," Midori lied, belatedly aware that everyone here watched one another.

"Go with her," one of the priests told the nun.

On the way to the privy and back, the nun never let Midori out of sight. Working beside Toshiko, Midori whispered, "You have to help me get away."

Toshiko sliced her knife between rows of printed characters. "I'll do something to distract everybody."

"When?" Midori asked anxiously.

"We'll have to wait for the right time. Just be patient and watch me. When I wink at you, run."

Now Midori was glad she'd taken Toshiko into her confidence. Toshiko was exactly the clever accomplice she needed.

"We should not have left Haru in jail," Reiko said to Sano.

It was late afternoon, and they were traveling through Nihonbashi toward Edo Castle. Reiko rode in her palanquin, while Sano walked beside its open window, leading his horse; Hirata and the detectives preceded them. A short time ago, Sano had finished his inquiries at Edo Jail, told Reiko the results, and said it was time to go home. Reiko hadn't wanted to leave

Haru, and she didn't agree with his version of events, but she couldn't disgrace her husband by challenging his authority at the jail, so she'd reluctantly kept silent until now.

"Haru will be fine," Sano said. "The two guards I stationed outside her cell will protect her, and Dr. Ito will tend her injuries. I've warned the warden that he'll be demoted if he allows any more harm to come to her. The jailers have been flogged for beating Haru. They won't bother her again."

"But you haven't found all the men responsible for the attack." Reiko described what Haru had told her. "Where's the third one?"

"There were only two men," Sano said as the procession slowed on its way through an outdoor marketplace.

Reiko heard firm conviction in Sano's voice and braced herself for an argument. "Haru says there were three."

"Hirata and I interrogated everyone at the prison, checked their whereabouts last night, and searched their quarters for clothes with fresh bloodstains," Sano said. "We found no cause to think that anyone else besides those two jailers was involved in the attack."

"Maybe not anyone else from the jail," Reiko said, though troubled by the discrepancy between his version of the story and Haru's. "The other man could have come from outside. I think he was a Black Lotus priest. He tried to threaten Haru into confessing to the arson and murders."

"Or so she told you," Sano said skeptically. "After the two jailers admitted beating Haru, I asked them what happened in that cell. They said they warned Haru to be quiet, but there was no other talk. The prisoners in the other cells heard nothing at all."

"The jailers are probably Black Lotus followers, trying to protect their leader," Reiko said. "The prisoners are probably lying because they're afraid of the jailers and don't want to get in trouble."

Sano shook his head; Reiko saw irritation harden his profile. "If anyone is lying, it's Haru. She's obviously trying to use a random incident to manipulate her way out of jail. I won't fall for that, even if you do."

Reiko thought of Haru's words about the murdered child, and lingering doubt resurfaced.

"What is it?" Sano said, peering suspiciously through the window at her.

"Nothing." Reiko turned away so he couldn't read her thoughts.

She should tell him that Haru had identified the boy as Chie's son, but she didn't want to invite questions about what else Haru had said. Reiko envisioned her relationship with Sano as a house they'd built together, and the secrets she hid as invisible flaws in the structure. Her decision to withhold a clue from him eroded its foundation. Every new development in the case further weakened the integrity of their marriage. Reiko experienced a powerful urge to surrender the battle over Haru, placate Sano, and try to restore the harmony between them, yet her crusade against the sect forced her to stand by Haru. And a part of her still believed she was right to defend the girl.

Frustrated by Sano's refusal to change his mind, she said, "Maybe you're eager to believe that the attack was random because if you'd left Haru at my father's house, it wouldn't have happened. You wouldn't like to think that you arrested the wrong person and let the real killers get her."

"What I like is not the issue. Evidence is." Asperity edged Sano's voice, and Reiko knew that her remark had pierced a sore spot in him. Clearly, he wasn't as sure of Haru's guilt as he wished to be, and the possibility that he'd caused undeserved harm to someone disturbed him. "The evidence says Haru is a criminal and that two jailers who enjoy molesting female prisoners attacked her."

"Maybe you've overlooked evidence that proves Haru's story," Reiko said, desperate to prevent him from letting the Black Lotus dupe him.

Sano stared at her in shock. "Are you saying that I contrived the investigation at the jail to serve my personal aims? Can you really be so smitten with Haru that you think I would do such a dishonest, selfish thing?"

Now Reiko realized she'd again pushed him too far. She was appalled that her attempt to sway him had backfired. "No, I'm just asking you to be objective and reconsider—"

"*You* dare tell *me* to be objective?" Sano's expression turned furious. "You're the one who's lost your objectivity where Haru is concerned. And you've forgotten where your loyalty belongs." He was shouting, oblivious to the presence of the people around them. "Don't you see that Haru has corrupted you? You're becoming as deceitful and wayward as she is. Well, go ahead and choose her over your husband. Let her destroy our life, because I don't care anymore—I'm sick of you both!"

His bitter fury seared Reiko. She was aghast to think he believed their trouble was solely due to her friendship with Haru, and that her reckless words had caused the final rupture between them. How could she explain that there was much more involved than a fight over the girl, and that his honor was at stake, without further angering him?

Sano gave her no chance to try. "I'll have no more of your criticism or interference," he said, his words cutting like a steel blade, his face taut with anger. "Either you come to your senses, treat me with respect, and stay out of this investigation, or—"

He seemed to notice that he was shouting in public for all to hear, and a look of mortification came over his face. He mounted his horse and galloped ahead, leaving Reiko sitting in her palanquin, amid the ruins of their life together. He was threatening to divorce her! Imagining consequences too terrible to contemplate, she suddenly realized how much she would hate to lose him.

As Sano rode beside Hirata, emotion contradicted his ultimatum. Reiko was his wife and the mother of his son. Though he hated her stubborn defense of Haru, they'd shared so many accomplishments, happy times, and dangers. He didn't really want to end their marriage, yet he refused to tolerate her misbehavior any longer, and if she refused to yield, there seemed no alternative except divorce. Sano maintained a stoic countenance that hid his regret and bewilderment.

Hirata said, "Maybe it's just coincidence, but every main road we've tried to follow has been blocked. We've been constantly having to take detours."

Sano had been too preoccupied to pay attention. Now his memory recalled images subconsciously noted: a burning trash heap at one intersection and a big stack of wood at another;

jugglers performing for a crowd. None of these things was unusual, but Hirata was right to bring the combination to Sano's notice.

"I don't like this," he said, looking around suspiciously.

The detours had diverted them into a labyrinth of narrow lanes between houses whose balconies almost touched overhead. Sano and his men had to ride single file, and Reiko's palanquin barely fit. The street they were on seemed oddly empty for such a populous district, with not a soul in sight.

"I smell a trap," Hirata said.

"Let's get out of here," Sano said. Slapping the reins, he called to the palanquin bearers and the guards at the rear of the procession: "Hurry."

The procession gathered speed. Ahead loomed the portals of a neighborhood gate. Through it rushed six men dressed in hooded cloaks, with cloths tied over the lower portions of their faces. They wore daggers at their waists and carried spears. They charged at the procession.

"It's an ambush!" Sano yelled. His party of twelve men outnumbered the attackers, but he didn't want to be stuck in this confined space. "Go back!"

He and Hirata and the detectives turned their horses, but the palanquin, with its long poles, was too big. The bearers hastily backed down the street. Eight more hooded, masked, armed men stormed in from the opposite direction. Now the attackers had the advantage, and Sano's party was trapped.

"Fight!" Sano shouted.

He saw the four bearers set down the palanquin and hurry to join the four guards in a rear defense. Drawing his sword, he leapt from his mount. Hirata and the detectives followed suit. An attacker rushed Sano, spear aimed at his heart. Sano dodged. He bumped into Hirata, who was parrying slices from the spears of two more attackers. Sano clashed blades with his opponent.

"Reiko!" he called. "Stay inside the palanquin!"

Another attacker joined the man battling Sano. They lunged and jabbed at him. Sano hacked at the wooden shaft of one opponent's spear. The shaft broke. Sano sliced the man across the throat. Blood spurted, and the man fell dead.

The other man lunged; Sano sidestepped, crashed against a

building, and the spear grazed his shoulder. Swinging his sword around, he struck at the man's hands. The man dropped the spear, ducked another cut from Sano, and drew a long-bladed dagger. As he slashed and parried, Sano noticed that another attacker lay facedown in a pool of blood nearby, slain by Hirata or the detectives. Through the narrow gap between the palanquin and the buildings he saw his men fighting the attackers on the other side of the palanquin. The remaining four on his side formed a line of offense. Thrusting spears crowded Sano and his men together, forcing them backward. Sano glimpsed the attackers' intent, merciless eyes above the masks.

Who were they? Why did they risk ambushing an armed Tokugawa procession?

The horses, frightened by the battle, neighed and circled, trying to escape, but the fighters and the palanquin hemmed them in. One of the horses reared; its flailing hooves struck the detective at Sano's right, and he stumbled. A spear pierced his middle. He screamed, collapsed, then lay still.

Outraged by the murder of a loyal retainer, Sano fought harder. Spears and swords flashed, battered, and rang in the air between his side and the attackers. Sano darted past spears and around to the rear of the offense. He sliced an attacker down the back. The man howled and died. Sano, Hirata, and the other detective circled the three remaining attackers and soon felled them, then ran to the back of the palanquin. There, two guards were wielding swords against the spears of two attackers. The corpses of the other guards, attackers, and the palanquin bearers lay strewn upon the road.

Sano called to the attackers, "Your comrades are dead. Surrender!"

They turned toward him, and he saw them realize that they were now outnumbered five men to two. They fled down the street. Hirata, the detective, and the guards raced off in pursuit. Reiko jumped out of the palanquin and gaped at the carnage.

"You're bleeding," she said to Sano, pointing at his shoulder.

Sano inspected the wound, which hurt but had stopped bleeding. "It's not serious. Are you all right?"

Reiko nodded, but her lips trembled. Sano worried that this trauma, so soon after the murders of the Fugatami, was too much for his wife. He felt an impulse to hold her, to reassure her that she was safe. Yet their strife had created a distance between them that precluded intimacy. Reiko averted her gaze from Sano and walked over to the corpse of an attacker.

The man lay sprawled on his back. Blood from the fatal gash across his belly drenched his garments; his hood and face cloth had fallen off. He was young, with coarse features, and a stranger to Sano. His head was shaved bald.

"A priest," Reiko said.

Leaning closer, she examined his neck, then pointed at a tattoo just below his throat. It was a black lotus flower.

"First the sect attacked Haru, and now us," Reiko said, her voice deliberately calm. "They must have followed us from the jail and set up the ambush. They wanted to keep us from discovering the truth about the Black Lotus."

Sano agreed with her logic, and he began reassessing his opinion of the attack on Haru, but before he could reply, his men returned. "You lost the last two?" Sano said.

"We cornered them in an alley," Hirata said, "but they cut their own throats to avoid capture." Eyeing the corpse beside Reiko, he added, "They're both priests, with that same tattoo."

Reiko turned a bleak gaze on Sano. "They'll stop at nothing to destroy their enemies and protect their secrets."

30

The land of the Bodhisattva of Infinite Power
Will be filled with treasures and heavenly palaces.
The faithful will be transformed,
Their bodies will glow with light,
They will feed on joy and unlimited knowledge.
——FROM THE BLACK LOTUS SUTRA

Iridescent pink cloud glowed in the twilight sky above the Zōjō temple district. Bells clamored, heralding evening rites. Peddlers and late worshippers trudged homeward from the marketplace, while nuns and priests streamed into temples. But the gates to the Black Lotus Temple were closed; no one passed in or out. Shrouded in secrecy, the walled compound gathered the night around itself.

Inside the temple precinct, monks armed with spears guarded the gates and patrolled the grounds. Lights burned behind the windows of the buildings. Flames flickered in stone lanterns along the main path, where a hundred nuns and priests stood in rows, each holding a wooden dagger. Priest Kumashiro, armed with a steel dagger, headed the group. He whirled, slashing the air in ritualistic combat. The nuns and priests imitated his actions like an army of shadows.

Midori clutched her dagger, panting as she tried to keep up with her comrades. She wondered why they needed to learn how to fight. Kumashiro had merely told them it was vital to their future. Her comrades mimicked him with rapt concentration, as if they shared his secret purpose. The lesson, which reminded Midori of military drills at Edo Castle, intensified her fears about the Black Lotus. As she darted and stabbed, she tried to keep an eye on Toshiko, in the next row.

All day she'd waited for her friend to create a diversion so she could escape the sect's supervision, but Toshiko had done nothing. She hadn't winked; she hadn't even spoken to Midori. Now Midori was starving because she didn't want to be poisoned by eating the sect's food. She wanted to finish spying and avoid spending another night at the temple, but she feared that Toshiko had changed her mind about helping.

Beyond the rows of moving figures Midori saw nuns stationed along both sides of the path, watching the group. She would never get past them without Toshiko's cooperation. Despair filled her.

The lesson halted, and the group stood at attention while three priests joined Kumashiro. Each carried a horizontal pole with a life-sized human dummy at the end. The dummies had wooden heads and wore men's kimonos and wicker hats.

"Watch carefully," Kumashiro ordered the group.

The priests moved in a staggered line toward him, dummies extended. Kumashiro charged at the dummies. He swung his dagger right, left, and right, slashing tears across the dummies' middles.

"Form a line, run up one at time, and do as I showed you," Kumashiro said.

Midori and the others jostled into position. The monk at the head of the line ran forward. The priests thrust the dummies at him, and he whacked his wooden dagger against the stuffed figures. Other monks and nuns followed his example. As the line moved up, Midori fidgeted in anxiety. The violence of the exercise disturbed her, as did the ferocity with which her com-

rades attacked the dummies. Dreading her turn, she watched
Toshiko, who stood four places ahead of her.

Suddenly Toshiko let out a loud cry. Midori's heart jumped.
Everyone looked at Toshiko as she dropped her dagger and
clutchéd her stomach.

"Ow, ow, it hurts!" she screamed, toppling to the ground.

The nuns on the sidelines hurried toward her. Toshiko rolled
back and forth, grimacing in pain, and her gaze briefly met
Midori's. She winked.

Overjoyed, Midori turned and ran into the grounds. Trees
screened the light from the moon and the buildings, and she
could barely see where she was going. She plunged into a passage between solid walls, then through a patch of woods, and
emerged into open space. Her foot struck a stone or fallen
branch. She tripped, sprawling flat on the grass.

The fall knocked the dagger out of her hand and the breath
from her lungs. Midori lay stunned for a moment, heart pounding. Then she scrambled up, aware that she hadn't thought what
to do after escaping. Where should she go? Uncertainty immobilized her. She felt very small and alone and scared.

Now that her eyes had adjusted to the darkness, she saw
that she was in a garden. Jagged pine trees stood out against
the indigo sky, and a pond reflected the moon's bleached circle.
Midori smelled the odor of burnt wood and saw a large square
of bare, charred earth. A chill tingled her skin. This must be
where the cottage had been burned with Commander Oyama,
the woman, and the little boy inside, and the debris cleared
away.

Rapid footsteps rustled through fallen leaves, coming toward
Midori. Panic ripped a gasp from her throat. She whirled, raising her hands to fend off the dark figure approaching her.

The person halted and whispered loudly, "It's me!"

"Oh!" Midori went limp with relief as she recognized Toshiko. "I'm so glad to see you. How did you get here?"

"I told them I had cramps," Toshiko said, "and then pretended to get better. After the lesson started up again, I sneaked
away. So, what's next?"

Before Midori could admit that she didn't know, a creaking
noise came from the site of the fire. They both started. Midori
saw an eerie glow issuing from the burnt ground.

"It's the ghosts of the people who died here!" she whispered as superstitious fright shot through her.

She and Toshiko hugged each other, cowering behind a tree. Up from the ground rose a hand, bearing a lantern; then an entire figure emerged. It was a woman dressed in a gray kimono and long white head drape: Abbess Junketsu-in. She held the lantern over a large hole out of which she'd climbed.

"That must be an opening to the underground tunnels Lady Reiko told me about," Midori whispered to Toshiko. Apparently, it had once led into the cottage.

As they watched, there were more creaking sounds, and two male figures climbed from the hole. They had shaved crowns and wore swords. Midori recognized the crest of the Kuroda clan on their glossy silk robes. They and Junketsu-in walked away down a path toward the main precinct.

"Do you want to see what's inside the hole?" Toshiko whispered.

Midori shuddered at the idea of going down there. "Let's find out what the abbess and those men are doing." Reiko would want to know why Junketsu-in had sneaked two high-ranking samurai from a powerful clan into the temple. "Come on!"

They followed the trio, creeping along behind the shrubs that bordered the path. The abbess led the samurai up the stairs to the veranda of a secondary worship hall. Dim light shone through the barred windows. Midori and Toshiko hid behind a prayer board outside and watched one samurai open the door.

"Not so fast," Junketsu-in said irately. "Aren't you forgetting something?"

The men reached inside their kimonos, removed objects too small for Midori to see, and handed them to the abbess. Then the three vanished into the building.

Midori said to Toshiko, "We'll listen at the windows."

They scurried over to the base of the building and crouched in the shadows. Midori heard footsteps inside, and the scrape of doors sliding. Then a male voice said, "I'll take her." Another said, "That one will do for me." Soon Junketsu-in exited the building, alone. She walked toward the main hall. Midori was torn between investigating the mysterious activities here, or spying on Junketsu-in. Afraid of the abbess, she decided to stay.

Low murmurs came through the window above; Midori couldn't make out the words. Toshiko rose, poked her finger through the bars, pierced the paper pane, and gingerly tore a hole in it. While Midori watched, daunted by her boldness, Toshiko peered into the hole.

"Look!" she whispered excitedly.

After glancing around to make sure nobody was watching, Midori stood and looked through the hole. Inside were a nun and one of the samurai who'd come with Abbess Junketsu-in. The samurai had stripped nude. He was kneeling, while the nun hunched before him, sucking his organ. He groaned, caressing her shaved head. Midori gasped in shock.

Toshiko tugged her arm. "Let's see what's happening in the other rooms."

They crept to the next window, where Toshiko tore another hole. In this room they saw a naked monk crouched on all fours. The other samurai knelt behind him, thrusting into his buttocks. Recalling the exchange she'd observed between Junketsu-in and the two samurai, Midori realized that the men had been paying for sexual services and choosing their companions. The temple was running a brothel for rich patrons.

"Have you seen enough?" Toshiko whispered. "Can we leave?"

Midori would have liked nothing better than to flee the temple, but she doubted that Reiko or Hirata would think much of what she'd learned so far. Prostitution outside the Yoshiwara licensed district was a crime, but it revealed nothing about the murders or the Black Lotus's plans.

"We can't go yet," Midori told Toshiko. "Come this way!"

They stole through the grounds, back to the site of the burned cottage. Crouching at the edge of the hole, they peered inside. Midori saw a shaft with plank walls; a wooden ladder extended down one side into a deep pit. Dim light shone at the bottom, and she heard a distant clattering noise.

"There's something in there. It's dark," Toshiko whimpered. "I'm afraid to go down."

So was Midori, but she must be brave. "You can wait for me here," she said with more confidence than she felt.

"But I'm afraid to be alone."

"Then you'll have to come with me."

Midori began climbing down the creaky ladder. The dark shaft enclosed her. As she descended, the air grew cooler and damper, exuding the odor of soil. A panicky, trapped feeling built inside Midori. She gripped the sides of the ladder and her feet fumbled for the rungs while she imagined hands reaching up from the darkness to grab her. Reaching the bottom, she found herself in a cave. The light came from oil lamps mounted on the reinforced walls of three tunnels that joined where she stood. A moment later, Toshiko came scrambling down the ladder.

Having her friend by her side renewed Midori's courage. "This way," she said, picking a direction at random.

Treading softly upon the earth floor, they started down a tunnel. The steady beat of the clattering noise echoed around them. Air gusted from holes in the ceiling, and a strong odor of fish and pickled radishes permeated the atmosphere. Rooms lined the tunnel. Midori peeked through the open doorway of one and saw ceramic urns stacked to the ceiling. The next rooms contained rice bales, and the next, water barrels.

"These must be the provisions we saw them bringing into the temple," Midori said. The cool temperature would preserve the food, but she didn't understand why the sect would amass so much, or bother hauling water underground.

Toshiko gazed down the tunnel, her eyes alert and frightened. "Someone's coming!"

Midori heard the footsteps in the distance. She ducked into the room containing the water barrels, pulling Toshiko with her. They watched six priests march by. After the group passed, they started down the tunnel again.

"Where are we going?" Toshiko whispered.

"I guess we'll follow the noise."

This grew louder as they wound deeper into the subterranean complex. They passed more pantries, rooms lined with mattresses set on wide shelves, and junctions where the tunnel branched. At one junction, a shaft rose to ground level. Four nuns came down its ladder. Midori and Toshiko leapt back into the tunnel just in time to hide.

"Let's go back up," Toshiko pleaded.

"Not yet."

The clatter rose to a shuddering racket. Through it Midori heard resounding metallic clangs and eerie cries. Now they came upon a spacious hollow. Inside, Midori saw what looked to be a gigantic machine composed of pleated, tubular cloth bellows, wooden wheels, and a vertical iron conduit as wide as a tree trunk running through the ceiling. Ten muscular priests pumped the bellows and turned cranks.

"They're pumping air in from outside so people can breathe down here," Midori deduced.

She and Toshiko slipped past the hollow. They rounded a corner, and a deafening cacophony burst upon them, accompanied by a powerful reek of urine and rank earth. Down the passage, shaven-headed men and women shoveled, swung pickaxes, erected beams and walls, and hoisted loads of dirt up a shaft, building new tunnels. Sweat and grime soiled their clothes; iron chains shackled their ankles. Torches flared through dust clouds. Priests armed with clubs strolled through the scene, hitting workers who paused to rest. Pained cries rent the air.

"I think I've seen enough," Midori said, appalled to discover that Reiko's tale of slavery in the temple was true, and increasingly afraid of getting caught. "Let's go back up."

Hurrying back through the tunnels with Toshiko, she followed the route by which they'd come, but somewhere she took a wrong turn into unfamiliar territory. Here, the passage stank of rotten fish, and Midori heard grinding noises coming from a room. Signaling Toshiko to stand back, she stole up to the doorway and peeked inside. A man stood at a long table against the wall, writing. It was Dr. Miwa.

Fear clenched Midori's stomach as she observed that the room was some sort of workshop, furnished with equipment strange to her. A nun was lifting small, dead fish from a basin of water and dropping them into a ceramic pot. Another nun pounded the fish with a sharp-bladed chopper, while more nuns strained slimy pulp through cloths and gathered the liquid in jars. Midori recognized the fish as fugu—puffer fish. Everyone knew that fugu was poisonous and its sale illegal in many places. What could the Black Lotus be planning to do with the extract?

Suddenly Toshiko gasped, clutching Midori's arm, as footsteps approached. The girls scurried around a corner, peered cautiously out, and watched three priests cross a junction some twenty paces away. One was High Priest Anraku. The others carried lanterns. Midori remembered the ceremony and Anraku's fathomless eyes, hypnotic voice, and unsettling touch, his sexual arousal and her own. She wanted to run fast and far from him, but he was the heart of the Black Lotus and important to her mission.

"We'll follow him," she told Toshiko.

They hurried after Anraku. Suddenly a group of nuns came around a corner and straight toward them. Toshiko shrank back, but Midori pulled her forward, murmuring, "Keep going. Act like you belong here."

The nuns passed, bobbing perfunctory bows, which Midori and Toshiko returned. Ahead, Anraku and the priests entered a room. Midori and Toshiko huddled near the door.

"How many pieces?" Anraku's voice said.

A priest replied, "Our samurai patrons have donated enough to arm everyone in the temple and all our brothers and sisters outside."

"Excellent."

Midori stole a look through the doorway, into a large cave where Anraku and the priests stood, their backs to her. An eerie radiance surrounded them. Midori saw that the radiance was light from the priests' lanterns, reflecting on the steel blades of thousands of swords, spears, daggers, and lances mounted in racks on the walls, hung from the ceiling, and stacked on the floor. The sight amazed her. There must be almost as many weapons here as in Edo Castle!

Anraku walked toward an ironclad door at the back of the cave. "Leave the lanterns here. We don't want to ignite the gunpowder bombs until we're ready."

The priests obeyed, following him into the dark cavern beyond the door, from which Midori overheard them discussing the quantity of bombs and the area they could destroy. A thrill of revelation and dread swept through her as she at last perceived the meaning of what she'd seen tonight.

"The Black Lotus is preparing for a war and siege!" Midori whispered excitedly to Toshiko. This was just the sort of discovery that would help Reiko and impress Hirata. "We must go up and warn people!"

She turned to her friend . . . and discovered that she'd spoken to empty air.

"Toshiko-*san*?" she said. "Where are you?"

The girl had disappeared. Midori fought panic; she wasn't sure she could get out by herself, and even if she could, she couldn't leave Toshiko in this awful place. Desperate to find her friend, she ran down the tunnel.

A gang of priests hurried toward her, shouting, "There's the intruder. Catch her!"

Terrified, Midori turned and ran in the other direction, but two figures standing in the passage blocked her escape. She skidded to a halt, alarmed to recognize Anraku and Toshiko.

"Such a pity." Anraku shook his head, regarding Midori with what looked to be genuine regret. "You had a wonderful future with me, but I regret to say that your betrayal of my trust has altered your destiny. They who oppose the Black Lotus must be punished."

A wave of nauseating horror washed over Midori, followed by remorse. "I'm sorry for dragging you into this," she said to Toshiko.

However, Toshiko didn't look frightened. Her face wore a smug smile. Anraku beamed down at her, and terrible comprehension dawned on Midori.

"This morning you asked me what Anraku-*san* promised me," Toshiko said. "When I joined the Black Lotus last year, he said that my purpose in life was to expose his enemies, and he would reward me with a life of luxury in his new kingdom."

Too late, Midori recalled warning signs: how easily Toshiko had befriended her, gone along with her plans, and gotten away from the combat lesson to accompany her here. Toshiko wasn't a fellow newcomer and victim; she was a Black Lotus spy, who must have been planted among the novices to watch them, her fear and reluctance a mere pose. When she'd vanished a moment ago, she'd gone to report Midori to her superiors.

Now, as the priests seized Midori and marched her down the tunnel, she rued her naïveté. Surely she would pay for it with her life.

31

*Beware of rulers, princes of kingdoms, high-ministers, and heads
of offices
Who stubbornly adhere to untruth.*

> —FROM THE BLACK LOTUS SUTRA

Huddled in her palanquin, Reiko heard shouts and clashing
blades from the battle raging outside. Then the world shifted,
and she was standing alone inside Minister Fugatami's house,
where the minister and Hiroko lay dead in their blood-spattered
chamber. Reiko fled through empty rooms and corridors, seeking a door that didn't exist, fleeing an unknown danger. She
came to a window and wrenched at the bars that covered it.

"Help!" she called.

Outside, in a garden eerily still in the gray dawn, stood Haru.
She held a flaming torch.

"Haru, let me out!" Reiko pleaded.

But the girl, whose face wore a look of blind, intense concentration, didn't seem to notice her. Haru raised the torch, and fire exploded around Reiko. She screamed.

The sound of her own voice startled her awake. She sat up in bed, her heart thudding. Now she recognized her own chamber, its windows pale with morning light. An afternoon, evening, and night had passed since the attack in Nihonbashi, but she again experienced the breathlessness and tremors of a delayed reaction that had set in after she'd arrived home.

Because her palanquin bearers had all perished in the battle, Reiko had ridden back to Edo Castle on a horse that had belonged to one of Sano's dead retainers, while Sano held the reins and rode beside her. She'd thought herself unaffected by the attack, until she and Sano were seated in the parlor of their mansion and she tried to discuss what had just happened.

"Surely now you must realize how dangerous and evil the Black Lotus is," she said.

"Yes, I know the sect is evil," Sano said. His matter-of-fact tone echoed hers, though he watched her with concern. "But so is Haru."

"Then you still mean to leave her in jail, awaiting her trial?" Reiko said, dismayed.

"I believe that the arson and murders were Haru's contribution to the Black Lotus's scheme, whatever it is," Sano said. "But let's not talk about this while you're upset."

"I'm fine," Reiko said, but a sudden onrush of tears contradicted her claim. "You can't condemn Haru to death when there's a chance that she's innocent and blaming her could leave the real killers free to do whatever they please!"

Sano had refused to continue the discussion, and insisted that Reiko go to bed. Toward dawn, she'd fallen into a restless sleep that had brought the nightmare. Now she drew deep breaths, willing away emotion. She couldn't bring the Black Lotus to justice unless she pulled herself together.

She tried to forget her dream about Haru, and everything it implied.

Reiko washed, dressed, and forced herself to swallow some tea and rice gruel. She fed Masahiro, then went to the palace. She found Lady Keisho-in in her chambers in the Large Interior, eating her morning meal.

"I've come to see Midori," Reiko said.

"She's not here." Slurping fish broth, Lady Keisho-in looked surprised. "I thought she was at your house."

"Not this time," Reiko said. "I haven't seen her since the night before last."

"Well, she told me she had important business, so I gave her a holiday," Keisho-in said. "She left here some days ago, early in the morning before I was up." Keisho-in turned to her attendants. "Midori-*chan* hasn't come back at all, has she?"

The women shook their heads. Keisho-in said in peevish disapproval, "I didn't mean for her to be gone so long, and a young lady has no business staying out all night. Midori-*chan* is probably gallivanting in town with disreputable folk. If you find her, tell her she must return at once."

"I will," Reiko said as anxiety stole through her. Midori wasn't the kind of girl who ran wild. Her extended absence boded no good.

After bidding Keisho-in farewell, Reiko went home and ordered a manservant to find out whether Midori had reentered the castle and might be somewhere inside. Reiko sent another servant to Lord Niu's estate in the daimyo district to see if Midori had stopped there to visit her family. Within an hour, Reiko received news that the gate sentries recalled Midori leaving, but she hadn't returned. She wasn't at her family's house, and Reiko doubted that Midori had anywhere else to stay. A dreadful suspicion burgeoned in Reiko's mind.

Then, as she paced in her chamber, oblivious to the sight of Masahiro and his nurses playing in the sunny garden outside her window, she caught sight of a scrap of paper lying on the floor. The wind must have blown it off her desk. Absently, Reiko picked up the paper, and the words she read on it turned suspicion to terrible reality.

Midori had broken her promise and gone to the Black Lotus Temple.

After seeing what the Black Lotus had done to Haru, after the Fugatami murders and the attack by the priests, Reiko knew the sect had no mercy. What if Midori had been caught spying at the temple? The sect would surely kill her. Reiko dreaded telling Sano what had happened, but she must.

She hurried to his office, interrupting him in a meeting with

Hirata and several detectives. "Please excuse my intrusion, but it's an emergency," she said, bowing to Sano.

Sano dismissed the detectives, but asked Hirata to stay. "What's wrong?" he asked quickly.

Reiko knelt and poured out the whole story of Midori's plan to spy on the temple and the note that Reiko had just found. She watched Sano's face reflect incredulity, then outrage.

"You brought Midori into a murder investigation?" he demanded. "You've done many foolish things during this case, but this is the worst!"

"No, I didn't. Midori begged to help," Reiko defended herself as Hirata stared at her in open-mouthed horror. "I told her not to go, but she went anyway."

Shaking his head, Sano smacked his palms down hard on his desk. "You must have given her the idea to go. She wouldn't have thought of it herself. This is all your fault. Midori's only fault is her ill-conceived loyalty to you."

Reiko didn't want to appear craven by making excuses, but neither could she let Sano misinterpret the situation and think the worst of her. She said, "I tried to talk Midori out of spying—"

"But you failed," Sano interrupted, rising as he glared at her. "Or perhaps you didn't really try. Perhaps you wanted to take advantage of your innocent, helpless friend and further your mistaken defense of Haru."

His words battered Reiko like blows. How she wished she could go back in time and restrain Midori from leaving by physical force instead of ineffectual words. Wretched, she gazed up at Sano. "All right, I'm sorry for whatever I did wrong." She felt the trembling and tears beginning again. "Now, please help me rescue Midori before it's too late!"

Hirata sat listening to Sano and Reiko argue, but he hadn't really heard anything after Reiko's announcement that Midori had gone to the Black Lotus Temple and not returned. A torrent of emotions had focused his thoughts upon things he'd forgotten or ignored.

He remembered how Midori had been a loyal friend to him,

and how the world had always seemed brighter and sweeter whenever he was with her. He remembered a rainy evening spent in her company, when he'd thought how happy he would be to have her as his wife. Hirata experienced a powerful surge of tenderness toward Midori.

Then he recalled his recent treatment of her. Caught up in the excitement of high society, he'd spared her little time. He thought of her hovering dejectedly on the fringes of his life, and shame filled him. Now he understood why Midori had changed: She'd been desperately trying to recapture his attention. Horror overwhelmed him as he wondered if she'd decided to be a detective and spy on the Black Lotus Temple so he would take new notice of her. Could he be responsible for whatever trouble Midori had gotten herself into? His mind echoed with stories he'd heard at police headquarters—tales of husbands, wives, and children swallowed up by the Black Lotus and never seen again. He didn't quite understand why he was so upset by Midori's disappearance, but he knew he had to do something.

Wild panic launched Hirata to his feet. "Please excuse me," he said, bowing hastily to Sano. "I must go to the Black Lotus Temple to rescue Midori."

Sano's expression was worried, conflicted. "The shogun has ordered me to stay away from the Black Lotus, and his order includes my retainers."

Reiko exclaimed in outraged alarm: "But we can't just leave her there!"

Hirata wished with all his heart that he could go back in time and treat Midori better so she wouldn't have felt a need to put herself in danger. Suddenly he recalled the warning given him by the police clerk Uchida: "By succumbing to pride and ambition, one may end up losing everything that really matters." Too late, he realized that his shallow new friendships meant nothing to him. What a blind, vain fool he'd been! Midori was all that mattered. He was in love with her, and now he stood to lose her. Hirata wanted to raise an army, storm the temple walls, and tear apart every building until he found Midori, then slay anyone who had hurt her.

Yet his samurai spirit could neither disobey his supreme lord's wishes nor jeopardize Sano, who would share the blame

for his disobedience. Torn between love and honor, overwhelmed by his helplessness, he dropped to his knees before
Sano.

"Please," he said in a voice that broke on a sob. "Help me
find a way to rescue Midori."

Sano decided that Midori's disappearance justified a search
of the Black Lotus Temple, which required the shogun's special
permission. He and Hirata hastened to the palace. There they
found Tokugawa Tsunayoshi seated on the dais in his reception
room. As various officials presented documents for his approval, he affixed his personal signature seal to each.

"Ahh, *Sōsakan-sama* and Hirata-*san*," he said, smiling wear-
ily. "This is such tedious, exhausting work that I, ahh, hope
you have come to refresh me with interesting news."

Sano and Hirata knelt below the dais and bowed. "Yes, we
do bring news, Your Excellency," Sano said. "Niu Midori, one
of your honorable mother's ladies-in-waiting and daughter of
the daimyo of Satsuma and Osumi Provinces, went to the Black
Lotus Temple two days ago. No one has seen or heard from
her since."

"Most puzzling," Tsunayoshi said, wrinkling his brow in an
obvious attempt to guess how this concerned him.

"Recently there have been some serious acts of violence
associated with the sect," Sano continued.

He glanced at Hirata sitting silently beside him. Hirata's face
was set in rigid lines that betrayed his desperation to get to the
point of the conversation. Yet asking the shogun to change an
order was an extreme step for which Sano must demonstrate
strong cause.

"Minister Fugatami and his wife were murdered and their
children kidnapped by the killers, who painted the Black Lotus
symbol in blood on the walls," Sano continued. "My entourage
and I were attacked and some of my men killed by armed Black
Lotus priests. Now it appears that Niu Midori is trapped in the
temple and is most probably in grave danger. I know that you
have ordered me to stay away from the Black Lotus sect, but

I must beg you to let us go into the temple to save an innocent, helpless young woman."

The shogun frowned in displeasure. The officials stirred uneasily, and Sano sensed their wish to flee. He himself wouldn't want to be around when some other foolhardy soul challenged the shogun's authority.

"Niu Midori is a good, kind, loyal girl," Hirata blurted. "She—I—"

As his voice faltered in his effort to convey how much Midori meant to him without expressing unseemly emotions, the shogun's expression softened.

"Ahh, I see that the young woman in question is important to you," Tsunayoshi said, perceptive regarding matters of love, if about nothing else. "Something certainly must be done to rescue her." Worry clouded his face. "However, I cannot allow anyone to interfere with the Black Lotus."

Sano thought of the powerful Tokugawa relatives intimidating the shogun into protecting their religious sect. His heart sank, and Hirata flashed him an agonized look.

"Also, I do not think I should, ahh, revoke my orders." The sho-gun pondered a moment, then said uncertainly, "But maybe just this once . . . ?"

Hope leapt in Sano; he heard Hirata inhale a deep breath. Then a panel of the landscape mural on a wall of the chamber swung open. Senior Elder Makino walked in from the adjacent room. The sight of the emaciated Makino gave Sano an unpleasant shock. Makino must have listened to the whole conversation, and his arrival signaled trouble.

"Ahh, Makino-*san*, how convenient that you should come now," the shogun said with a glad smile. "Maybe you can help me resolve a dilemma that has just arisen."

With a covert, hostile glance at Sano, the senior elder knelt near the dais and bowed to Tokugawa Tsunayoshi. "Certainly I shall do my best."

Sano inwardly cursed the bad luck that Makino had happened to be around when he could least afford a battle over their lord's favor.

The shogun explained the situation; obviously, he had no idea that Makino eavesdropped on him. "I think maybe I should allow the *sōsakan-sama* to go to the temple and fetch Niu Midori as he wishes to do, but I have already banned him from the temple." He addressed Makino with timid entreaty: "What is your opinion?"

"I advise against granting the *sōsakan-sama*'s wish," Makino said, just as Sano had expected. "The lady may or may not be at the temple, and in any case, his suppositions about the Black Lotus do not signify that she is in any need of rescue or that you should revoke your order."

"We shouldn't spend valuable time debating theories when the wisest course of action would be to remove Niu Midori from the temple at once," Sano said, fighting impatience.

He wondered whether Makino was one of the high-ranking officials who belonged to the Black Lotus and protected it, then thought not. Makino was too selfish for fanatical loyalty to a religious order. More likely, he just wanted to prevent Sano from getting a special concession from the shogun.

Tsunayoshi gave Sano a confused, benevolent look, as though he might agree with Sano just to end this conversation, which taxed his limited mental powers.

Makino said hastily, "But there is proof that the *sōsakan-sama* wishes to defy your orders for a reason that has nothing to do with a missing lady. In fact, I venture to say that the lady is not missing at all, and the *sōsakan-sama* has made up the story to further his own sinister purpose."

As Sano wondered what on earth Makino was talking about, the senior elder slipped his bony fingers beneath the sash at his waist and removed a folded sheet of paper.

"This document reveals the *sōsakan-sama*'s true motives." With a flourish, Makino unfolded the paper and held it up for the assembly's inspection.

Sano saw his own calligraphy and recognized a letter he'd recently written. An awful prescience chilled him.

"It is a letter sent by the *sōsakan-sama* to the Honorable Chamberlain Yanagisawa," said Makino. He flashed Sano a sly look, adding, "Sometimes routine inspections at highway checkpoints turn up the most interesting items."

Makino's minions had confiscated the letter from the messenger, Sano realized. He saw Hirata anxiously watching him, but in his sudden panic, he couldn't think how to forestall impending disaster.

"Your Excellency, shall I read you the relevant passage of the letter?" Makino said.

"Yes, do," the shogun said, sounding mystified but curious. Exuding satisfaction, Makino read:

"Honorable Chamberlain, I must bring to your attention a matter that poses a serious threat to the Tokugawa regime. While investigating a case at the Black Lotus Temple, I discovered that the sect has gained followers among the upper echelon of the *bakufu,* and much influence over the shogun. I believe the sect is responsible for the recent murder of the Minister of Temples and Shrines, who opposed it. Citizens have accused the Black Lotus of kidnapping, extortion, and violent attacks on the public, and these accusations are too many to disregard. However, the shogun has prohibited me from investigating the Black Lotus Temple, apparently because he has been persuaded to shield its secret activities. Therefore, I beg you to return to Edo and join forces with me to learn what the Black Lotus is up to and combat its rise to power."

The ominous quiet that followed his reading seemed to reverberate like the echo of a bomb just exploded. Sano realized that the senior elder had been hoarding the letter to use when the right opportunity arose. He guessed what Makino meant to do to him, and his mind raced to construct a defense.

The shogun exclaimed in bafflement, "But what does this mean?"

"I was informing Chamberlain Yanagisawa about the Black Lotus situation," Sano said, striving to stay calm. "I hoped that he could persuade Your Excellency that the sect is dangerous and we must protect the nation from it."

"What you were really doing was inviting the honorable chamberlain to join you in persecuting a subsidiary of the Tokugawa family temple," Makino countered. "You want him to help you destroy the Black Lotus and thereby eliminate a rival in your quest for control over the *bakufu.*" Makino turned to the shogun. "Your Excellency, this letter is conclusive evidence that the *sōsakan-sama* is plotting against you."

Pressing a thin, delicate hand to his chest, the shogun stared at Sano. His eyes reflected the appalled horror that Sano felt. "Is this true?"

"No!" Hirata burst out in impassioned outrage. "My master is your loyal, devoted servant!"

"Of course he would deny the truth, Your Excellency," Makino said reasonably. "As the *sōsakan-sama*'s chief retainer, he is part of this treasonous plot."

Sano could hardly believe that he'd come here for permission to rescue Midori and ended up accused of a crime for which execution was the punishment. Makino was a clever, ruthless adversary, and Sano had to fend him off without injuring him and provoking future retribution.

"There's been a misunderstanding," he said. "The honorable senior elder has read into my letter a meaning I never intended. It was an honest mistake, and I suggest that we all agree to forget his accusation and resume discussing the rescue of Niu Midori."

"We cannot forget treason," Makino huffed. "Your Excellency, he is trying to talk his way out of punishment like the cowardly, dishonorable traitor he is."

"Don't you insult my master!" Hirata glared at Makino.

The senior elder continued railing against Sano while Hirata shouted angry objections and Sano tried to quiet him. The argument raged until the shogun flung up his arms and shouted, "Stop! I cannot take any more of this noise!" Abrupt silence fell. Pressing his palms against his temples, the shogun winced. "You have given me a terrible headache. I cannot believe that my, ahh, *sōsakan-sama* would plot against me, but neither can I believe that Senior Elder Makino would, ahh, slander a comrade. I do not know what to think!"

He fluttered his hands at the assembly. "Get out! Everyone! Leave me in peace!"

Sano, Hirata, Makino, and the frightened officials bowed hastily and leapt to their feet.

"Your Excellency," Makino ventured cautiously.

"If you, ahh, really believe that Sano-*san* is a traitor, then show me some, ahh, proof besides that letter," Tokugawa Tsunayoshi said with uncharacteristic decisiveness born of pique.

To Sano he said, "And if you want me to let you fetch the lady from inside the Black Lotus Temple, then bring me proof that she needs rescuing. For now, I refuse to think any more about either subject!"

32

Those who will not accept the true law of the Black Lotus
Will be plunged into the deepest hell,
A place dark and foul,
Beset by evil spirits,
To suffer for countless eons.

— FROM THE BLACK LOTUS SUTRA

"We can't rescue Midori without defying the shogun and dishonoring ourselves, but we can't leave her at the mercy of the Black Lotus," Hirata said in despair. "What are we going to do?"

Sano walked beside his chief retainer through the stone-walled passage leading downhill through Edo Castle. Though still shaken by Makino's surprise attack on him, he applied his mind to their immediate problem.

"Haru is our key to solving the case, defeating the Black Lotus, and saving Midori," he said.

Hirata stared, incredulous. "But she's proved herself good for nothing except telling lies and turning you and Lady Reiko against each other. We can't stake Midori's safety upon her!"

"There's one last way to get the truth out of Haru and get Midori out of the temple with the shogun's permission," Sano said.

When they entered the courtyard of his estate, he called a groom to bring their horses.

"Where are we going?" Hirata asked.

"To see Magistrate Ueda."

Soon they were in the Hibiya official district, seated in the magistrate's office. Sano said to his father-in-law, "I wish to convene Haru's trial. Will you oblige?"

"Certainly," said Magistrate Ueda. "Have you found definitive evidence of her guilt?"

"No," Sano admitted, "but there are compelling reasons for forcing Haru to reveal what she did and what she knows about the Black Lotus." He described how Midori had disappeared, the shogun had ordered him to stay away from the temple, and Senior Elder Makino had accused him of plotting against the shogun. "A trial could produce facts that will convince the shogun that Midori is in danger, before Makino can manufacture evidence to prove I'm a traitor."

"Putting Haru on trial will work only if she is in possession of the facts and can be persuaded to reveal them," Magistrate Ueda pointed out.

"I know she knows more than she's admitted." Deep instinct told Sano he was right. "And a trial can pressure a person into cooperating when all other methods have failed."

"When would you like me to conduct the trial?" Magistrate Ueda asked.

"This evening, at the hour of the rooster."

"But that's too long to wait!" Hirata burst out. "Every moment Midori stays at the temple endangers her more." He looked anxiously from Sano to Magistrate Ueda.

"We can't rush things and ruin our last chance to secure Haru's cooperation," Sano said. "We must prepare carefully, which will take time."

He only hoped that Midori would survive the delay.

*   *   *

The absolute darkness of the Black Lotus's underground prison was like a monstrous live creature, breathing a draft redolent of human misery, its heartbeat the pulsing bellows. It filled the cell where Midori lay curled in a corner. The chill dampness penetrated her thin robe, and she shivered. No one had said what her punishment would be for spying on the sect, or spoken to her at all after the priests had imprisoned her here. Would they torture her, force her to dig tunnels, or use her in evil rites? Would they kill her, or just leave her to go mad?

At first Midori had mustered her courage and tried to escape. She'd pounded at the heavy wooden door, which refused to yield. Groping in the darkness, she'd located a square opening high in the door, and an air vent in the wall, but both openings were too small to crawl through. Midori had torn planks off the low ceiling and tried to dig her way up, but the clay was too hard. She'd shouted for help, but no one aboveground could hear her. There seemed to be no other prisoners in this branch of the tunnel, and finally Midori had wept in exhausted, helpless solitude.

Now she had no idea how many hours she'd spent in this cell. Once, she'd seen light outside, and someone had shoved a meal tray through the crack under the door. Too famished to worry about poison, Midori had devoured the rice, pickles, and dried fish. She'd slept, then awakened blind and terrified in the darkness. Midori did not know whether each passing moment bettered her chances of survival or brought her closer to death. Her hope of deliverance rested upon Reiko.

Reiko was the only person who had any way of knowing she'd come to the temple and figuring out that she'd been caught. Surely Reiko would come looking for her. Yet even as Midori sought comfort in the idea, doubts plagued her mind. What if Reiko didn't find the note? Even if she did, and even if she sent a rescue party, how would it find Midori?

She thought of Hirata, and her heart ached. If only she'd been satisfied with the crumbs of attention he'd tossed her! Now she would probably never see him again.

Footsteps approached her cell. Hope and terror collided within Midori. She yearned for human contact, yet she feared the punishment that High Priest Anraku had promised. Light shone through the square hole in the door, brightening as the footsteps neared. Sitting up, Midori fought an urge to leap toward the welcome illumination. She wrapped her arms around her knees, helplessly waiting for whatever would happen.

In the opening appeared the side of a round paper lantern, like the curve of the moon. It shone into Midori's cell, momentarily blinding her. Then her vision returned, and she saw beside the lantern a portion of a face, containing a single eye focused on her with dark, gleaming concentration. It belonged to Anraku.

A whimper issued from Midori; her heart thudded in terror. She wanted to look away, but Anraku's gaze held hers captive. Pleas for mercy rose to her lips, but she couldn't speak.

Then a woman said, "Why must we keep her?" Midori recognized the sharp, irritated voice of Abbess Junketsu-in.

"She is special," Anraku said quietly.

Midori realized that they were talking about her.

"What makes her different from anyone else?" Junketsu-in said. "And haven't you enough women already?" Midori heard jealousy in her tone. "I think you should have gotten rid of her as soon as we found out she was a spy."

The high priest didn't answer. Alarm flared in Midori.

"She's no problem as long as she's down here," said a man's rough voice. It was Priest Kumashiro. "But if she somehow escapes, she could cause trouble. Keeping her alive is too risky. Please allow me to eliminate her at once."

Midori's alarm turned to horror. But Anraku spoke again. "Remember what my vision has foretold. Three signs shall herald our day of destiny. We have already witnessed human sacrifice and persecution against our kind, but we still await the third sign. And I have had a new vision."

Anraku exuded mystical energy like a fire radiating heat through the door. Midori cringed from it.

"The Buddha said that the capture of Niu Midori presages the third sign," Anraku continued, "and we shall not achieve glory unless she remains alive to perform a critical role."

"What role? Why her?" demanded Junketsu-in.

"How long must we tolerate an enemy in our midst?" Kumashiro said, clearly displeased.

Anraku's tactile stare probed Midori. "Question me no more. You shall know soon enough."

His face and the lantern vanished from the peephole. Darkness immersed the cell as footsteps receded down the corridor. Anraku's spell over Midori relaxed like kite strings when the wind ceases, and she hurled herself against the door.

"Please don't leave me! Come back!" she cried.

The darkness and solitude seemed even worse now. Her terror was more acute because although she now knew she would live awhile, she didn't know how much longer, or for what terrible purpose.

"Help, help!" Midori screamed. Bursting into wild sobs, she pounded on the door. "Let me out!"

There was no response except the echo of her own desperate voice resounding through the tunnels.

33

If you among the faithful should encounter trouble with the
law,
Face punishment, about to forfeit your life,
The Bodhisattva of Infinite Power will break the
executioner's sword in pieces.

—FROM THE BLACK LOTUS SUTRA

"The trial of Haru shall commence," announced Magistrate Ueda.

He was seated upon the dais in the Court of Justice, a cavernous hall with barred windows set in paneled walls, illuminated by lanterns. Sano sat at his right; secretaries flanked them. All wore black ceremonial robes.

The magistrate continued, "Haru is accused of four crimes: arson, and the murders of Police Commander Oyama, a peasant woman named Chie, and a small boy of unknown identity."

The secretaries wrote, recording his words. Sano hid anxiety behind a cool façade. He'd spent the day preparing for the trial. Now, as twilight dimmed the windows, he hoped to secure a conviction and elicit facts that would convince the shogun to authorize a rescue expedition to the Black Lotus Temple, but the outcome of the trial was by no means certain.

A large audience sat in rows on the floor, in a haze of smoke from tobacco pipes. Sano eyed Hirata, who knelt among other Tokugawa officials, apart from a delegation of civilian town leaders. Hirata's features were strained with worry about Midori.

Magistrate Ueda addressed the guards stationed at the door at the far end of the court: "Bring in the defendant."

The guards opened the heavy, carved door. Through it walked two soldiers, with Haru between them. Her hands were bound by ropes, and her ankles shackled in iron cuffs joined by a thick chain. She wore a gray muslin kimono and straw sandals, and her hair was braided. The bruises around her eyes had darkened to violet; her puffy nose and raw, split lips rendered her face almost unrecognizable to Sano. As the guards led her toward the dais, she moved stiffly, as if in pain.

Uneasy murmurs swept the audience. Magistrate Ueda's calm didn't waver, yet Sano doubted that this father of a beloved daughter could remain unmoved by the injured girl. She might induce sympathy in the man designated to judge her.

The guards positioned Haru on her knees on a straw mat on the *shirasu,* an area of floor directly before the dais, covered by white sand, the symbol of truth. Haru bowed low. Looking down at her bent back, Sano could pity her himself.

"Look up," Magistrate Ueda ordered her.

Haru lifted a woeful face.

"Do you understand that the purpose of this trial is to determine whether you are guilty of the arson and murders for which you were arrested?" Magistrate Ueda said.

"Yes, master." Haru's voice was a barely audible whisper that the audience strained forward to hear.

"First we shall hear the facts of the crimes and evidence against you, presented by His Excellency the Shogun's *sōsakan-sama,*" said Magistrate Ueda. "Then you may speak in your own defense. Afterward, I shall render my decision." He nodded to Sano. "Proceed."

"Thank you, Honorable Magistrate." Sano described the fire at the Black Lotus Temple, how the victims found in the cottage had died, then how the fire brigade had discovered lamp oil, a torch, and Haru at the scene. "Haru claimed to have lost her memory of the time preceding the fire. She insisted that she didn't set the fire or kill anyone. But my investigation has proved that she is a liar, arsonist, and murderess."

Haru sat with eyes humbly downcast, like a martyr resigned to persecution. Sano was glad that Reiko wasn't here. He hadn't seen her since morning, when she'd told him Midori was missing; he hadn't told her about the trial because he didn't want her around to interfere. Next he related Haru's probable involvement in her husband's death, and what Abbess Junketsu-in and Dr. Miwa had said about her misbehavior at the temple. He mentioned that the two girls from the orphanage had seen Haru go to the cottage.

"Therefore, Haru had both the bad character and the opportunity necessary to commit the crimes," Sano said.

Still, he feared that his argument would be weakened by his failure to produce the witnesses to speak for themselves. Magistrate Ueda understood that the shogun had prohibited him from contact with Black Lotus members, but if he had the least uncertainty about whether the witnesses had told the truth or Sano had accurately reported their statements, he might give Haru the benefit of the doubt.

"Now I shall show that Haru also had reason to kill," Sano said. "After further interrogation, she admitted that Commander Oyama once forced her to have sexual relations with him. There is a witness who can prove that she hated him for mistreating her. Will Oyama Jinsai please come forward?"

The young samurai rose from the audience, knelt before the dais, and bowed. Under Sano's questioning, Jinsai described how Commander Oyama had used the girls at the Black Lotus Temple and introduced him to Haru, who had glared and spat at the commander.

"I say that on the night of his murder, Commander Oyama again violated Haru, and she killed him in revenge," Sano concluded. "Afterward, she set fire to the cottage to disguise the circumstances of his death."

Just then, the door opened, and Reiko slipped into the room. Sano beheld her in dismay. As she knelt behind the audience, her level gaze met his. Sano experienced a stab of alarm.

"Honorable Magistrate, I recommend that Haru be condemned," Sano said, hiding his concern about what Reiko might do.

"Your counsel will be given serious consideration," Magistrate Ueda said.

Yet Sano knew that Haru's lack of apparent connection with the other victims was the major flaw in his case, which Magistrate Ueda wouldn't miss. Because the murders were obviously connected, if she hadn't committed them all, then perhaps she hadn't committed any of them. As much as the magistrate wanted to serve justice, he required evidence to support a guilty verdict.

The men in the audience whispered among themselves. Reiko leaned forward, her expression avid. Haru sat meekly, the picture of wounded innocence. Sano fought rising anxiety as he observed the desperation on Hirata's face. Time was speeding by; Midori was still inside the temple, and he might neither secure Haru's conviction nor extract the truth from the girl.

"I shall now hear the defendant's story," Magistrate Ueda said.

An expectant hush descended upon the audience. Reiko clasped her hands tightly under her sleeves. Anger at Sano twisted inside her. How could he waste time persecuting Haru when he should be trying to rescue Midori? And he hadn't even done Reiko the courtesy of telling her he'd scheduled the trial! She'd learned about it by chance, when she'd come to ask her father to use his influence to get Sano permission to enter the Black Lotus Temple, and a clerk had told her the trial was under way. But of course Sano didn't want her to interfere with his destruction of Haru. He was cutting her out of the final stage of the investigation and ending her involvement in his work forever.

Yet Reiko wouldn't give up her vocation without a fight. Nor could she let Haru suffer for the crimes of the Black Lotus while there was any chance that the girl was innocent. Might Reiko still ensure that her last investigation ended in justice?

The flaws in Sano's argument gave the girl a chance for reprieve, and Reiko wondered why he'd rushed the trial. Still, his haste favored her and Haru. Reiko hoped that Haru would make a good showing.

Magistrate Ueda turned to Haru. "What have you to say for yourself?"

"I didn't do it." Head bowed, the girl spoke in a low but distinct voice.

"Say specifically what you did not do," Magistrate Ueda instructed her.

"Kill Commander Oyama."

"What about the woman and boy?"

"I didn't kill them, either," Haru said, and Reiko could see her trembling with fear.

"Did you set fire to the cottage?" Magistrate Ueda asked.

"No, master."

The magistrate seemed unaffected by Haru's pained earnestness. "There has been much evidence presented against you," he said gravely, "and in order to prove your innocence, you must refute it. Let us begin with the death of your husband. Did you burn his house?"

"No, master." Haru sniffled, weeping now. Reiko saw Sano betray his disdain with a slight compression of his lips, but her father's expression remained inscrutable.

"Did you go to the cottage the night before the fire?" the magistrate asked.

"No, master."

"Then how did you come to be found there?"

"I don't know."

"What had you been doing previously?"

"I can't remember."

Reiko listened, upset that Haru was repeating the same story that hadn't convinced Sano. It probably wouldn't convince the magistrate, either. Reiko believed more strongly than ever that Haru did know something about the crimes and wished the girl would tell the truth, rather than forfeit her last chance to clear herself and take her secrets to the grave.

Magistrate Ueda thoughtfully regarded Haru. "If you expect me to believe in your innocence, then you must offer some

explanation for why you were at the cottage and how three
people died in your vicinity."

Cowering, the girl shook her head. Reiko watched in anxious
dismay. Surely Haru realized what a poor impression she was
making. Was she concealing facts that would incriminate her?

"Have you anything more to say?" Magistrate Ueda said.

"I don't know why I was there," Haru mumbled. "I didn't
set the fire. I didn't kill anyone."

The magistrate frowned, clearly weighing her denials against
the case Sano had presented. Reiko felt her heart pounding as
she hoped her father would see that there wasn't enough evidence to convict Haru. Yet she feared that Haru deserved conviction.

At last Magistrate Ueda said, "I shall now render my verdict."

And his verdict would be final, Reiko knew, whether justice
was served or contravened. Suddenly Reiko couldn't watch
passively any longer. "Excuse me," she blurted.

Everyone stared in astonishment at the spectacle of a woman
talking out of turn. Reiko, who had never spoken in a public
assembly, experienced a daunting embarrassment.

"What is it?" Magistrate Ueda's cold manner said that she'd
better have a good reason for interrupting the trial.

Seeing Sano eye her with consternation, Reiko understood
that what she intended to do would probably destroy any hope
for a reconciliation between them. Sano would divorce her and
keep their son, as he had the legal right to do. Her courage
almost failed, until she thought of what would happen if she
didn't act. Haru would be convicted; the Black Lotus would
go on to commit more attacks and murders; Sano would be
blamed for failing in his duty to protect the public. The shogun
would order Sano, Reiko, Masahiro, and their relatives and
close associates executed as punishment. Only Reiko could
save them all, by doing her best now.

Reiko forced herself to say, "I wish to speak on behalf of
the accused." She saw gladness dawn on Haru's bruised face,
as though the girl anticipated salvation.

"Honorable Magistrate, unsolicited witnesses should not be
allowed to interfere with justice," Sano hastened to say.

He believed that the magistrate had intended to decide in his favor, Reiko thought. Magistrate Ueda addressed her with polite formality: "What can you add to that which has already been said?"

"I—I can present evidence that indicates the crimes were committed by someone other than the accused," Reiko faltered, intimidated by the audience's stares.

Sano hadn't presented this evidence because the law didn't require him to do so. Reiko's chest constricted with hope that her father would agree to weigh her testimony in his decision, and dread that he wouldn't.

"Spurious accusations against other persons are neither evidence nor relevant to the trial of Haru," Sano argued.

A fleeting, pained expression clouded Magistrate Ueda's features: He was loath to take sides in a public dispute between Reiko and Sano. Then he said, "Since a life is at stake, I shall grant Lady Reiko the privilege of speaking."

Rejoicing that his mercy had prevailed over Sano's objections, Reiko rose and walked toward the dais. As she passed Hirata, she glimpsed his undisguised horror. She knelt beside the *shirasu,* and Haru welcomed her with a grateful smile. Sano fixed on her a look that seemed to say, Please don't do this. Trust me, and soon you'll understand.

Reiko ignored him. In a voice that quavered with nervousness, she described her impressions of Haru as troubled but harmless. She drew courage from her certainty that she was doing the right thing, no matter what Sano thought, and clung to her persistent feeling that events would somehow exonerate Haru. She told about Abbess Junketsu-in, Dr. Miwa, and Kumashiro's suspiciously determined efforts to blame Haru for the crimes and prevent Reiko from making inquiries into the Black Lotus sect. Reiko mentioned her encounter with Pious Truth and his story of torture, slavery, and murder at the temple.

Mutters of surprise rumbled in the audience. Magistrate Ueda listened in stoic silence, while Sano watched Haru. The girl's face acquired a strange expression that momentarily unbalanced Reiko. It almost seemed as if Haru didn't want the Black Lotus maligned. Didn't she understand that incriminating the sect was to her advantage?

Recovering, Reiko described the murder of Minister Fugatami and his wife, the beating Haru had received in Edo Jail, and the attack on herself and Sano.

"Honorable Magistrate, these incidents represent the Black Lotus's efforts to destroy its enemies," she concluded breathlessly. "The sect killed Minister Fugatami to prevent him from censuring it, and tried to assassinate the *sōsakan-sama* and myself because we were probing its affairs. Its thugs hurt Haru because she refused to confess." Now Reiko's voice rang out in a passionate conviction she didn't feel: "The Black Lotus, not Haru, committed the arson and murders, and has framed her to protect itself."

A short silence followed. Then Magistrate Ueda said in a neutral tone, "Your points are noted. Now I offer the *sōsakan-sama* the opportunity to address them."

Reiko felt her heart sink at the thought that Sano might undo whatever good she'd accomplished.

"Lady Reiko has portrayed you as the innocent victim, slandered and framed by Black Lotus members," Sano said quietly to Haru. "But it's not just they who have seen you for what you are."

Haru gazed up at him, wary and uncomprehending.

"The people who know you best can also attest to your evils," Sano said, then turned to Magistrate Ueda. "There are two witnesses I didn't present earlier because their personal situation is sensitive. I request permission for them to testify now."

Alarm shot through Reiko. Who were these witnesses? What was Sano up to?

"Permission granted," Magistrate Ueda said.

Sano nodded to Hirata, who left the court, then returned with a middle-aged couple. Both man and woman wore the modest cotton kimonos of peasants. They huddled together, their faces apprehensive.

"I introduce Haru's parents," Sano said.

Haru cried joyfully, "Mother! Father!" Shedding her meek, frightened demeanor, she rose up on her knees and leaned toward the couple. "Oh, how I've missed you! And now you've come to save me!"

But Reiko guessed why Sano had brought them. Filled with dismay, she watched helplessly as Hirata led Haru's parents up to the dais. They averted their eyes from Haru. Kneeling, they bowed to the magistrate. The mother began weeping quietly; the father hung his head.

"What's wrong, Mother?" Haru said in confusion. "Aren't you glad to see me?"

"Your cooperation is much appreciated," Sano said.

His tone conveyed sympathy for the shame the couple obviously suffered from public exposure at their child's trial. In response to gentle questions from him, the parents described how they'd married Haru off, and her contradictory stories about the fire that had killed her husband.

"Why are you saying those things?" Haru interrupted, and hurt eclipsed the happiness on her face. "I told you I didn't set the fire. Why do you want to turn everyone against me?"

Her father regarded her sadly. "We were wrong to hide what we know about you. Now we must tell the truth."

"And you must face up to what you've done," said her mother, turning a tear-streaked face toward Haru. "Repent, and cleanse the disgrace from your spirit."

"I haven't done anything wrong," Haru protested, beginning to wheeze as she glared at her parents. "You never loved me. No matter how hard I tried to please you, I was never good enough. It's all your fault that I'm in trouble."

Sano had kept quiet during this exchange. He'd identified Haru's feelings for her parents as a vulnerability, Reiko thought, deploring the cruel tactic by which he'd exposed a dark side of Haru. Now he said, "But it wasn't your parents who committed murder and arson. It was you."

"They made me marry that horrible old man. I told them how badly he treated me and begged them to let me come home, but they wouldn't listen." Louder wheezes rasped from Haru; she squirmed, straining at her bonds. "You didn't care how I suffered," she shouted at her parents, who cringed. "All you cared about was the money the old man gave you. I had to protect myself."

"And that's why you killed your husband?" Sano said.

"No, no, no!" Haru shrieked, rocking back and forth. "The night he died, he got angry at me for serving him cold tea. He hit me, and his arm knocked over a lamp. It set his clothes on fire. I ran away and let him and his house burn. He deserved to die!"

The confession descended upon Reiko like a vast iron bell that resonated with her shock and horror. She barely heard the audience's outcry. Everything seemed hazy. She felt sick because she no longer believed anything Haru said.

"More lies." Sano addressed the girl with scornful contempt. "I suggest that you threw the lamp at your husband and set him on fire. Did you kill Commander Oyama, too?"

Haru's resistance suddenly broke into hysteria. "Yes," she moaned. "Yes, yes!"

Reiko bowed her head, mournfully resigned to the knowledge that Haru had deceived her from the start. She'd compromised her marriage and her vocation over a liar and criminal. There would be no exoneration of Haru, no ultimate justification of Reiko's defense of the girl. Reiko had made a fool of herself in public and failed to direct the power of the law toward the Black Lotus. Mortified, she looked to see if Sano would acknowledge his victory over her, but he was watching Haru.

"What happened that night at the Black Lotus Temple?" he said.

"Commander Oyama told me to meet him in the cottage. I didn't want to, but the Black Lotus needed his patronage." The words rushed from Haru like water pouring through a broken dam. "So I sneaked out of the orphanage. When I got to the cottage, he was already there, naked on the bed. He ordered me to—" Haru's voice dropped in shame "—to suck on him.

"He said that unless I obeyed, he would stop giving money to the Black Lotus, and Anraku would be angry with me and expel me from the temple. I was afraid he was right, so I knelt and took him in my mouth." Haru gulped, as if swallowing nausea engendered by the memory. "Suddenly his legs came up around my neck and started squeezing, choking me. I begged him to let go, but he just shouted at me to keep sucking. I broke free, and he started hitting me. He pinned me down on the floor and rammed himself inside me. He was strangling me. Everything started going dark. I was so frightened that he was going to kill me."

Through her emotional turmoil, Reiko absorbed the fact that

Oyama had caused Haru's bruises. But what did it matter that Reiko had correctly believed Haru had been the victim of an attack that night, when she'd been mistaken about too much else?

Haru began to cry in loud, whooping sobs. "I had to stop him. There was an alcove in the wall, with a little brass statue of Kannon inside. I grabbed the statue and struck at his face with it. He ducked, but he let go of my neck and fell off me. I kicked him in the crotch. He howled and doubled up in pain. Then I hit him on the back of the head with the statue. All of a sudden his voice stopped. His eyes were open, but he didn't move. There was blood all over his head, on the floor, on the statue. I knew he was dead."

Whether Haru had really killed Oyama in self-defense, or was twisting the truth again, Reiko didn't know what to think, for she could no longer trust her instincts. They'd failed her, and she perceived the worst of what she'd done. Instead of serving justice, she'd sabotaged Sano's work and dishonored her vocation. Self-hatred tormented Reiko.

"I was so terrified that I couldn't move," Haru went on. "I sat there for a long time, crying and wondering what to do. I thought of going to High Priest Anraku for help, but I was afraid he would get angry at me for killing an important patron. Finally I decided to make it look like an accident. I picked up the statue, left Commander Oyama lying in the cottage, and ran to the main hall. I wiped off the statue and set it in a niche with a lot of other statues like it. Then I got the idea that Commander Oyama was still alive. I had to see, so I went back to the cottage. That was when someone came up behind me and hit my head. I didn't see who it was. The next thing I knew, the firebell was ringing, I was lying in the garden, and it was morning."

Tears streaming down her face, Haru cast a beseeching gaze up at Sano. "Yes, I killed Commander Oyama. But not the others. I didn't even know they were there. That's the truth, I swear!"

It sounded as if someone else had killed Chie and the boy, then framed Haru for their murders by knocking her unconscious so that she would be found at the scene. Their bodies must have been put in the cottage while Haru was hiding the statue, or while she lay oblivious. Perhaps someone else had indeed set the fire. Yet Reiko had little hope of this, and even if the girl was telling the truth now, it would make little difference to her fate.

"Honorable Magistrate," Sano said, "whether or not Haru is responsible for the deaths of the woman and boy, she has confessed to killing an important man. She deserves punishment."

Nor did the possibility of a second murderer change the fact that Reiko had been wrong to ever believe in Haru's innocence. Sick with shame and regret, Reiko wanted to rush from the room, but a stubborn need to see the case through to the end compelled her to stay.

"Haru, I pronounce you guilty of two instances of murder and arson," Magistrate Ueda said solemnly. Reiko saw in his face his personal conviction that he'd chosen the correct verdict. "The law requires that I sentence you to death by burning."

"No!" Haru's shrill, terrified protest pierced the quiet of the courtroom. She writhed, as if already beset by flames. "Please, I can't bear it." She turned to Reiko, begging, "Help! Don't let them burn me!"

Reiko wordlessly shook her head because she couldn't help Haru even if she'd wanted to.

Sano exchanged glances with Magistrate Ueda. When the magistrate nodded, Sano said to Haru, "There is one way you can earn a quicker, more merciful death, if you wish."

The girl exclaimed in desperate relief: "Yes! I'll do anything!"

"You must tell me everything you know about what's going on inside the Black Lotus Temple and what the sect plans to do," Sano said.

Comprehension stunned Reiko. Now she knew why Sano had convened the trial, then pushed so hard for Haru's conviction. He'd meant to break Haru, thus forcing her to inform on the Black Lotus. Reiko wished he'd told her his intentions even as she inwardly berated herself for not guessing them. By defending Haru, she'd almost ruined Sano's attempt to get the facts needed to justify an inspection of the temple. She remembered the look he'd given her: He'd been trying to let her know what he was doing. By disregarding his silent plea, she might have cost Midori her life!

"But I can't tell," Haru said, recoiling in horror. "I mean, I don't know anything."

"Very well," Sano said. "Then you must endure your original sentence." He signaled to the guards. "Convey her to the funeral pyre at the execution ground."

The guards moved toward Haru, who cried, "No! Wait!"

Sano's raised hand halted the guards. Reiko watched Haru struggle against whatever loyalty or fear kept her in thrall to the Black Lotus. Her eyes flicked from side to side; she bit her lips. Sano looked directly at Reiko for the first time since before Haru had confessed; his frown warned Reiko to keep silent. She bowed her head, miserably aware that she'd already done too much wrong for her to even consider intervening. Haru's fate was in her own hands now.

At last Haru slumped, her resistance gone. "The mountains will erupt," she mumbled. "Flames will consume the city. The waters will flow with death, and the air will breathe poison. The sky will burn and the earth explode."

A chill passed through Reiko as she recognized the words spoken by Pious Truth when the priests captured him. Puzzled exclamations broke out among the audience.

Haru spoke in an emotionless monotone, as if reciting a lesson: "High Priest Anraku has transformed his followers into an army of destroyers who will set fires and bombs around Edo and poison the wells. They will slay the citizens in the streets. The conflagration of death and destruction will spread all across Japan. Only the true believers of the Black Lotus will survive. They shall achieve enlightenment, acquire magical powers, and rule a new world."

34

When the faithful hear the prophecy,
They will rush to meet their destiny,
And in body and mind be filled with joy.
—FROM THE BLACK LOTUS SUTRA

The highway approaching the Zōjō temple district lay beneath a clouded indigo night sky. Faint radiance from the full moon behind the clouds touched the hilltops. The forest bordering the road loomed still in the windless air. Hoofbeats and the steady rhythm of marching steps came from the direction of Edo to the north.

Sano, clad in full armor, rode beside Hirata near the head of a procession that numbered two hundred troops mounted and on foot, including all his detectives and guards, plus other Tokugawa soldiers from Edo Castle. Their lanterns illuminated grim faces beneath iron helmets.

"What if we're too late?" Hirata said anxiously. "If the Black Lotus has hurt Midori . . ."

"We're almost there. She'll be fine," Sano said.

Yet he, too, was worried that they wouldn't reach the temple soon enough to rescue Midori. The necessary preparations for this expedition had consumed hours that might have cost Midori her life.

After Haru had confessed and agreed to inform on the Black Lotus, Magistrate Ueda had adjourned the trial. Sano and Hirata had thoroughly interrogated Haru about the sect's activities. She'd confirmed Pious Truth's story and admitted that she'd been among a group of sect members responsible for the trouble in Shinagawa, which was a rehearsal for an attack on Edo. She'd claimed to know where High Priest Anraku's underground arsenal and prison were, and agreed to guide Sano there.

Next, Sano had reported the news to the shogun. Tokugawa Tsunayoshi had vacillated, torn between fear for his regime and fear of his relatives' disapproval. In desperation, Sano had resorted to a ploy that Chamberlain Yanagisawa often used. He had praised the shogun for his wisdom and flattered his pride, then gently hinted that he would be making a terrible mistake to ignore the threat of the Black Lotus. When the shogun had begun yielding to Sano's stronger will, Sano had described in lurid detail the widespread destruction that would occur unless they crushed the sect now. Finally, the frightened shogun had signed an edict granting Sano permission to do whatever was necessary to protect the regime.

Sano, ashamed of his manipulative, dishonorable behavior, had taken the edict and fled before the shogun could change his mind. Then Sano had gathered troops for an invasion of the temple. Things had turned out better than he'd expected— with one hitch.

Haru had balked at going to the temple. She'd cried, screamed, and struggled against his troops as they tried to put her in a palanquin, and called for Reiko. Even though they threatened to burn her, she still resisted, and she had the advantage because Sano needed her to guide him through the Black Lotus underground. Sano didn't want Reiko involved in the expedition; nor did he welcome further association between her and Haru. But he feared that he wouldn't get the promised cooperation from Haru unless someone calmed her down, so he'd hurried home to fetch Reiko.

He'd found her sitting alone in her chamber. Her eyes were red from crying, and she regarded him with wariness, but Sano had no time to indulge emotions or attempt a reconciliation. He wasn't sure that the latter was possible; Reiko's speech in the Court of Justice represented the final, intolerable act against him.

"Haru is being difficult," Sano said. "She's calling for you. I want you to coax her into going to the Black Lotus Temple. Then you're coming along to help me control her."

Reiko gaped, momentarily stricken speechless. "I can't," she said in a hoarse, unsteady voice. "I don't ever want to see Haru again."

"This is the least you can do to make up for your interference," Sano said, unrelenting.

Reiko had unhappily assented. She'd soothed Haru, coaxed her into a palanquin, then climbed in with her. Now Sano turned in his saddle, looking backward at the palanquin, which trailed near the end of the procession. The trial should have destroyed Reiko's sympathy for Haru, but still . . . Had he made a mistake by bringing his wife?

The forest gave way to fields and thatched houses, and finally the procession entered the narrow lanes of the temple district. Reiko sat in the palanquin, enduring the rapid, jouncing motion of the bearers' steps. She fixed her gaze on the temple walls moving past the open window because she couldn't stand to look at Haru, seated opposite her. Imprisoned with the girl, Reiko felt ill with hatred, polluted by the acts of violence Haru had committed. Whether or not Commander Oyama or the husband deserved punishment for hurting Haru, she was a criminal, marked for death. Yet Haru remained a living presence impossible to ignore. The warmth from her body, the smell of her sweat and sour breath, nauseated Reiko.

Several times during the trip, when Haru had started to

speak, Reiko maintained a frosty silence, but as they neared the Black Lotus Temple, she turned to face Haru. "I suppose you're proud of the way you tricked me," she said in a quiet voice that shook with rage.

Huddled miserably in the corner of the palanquin, Haru mumbled, "No, I'm not proud. I'm ashamed."

"The first time we met, you guessed that I would be useful to you," Reiko said bitterly. "All along, you must have been congratulating yourself on how smart you were to take advantage of the *sōsakan-sama*'s gullible wife."

"That's not true." Haru's eyes reflected hurt and alarm. "I was sorry I had to lie to you. I only did it because you wouldn't have helped me if you knew what I'd done."

"Oh, stop making excuses," Reiko said, furious. "You accepted my hospitality and the things I gave you, all the while laughing behind my back."

"I never laughed," Haru protested.

"How it must have pleased you to see me make a fool of myself defending you in court!" The memory humiliated Reiko.

"It didn't please me," Haru said vehemently. "I hate myself for deceiving you, after you were so kind to me. You're my friend, and I love you." Her face crumpled. "I'm so sorry for hurting you. Please forgive me."

Reiko expelled her breath in a gust of contempt and folded her arms. She supposed that Haru's company was the least punishment she deserved. And Reiko foresaw no opportunity to cleanse the dishonor from her spirit, or to reclaim what she'd lost.

Before they'd left Edo, Sano had told her to watch over Haru and make sure she behaved well, but not to do anything else whatsoever. He'd spoken as if he doubted whether Reiko could perform this simple task. And he was right to doubt her, Reiko thought miserably, after she'd defied him and failed at the investigation for which she'd had such high hopes.

"I want to make up to you for the trouble I caused," Haru said, "so I'm going to tell you something." She laid her hand on Reiko's. "We can't go to the temple—it's dangerous. You must tell your husband to turn back."

Outraged, Reiko recoiled from Haru's touch. "You must be mad to think I'll believe more of your stories! It's obvious that you want to get out of leading us to Midori and the arsenal, and you want me along to help you shirk your obligations and run away. Well, expect no more favors from me."

"But I'm not lying this time," Haru said, frantic. "You'll get hurt if we go inside the temple. Please, heed my warning."

She clutched at Reiko, babbling, "We're the third sign. An-raku will send forth his army to destroy the world. If we don't turn back, you'll be the first to die."

"Be quiet! Leave me alone!" Pulling away, Reiko pressed her hands over her ears. "I won't listen to any more of this!"

The Zōjō temple district was dark except for a halo of light crowning the Black Lotus precinct.

"It's as if they're expecting us," Sano said, disturbed to think that spies within the *bakufu* had forewarned the sect. He'd hoped to take it by surprise and thereby quickly subdue the members.

"They won't keep me away from Midori," Hirata said in a hard voice.

The procession reached the temple gate, which stood wide open and unguarded. Although Sano sensed danger in the temple, Midori's presence there beckoned him. He led the procession into the precinct. The lanterns along the main path burned; light shone in the windows of all the buildings. As Sano, Hirata, and the other mounted samurai filed up the path, their horses' hooves clattered on the paving stones, echoing across hushed, vacant grounds. The foot soldiers and palanquin followed. Sano's detectives had orders to take troops into the buildings and arrest the occupants while Haru led Sano, Reiko, and Hirata on a search for Midori, but before they could proceed with these plans, a wild cry shattered the night.

Out of the gardens and woods stormed hundreds of nuns and priests, their voices raised in a deafening chorus of howls, white robes flying. Brandishing swords, daggers, spears, torches, and clubs, they charged the procession.

Alarmed, Sano drew his sword and shouted to his troops: "Prepare for battle!"

Nuns and priests surrounded them. Sano had expected resistance from the Black Lotus, but not this full-scale attack. Dismay flooded him. He'd hoped to rescue Midori and dissolve the sect without anyone getting hurt, but the Black Lotus gave him no choice except to fight back. Now his men fended off priests and nuns. The air resounded with wild yells and the clang of striking blades.

"Stay together!" Sano ordered his troops, but they scattered, forced apart by the mob. He saw white-robed figures swarming around the palanquin, and horror gripped his heart.

Reiko, though probably armed with her dagger as usual, was no match for so many attackers. The intensity of his fear for her told Sano how much he loved his wife, in spite of everything. And he needed Haru alive to locate Midori. Anxious to protect the women, he urged his horse through the melee, toward the palanquin.

A young priest assailed him with a spear. Sano parried and reined in his rearing horse. He slashed the priest's chest. The youth dropped his spear; blood spread across his robe, and rapture illuminated his face.

"Praise the glory of the Black Lotus!" he cried, then fell dead.

Sano saw Hirata and his detectives cutting down more priests and realized that the sect members were inept fighters—probably peasants, without the benefit of long-term training. He was loath to slay weaker opponents, despite their determination to kill him.

"Surrender, or you'll all die," Sano shouted at the horde.

But the priests and nuns continued attacking. More cries of praise arose from the defeated. They seemed like mindless puppets sacrificing their lives to defend their leader's territory. Still, their sheer numbers overwhelmed Sano's forces. Each samurai battled multiple attackers. Several soldiers lay dead, trampled by the mob. New legions of armed nuns and priests poured from buildings to replace those killed. Blades jabbed and clubs pounded at Sano, and he cut down more sect members as his horse plowed a path to the palanquin. Then he noticed nuns and priests moving toward the gate. Some carried only weapons or torches, but others lugged bulky bundles on their backs.

Sano realized that his arrival at the temple had set in motion the Black Lotus's deadly scheme. The members were heading off to attack the city.

"Stop them!" Sano yelled to his troops. "Don't let them out of the temple!"

"Merciful gods," Reiko said, horror-stricken as she gazed through the palanquin's window at the battle outside.

"See? I told you the truth," Haru said eagerly. "Now can you believe what I say?"

The bearers had set down the palanquin, which now sat stranded on the ground, its thin walls offering scant protection from the horde. Reiko relived the terror of the ambush in Nihonbashi, yet this was far more serious. The troops formed a protective circle around the palanquin, but the nuns and priests fought them ruthlessly. Reiko and Haru were sitting targets for savagery.

"If you knew this would happen, then why didn't you say so before we left town?" Reiko demanded of Haru.

The girl shook her head in chagrin.

"We could have brought more troops," Reiko said, "but now it's too late. And do you know what I think?" She grabbed the front of Haru's robe, yanked the girl close, and shouted, "You didn't really know what would happen. You're just trying to turn circumstances to your own advantage."

Then a disturbing alternative occurred to Reiko. "No. You knew, and you wanted us to come and be killed!"

She let go of Haru and peered out the window, looking for Sano. She heard him shouting, but she couldn't see him in the chaos of darting figures. Blood-spattered corpses lay strewn across the ground, mostly Black Lotus, but some samurai; horses ran free, their saddles empty. Fires smoked in the grass, ignited by fallen torches.

"High Priest Anraku's day of destiny is here," Haru said in a wondering, exultant voice.

As fear for her husband's life chilled Reiko, she became

aware of a compelling need to set things right with Sano. She loved him and desperately wanted him to love her again. The thought of them dying estranged from each other tore at her heart. She longed to help him fight the Black Lotus, but she'd promised to watch over Haru.

A gang of nuns broke through the defense and stormed the palanquin, their faces contorted in maniacal fury. Shrieking, they beat clubs against the vehicle. Some grabbed the poles and rocked the palanquin, throwing Reiko and Haru from side to side. Others thrust spears through the window. Haru screamed. Reiko drew the dagger strapped to her arm and struck at the blades. Soldiers closed in, slashing at the nuns. Reiko saw women release their spears as their eyes went blank and they fell away from the window. But one nun lunged through the window, snarling and clawing.

Reiko struck out with her dagger and gashed the nun's throat. Warm, thick blood spurted on Reiko. She cried out as the dead nun collapsed across her legs. Then she heard the palanquin's door open. Turning, she saw Haru scramble out.

"Haru!" Reiko called in alarm.

She grabbed for the girl, but missed. Thoughts raced through her mind: If Haru got away, Sano would never forgive Reiko. In a flash, she was out of the palanquin.

35

Follow me, and I will lead you
Out of the wilderness of illusion
To the place where you can attain wisdom.

——FROM THE BLACK LOTUS SUTRA

Reiko cast a frantic glance around the precinct and saw Haru scurrying through the battle. Small and unobtrusive, the girl dodged fighters who took no notice of her. Reiko sped off in pursuit, shouting, "Stop, Haru!"

Haru kept going. A screaming nun charged at Reiko, swinging a club. Reiko lashed out with her dagger and cut the nun across the abdomen. More nuns chased Reiko. She saw Sano, astride his horse, battling four priests.

"Haru has escaped," Reiko called to him. "I'm going after her."

But Sano didn't even look toward Reiko: He couldn't hear her over the noise. The deranged nuns chased her away from him. A mob of priests and mounted troops blocked her path, and by the time she'd detoured around them, she'd shaken off the nuns, but lost Haru. Then she spotted the girl running into a thicket of trees at the north side of the temple. Reiko hurried toward her.

This area was deserted. The dense foliage screened out the battle noises and the light from the buildings. Reiko saw her quarry's shadowy figure race down a gravel path and disappear beneath an arbor. She followed through the leafy tunnel and emerged into open space. Before her loomed the abbot's two-story residence. Reiko halted, gasping in exertion and anxiety. Haru was nowhere in sight, but the door to the residence stood ajar.

Reiko raced up the steps. She hesitated at the door, fearing that there were Black Lotus members inside. Emboldened by her determination to catch Haru, she slipped through the door. Beyond the entryway, a corridor encircled the building's interior, which was dark except for a dim glow visible through openings in the partitions that divided the rooms. Listening, she perceived wheezes coming from the direction of the light: Haru was there. Reiko groped her way through the chambers.

The light was a lamp that shone through a paper wall. The wheezes were louder now, accompanied by the scrape of something heavy against the floor. Then came scuffling noises, and creaks. Reiko looked into a room that was empty except for a cabinet, a lacquer chest, and a table upon which the oil lamp burned, and quiet except for a hollow, rhythmic clattering noise.

"Haru?" Reiko said, puzzled because the girl had mysteriously vanished.

Then she noticed that the chest stood at an odd angle across the floor, and the shadow beside it wasn't really a shadow, but a hole from which the clattering emanated. Dismaying realization struck her. Haru had moved the chest and gone through a secret entrance to the temple's underground realm.

Moving to the edge of the hole, Reiko spied a ladder leading down to a dimly lit cavern. She considered and rejected the idea of fetching Sano. If the tunnels extended beyond the temple district as Pious Truth claimed, Haru could be far away before Reiko returned with help. Besides, it was Reiko's fault that Haru had gotten away, and Reiko's responsibility to get her back. Donning courage like an armor tunic over her fear, Reiko slipped her dagger into the scabbard strapped to her arm and descended.

She had an unsettling sense of the earth swallowing her. Her heart hammered, and a chill draft shivered her skin. The underground seemed alive, breathing pure malevolence. Reiko alighted in a junction of three tunnels. Drawing her dagger, she looked around, expecting to see a horde of armed nuns and priests, but no one appeared. The clattering pulsation accompanied rushes of air that wavered the flames in oil lamps on the walls. Haru's wheezes and footsteps echoed from one branch of the tunnel.

In the temple precinct, Sano lashed his sword at the priests clamoring around him and his horse. "Get away!" he shouted, trying to clear a path to Reiko's palanquin.

White-robed figures poured out the open gate, chased by soldiers. Wounded sect members gulped the contents of vials that hung on strings around their necks and expired in violent convulsions, having poisoned themselves to avoid capture. Though the grounds were covered with fallen priests and nuns, the temple yielded up a seemingly endless supply of new attackers. The fires caused by the torches had lit the shrubbery. Anraku's conflagration had begun. Sano feared that his army wouldn't be able to contain the violence, and he would fail in his duty to prevent the destruction of Edo.

As he fought his way closer to Reiko's palanquin, an object the size of a teapot soared through the air ahead of him, trailing a short tail with a burning end. It thudded to the ground amid a nearby group of combatants and exploded with a tremendous boom and blinding flash of light.

Sano exclaimed in shock. His horse reared. A huge smoke cloud burgeoned at the site of the explosion. Out of this flew bodies hurled by the blast. Agonized screams arose. The Black Lotus had begun deploying gunpowder bombs intended for the destruction of Japan. All around the temple, priests ignited fuses and flung more bombs. More explosions produced more screams and maimed corpses. Injured survivors moaned. Then Sano saw a bomb land on the roof of the palanquin.

"Reiko!" he yelled, horrified. "Get out! Run!"

He vaulted from his saddle, over the priests around him, and landed hard in a crouch. The impact rolled him heels over head, across rough grass, until he halted some ten paces from the palanquin. Still gripping his sword, he leapt to his feet, just as the palanquin exploded.

The blast threw him backward. He felt intense heat. Broken boards showered down upon him. Gunpowder fumes seared his lungs. Then he was crawling through the smoke, frantically pawing the wreckage of the palanquin.

"Reiko!" His ears were ringing from the explosion; he could barely hear himself. A dark afterimage of the flash obscured his vision. "Where are you? Answer me!"

Heedless of the flames that licked his hands, he flung aside splintered panels. A motionless, bloody form appeared.

"No!" The violent denial erupted from Sano.

Then he noticed the corpse's shaved head: It was a nun. Yet Reiko must be here somewhere. Willing her to be alive, Sano worked furiously until he'd cleared all the debris off the palanquin's shattered base. But he found no trace of Reiko, nor Haru. Sano's relief was transient, obliterated by fresh horror. He looked up and saw Hirata running toward him.

"They're gone," he shouted over the noise of more explosions.

"What?" Hirata, grimy and sporting cuts in his armor, halted and looked at Sano in confusion. "Who?"

"Reiko and Haru."

"Where?"

"I don't know." As Sano looked around for the women, dread sank icy roots deep in his heart. "Help me gather some troops. We've got to find them."

Gripping her dagger, Reiko hurried down the tunnel, stumbling over rocks embedded in the floor, past closed doors. The lamps cast her fleeting shadow on the walls; the passage wound on. Reiko couldn't see Haru, but the tunnels amplified noises, and she followed Haru's wheezes. She became aware of other, distant noises—marching footsteps, garbled voices, and the ring of metal on stone. Her heart seemed to expand with her fear, thudding against her rib cage. If the Black Lotus discovered her, they would surely kill her. But she had to catch Haru.

A turn brought Reiko to a fork in the tunnel. From one branch came the unexpected, chilling sound of children laughing and chattering. The Black Lotus had evidently hidden their young underground. From the other passage came a loud pounding, and Haru's voice shouting, "Let me in!"

Reiko ran down that passage. She rounded a curve and saw Haru banging on a door. It opened inward, and Haru tumbled through it. The door creaked shut. Reiko halted, panting. Her terror burgeoned as she wondered who had taken Haru in and a likely answer occurred to her. Still, she was duty bound to stick with Haru. She crept to the door.

It wasn't completely closed, and there was a small, barred window at eye level in its iron-banded surface. Cautiously, Reiko peered through the window. Color dazzled her eyes. The spacious room inside was lined with curtains printed in brilliant, swirling abstract patterns of crimson, orange, and purple. The curtains shimmered in the light of lanterns, bathing in garish radiance the people in the room.

At the back, High Priest Anraku sat cross-legged on a platform. His white robe glowed ruddy; his brocade stole sparkled. To his right stood Priest Kumashiro, like a bronze statue in saffron robe and armor tunic, swords at his waist. Abbess Junketsu-in, clad in white robe and head drape, was kneeling on the tatami at the left side of the room. Opposite her knelt Dr. Miwa, in formal dark kimono.

Reiko realized that this was where the Black Lotus leaders planned to wait out the conflagration they'd devised. Eight priests—evidently high sect officials—stood along the walls. Everyone stared at Haru, crouched on hands and knees in the center of the room, facing Anraku.

Dr. Miwa said to her, "How did you get here?"

"The *sōsakan-sama* brought me. I sneaked away." Haru spoke as if proud of her cleverness.

"Did anyone see you enter the tunnels?" Kumashiro said,

obviously concerned about security in the temple's underground.

He looked toward the door, and Reiko ducked beneath the window. She heard Haru say, "No, there was so much confusion, nobody knows I left." Haru was still lying, Reiko observed with irony; the girl couldn't have forgotten that there was one person who would have noticed her absence. "Oh, Anraku-*san,* I'm so glad to be with you again." Haru's voice trembled with emotion, then faltered, "Aren't you glad I came back?"

"After you traded our secrets to get better treatment for yourself?" Junketsu-in said incredulously. Reiko understood that the sect had learned the results of Haru's trial. "You betrayed us. And now you expect us to welcome you? Hah!"

Reiko risked another peek through the window and saw Anraku appraising Haru in thoughtful silence. Haru beseeched him, "Please let me explain. I only did what I did because they made me." Though Reiko couldn't see Haru's face, she could picture its expression of wounded innocence. Haru was still making excuses, Reiko noted in disgust, and still blaming other people for her actions.

"Wicked little traitor," Junketsu-in hissed at Haru.

"I'll get rid of her," Kumashiro said. Striding over to Haru, he grabbed her arm.

"Let me go," Haru cried. As Kumashiro hauled her toward the door, she appealed to Anraku, who sat grave and still on his altar: "I can't bear to be separated from you again. If you throw me out, they'll catch me and kill me. I'm sorry for causing you trouble. I beg you to forgive me. If you let me stay, I'll prove how loyal I am." She was crying now, and Reiko glimpsed her panic-stricken face. "I promise!"

Anraku spoke with quiet authority: "Release her."

Kumashiro hesitated; his brows slanted downward in displeasure, but he obeyed. Haru thudded onto the floor. Anraku held out his hand to her.

"Come," he said.

With a glad cry, Haru crawled over to him, seized his hand, and pressed it to her face. "I knew you wouldn't forsake me." Now she wept for joy. "I'll do anything to repay your mercy."

"My lord, don't you see that she's playing on your sympathy, just as she's always done?" Junketsu-in said. "How can you still be so blind to her evil ways?" She leaned anxiously toward Anraku. "Please don't take her back. She'll destroy us all—if she hasn't already."

"I'm afraid the abbess is right," Dr. Miwa said timidly, sucking breath through his teeth.

Reiko watched Anraku draw Haru close, and anger glint in his eye. "Do not accuse me of blindness or gullibility," he said. "I see and understand all that mortal fools such as you cannot." Miwa and Junketsu-in cringed from his wrath; Haru sat below the platform, snuggling against his knees. "Haru has played the role for which she was destined. She performed the blood sacrifice necessary to set the cosmic forces in motion. She occasioned the persecution that generated spiritual energy within the Black Lotus. And now she has ushered in the third sign heralding our day of glory: The siege of the temple."

Reiko marveled at how the high priest had interpreted events to fit his prophecies. Indeed, he seemed to believe his own insane logic. His faith in it, plus the force of his personality, had turned his followers' desire for spiritual fulfillment into a desire to kill and die for him.

Regarding Haru fondly, Anraku caressed her hair. "My child, you are indeed an instrument of fortune. Because of you, the triumph of the Black Lotus is at hand."

And he viewed mortal crimes as steps toward spiritual enlightenment. The magnitude of his madness and his perversion of Buddhism astounded Reiko.

Haru preened like a child praised for good behavior and directed a triumphant gaze toward Junketsu-in. "You always hated me because I'm more important to him than you are. Now I'm going to tell you exactly what I think of you. You're a mean, jealous, stupid whore." As Junketsu-in sputtered indignantly, Haru laughed, then turned to Dr. Miwa. "And you're a dirty, disgusting lecher."

Dr. Miwa glowered; Haru's contemptuous stare encompassed him and the abbess. "You tried to get rid of me, but it didn't work," Haru taunted. "You'll both be sorry you said bad things about me." Then, while Anraku beheld his followers with lofty amusement, she glared at Kumashiro. "And you'll be sorry you tried to scare me into confessing."

Reiko was appalled by Haru's selfish spite. The girl had committed murder and arson, and people were dying by the score, yet all she seemed to care about was regaining Anraku's esteem and taking revenge on her enemies. Reiko felt fresh shame over befriending Haru.

"I must contradict your opinion of how well things have turned out," Kumashiro said to Anraku. "I've been above-ground and seen what's happening. Our people are being slaughtered. There won't be enough of them left to conquer Edo, let alone the rest of Japan. Our mission is doomed."

"It wouldn't be, if you'd trained the nuns and priests into a better army." Junketsu-in vented on Kumashiro the animosity she dared not express toward Haru now that the girl had Anraku's favor. "You've only yourself to blame for our defeat."

"Peasants are no match for samurai," Kumashiro said defensively. "I taught them as well as anyone could."

"The poison I concocted is very potent," Dr. Miwa said in a voice timid yet prideful. "If even a few of the couriers reach the city, the result will be most gratifying."

Junketsu-in gave a disdainful laugh. "A few doses of your stinking goo will accomplish too little to matter. If you'd perfected the poison gas, it would have spread on the wind. But Shinagawa proved that you're a miserable failure."

Dr. Miwa muttered. Kumashiro walked over to Junketsu-in, his fists clenched. "What right have you to berate us?" he demanded. "You, who are a weak, ignorant female, and good for nothing. Hold your tongue, or I'll cut it out of your head."

The antagonists either still trusted Anraku and didn't blame him for the havoc he'd wrought, or were afraid to criticize him, Reiko thought.

"My lord." Kumashiro addressed Anraku in respectful entreaty. "The soldiers will soon come looking for us. We must leave at once."

Panic shot through Reiko. If they left, what would she do?

"We will stay," Anraku said, his expression obstinate. Haru rested her head on his knee, blissfully oblivious to the argument. "My army shall triumph. We shall achieve enlightenment here, on this night, as my vision has foretold. I'll not let the enemy drive me away."

Yet Junketsu-in's face displayed fear and shock. She said,

"They might be coming even now. They'll kill us all. I want to go."

"You wish to desert me at the advent of my new world?" Impervious to reason, Anraku frowned. "Is this how you repay me for the wealth and privilege I've lavished upon you? With cowardice and disloyalty?" He flung out a hand, waving Junketsu-in away. "Then by all means, go. But if you do, our paths shall never again converge."

"No," Junketsu-in cried, "I don't mean to desert you." She lurched toward Anraku, as if to throw herself into his arms, but Haru already occupied them. "I want you to come with me."

A loud boom from aboveground shuddered the tunnel. Reiko gasped. Crouching, she covered her head with her arms as dirt trickled through the rafters and startled exclamations arose from Anraku's chamber. She heard Dr. Miwa cry, "They're setting off the bombs," and Junketsu-in's panicky voice: "The temple will come down and crush us!"

The idea terrified Reiko, yet the thought of Sano up there in the explosions terrified her even more. A burning smell drifted through the tunnel—the temple must be on fire. Reiko fought the urge to run to Sano. Looking through the window, she saw Junketsu-in, Miwa, Kumashiro, and the priests huddling near Anraku as if craving shelter from him.

Another blast rocked the hanging lanterns. As Reiko braced herself against the lurch of the ground under her feet, Anraku said suavely, "Perhaps it would be best to pursue destiny elsewhere."

So he still had some sense of self-preservation, Reiko thought, quailing at the calamity that his flight posed for her. If Haru went with him, Reiko must follow.

"I've ordered provisions packed for a journey," Kumashiro said. "There's enough money for us to live on indefinitely. Your followers in the provinces will shelter us. We'll hide until the hunt for us dies down, then take on different names and recruit new followers. You and I will revive the Black Lotus and found another temple."

Reiko saw shock freeze the countenances of the abbess and doctor as they absorbed Kumashiro's meaning. Haru, still seated close to Anraku, looked around, confused. Junketsu-in demanded of Kumashiro, "You think you're going to take him away with you and leave the rest of us here? Well, I won't stand for that. Where he goes, I go."

Dr. Miwa said with a nervous smile, "Honorable High Priest, surely you'll need me to help you start over."

As Anraku surveyed the group, cunning gleamed in his eye. "We'll all go," he said. Reiko supposed that he needed devoted attendants to help him survive, and thrived on the discord among them. He rose and stepped off his platform, raising Haru to her feet.

"Not her," Kumashiro said.

Haru's brow puckered; Anraku hesitated. Junketsu-in chimed in eagerly, "She can't keep secrets. If she travels with us, she'll tell the wrong people who we are. The *bakufu* will find us. We'll never be safe with her around."

"She's an escaped criminal," Dr. Miwa said. "The police will hunt us even harder, to get her. We must abandon her to improve our chances of survival."

If they did abandon Haru, then Reiko would be spared the trouble of pursuing them. Reiko held her breath, hoping she could capture Haru after Anraku and his officials departed, then warn Sano before they got too far.

Haru stared at her enemies, aghast. She clutched Anraku's arm. "But I want to go with you. You won't leave me?"

"The fewer who go, the easier to hide," Kumashiro said.

Anraku shook off Haru and stepped away from her.

"No!" Haru screamed. Dropping to her knees, she hugged Anraku's legs and babbled, "Nothing can separate us. My path is the path that unites all others—you said so, don't you remember? The future of the Black Lotus depends on me. We were meant to be together, forever. You must take me with you."

Watching, Reiko exhaled, silently imploring Anraku to leave Haru and take the others away. Anraku focused a speculative, searching gaze on Haru. He said to the priests, "Bring our prisoner."

His order, which seemed to have no bearing on the circumstances, baffled Reiko.

"Not her, too," Junketsu-in protested.

A pair of the priests vanished through a doorway behind the curtains at the back of the room. They reemerged carrying a limp, horizontal figure clad in a gray robe. The arms dangled; long hair trailed on the floor. The head lolled toward Reiko.

It was Midori, Reiko realized in shock.

Midori's eyes were closed, her lips slack. Unconscious, she didn't stir when the priests laid her on the floor near Anraku's platform. She lay motionless except for the slow rise and fall of her bosom as she breathed. The sect must have drugged her with sleeping potion, Reiko supposed. Even as she experienced the joy of finding her friend, fear knifed through her. What did Anraku mean to do with Midori?

Junketsu-in said vehemently to Anraku, "She's a spy. You can't bring her along."

"I've enough potion to keep her unconscious for a long time," Dr. Miwa said, ogling Midori's body.

Now Reiko realized with dreadful certainty that she must follow the fugitives. She couldn't leave Midori to them, and there would be no time to fetch Sano. Yet new hope awakened inside her, fragile and vibrant as butterfly wings. At least she'd located Midori. Might she somehow rescue her friend?

"Lady Midori still has an important purpose to serve," Anraku said, unperturbed.

"You're going to take her and not me?" Haru shrilled in panic. She clutched Anraku tighter. "But you can't!"

"If we have to carry her, she'll slow us down," Kumashiro point-ed out.

Another bomb exploded. Junketsu-in screamed; everyone ducked. There was a rumbling sound like a flood of rocks: a tunnel had collapsed nearby.

"Let's go now, before it's too late," Junketsu-in pleaded. "We can just leave Lady Midori here with Haru."

As Reiko's heart leapt at the possibility, Midori slept on, oblivious. A strange smile shimmered on Anraku's lips.

"A new vision has just revealed to me the final purpose for which Lady Midori is destined." He stared down at Haru. "Do you truly wish my forgiveness?"

"Yes," she gasped, lifting a hopeful face to him, "more than anything in the world."

"You wish to prove your loyalty to me?"

"Oh, yes." Haru was wheezing, pathetic in her eagerness.

"You would do anything to earn the privilege of accompanying me?"

"Anything!" Haru cried, as Reiko tried to figure out where the conversation was leading.

The high priest's smile broadened. "Then kill Lady Midori."

Horror reverberated inside Reiko like the toll of a shattered bell. Through her panic she saw Junketsu-in's and Miwa's faces go blank with surprise at Anraku's order. Kumashiro frowned, as though disappointed to be deprived of killing Midori himself, or perhaps doubtful that Haru could accomplish the task. Haru slowly unclasped her arms from Anraku and sat back on her heels. Reiko read trepidation in the furrowed lines of the girl's profile.

Then Haru nodded, murmuring, "If you wish, Anraku-*san*."

She stood and walked toward Midori. Reiko, aghast to see her friend's life placed in the hands of a murderer who cared about nothing except appeasing Anraku, felt a shout of protest rise in her: *Haru, no!*

Anraku mounted his platform. "Give her your sword," he said to Kumashiro.

Reiko watched in shock as the priest drew his long sword and offered it to Haru. She clumsily grasped the hilt in both hands. Raising the blade over her head, she positioned herself a few paces from Midori's neck. She drew a deep breath and gradually lowered the blade, looking sideways at Anraku.

He nodded and smiled encouragingly. Kumashiro and Dr. Miwa watched the moving blade, while Junketsu-in turned away and clapped a hand over her mouth. A nightmarish state of paralysis gripped Reiko, numbing her thoughts and muscles. She couldn't move; she could only watch. Haru's wheezes and the clattering in the tunnels marked the slow passage of time. Midori's eyelids fluttered. The blade hovered low over her throat. Haru winced. Her knuckles tightened convulsively on the sword.

The undeniable knowledge that Midori's death was imminent jarred Reiko out of her paralysis. "Stop!" she shouted.

Pushing the door open, she burst into the room.

36

Go with fearless heart,
Begrudge neither limb nor life,
But with a single mind concentrate
On the pursuit of ultimate enlightenment.
— FROM THE BLACK LOTUS SUTRA

Startled faces turned toward Reiko. Haru jerked the sword away from Midori. During a brief silence, Reiko saw herself through everyone else's eyes—a lone, scared young woman brandishing a dagger.

Then the stillness shattered. Abbess Junketsu-in exclaimed, "It's Lady Reiko, the *sōsakan-sama*'s wife!" Kumashiro and the other priests advanced on Reiko.

"Stay away from me," she commanded with shaky bravado. "I'm taking Lady Midori out of here." She turned to Haru, who gawked at her. "You're coming with us."

Her words sounded foolhardy to herself. Anraku ordered calmly, "Subdue her."

The priests surrounded Reiko. She stabbed at them, and a tumultuous chase ensued. Reiko whirled and darted, slashing bloody cuts on the arms grabbing at her. The injured men cursed. Kumashiro seized her around the waist, clamped a hand around her right wrist, and wrenched. Pain skewered through her hand, and she cried out in pain, dropping the dagger. Kumashiro's steely arms encircled her, pinning her arms against her sides. He turned her to face Anraku.

"How rude of you to trespass in my private domain, Lady Reiko," the high priest said with a sardonic smile.

"You'd better let me go, and Midori, too," Reiko said, breathless and terrified. "My husband and his troops have invaded the underground. They'll be here any moment."

Anraku received her lie with cool amusement, then said to Haru, "So no one saw you enter the underground?"

She shrank from the accusation in his voice. "They didn't. I swear."

"Then how did Lady Reiko find us?" Anraku said.

". . . I don't know."

"Obviously, you showed her the way," Junketsu-in said spitefully. "You brought her here to attack us."

"But I didn't mean to," Haru protested. "I never thought she would come after me, honest."

Reiko jerked and grunted, trying in vain to break free of Kumashiro. She'd delayed Midori's death, but now they were both captives of the Black Lotus.

"The *sōsakan-sama* will come looking for his wife," Kumashiro said to Anraku. "We have to get out before he finds his way down here. What do you want me to do with her?"

Anraku raised a hand, counseling patience. "It seems you have betrayed me yet again, Haru," he said. "Therefore, the task I assigned you is no longer sufficient to demonstrate your loyalty." He said to Kumashiro, "Place Lady Reiko by our other prisoner."

Kumashiro propelled Reiko across the room. She resisted, but he shoved her into place, facing Haru. The other sect members grouped together along the wall behind the girl.

"Another act of disloyalty requires an additional test," Anraku told Haru. "To secure the privilege of staying with me, you must now kill both Lady Midori and Lady Reiko."

As her heart pumped wildly and her lungs heaved, Reiko realized that she and Midori would die together, by the hand of the girl Reiko had tried to save.

Anraku said to Haru, "You may dispose of Lady Reiko first."

Through dizzying faintness, Reiko saw Haru looking everywhere except at her. The girl raised the sword, and Kumashiro walked Reiko forward until her throat met the tip of the blade. The cold prick of steel interrupted her breath. She experienced a strong urge to vomit and a terrible despair. Her thoughts flew to her son.

Images of Masahiro's lively face filled her mind. Memory recalled the sound of his laughter, the feeling of holding his warm little body. Reiko also remembered herself and Sano and Masahiro happy together at home. With a fierce intensity, she longed for her husband and son. Love of them strengthened her will to survive. The desire to save Midori and see Sano and Masahiro again revived her courage and her wits. She must forestall death and hope for a miracle.

Sano, Hirata, and four detectives ran through the Black Lotus precinct, skirting buildings and trees. While they fought off priests, Sano looked for Reiko, to no avail. The smoke stung Sano's eyes; he ached from strikes to his armor. Another explosion flared. And Sano knew with a sudden, sobering certainty what had happened to Reiko and Haru.

"They've gone underground!" he shouted to Hirata, who was battling three priests.

Reasoning that the buildings must contain entrances to the tunnels, Sano raced up the steps of the main hall. The door was open, the cavernous interior unoccupied. Incense and lamps burned on a raised altar before a mural of a black lotus flower. As Sano halted inside and scanned the room, his men joined him. He saw that the altar's base was fronted by carved panels. The center one hung open on hinges. Darkness yawned behind it.

"Over there," Sano said, hurrying to the portal that the Black

Lotus hordes had apparently neglected to close after emerging from the tunnels.

He and his men ducked beneath the altar and dropped into the earthy-smelling space under the building. Walking crouched beneath the floor joists, they found a hole in the ground. Sano saw a ladder reaching down the shaft to a lighted pit, heard tortured wails and a mechanical pulsation.

"Be careful," he said. "There's someone down there."

"Midori." Hirata's voice exuded fear and the hope that she was within reach. "I'll go down first."

He sheathed his sword and hurtled down the ladder. Sano and the detectives followed. When they reached the bottom and paused to rearm themselves, Hirata was already racing down a tunnel. An overpowering stench hit Sano as he sped after Hirata. A din of voices crying, "Help! Let us out!" erupted. Down the tunnel, Hirata skidded to a stop and exclaimed, "Merciful gods!"

Catching up, Sano saw doors, bolted with thick iron beams, lining the tunnel. From inside the chambers, skeletal hands reached outward through tiny barred windows in the doors. This was the Black Lotus's secret prison.

"Midori! I've come to get you!" Hirata yanked the bolt away from one cell and threw open the door.

Cheers arose. Out of the cell stumbled some twenty emaciated young men dressed in dirty rags. Their faces were gaunt, their hair shaggy. Sano and the detectives opened other cells, releasing hundreds more men and women in similar condition, who'd apparently run afoul of the Black Lotus. Hirata pushed through the crowd, calling, "Midori!"

Prisoners stampeded toward the exit. Sano and Hirata inspected the cells. They found a few remaining prisoners, too weak to move, but no Midori.

"She's not here," Hirata said, stricken by disappointment.

"Stay calm. We'll find her," Sano said, although he, too, had hoped to find Midori among the prisoners and was worried about why she wasn't there. "Midori is alive," he said, hoping he was right. "We'll save her, and Reiko too."

He felt panic erode his own self-control, but his words calmed Hirata, who nodded and assumed a stony composure. They and the detectives hurried deeper into the tunnels. Enter-

ing a three-way junction, Sano heard fierce yells. He and his
party froze, trapped, as priests waving swords charged toward
them from all directions.

"Haru-*san*," Reiko compelled herself to say through her terror, "look at me."

Emitting a frightened mewl, Haru stared at the sword in her
hands. Then her gaze slowly rose, drawn by Reiko's desire to
reestablish a connection between them.

"You don't really want to kill me, do you?" Reiko said,
feigning calmness while Kumashiro held her tight and the
sword's sharp touch contracted her throat muscles.

Haru said with defiant bravado, "I have no choice."

Reiko's heart sank. Haru's choice was between their friendship and Anraku, and Reiko knew how the odds lay. "We all
have choices," Reiko said, improvising fast. "I chose to take
your side when no one else did. I chose to help you against
my husband's wishes. Don't you owe me a favor?"

Haru's mouth worked; uncertainty clouded her eyes. But as
Reiko dared to hope, Kumashiro said to Anraku, "Time is
short. If Haru won't kill Lady Reiko, I can."

Reiko sensed his blood lust in the hot pressure of his flesh
against hers. Suddenly the clattering noise stopped. Quiet settled upon the underground; everyone looked around in surprise.

"The slaves have deserted the air bellows," Kumashiro said.
"Soon we won't be able to breathe down here. Let me dispose
of the prisoners so we can go."

"No. It is Haru's duty," Anraku said firmly.

A new resolve set Haru's jaw. Anraku fixed a tantalizing
stare on Reiko. She saw that this had become a contest between
them. He cared less about making a timely escape than about
controlling his followers, because his desire for power over
them outweighed all other concerns. But Reiko was competing
for her life.

"Haru-*san*, he doesn't deserve your loyalty," she said. "After
the fire, did he try to protect you? No—he let you shift for
yourself. When you were in jail, did he comfort you?" Reiko
shook her head regretfully. "He never came near you. Did he

try to clear your name and save you from execution? On the contrary: He left you to the law."

"I don't care about the past," Haru said belligerently. "All that matters is that Anraku-*san* and I are together again."

But Reiko could tell that Haru did mind his desertion. "He and his followers did everything possible to incriminate you," Reiko said. "Dr. Miwa and Abbess Junketsu-in revealed your bad reputation. Kumashiro tried to force you to confess. The orphans placed you at the scene of the crime. Black Lotus priests attacked you in jail."

"That was their own doing," Haru faltered.

Anraku radiated a confidence that scorned Reiko's plan to break his hold on Haru.

"But Anraku knows everything, doesn't he?" Reiko said.

Haru hesitated, then nodded.

"And everyone in the Black Lotus serves and obeys him?"

". . . Yes." Haru's expression turned wary.

"Then he not only knew how your enemies tried to destroy you," Reiko said, "he must have ordered them to do it."

"No!" Glaring at Reiko, Haru said, "He wouldn't."

Yet she withdrew the sword and stole an uneasy glance at Anraku. Displeasure darkened his aspect.

"Oh, yes, he would." Reiko listened for sounds indicating that Sano's troops had invaded the tunnels, but heard none. Since the bellows had stopped, the atmosphere had become stale; the suffocating smoke from the lamps increased her sense of urgency. Midori stirred, yawning: she would soon awake. Reiko tried to believe that rescue was near. "I'll tell you why."

"You're just trying to mix me up." Haru took an aggressive step toward Reiko. Fresh terror pumped through Reiko's blood as she strained away from the blade and Kumashiro immobilized her. Haru appealed to Anraku: "I don't have to listen to her, do I?"

"No, indeed," Anraku said. "Just kill her, and she'll speak no more."

"He wanted to make sure you were blamed for Commander Oyama's death." Reiko swallowed desperation. "But he also wanted you blamed for the crimes you didn't commit." She saw Haru's forehead contract in bewilderment, and hurried on,

"Remember Nurse Chie and the little boy. You really didn't kill them, did you?"

The trial hadn't filled in the major gap in Sano's case against Haru—her lack of motive for the other two murders. Reiko had never believed that Haru had killed the woman and child, and in spite of her disillusionment with Haru, she still didn't believe it.

Haru was nodding, though wariness lurked in her eyes. Reiko said, "If you didn't kill Chie and the boy, then someone else in the Black Lotus did."

As Haru looked around at the other people in the room, her features sharpened with suspicion.

"Someone set you up to be punished for his crimes," Reiko said, feeling sudden tension in Kumashiro's body. "Someone wanted you executed so he—or she—could go free."

The eight priests seemed indifferent to Haru's scrutiny, but Abbess Junketsu-in and Dr. Miwa averted their eyes from her, their expressions suddenly guarded. Haru's gaze came to rest on Anraku, whose face took on an ominous intensity.

"Yes," Reiko said. "Even if he didn't kill Chie and the boy with his own hands, he ordered their deaths. He meant for you to die, too." Haru shook her head vigorously, but her stricken countenance belied the denial. Reiko challenged the high priest: "Didn't you?"

Anraku's tongue rolled inside his cheek, and Reiko saw from his discomfiture that she'd placed him in an intolerable position, as she'd meant to do. Either he must acknowledge his guilt and weaken his influence over Haru, or admit that he didn't control everything that happened. He didn't want to lose this contest with Reiko, but neither could he afford to have his omnipotence exposed as a fraud.

Wicked inspiration glinted in the high priest's eye. He spoke to Abbess Junketsu-in: "You shall tell us about the events leading up to the fire in the cottage."

"Me?" Junketsu-in blanched as everyone looked at her. "But—I don't know anything. I—"

Anraku's gaze captured hers, and she halted. Her resistance dissolved as his will subdued her. She said meekly, "That night I was walking alone in the precinct, when I saw two girls sneak out of the orphanage."

So she hadn't been in her quarters with her attendants as she'd claimed, Reiko observed. She realized that Anraku had cleverly diverted Haru's suspicion from himself to the abbess, and she'd lost a round in her fight for her life. But here was her chance to learn the truth about the murders and fire, and the telling of the story bought her more time.

"I meant to send the girls back to bed," Junketsu-in went on, "but then I spotted Haru walking ahead of them. They were following her. I wanted to know what she was doing, so I followed, too. When we got near the cottage, the other two girls turned and headed back toward the orphanage. I hid behind a tree so they wouldn't see me. Then I continued after Haru.

"There was a light in the cottage. She slipped through the door. I stood outside and watched through the window. I saw Haru with Commander Oyama. His legs were around her neck, and she was screaming. He shouted at her. Then they were fighting, and she hit him on the head with a statue and killed him."

While Junketsu-in described watching Haru come out of the cottage, hide the statue, and return to the scene of Oyama's death, Reiko listened in utter amazement. Here was Haru's exact story, confirmed by a witness who had no reason to lie for the girl's benefit. Haru had told the truth about how Oyama died!

"I thought of how Commander Oyama had arrested me and doomed me to whoredom in the Yoshiwara and forced me to service him here, and I was so delighted by his death that I laughed." Vindictive glee shone in the abbess's eyes. "And at last I'd caught Haru at something bad enough to persuade Anraku to throw her out of the temple."

Clearly, the abbess had hated Oyama and relished the turn of fate that had not only punished him, but placed Haru in her power. Junketsu-in hadn't cared whether Haru was punished by the law, as long as the girl no longer troubled her, and Reiko guessed why she hadn't reported Haru later.

"Then I remembered that I was the only one who'd seen Haru kill Oyama," the abbess said, confirming Reiko's guess. "She could deny everything. It would be my word against hers, and Anraku might take her side. She could get away with murder!"

Outrage shook Junketsu-in's voice. "But I wouldn't let her. After I followed her back to the cottage, I slipped off my sandals, which had thick wooden soles, and grabbed one." The abbess raised her hand, the fingers curled around an imaginary shoe. "I stole up behind Haru, and I hit her on the head with my sandal."

Junketsu-in pantomimed the blow. "Haru fell down and didn't move, but she was breathing. I went to the storehouse and got some oil and rags. I tied the rags around a stick to make a torch. Then I returned to the cottage. Haru was still unconscious. The lantern was still burning in the room where she'd left Commander Oyama, and I lit the torch there. I poured oil on the floor and along the corridor, and I ran around splashing more kerosene on the outside of the cottage. I touched the torch to the wall, and it burst into flames. I tucked the oil jar in the bushes and put on my shoes. Then I went back to my quarters, leaving Haru lying in the garden. I knew that her husband had died in a fire, and I wanted people to think she'd burned Oyama to death."

This was how Haru had come to be found at the scene, ready to receive the blame for the fire and Oyama's murder, Reiko understood at last. A wondrous sense of vindication momentarily lifted her above her fear. Haru hadn't murdered Oyama in cold blood; she hadn't set the fire. That she was innocent of those crimes indicated that her husband's death had been accidental, as she'd claimed. Haru was indeed a liar and troublemaker, yet also a victim. Reiko's instincts had been true all along.

Haru had been listening with an expression of mingled disbelief and confusion. She said to Junketsu-in, "It was you who framed me."

The abbess sneered. "I just made you face the consequences of your actions."

"And you killed Chie and Radiant Spirit." Now Haru spoke in a tone of angry realization. "You were jealous of them because Anraku liked Chie, and Radiant Spirit was his son."

"I had nothing to do with their deaths," Junketsu-in retorted. "They weren't even in the cottage when I was there."

Reiko, elated by personal triumph, seized the chance to reintroduce the issue of Anraku's culpability. "The abbess's story explains why you were unconscious in the garden and couldn't remember anything about the fire," she said, "but not how Chie and the boy died. That was Anraku's doing."

Haru swiveled her head toward Anraku, refocusing her fury on him. New hope kindled in Reiko, but he gave her a disdainful smile and said, "Dr. Miwa shall tell the rest of the story."

Behind Haru, the doctor started in fear; air whistled through his teeth. "Oh, but—" Anraku's gaze impaled him, and he surrendered. "Chie became unhappy here after she bore her son. She wanted to care for Radiant Spirit herself, but the nuns took him away to raise with the other children and rarely allowed her to see him. She disliked the way the children were trained. She couldn't understand that prayer and fasting builds their spirits, and she complained whenever Radiant Spirit was beaten for disobeying."

Reiko thought of the boy's bruises and emaciated body, the result of the cruel indoctrination.

"Soon Chie began questioning our other practices," Dr. Miwa said. "She objected to my experiments—she said it was wrong to give helpless people medicines that made them sick instead of healing them. She demanded to know the purpose of the potions we mixed. When she learned that they were poisons for contaminating the wells in Edo, she tried to persuade me that what we were doing was wrong. She begged me to stop. We argued, and she ran from me."

The maltreatment of the child had broken down Chie's loyalty to the sect, Reiko noted. The argument that Haru had described to Sano really had occurred, although he'd misinterpreted it.

"But I didn't kill Chie," said Dr. Miwa, quailing as Haru wheeled around and pointed the sword at him. "All I did was tell Kumashiro that she was becoming a problem."

A chill coursed through Reiko. The doctor had passed along the "problem" to the man holding her—the man responsible for the deaths of Chie and son. Now, as Anraku fixed his compelling gaze on Kumashiro, Reiko felt the priest stiffen, then yield.

"I had Chie watched," Kumashiro said. "Just before dawn on the day of the fire, she stole her son from the nursery. My men and I caught them as they were running toward the gate. I dealt with them according to the usual procedure for handling escapees."

By strangling them, Reiko thought, appalled by Kumashiro's callousness and abhorring the close physical contact with him.

"As my men and I carried the bodies to the tunnel entrance, a watchman ran up and said the cottage was on fire. He'd found Haru unconscious outside. That gave me an idea. We took the bodies to the burning cottage and put them inside. We saw Commander Oyama lying dead in the other room. It seemed that Haru had killed him and set the fire to cover up what she'd done. Why not implicate her in the other deaths? Then the police would be sure to arrest her. I organized the attack on her in jail, to make sure she confessed."

At last Reiko fully understood why Haru had known nothing about the other murders. She also understood why Kumashiro, Junketsu-in, and Miwa had been so eager to incriminate Haru, yet so evasive when she'd questioned them. They'd all played roles in the crimes, while Kumashiro and Junketsu-in had separately taken advantage of Haru's actions.

The girl regarded her enemies with hatred. She said to Anraku, "They all hurt me. You'll punish them, won't you?"

"Of course," Anraku promised gravely, "after you pass your test." He canted his chin toward Reiko.

"If Anraku is all-powerful, then he caused the wrongs they did you," she said. "He let you down then; if you stay with him, he will again. Don't do his dirty work."

Haru moaned, and the sword shuddered in her hands. A malicious smile thinned Anraku's mouth. "Lady Reiko only helped you as a means of attacking me. What does she offer you in exchange for sparing her life?" he said to Haru. "Freedom?" He laughed. "She came here to capture you. Unless you earn my protection, she'll turn you over to the law."

He'd spoken the damning argument that Reiko had hoped he wouldn't get a chance to use. Despair washed over her while she watched Haru absorb his words. The girl looked momentarily nonplussed, then beheld Reiko with hurt and dawning anger.

"His protection is just an illusion," Reiko said quickly. "He can't escape justice. He can't save you."

"Shut up!" Haru yelled, furious. "Stop keeping me from doing what I have do!"

With the sword wavering between her and her executioner, Reiko rushed on: "Anraku is an evil madman. He would kill you and everyone else in the world to please himself. He's ultimately responsible for all the ills that you've suffered since you came to the Black Lotus Temple." Encouraged by Haru's hesitancy, Reiko said, "You called me your friend. You said you loved me and want to make up for the trouble you caused me. Now is your chance."

The girl began shaking violently, wracked by opposing impulses, but she kept the sword aimed at Reiko. Her eyes blazed with blind compulsion; a growling sound issued through her bared teeth. Reiko saw Anraku's smug smile; the other sect members waited, their gazes averted from her and Haru, expecting violence. Haru, wheezing furiously, moved the weapon sideways and stood poised to strike. And Reiko realized with helpless futility that she'd lost the contest. She was going to die. She'd failed to capture Haru and save herself and Midori; she would never see Sano or Masahiro again.

Reiko wanted to scream out her terror, to shut her eyes in anticipation of the blade slicing her throat. But a samurai woman must face death with courage and dignity. Trembling in Kumashiro's grip, Reiko silently prayed that fortune would bless her husband and son and she would be reunited with them someday. She looked straight at Haru and steeled herself for the pain, the spill of her blood, the plunge into oblivion.

Suddenly Haru's growl erupted into a loud roar. She whirled, swinging the sword around. The blade cut Dr. Miwa deeply across the stomach. Uttering a cry of dismay, he clutched the bleeding wound. Junketsu-in screamed. Reiko gaped in stunned disbelief. Shock and anger erased Anraku's smile. He barked out, "Haru!"

Shrieking as if insane, the girl spun and lunged, slashing at random. The priests shouted, "Look out!" They scattered, bumping one another, trying to avoid Haru.

"Stop her," Anraku ordered.

Kumashiro let go of Reiko, drew his short sword, and

charged after Haru. Reiko hurriedly crouched beside Midori and shook her. "Midori-*san*, wake up. We've got to get out."

"Reiko-*san*?" Midori mumbled sleepily. Opening bleary eyes, she frowned. "Where am I? What's going on?"

"Never mind." Reiko hauled Midori upright. "Come on."

Supporting her friend's limp, heavy body, she staggered toward the door. She heard Anraku call, "Catch them!" Kumashiro turned, saw them, and swiftly blocked their way.

"Put her down," he said, pointing his sword at Reiko. "Stay where you are."

Reiko floundered backward, dragging Midori with her. Around them, Haru continued her rampage. Dr. Miwa lay dead on the floor next to Junketsu-in, who struck out her foot so that Haru tripped and went sprawling. The sword, knocked out of her hand, slid across the floor toward Reiko. Quickly, Reiko bent and snatched up the weapon.

"Get out of our way," she commanded Kumashiro.

Then she heard shouts, metallic clashes, and a stampede of footsteps outside the room. Through the door burst six samurai battling as many sword-wielding priests. Reiko recognized Sano and his men. Her heart leapt with joy.

"Hirata-*san*!" Midori cried.

Hirata's face lit up at the sight of Midori. He shouted her name, then continued striking at his opponents. As the room became a maelstrom of flashing blades and colliding combatants, Anraku stayed on his platform, watching with a peculiar euphoria. His eight priests fled out the door, while the abbess cowered in a corner. Kumashiro joined in the battle.

"Reiko-*san*," Sano shouted, dodging Kumashiro's strikes. "Protect Midori."

Clutching her friend's hand, Reiko wielded her sword against the priests, while Midori huddled behind her.

"Haru." Anraku's voice, eerily calm, rose above the noise.

The girl was scrambling for cover, but she paused and turned toward the high priest.

"Come here," Anraku said.

She rose and walked to his platform. Her step was hesitant, but she seemed irresistibly drawn to Anraku.

Sano cut down one priest and Hirata another. Four remained;

the battle raged on. Reiko, guarding Midori, risked a glance at Anraku. What was he doing?

"You have failed the test," Anraku said to Haru, his silky tone replete with disapproval.

"Please, give me another chance," Haru begged.

Anraku shook his head; his smile mocked her anxiety. "Your betrayals number too many for forgiveness. You must be punished." Pointing at Haru and gazing deep into her eyes, he intoned, "I plant inside you the seed of the Black Lotus."

Haru pressed a hand to her abdomen, looking disturbed, as if she really felt something enter her body.

Now Sano, Hirata, and the other samurai had slain all their opponents except Kumashiro, who fought ferociously. Junketsu-in dashed toward the door, but a soldier caught her.

"The seed sprouts roots that invade you." Spreading his fingers in illustration, Anraku elicited pained yelps from Haru. "The seedling sends forth shoots, filling your veins, entwining your bones, and piercing your muscles."

Haru began to tremble and moan; terror glazed her eyes as she clutched at herself, feeling for the alien growth.

With amazement, Reiko saw that Haru believed so strongly in Anraku's powers that the spell could physically hurt her. Reiko hurried the dazed Midori to a corner and sat her down. "Stay here," she said, then rushed toward the platform.

Anraku's hypnotic voice continued, "The leaves unfurl, their knifelike edges tearing and penetrating, spilling blood. The stalk pierces your heart. A huge bud forms."

Haru grabbed her chest, wheezing loudly. "It hurts. I can't breathe!" she cried in panic.

"The bud grows larger and larger," Anraku said. His eye glowed brighter; his smile reflected enjoyment of her suffering.

"It's killing me." Spasms jarred Haru, and her complexion turned livid. She dropped to her knees. "Please, take it out!"

"Stop," Reiko shouted at Anraku. Raising her sword, she ordered, "Leave Haru alone."

The high priest ignored Reiko. "Feel the lotus bud begin to flower," he told Haru. "The petals are pure black and razor-sharp. As they spring open, they lacerate your heart."

Out of the corner of her eye, Reiko saw Sano's blade cut deeply into Kumashiro's thigh. The priest stumbled and sank to his knees. With his face set in a scowl of desperation and the cut spurting blood, he lashed his blade at the samurai surrounding him, until Hirata wounded his arm. His sword went flying. Sano and Hirata wrestled him down.

Frantically gasping for air, Haru sobbed. "I'll die!"

"That is the fate of enemies of the Black Lotus," Anraku said, gloating. He extended his fists, knuckles facing Haru. "When the flower reaches full bloom, your life shall cease."

Reiko grabbed Haru's shoulder, urging, "Look away. Don't listen. He's a fraud. He can't hurt you unless you let him."

But Haru's gaze seemed magnetically locked onto Anraku's. Keening in agony, the girl clawed open her robe, trying to tear the flower out of her chest. Her fingernails left bloody scratches on her skin. Reiko leapt up on the platform.

"Stop, or I'll kill you!" she told Anraku.

"Your time has come," he said with a triumphant smile at Haru.

His fingers shot open. Haru screamed, as if pierced by invisible blades. Her back arched and her limbs splayed. Incensed, Reiko slashed Anraku down his chest. He lurched, then crumpled onto his side. His face was luminous with rapture, his eye focused on some faraway vista.

"Enlightenment at last," he whispered.

A spasm contorted his features and body. His radiance dimmed, and death veiled his eye. Anraku had met the destiny he'd prophesied.

Reiko dropped the sword and leapt off the platform. "Haru-san." Kneeling, she touched the girl's cheek. "What's happened to you?"

No answer came. Haru's open eyes were sightless; blood trickled from her mouth. Gravity relaxed her features, and her terrified expression faded as Reiko watched. She was dead.

A terrible grief seized Reiko as she cradled Haru's head in her lap. The girl had remained in the thrall of the Black Lotus and ultimately succumbed to Anraku. They had indeed shared a destiny; they would be together always, as she'd wished. But Haru had chosen friendship for Reiko over her devotion to the high priest. By saving Reiko's life at the expense of her own, she'd atoned for her evils. And Reiko hadn't even had a chance to thank Haru. Now it was too late.

It was too late for all the disturbed souls who'd fallen under the influence of the Black Lotus and died tonight.

Suddenly overwhelmed by the horrors of the day, Reiko sobbed. Nearby, she saw Hirata embracing Midori, but there was no consolation for herself.

Then Reiko felt a gentle touch on her shoulder. Looking up, she saw Sano standing beside her. His eyes were filled with a compassion for her that she'd thought gone forever. He drew her to her feet and held her close. As she wept against the hard plates of his armor, he led her out of the room.

37

In the age that will follow the passing of the Bodhisattva of
*   Infinite Power,*
His disciples will turn the wheel of his truth,
Beat the drum of his truth,
And sound the conch trumpet of his truth,
Until he manifests himself to the world again.

—FROM THE BLACK LOTUS SUTRA

"Priest Kumashiro, I pronounce you guilty of multiple assaults and murders," said Magistrate Ueda.

It was the end of the fourth day of the Black Lotus trials. The magistrate sat with Sano, Hirata, and the secretaries on the dais in the Court of Justice. On the *shirasu* knelt Kumashiro and Junketsu-in, their wrists and ankles shackled. The priest glowered; the abbess hung her head and sniveled. A large audience of officials filled the room behind them.

"Abbess Junketsu-in," the magistrate said, "I pronounce you guilty of arson." His stern gaze rebuked the defendants. Both had confessed after Sano had interrogated them and witnesses from among the captured sect members had testified against them. Kumashiro had admitted murdering Chie, Radiant Spirit, and Pious Truth and his sister Yasue, among many others. "I pronounce you both guilty of harmful religious practices and conspiracy to destroy Edo and massacre the citizens. You are hereby sentenced to death by decapitation."

Guards dragged the pair out of the building. Junketsu-in wept; Kumashiro scowled. The crowd that had occupied the street outside Magistrate Ueda's estate since the trials had begun greeted them with angry jeers, curses, and waving fists. The weather had turned cold and stormy, but the victims of Black Lotus attacks and the families of abducted, enslaved, and murdered followers had stayed to see justice done.

In the court, the audience and secretaries had departed. Sano, Hirata, and Magistrate Ueda lingered inside the doorway.

"This is a sorry business," the magistrate said. "I hope that a disaster of such magnitude never happens again."

The death toll from the battle at the temple numbered six hundred forty Black Lotus members and fifty-eight of Sano's troops. A later search of the tunnels had turned up the ashes and bones of countless cremated bodies. And two hundred ninety captured sect members had been executed.

"Still, it could have been worse," Sano said. "My men captured most of the fugitives near Zōjō Temple, and the police have caught more on the outskirts of Edo. Hopefully, that's all there are."

He heard the hollow note in his own voice. The experience had left him drained and shaken. Memories of the carnage robbed him of appetite and sleep. He didn't know the identities of the people he'd slain, and it bothered him that he could take lives and not know whose, or how many. Yesterday he'd attended a mass funeral for his retainers killed in the battle; he mourned their deaths. He'd solved the murder case and eliminated a threat to the nation, but he had no sense of accomplishment, despite the shogun's praise of his valor. And his difficulties with Reiko were still unresolved.

Busy from dawn until late at night every day, interrogating captured sect members, testifying at their trials, and supervising the dismantling of the Black Lotus Temple, he'd hardly seen his wife since he'd brought her home from the temple. Reiko had told him some of what had happened in Anraku's hideout before his arrival there, but otherwise, they'd barely spoken.

"There have been a few minor fires, but no explosions or instances of poisoning," Hirata said. He wore the same haunted look as did all Sano's men who'd survived the raid. "And many innocent people have been saved."

After the battle, Sano's troops had escorted home to the city the two hundred thirty-four prisoners they'd liberated. A hundred fifty children found underground had been returned to their families or placed in orphanages. The two sons of Minister Fugatami now resided with relatives.

"The shogun has issued an edict outlawing the sect," Sano said. "Lady Keisho-in has, on the advice of Priest Ryuko, denounced the Black Lotus. And with Anraku dead, there seems little chance of its revival." Whether or not the high priest had really possessed supernatural powers, Reiko had rid the world of a great evil. "Tokugawa troops have occupied the temple, confiscated Anraku's gold, and begun demolishing the buildings and filling in the tunnels. And the *bakufu* will conduct more rigorous monitoring of other religious orders in the future."

Yet Sano bitterly rued that the shogun had waited so long to quell the Black Lotus. He also wondered how much of the blame he himself deserved for the disaster. If he had believed Reiko when she'd told him Pious Truth's story, could the sect have been disbanded sooner and peacefully?

He would never know.

"How does the elimination of Black Lotus influence from within high levels of society progress?" said Magistrate Ueda.

"Kumashiro and Junketsu-in have revealed names of *bakufu* officials who belonged to the sect," Sano said. Among them was his own Detective Hachiya, who'd betrayed the spy team he'd sent to the temple. "Some had joined Anraku's army and have turned up among the captured priests, or the dead. The survivors included the men who murdered the Fugatami. They'll all be allowed to commit seppuku. Others who didn't directly participate in the attack will be exiled." A quiet purge had already begun in Edo Castle. "We've also gotten names of Black Lotus followers among the daimyo, merchant, and lower classes."

"I am prepared to conduct as many more trials as necessary," Magistrate Ueda said, resigned.

The process of meting out justice to the Black Lotus seemed
endless. Disheartened by the thought of all the work that was
yet to be done, Sano said, "Hirata-*san* and I must be going.
We have a jail full of prisoners to interview."

They'd already spent many hours questioning the captured
priests and nuns, who numbered so many that they'd over-
flowed the jail cells and had been housed in tents in the compound. Day and night they chanted, "Praise the glory of the
Black Lotus." So far none of them had shown remorse for the
attack. All refused to accept the fact that Anraku was dead, and
all still believed themselves destined for glorious enlightenment. Interrogating them, Sano had looked into souls consumed
by fanaticism—Anraku's legacy. The experience unnerved
Sano, and he longed for it to be over.

"May I offer a word of advice?" Magistrate Ueda asked. At
Sano's nod, he said, "Please spare the time to take care of
matters at home. You'll be better off for it."

Trepidation daunted Sano, but he nodded, because he knew
the magistrate was right. It was time for a talk with Reiko.

At Sano's estate, Midori sat in the nursery, watching Reiko
and the maids give Masahiro his supper. The room was bright
with lanterns; charcoal braziers warmed the chill, damp twilight. Masahiro gobbled rice gruel and chattered happily.

"That's a good boy." Reiko smiled at her son. "Eat plenty.
Grow big and strong."

Midori, who had received permission from Sano and Lady
Keisho-in to stay in the mansion for as long as she needed to
recuperate from her ordeal, tried to enjoy the cozy, familiar
scene, but a restless melancholy disturbed her spirit. Everything
looked the same as before the fire and murders at the Black
Lotus Temple, yet so much had changed.

Reiko and Sano seemed permanently divided. Midori knew
that Reiko was upset about this and the disaster at the temple,
although she put on a cheerful front. And Midori herself had
lost her usual brightness of outlook and buoyancy of heart.

After meeting Anraku, after seeing what he'd done to people and made them do for him, the world seemed a darker place. Midori now knew herself to be susceptible to evil influences—and death. Worse, she hadn't even accomplished the purposes that had driven her to spy on the sect.

Sano had told her that she needn't bear witness against the Black Lotus because the war at the temple had provided the shogun enough proof of its evil to disband the sect. Thus, Midori had been spared the public disgrace of telling about her experiences in the temple and her reputation saved from scandal. Yet she regretted that her suffering had been in vain, and she'd helped Reiko not at all. And Hirata had been too busy to see her during the time since he'd brought her here from the temple. Because of the drug given her there, Midori had little recollection of that night. She thought she remembered Hirata hugging her and exclaiming, "Thank the gods you're alive!" But maybe it had been a delusion. Certainly, she was as far from winning Hirata as ever.

As Midori tried to feel glad to be alive and forget her ordeal, she heard footsteps in the corridor. Sano and Hirata appeared in the doorway. Midori's heart began hammering in painful, joyous agitation that she hid by casting her eyes downward. Masahiro called out gaily to his father, but an uneasy silence descended upon everyone else.

Reiko spoke first. "I wasn't expecting you home so soon."

"Yes, well." Obviously at a loss for words, Sano hesitated.

The maids gathered up Masahiro and left the room. Hirata said in a somber voice, "Midori-san, will you come for a walk with me?"

Wild hope leapt in Midori, but she was so nervous that she could barely look at Hirata. She murmured, "All right. Let me put on my outdoor things."

Soon she was walking beside Hirata along a path through the garden. They looked at the ground instead of at each other. Murky clouds in the twilight sky promised more rain; lights from the house shone through the sodden trees. Trembling with love and anxiety, Midori clasped her hands tightly under her sleeves.

"How are you feeling?" Hirata asked. He'd lost his cockiness; he sounded young and uncertain.

Midori drew a calming breath of moist, pine-scented air. "Much better, thank you."

They walked for a while without speaking. Hirata picked a leaf off a bush and examined it studiously. "About what you did at the temple . . ." he began.

Desperate to forestall the humiliation of a scolding from Hirata, Midori blurted, "I know it was wrong. I shouldn't have gone." Her voice shook. "You were right—I was stupid to think I could be a detective."

Hirata halted, flung away the leaf, and faced Midori. "That's not what I was going to say," he said urgently.

"I thought I was so clever, getting into the temple, but they only took me in because I'm the kind of person they wanted." Midori had figured out that her simple, submissive, vulnerable nature had won her admission to the sect. "And they caught me before I could even report what I'd seen!"

Tears welled in her eyes. "I thought I could be brave, but I was so scared." Overcome by emotion, Midori confessed what she'd never intended Hirata to know: "I did it to get your attention. I'm sorry I caused so much trouble."

"Midori-*san*." Hirata grasped her shoulders. "Listen."

Gulping back a sob, Midori looked up at his face. The concern and warmth she saw there startled her.

"You were clever and brave," Hirata said, his voice rough with sincerity. "You got inside the temple when professional spies had failed. You risked your life to find evidence against the Black Lotus. Of course you were scared; who wouldn't have been? But you endured your fear. You survived."

Suddenly shy, he released Midori and stammered, "What I wanted to tell you is that—even though I would have stopped you from going if I could have—and I hate that you suffered—I admire you."

"You do?" Midori stared, confused. "But I don't deserve your admiration. I was such a fool to get caught."

"No, no." Hirata waved his hands in eager contradiction. "You weren't caught because you're a fool. You were caught because you're good and kind. You couldn't leave that girl Toshiko in danger, and I think you would have tried to save her even if you'd guessed she was a spy." He bowed his head, mumbling, "I'm the one who doesn't deserve your admiration."

Rain spattered through the trees. Hirata hurried Midori into the pavilion that had sheltered them from another storm two years ago. Side by side, hands clasped, they watched the rain, as they'd done then. Midori's heart raced with the same anticipation.

"It's I who should apologize to you—for the way I've treated you," Hirata said humbly. "I was the fool, to throw away your friendship, and to think that all those other women mattered, or that moving up in society was so important. Now I know there's no one else in the world who would do for me what you would. When I found out you'd gone to the temple and hadn't come back, I realized—"

Turning to her, he said in an ardent voice, "How much I love you."

Midori felt a radiant smile erase the misery from her face. Her tears spilled, for joy.

"Then it's not too late?" Hirata said, gazing hopefully at her. "You still care for me?"

Midori blushed and nodded. Hirata's face brightened. The rain streamed down, blurring the world outside the pavilion. Then Hirata turned serious.

"I want us to be together always," he said.

Too shy to echo his bold declaration, Midori signaled her agreement with an adoring glance and heartfelt smile. But a marriage between them required their families' approval. "What shall we do?" she whispered.

Hirata tightened his warm grip on her hand. "Whatever it takes," he said.

Alone together in the nursery, Sano and Reiko sat facing each other. The distant sound of Masahiro's laughter emphasized the uncomfortable silence between them. Reiko, rigid with apprehension, braced herself for recriminations. She deserved punishment for her mistakes, and for her disobedience to Sano. It was his right to divorce her and send her away from Masahiro if he chose. That he hadn't yet done so might only mean he'd been too busy working. Fearing heartbreak, she waited with dread to learn her fate, just as she'd waited for the past four days.

She'd spent that time going through the motions of domestic life. For Masahiro's sake she'd tried to act as if nothing had happened, while the unfinished business from the investigation hovered over her like a storm cloud. She felt suspended in time, still caught up in the horror of her experience at the temple. Her mind was a shifting collage of terrible scenes—savage nuns and priests, bloody corpses, flashing blades, fire, dim tunnels, and Anraku slain by her hand. But the image of Haru's death was more vivid, more persistent than any other.

Even now, with her future threatened, Reiko couldn't forget Haru. The girl's spirit was still here between Reiko and Sano, a haunting reminder of Reiko's errors of judgment, a debt unpaid, and a relationship severed without conclusion.

"It's natural to grieve for her," Sano said quietly.

Reiko was surprised that he'd guessed she was thinking of Haru, and that she mourned the girl. Though still fearful, she drew cautious hope from Sano's apparent sympathy. "But Haru was a selfish, immoral person. Why should her death haunt me more than all the others?" Reiko lifted empty hands. "Why do I miss her?"

"Because you were her friend. And she proved herself yours in the end."

"How did you know?" Reiko said, puzzled; she hadn't told Sano about Haru's choice.

"When I interrogated Abbess Junketsu-in, I learned that you're alive because of Haru," Sano said. Irony tinged his faint smile. "To think that after I worked so hard to convict her, she did me a great favor."

His implication set Reiko's heart racing. She murmured, "Was it a favor?"

Sano's expression turned tender. Wordless communication crumbled a barrier, filling Reiko with relief and joy. Difficulties still precluded complete reconciliation, but now Reiko had the courage to confront them.

"You were right all along to believe that Haru was dishonest," she said. "I regret all that I said and did to hurt you. Please accept my apologies."

"If you'll accept mine," Sano said with equal, pained contrition. "You were right that Haru didn't kill Chie or the boy, or set the fire. I should have heeded your suspicions about the Black Lotus sooner, instead of concentrating so hard on her. I drove you to protect her."

Humbled by his honesty, Reiko said, "But she was manipulating me, just as you thought." Even as she acknowledged Haru's fault, sorrow for the girl overwhelmed her.

"It turned out to be a good thing that you did form a bond with Haru," Sano pointed out. "Her feelings for you saved your life, and Midori's."

His willingness to assuage her humiliation didn't excuse her other mistake. "I let Midori see how much I wanted a spy in the temple. I should have guessed she would go, and I'll never forgive myself for what happened to her," Reiko said.

As Sano's features clouded, despondency undermined her happiness at discovering that their love had survived. Certainly her lapse of caution regarding Midori had cost her the privilege of ever again participating in investigations.

Then Sano said grimly, "Midori is alive. But Minister Fugatami, whom I might have helped, was murdered. As was his wife. And their children are orphans."

They sat in shared self-recrimination until Sano said, "The worst of our problems wasn't that you made mistakes or that I did, but that we worked against each other. No good will come of accepting blame unless we learn from our experience and do better next time."

"Next time?" Reiko thought she hadn't heard him right. Doubt vied with excitement. "Do you mean . . . you still want my help, after what happened?"

"A few days ago I would have said no," Sano admitted. "But I've come to understand that I'm no less susceptible to bias than you, and my errors can have serious consequences, too. I need someone to oppose me when I'm too quick to draw conclusions." He said with a wry smile, "Who better than you?"

Reiko beamed at him, savoring the exhilaration of wishes fulfilled, harmony restored. Bad memories began to pale in the light of her happiness, and Sano looked less exhausted. Perhaps their partnership would be better for accommodating differences of opinion; perhaps someday the thought of Haru would cease to torment her. But experience had taught Reiko caution. There would be other suspects, other disagreements.

"Can we prevent a future investigation from dividing us again?" she said.

Sano took her hands in his. "We can pledge to try our best."

The warm contact with her husband stirred in Reiko a powerful sense of all they'd experienced together during their marriage—the dangers faced and surmounted, the birth of Masahiro, the love for each other and their child that had sustained and gladdened them. She felt Sano's strength and hers join to meet the challenges yet to come.

"And we shall succeed," she said.

Read on for an excerpt from
Laura Joh Rowland's next book

THE PILLOW BOOK OF LADY WISTERIA

Available in hardcover from St. Martin's Minotaur

Northwest of the great capital of Edo, isolated among marshes and rice paddies, the Yoshiwara pleasure quarter adorned the winter night like a flashy jewel. Its lights formed a bright, smoky halo above the high walls; the moon's reflection shimmered silver on the encircling moat. Inside the quarter, colored lanterns blazed along the eaves of the teahouses and brothels that lined the streets. Courtesans dressed in gaudy kimono sat in the barred windows of the brothels and called invitations to men who strolled in search of entertainment. Roving vendors sold tea and dumplings, and a hawker beckoned customers into a shop that sold paintings of the most beautiful prostitutes, but the late hour and chill weather had driven most of the trade indoors. Teahouse maids poured sake; drunken customers raised their voices in bawdy song. Musicians played for guests at banquets in elegant parlors, while amorous couples embraced behind windows.

The man in an upstairs guest chamber on Ageyachō Street lay oblivious to the revelry. A drunken stupor immobilized him on the bed, which seemed to rock and sway beneath him. Singing, samisen music, and laughter from the parlor downstairs echoed up to him in waves of discordant sound. Through his half-open eyes he saw red lights glide and spin, like reflections in a whirlpool. A painted landscape of gardens slid along the periphery of his vision. Dizzy and nauseated, he moaned. He tried to recall where he was and how he'd gotten here.

He had a faint memory of a ride through winter fields, and cups of heated sake. A woman's beautiful face glowed in lamplight, eyes demurely downcast. More sake accompanied flirtatious conversation. Next came the hot, urgent intertwining of bodies, then ecstatic pleasure, followed by much more drink. Because he possessed a hearty tolerance for liquor, he couldn't understand how the usual amount had so thoroughly inebriated him. A peculiar lethargy spread through his veins. He felt strangely disconnected from his body, which seemed heavy as stone, yet afloat on air. A pang of fear chimed in his groggy consciousness, but the stupor dulled emotion. While he tried to fathom what had happened to him, he sensed that he wasn't alone in the room.

Someone's rapid footsteps trod the tatami around the bed. The moving hems of multicolored robes swished air currents across his face. Whispers, distorted into eerie, droning gibberish, pervaded the distant music. Now he saw, bending over him, a human figure—a dark, indistinct shape outlined by the revolving red light. The whispers quickened and rose to a keening pitch. He sensed danger that shot alarm through his stupor. But his body resisted his effort to move. The lethargy paralyzed his limbs. His mouth formed a soundless plea.

The figure leaned closer. Its fist clenched what looked to be a long, thin shaft that wavered in his blurry vision. Then the figure struck at him with sudden violence. Pain seared deep into his left eye, rousing him to alertness. A squeal of agony burst from him. Music, laughter, and screaming rose to a cacophonous din. Turbulent shadows rocked the chamber. He saw a brilliant white lightning bolt blaze through his brain, heard his heart thunder in his ears. The impact heaved up his arms and legs, which flailed as his body convulsed in involuntary spasms. But the terrible pain in his eye pinned him to the bed. Blood stained his vision scarlet, obliterated the person whose grip on the shaft held him captive. His head pounded with torment. Gradually, his struggles weakened; his heartbeat slowed. Sounds and sensations ebbed, until black unconsciousness quenched the lightning and death ended his agony.

*   *   *

The summons came at dawn.

Edo Castle, reigning upon its hilltop above the city, raised its watchtowers and peaked roofs toward a sky like steel coated with ice. Inside the castle, two of the shogun's attendants and their soldiers sped on horseback between barracks surrounding the mansions where the high officials of the court resided. A chill, gusty wind flapped the soldiers' banners and tore the smoke from their lanterns. The party halted outside the gate of Sano Ichirō, the shogun's *sōsakan-sama*—Most Honorable Investigator of Events, Situations, and People.

Within his estate, Sano slept beneath mounded quilts. He dreamed he was at the Black Lotus Temple, scene of a crime he'd investigated three months ago. Deranged monks and nuns fought him and his troops; explosions boomed and fire raged. Yet even as Sano wielded his sword against phantoms of memory, his senses remained attuned to the real world and perceived the approach of an actual threat. He bolted awake in darkness, flung off the quilts, and sat up in the frigid air of his bedchamber.

Beside him, his wife, Reiko, stirred. "What is it?" she asked sleepily.

Then they heard, outside their door, the voice of Sano's chief retainer, Hirata: "*Sōsakan-sama*, I'm sorry to disturb you, but the shogun's envoys are here on urgent business. They wish to see you at once."

Moments later, after hastily dressing, Sano was seated in the reception hall with the two envoys. A maid served bowls of tea. The senior envoy, a dignified samurai named Ota, said, "We bring news of a serious incident that requires your personal attention. His Excellency the Shogun's cousin, the Honorable Lord Matsudaira Mitsuyoshi, has died. As you are undoubtedly aware, he was not just kin to the shogun, but his probable successor."

The shogun had no sons as yet; therefore, a relative must be designated heir to his position as Japan's supreme dictator in case he died without issue. Sano had known that Mitsuyoshi—twenty-five years old and a favorite of the shogun—was a likely candidate.

Ota continued, "Mitsuyoshi-*san* spent yesterday evening in Yoshiwara." This was Edo's pleasure quarter, the only place

in the city where prostitution was legal. Men from all classes
of society went there to drink, revel, and enjoy the favors of
the courtesans—women sold into prostitution by impoverished
families, or sentenced to work in Yoshiwara as punishment for
crimes. The quarter was located some distance from Edo, to
safeguard public morals and respect propriety. "There he was
stabbed to death."

Consternation struck Sano: This was serious indeed, for any
attack on a member of the ruling Tokugawa clan constituted
an attack on the regime, which was high treason. And the murder of someone so close to the shogun represented a crime of
the most sensitive nature.

"May I ask what were the circumstances of the stabbing?"
Sano said.

"The details are not known to us," said the younger envoy,
a brawny captain of the shogun's bodyguards. "It is your responsibility to discover them. The shogun orders you to investigate the murder and apprehend the killer."

"I'll begin immediately." As Sano bowed to the envoys,
duty settled upon his shoulders like a weight that he wasn't
sure he could bear. Though detective work was his vocation
and his spirit required the challenge of delivering killers to
justice, he wasn't ready for another big case. The Black Lotus
investigation had depleted him physically and mentally. He felt
like an injured warrior heading into battle again before his
wounds had healed. And he knew that this case had as serious
a potential for disaster as had the Black Lotus.

A long, cold ride brought Sano, Hirata, and five men from
Sano's detective corps to the pleasure quarter by mid-morning.
Snowflakes drifted onto the tiled rooftops of Yoshiwara; its
surrounding moat reflected the overcast sky. The cawing of
crows above the fallow fields sounded shrilly metallic. Sano
and his men dismounted outside the quarter's high wall that
kept the revelry contained and the courtesans from escaping.
Their breath puffed out in white clouds into the icy wind. They
left the horses with a stable boy and strode across the bridge
to the gate, which was painted bright red and barred shut. A
noisy commotion greeted them.

"Let us out!" Inside the quarter, men had climbed the gate and thrust their heads between the thick wooden bars below the roof. "We want to go home!"

Outside the gate stood four Yoshiwara guards. One of them told the prisoners, "Nobody leaves. Police orders."

Loud protests arose; a furious pounding shook the gate's heavy wooden planks.

"So the police have beat us to the scene," Hirata said to Sano. An expression of concern crossed his youthful face.

Sano's heart plunged, for in spite of his high rank and position close to the shogun, he could expect hindrance, rather than cooperation, from Edo's police. "At least they've contained the people who were in Yoshiwara last night. That will save us the trouble of tracking down witnesses."

He approached the guards, who hastily bowed to him and his men. After introducing himself and announcing his purpose, Sano asked, "Where did Lord Mitsuyoshi die?"

"In the Owariya *ageya*," came the answer.

Yoshiwara was a world unto itself, Sano knew, with a unique protocol. Some five hundred courtesans ranked in a hierarchy of beauty, elegance, and price. The top-ranking women were known as *tayu*. A popular epithet for them was *keisei*—castle topplers—because their influence could ruin men and destroy kingdoms. Though all the prostitutes lived in brothels and most received clients there, the *tayu* entertained men in *ageya*, houses of assignation, used for that purpose but not as homes for the women. The Owariya was a prestigious *ageya*, reserved for the wealthiest, most prominent men.

"Open the gate and let us in," Sano ordered the guards.

They complied. Sano and his men entered the pleasure quarter, while the guards held back the pushing, shouting crowd inside. As Sano led his party down Nakanochō, the main avenue that bisected Yoshiwara, the wind buffeted unlit lanterns hanging from the eaves of the wooden buildings and stirred up an odor of urine. Teahouses were filled with sullen, disheveled men. Women peeked out through window bars, their painted faces avid. Nervous murmurs arose as Sano and his men passed, while Tokugawa troops patrolled Nakanochō and the six streets perpendicular to it.

The murder of the shogun's heir had put a temporary halt to the festivities that ordinarily never ended.

Sano turned onto Ageyachō, a street lined with the houses of assignation. These were attached buildings, their façades and balconies screened with wooden lattices. Servants loitered in the recessed doorways. Smoke from charcoal braziers swirled in the wind, mingling with the snowflakes. A group of samurai stood guard outside the Owariya, smoking tobacco pipes. Some wore the Tokugawa triple-hollyhock-leaf crest on their cloaks; others wore leggings and short kimonos and carried *jitte*—steel parrying wands, the weapon of the police force. They all fixed level gazes upon Sano.

"Guess who brought them here," Hirata murmured to Sano in a voice replete with ire.

As they reached the Owariya, the door slid open, and out stepped a tall, broad-shouldered samurai dressed in a sumptuous cloak of padded black silk. He was in his thirties, his bearing arrogant, his angular face strikingly handsome. When he saw Sano, his full, sensual mouth curved in a humorless smile.

"Greetings, *Sōsakan-sama*," he said.

"Greetings, Honorable Chief Police Commissioner Hoshina," Sano said. As they exchanged bows, the air vibrated with their antagonism.

They'd first met in Miyako, the imperial capital, where Sano had gone to investigate the death of a court noble. Hoshina had been head of the local police, and pretended to assist Sano on the case—while conspiring against him with Chamberlain Yanagisawa, the shogun's powerful second-in-command. Yanagisawa and Hoshina had become lovers, and Yanagisawa had appointed Hoshina as Edo's Chief Police Commissioner.

"What brings you here?" Hoshina's tone implied that Sano was a trespasser in his territory.

"The shogun's orders," Sano said, accustomed to Hoshina's hostility. During their clash in Miyako, Sano had defeated Hoshina, who had never forgotten. "I've come to investigate the murder. Unless you've already found the killer?"

"No," Hoshina said with a reluctance that indicated how much he would like to say he had. Arms folded, he blocked the door of the *ageya*. "But you've traveled here for nothing, because I already have an investigation underway. Whatever you want to know, just ask me."

The Miyako case had resulted in a truce between Sano and

Yanagisawa—formerly bitter enemies—but Hoshina refused to let matters lie, because he viewed Sano as a threat to his own rise in the *bakufu*, the military government that ruled Japan. Now, having settled into his new position and cultivated allies, Hoshina had begun his campaign against Sano. Their paths crossed often when Sano investigated crimes, and Hoshina always sought to prove himself the superior detective while undermining Sano. He conducted his own inquiries into Sano's cases, hoping to solve them first and take the credit. Obviously, Hoshina meant to extend their rivalry into this case, and there was little that Sano could do to stop him. Although Sano was a high official of the shogun, Hoshina had the favor of Chamberlain Yanagisawa, who controlled the shogun and virtually ruled Japan. Thus, Hoshina could treat Sano however he pleased, short of causing open warfare that would disturb their superiors.

"I prefer to see for myself." Speaking quietly but firmly, Sano held his adversary's gaze.

Hirata and his detectives clustered around him, as the police moved nearer Hoshina. The wind keened, and angry voices yelled curses somewhere in the quarter. Then Hoshina chuckled, as though his defiance against Sano had been a mere joke.

"As you wish," he said, and stepped away from the door.

But he followed Sano's party into the *ageya*. Beyond the entryway, which contained a guard stationed at a podium, a corridor extended between rooms separated by lattice and paper partitions. A lantern glowed in a luxurious front parlor. There sat two pretty courtesans, eight surly-looking samurai, several plainly dressed women who looked to be servants, and a squat older man in gray robes. All regarded Sano and Hirata with apprehension. The older man rose and hurried over to kneel at Sano's feet.

"Please allow me to introduce myself, master," he said, bowing low. "I am Eigoro, proprietor of the Owariya. Please let me say that nothing like this has ever happened here before." His body quaked with his terror that the shogun's *sōsakan-sama* would blame him for the murder. "Please believe that no one in my establishment did this evil thing."

"No one is accusing you," Sano said, though everyone present in Yoshiwara at the time of the murder was a suspect until proven otherwise. "Show me where Lord Mitsuyoshi died."

"Certainly, master." The proprietor scrambled up.

Hoshina said, "You don't need him. I can show you."

Sano considered ordering Hoshina out of the house, then merely ignored him: Antagonizing Chamberlain Yanagisawa's mate was dangerous. But Sano must not rely on Hoshina for information, because Hoshina would surely misguide him.

Eyeing the group in the parlor, Sano addressed the proprietor: "Were they in the house last night?"

"Yes, master."

Sano ascertained that four of the samurai were Lord Mitsuyoshi's retainers, then glanced at Hirata and the detectives. They nodded and moved toward the parlor to question the retainers, courtesans, other clients, and servants. The proprietor led Sano upstairs, to a large chamber at the front of the house. Entering, Sano gleaned a quick impression of burning lanterns, lavish landscape murals, and a gilded screen, before his attention fixed upon the men in the room. Two soldiers were preparing to move a shrouded figure, which lay upon the futon, onto a litter. A samurai clad in ornate robes pawed through a pile of clothes on the tatami; another rummaged in a drawer of the wall cabinet. Sano recognized both as senior police commanders.

"*Yoriki* Hayashi-*san*. *Yoriki* Yamaga-*san*," he said, angered to find them and their troops disturbing the crime scene and ready to remove the body before he'd had a chance to examine either. "Stop that at once," he ordered all the men.

The police halted their actions and bowed stiffly, gazing at Sano with open dislike. Sano knew they would never forget that he'd been their colleague, nor cease resenting his promotion and doing him a bad turn whenever possible. He said sternly, "You will all leave now."

Hayashi and Yamaga exchanged glances with Chief Commissioner Hoshina, who stood in the doorway. Then Yamaga spoke to Sano: "I wish you the best of luck, *Sōsakan-sama*, because you will surely need it." His voice exuded insolence. He and Hayashi and their men strode out of the room.

The proprietor shrank into a corner, while Hoshina watched Sano for a reaction. Sano saw little point in losing his temper, or in regretting that his old enemies now worked for his new one. He crouched beside the futon and drew back the white cloth that covered the corpse of Lord Mitsuyoshi.

The shogun's heir lay on his back, arms at his sides. The bronze satin robe he wore had fallen open to expose his naked, muscular torso, limp genitals, and extended legs. A looped top-knot adorned the shaved crown of his head. From his left eye protruded a long, slender object that looked to be a woman's hair ornament—double-pronged, made of black lacquer, ending in a globe of flowers carved from cinnabar. Blood and slime had oozed around the embedded prongs and down Mitsuyoshi's cheek; droplets stained the mattress. The injured eyeball was cloudy and misshapen. The other eye seemed to stare at it, while Mitsuyoshi's mouth gaped in shock.

Sano winced at the gruesome sight; his stomach clenched as he made a closer observation of the body and recalled what he knew about the shogun's cousin. Handsome, dashing Mitsuyoshi might have one day ruled Japan, yet he'd had little interest in politics and much in the glamorous life. He'd excelled at combat, yet there was no sign that he'd struggled against his killer. A reek of liquor suggested that he'd been drunk and semiconscious when stabbed. Sano also detected the feral smell of sex.

"Who was the woman with him last night?" Sano asked the proprietor.

"A *tayu* named Lady Wisteria."

The name struck an unsettling chord in Sano. He had met Lady Wisteria during his first case, a double murder. One victim had been her friend, and she'd given Sano information to help him find the killer. Beautiful, exotic, and alluring, she'd also seduced him, and memory stirred physical sensations in Sano, even though four years had passed since he'd last seen her and he'd married the wife he passionately loved.

Hoshina narrowed his heavy-lidded eyes at Sano. "Do you know Wisteria?"

"I know of her." Sano wished to keep their acquaintance private, for various reasons. Now unease prevailed over nostalgia, because he had reason to know Wisteria had left Yoshiwara soon after they'd first met. He himself had secured her freedom, as compensation for wrongs she had suffered because she'd helped him. Afterward, he'd visited her a few times, but his life had grown so busy that he'd let the connection lapse. Later he'd heard that she had returned to the pleasure quarter, though he didn't know why. Now he was disturbed to learn that she was involved in this murder.

"Where is she now?" he said.

"She's vanished," Hoshina said. "No one seems to have seen her go or knows where she went."

Sano's first reaction was relief: He wouldn't have to see Wisteria, and the past could stay buried. His second reaction was dismay because an important witness—or suspect—was missing. Did her disappearance mean she'd stabbed Mitsuyoshi? Sano knew the dangers of partiality toward a suspect, yet didn't like to think that the woman he'd known could be a killer.

"Who was the last person to see Lady Wisteria and Lord Mitsuyoshi?" Sano asked the proprietor.

"That would be the *yarite*. Her name is Momoko." The man was babbling, overeager to please. "Shall I fetch her, master?"

A *yarite* was a female brothel employee, usually a former prostitute, who served as chaperone to the courtesans, teaching new girls the art of pleasing men and ensuring that her charges behaved properly. Her other duties included arranging appointments between *tayu* and their clients.

"I'll see her as soon as I'm finished here," Sano said, conscious of Hoshina listening intently to the conversation. The police commissioner was a skilled detective, but glad to take advantage of facts discovered by others. "Did anyone else enter this room during the night?"

"Not as far as I know, master."

But if Lady Wisteria had left the house unobserved, so could someone else have entered secretly, and committed murder. Sano drew the cloth over the body and rose. "Who found the body, and when?"

"Momoko did," the proprietor said. "It was a little after midnight. She came running downstairs, screaming that Lord Mitsuyoshi was dead."

All the more reason to question the *yarite*, thought Sano. She might have noticed something important, and in some murder cases, the culprit proved to be the person who discovered the crime. He bent to sort through the clothes on the floor, and found a man's surcoat, trousers, and kimono, presumably belonging to the victim, and a woman's ivory satin dressing gown. The gown was soft to his touch, and Sano recognized its odor of musky perfume. Closing his mind against memories of Wisteria and himself together, he moved to the dressing table behind the screen. The table held a mirror, comb, brush, jars of face powder and rouge. On the floor around the table lay a red silk cloth and a few strands of long black hair.

Sano addressed Hoshina: "What have you done to locate Wisteria?"

"I've got men out searching the quarter, the highways, and the surrounding countryside." Hoshina added, "If she's there, I'll find her."

Before you do, said his inflection. And Hoshina might indeed, because he had a head start. Sano felt an urgent need to find Wisteria first, because he feared that Hoshina would harm her before her guilt or innocence could be determined.

"Did Lady Wisteria often entertain clients here?" he asked the proprietor.

"Oh, yes, master."

Then she would have kept personal possessions at the Owariya, instead of just bringing a set of bedding with her for a night's visit, as courtesans did to houses they rarely used. "Where is her *kamuro*?" Sano said.

A *kamuro* was a young girl, in training to be a prostitute, who waited on the courtesans to learn the trade and earn her keep. Her chores included tending the courtesans' possessions.

"In the kitchen, master."

"Please bring her up."

The proprietor departed, then soon returned with a girl of perhaps eleven years. Small and thin, she had an oval face made up with white rice powder and red rouge, and wispy hair. She wore the traditional pine-leaf-patterned kimono of her station.

"This is Chidori-*chan*," the proprietor told Sano, then addressed the *kamuro*: "The master wants to talk to you."

Her frightened gaze veered around the room, then downward; she bobbed a clumsy bow.

"Don't be afraid," Sano said in a reassuring tone. "I just want you to look over Lady Wisteria's things with me."

Chidori nodded, but Sano saw her tremble. He pitied her, trapped in Yoshiwara, destined for a life of sexual slavery. She might someday attract a patron who would buy her freedom, but could instead end up begging on the streets, as did many courtesans when they got too old to attract clients. Sano gently led Chidori over to the cabinet, where they examined the folded garments and pairs of sandals on the shelves. Hoshina watched, leaning against the wall, his expression attentive.

"Is anything missing?" Sano asked Chidori.

". . . The outfit Lady Wisteria had on last night." Chidori risked a glance at Sano, seemed to discern that he wouldn't hurt her, and spoke up more boldly: "She wore a black kimono with purple wisteria blossoms and green vines on it."

Her conspicuous costume would aid the search for her, Sano thought, and saw the idea register on Hoshina's countenance. Opening the cabinet's other compartments, Sano revealed quilts, bath supplies, a tea service, a sake decanter and cups, a writing box containing brushes, inkstone, and water jar. A drawer held hair ornaments—lacquerware picks, silk flowers mounted on combs, ribbons. Chidori attested that all the possessions were present as she remembered from when she'd tidied the cabinet yesterday. This left Sano one last task for the girl.

"Chidori-*chan*, I must ask you to look at the body." Seeing her blench, he added, "You need only look for a moment. Try to be brave."

The *kamuro* gulped, nodding. Sano stepped to the bed and peeled back the cloth just far enough to reveal the upper part of Mitsuyoshi's head. Chidori gasped; she stared in horror at the hairpin stuck in the eye.

"Does the hairpin belong to Lady Wisteria?" Sano said.

Emitting a whimper, Chidori shook her head. Sano experienced a cautious relief as he replaced the cloth. That Wisteria didn't own the hairpin was evidence that hinted at her innocence. "Do you know who it does belong to?"

"Momoko-*san*," the girl whispered.

The *yarite* again, thought Sano. Revealed as the last person to see Wisteria and Lord Mitsuyoshi, discoverer of the body and now, owner of the murder weapon, she seemed a better suspect than Wisteria. He said to Chidori, "Look around the room again. Are you sure nothing is missing?"

"Yes, master." Then a frown wrinkled Chidori's brow.

Sano felt his instincts stir, as they did when he knew he was about to hear something important. Hoshina pushed himself away from the wall, eyeing the *kamuro* with heightened interest.

"What is it?" Sano said.

"Her pillow book," said Chidori.

A pillow book was a journal in which a woman recorded her private thoughts and the events of her life, in the tradition of Imperial court ladies. "What was in the book?" Sano said, intrigued to learn that Wisteria had followed the centuries-old custom.

"I don't know. I can't read."

More questioning revealed that the pillow book was a pack of white rice paper, bound between lavender silk covers tied with green ribbon. Wisteria wrote in it whenever she had a spare moment, and if she heard someone coming, she would quickly put it away, as though fearful that they might read it. She took the book with her whenever she left the brothel, and Chidori had seen her tuck it under her sash yesterday evening, but although Sano searched the entire room, the pillow book was indeed gone.

"Wisteria could have removed it when she left," Hoshina suggested.

Or someone had stolen the pillow book, Sano thought, resisting Hoshina's attempt to draw him into a discussion and elicit ideas from him. He considered possible scenarios for the crime. Perhaps the killer had entered the room while Wisteria and Mitsuyoshi slept, stabbed Mitsuyoshi, kidnapped Wisteria, and stolen the pillow book. But perhaps Wisteria herself had killed Mitsuyoshi, then fled, taking her book with her. Each scenario was as plausible as the other, and Sano realized how little he knew about his former lover. What had happened to her since they'd parted ways? Was she capable of such a grisly murder? The idea alarmed Sano, as did the suspicion that this case would bring him and Wisteria together again, with unpredictable consequences.

Hiding his uneasiness, Sano turned to the proprietor and said, "I'll see the *yarite* now."

GET A $5 REBATE ON LAURA JOH ROWLAND'S NEW HARDCOVER!

Send in this coupon, along with your store receipt(s) for the purchase of *Black Lotus* in paperback and Laura Joh Rowland's new hardcover *The Pillow Book of Lady Wisteria*, to receive a $5.00 rebate.

The shogun's dashing young cousin and heir apparent is found dead —stabbed through the eye with a long hairpin— in the bed of Lady Wisteria, a beautiful courtesan. When both Lady Wisteria and her pillow book, a journal of her private life and thoughts, turn up missing, Sano Ichiro is called upon to find her and unmask a cunning killer . . .

To receive your $5.00 rebate, please send this form, along with your original dated cash register receipt(s) showing the price for purchase of both the paperback edition of *Black Lotus* and the hardcover edition of *The Pillow Book of Lady Wisteria* to: St. Martin's Press, Dept. AN, Suite 1500, 175 Fifth Avenue, New York, NY 10010.

NAME:

ADDRESS:

CITY:

STATE/ZIP:

Coupon and receipt(s) must be received by October 31, 2002. Purchases may be made separately. One rebate per person, address, or family. U.S. residents only. Allow 6–8 weeks for delivery of your rebate. St. Martin's Press is not responsible for late, lost or misdirected mail. Void where prohibited.

 St. Martin's Press